Turner's shoulders shifted uneasily. "The job is simple: find the psychiatrist and his patient; persuade the guy to work with her under our supervision. Failing that, you are to use your . . . skills, as needed . . . to debrief Jane Doe yourself. That won't be easy. She's part wonder-worker and part time bomb. Four men dead behind her, two of 'em the Crow Wing cops who found her, two of 'em mine."

Nordstrom smiled. "I deliver the goods. And government imperatives allow me to push the human psyche to its limits—my own as much as anybody's. Everything that makes *Homo sapiens* civilized is useless when the ruling order requires a specific behavior. Useless to the victim, that is. Civilization has many uses to the hunter . . ."

———

"Fans of all genres will more than enjoy this thrilling adventure."

—Praise for PROBE, *Romantic Times*

Tor Books by Carole Nelson Douglas

Probe
Counterprobe

Sword & Circlet

Keepers of Edenvant
Heir of Rengarth
Seven of Swords

CAROLE NELSON DOUGLAS
COUNTERPROBE

A TOM DOHERTY ASSOCIATES BOOK
NEW YORK

COUNTERPROBE

Copyright © 1988 by Carole Nelson Douglas

A TOR BOOK
Published by Tom Doherty Associates, Inc.
49 West 24 Street
New York, NY 10010

Cover art by Jael

ISBN: 0-812-53596-0   Can. ISBN: 0-812-53597-9

Library of Congress Catalog Card Number: 88-12176

First edition: November 1988

First mass market edition: March 1990
Printed in the United States of America

0 9 8 7 6 5 4 3 2 1

For Judy Delton,
enthusiastic writer and teacher,
whose encouragement
started it all

Prologue: January 11
After

Snowflakes fell like shooting stars coming unglued from the midnight-black sky. They brushed the van's windshield with regularity—ice-cold butterfly kisses from the winter night.

The bluff top lay white and deserted except for the oblong of the van, silent except for the van's slow idling cough, motionless except for the stream of exhaust that oozed from the van's tail pipe.

The temperature wasn't much warmer inside the van, despite the idling motor. The man and woman within it huddled loverlike against the cold.

She wore a fur coat, her feet curled under her on the passenger seat. She shivered anyway—a dark-haired young woman with a lost look.

He crouched in the well between their bucket seats, his arms around her, a tattered down vest like some scarecrow's hand-me-down barely disguising his staccato shudders.

The van's side windows were cracked just enough to admit thin slabs of almost tangible January cold. The couple's breaths wove fog castles in the air, and their teeth chattered.

"Can we go?" she asked at last.

"Go? Sure. Where—I don't know."

"Home?" she suggested in a husky, tentative voice.

He laughed, a bit bitterly. Her expression sharpened.

"Kevin? Have you . . . changed?"

"Me? Me, change? Hell, no. I'm the same lovable, slightly insane shrink I always was. It's *all* the same—the world, I mean. You're the same. Maybe."

"The same . . ." She withdrew inside herself to see, then nodded gravely. "The same but different. I don't know how, in what way; I don't know what . . . they . . . left me—"

"They *left* you—that's the main thing!" He squeezed her shoulders encouragingly, blew his warm breath across the fur collar until its ruddy hairs tickled her pale cheek.

She smiled as palely. "There's so much I don't know—"

"Me, too." He hugged her again, not seeming to want to talk about it, about anything.

His clothes snapped like cracking ice as he pushed himself away and into the driver's seat. Her hand clung to his withdrawing arm.

"Keep your hands warm. It's going to be a long, cold drive." Kevin pushed her hand deep into the fur's side pocket, softening the gesture with a smile. "I hope you kept some of your—talents. They may follow us," he muttered.

She wrenched forward to press her face to the windshield and stare up at the bottomless well of night. *"They* might come again?"

"No! Not them. *My* masters. Bureaucratic bloodhounds with their own secret ways. Men on the road beside us, at the filling station pumps, in the city streets."

"Like the ones . . . behind us?"

He nodded grimly.

"But they—"

"Forget it." Command and plea interwove in his tone.

A smile brushed her tense features, turning her briefly beautiful. "Once, you wanted me to remember."

The van was churning into serious operation now, and warming. Random snowflakes kissing the windshield dissolved into tear tracks. Kevin's expression melted, too, then hardened. He thrust the woman's bare foot back under the swath of fur.

"You're living in a real world now, Jane. You've become real, too. Some things are too dangerous to remember."

2

"But . . . I remember everything I see. Except—"

"Forget it."

Kevin twisted the van's stiff steering wheel in a slow circle. The vehicle's tires dug into the drifts, squeaking as they tamped down snow. He braked at the mouth of the steep road leading down from the bluff, then looked back.

A feathery dusting of fresh snow was already riffling across the tonsure of bare rock at the bluff top's center.

"It'll look the same by morning," he said. "Just empty snow under an empty sky. As if it had never—"

"The same," Jane agreed, "but different."

Kevin's foot pushed the pedal, pouring gas down the engine's chilled throat.

The van lurched down into the dark and the deep snow, spiraling along the corkscrewed road, headlights slashing at a passing background of identical-seeming snow-hooded trees and bushes. Now and then the lights pinned a single snowflake in the glare of their yellow eyes. For an instant before shattering on the thick headlight glass, the snowflake went nova.

Jane winced and blinked her eyes.

Kevin steered them down into the rough, bucking dark —away from the naked bluff top and back to civilization, back down to the placid Minnesota town of Crow Wing, where a January night came as cold as God can make it and man can take it.

Where everything was always the same. Everlastingly the same.

The Retracing
January 8

*   *   *

"... the anguish of the marrow ..."

—T. S. Eliot
"Whispers of Immortality"

Chapter One

"Jeez, they look like burnt toast . . . what coulda done it?"

Turner winced visibly.

"Blowtorch maybe, you think?" The local sheriff stuffed wind-chapped hands into his parka pockets to dig out battered gloves.

Beneath them, snow squeaked as the men stuttered from booted foot to booted foot, tamping down the once-pristine surface.

Besides Turner and the sheriff in his teddy-bear parka and flap-eared red-plaid wool cap that made him resemble a cartoon hound dog, five other men had gathered in the deep woods clearing. Six were out-of-state government troubleshooters with cold-rouged ears and noses.

Then there were the two dead bodies sprawled across the hood of a heat-blistered government-issue Ford. Only months before, the automobile had left a plant assembly line painted a lackluster bottle-green; now its husk was singed to the color of tobacco spit.

"Burnt toast," the sheriff mourned again, shaking his head. "Musta been *some* heat wave."

Turner looked away into the low steady whine of the January wind. The worst were the fingers—swollen, split, char-broiled. They didn't look quite human, the bodies, Turner thought. His job came easier when the dead had the decency to look human.

"Go right ahead and do your stuff," the sheriff urged. "I like to see how the big-city boys do it."

The sheriff's name was Leonard Kustovich. Turner knew

his type—red-neck, blue-collar rube. This particular model was a third-generation Slav who should have been mining northern Minnesota's Iron Range taconite strips like his immigrant ancestors. Instead, the world's need for taconite had blown south down Highway 61 twenty-five years earlier, leaving with a harmonica-toting hitchhiker from Hibbing who called himself Bob Dylan.

Now northern Minnesota beer joints thronged with unemployed men stewing in the stench of wet wool and sour expectations. Leonard Kustovich, being smarter than he looked, an advantage for a low-level public servant, had gotten a job as sheriff.

"Don't see much in the way of capital offenses up here," Kustovich remarked. The sheriff eyed the team of technicians documenting the trampled snow around the burnt car. "Nothin' that calls for six men. What department badge you flash again?"

Turner patiently tugged off his new wool-lined leather gloves and flashed a discreet identity card in a small, two-sided case.

The brown leather cracked audibly in the subzero cold; so did the brittle clear plastic entombing his name, rank and serial number. Goddamn world's end of a place to end up in, Turner swore to himself, the only person he allowed to overhear his own profanity. Fucking foolish place to die in. To start a manhunt from, with a trail as cold as all outdoors.

Kustovich's seamed face waggled from side to side. "CIA. FBI. ATF. Now here's the PID. Never heard of you guys."

"We like it that way."

Turner stared at the sky, a stonewashed denim expanse speared by dark, jousting pinetops. Along a route demarcated by fluorescent pink string, the recording crew was videotaping the evidence—or rather, the absence of it.

Turner paced along the path, leaving behind two of his men, Kerr and Frakowski, but not the local sheriff.

"You kin see they had some sort of oversized vehicle here." Sheriff Kustovich's heavy-duty gloves, the fingers thick and stiff as the dead men's digits, traced a lopsided circle of footprints wading through the knee-high drifts. Nearby ran the deep parallel impressions of tire ruts. "Not equipped for back country snow, though."

"A van," Turner said flatly. "Beige '78 Chevrolet."

"Those boys of yours we picked off the highway ravine last night; they must be doin' okay in the hospital, if they kin remember that."

"Not really. But they're alive and probably'll stay that way. Watch where you're walking!"

"Hey, I know how to tippy-toe around a crime scene." Kustovich twisted to survey the ruined car shrinking into a blot of black on the white-washed winter landscape.

Snow sparkled in the brittle noonday sunlight. The tech team clicked and panned away, black boxes masking their faces. They didn't look quite human, Kustovich thought a little creepily, but then, neither did the dead men, and they were all stamped out from the same, government-issue cookie cutter.

Where the long-gone van had paused, the trail lurched toward a dark fence of surrounding tree trunks. Footprints —confused enough to indicate the coming and going of more than one person—pocked the snowdrifts.

"Who are these fugitives, anyway?" Kustovich probed. "Don't tell me we got Russky spies slippin' through the Mapleleaf Curtain? Or 'Nam draft dodgers finally comin' home? Hey! Undeclared aliens? Drug smugglers, maybe?"

"Maybe." Amusement crisped Turner's cold-cracked lips. Time had taught him that denying local authorities the pleasure of speculation created more stir than letting them pursue any number of wild tangents.

Kustovich eyed the city man, sizing him up as he himself had been so swiftly typecast. He liked to play into off–Iron Range prejudices, but wasn't half so dumb as he looked. Neither was the taut-lipped Turner. Mid-forties, without that beefy, hungry look you found among Iron Range men. Smooth in a way that didn't mean slick. Invisible. Except here.

The sheriff let his bright brown eyes carom off the busy men—all duded up in their nylon-shelled *this* and down-filled *that* with nothing on their heads but what hair God left 'em and with their exposed, note-taking, picture-taking hands turning lobster-scarlet in the icebox that was a Minnesota mid-January.

Amateur experts, he scoffed to himself. Still, he followed Turner to trail's end. At a clearing fenced by whip-thin brush, the footsteps ended in a cul-de-sac of drifts.

"How many perpetrators, you figure, Mr. Turner?"

"Just . . . two."

"—and whatever weapon fried those stiffs back there."

Turner winced without showing it this time. "And whatever."

"Musta been big, somethin' to do that kind of damage."

"Maybe not."

Kustovich's eyes narrowed hungrily, but Turner gave the sheriff his back as an aide plodded over for a whispered consultation.

Kustovich, not one to hide his weaknesses, eavesdropped openly.

"It's a puzzler, sir," the subordinate was saying.

Kustovich envied that "sir."

"We knew that when we came up here," Turner said.

"I mean . . . this. These marks in the snow."

Turner and Kustovich looked where the man pointed.

"Someone fell," Turner dismissed the discovery.

"Fell . . . maybe, sir. But why that? That . . . blurring around the impact point? It just grazes the snow's surface at torso level but it's deeper by the legs, like it was made deliberately. Weirdest thing I've ever seen."

Turner would have answered, but Kustovich loosed a laugh reminiscent of a stalled snowmobile engine. As many big men do, he gargled his mirth like raw razor blades, making quite a show of it.

"What's so funny?" Turner clipped out, annoyed at last.

"'Weird.' 'Puzzler.' Jesus H. Christ, where you boys come from originally, anyhow?" Kustovich sputtered amiably.

"My parents and Michigan," Turner snapped.

"Nevada," said the other man.

Kustovich's ear-flapped head wagged roguishly. "Hell, I

10

can see why a desert rat might be snowed by this, but a Michigan man . . . didn'cha *ever* play in the snow in Michigan, Mr. Turner?"

"Play?" Turner's enunciation made it evident that he never had played—then . . . or now.

"Didn'cha kids make winter snow forts years ago? Make icicles outa clothes poles by pouring water from the house down 'em? Didn'cha drag your feet through clean-fallen snow and make big pie shapes to play tag in?

"Hell, there ain't nothin' weird about that mark! It's a snow angel, that's all. We see 'em around here all the time, usually on the neighborhood lawns after a fresh fall."

"Snow angel?" The underling from Nevada echoed Kustovich's bizarre phrase when Turner wouldn't.

"Snow angel." Kustovich's laugh subsided to a chuckle. "Lead me to a safe mussing spot and I'll show yah how it's done."

The Nevada man gestured him beyond the staked-out string. Turner followed.

Before their eyes, Kustovich plopped ass-down in a virgin snowbank. He lay back in the bright white blanket of undented snow, chuckling with Santa-like glee, and began windmilling his arms and legs, sweeping them up and down, in and out, like a demented traffic cop.

Neither watching face betrayed reaction, but the Nevada man finally let his jaw drop enough to speak.

"That's the same shape, all right. You mean somebody laid down there in the subzero temperatures in the dark last night—with two men fried a few yards away—and did *that?*" He glanced incredulously to Turner.

Kustovich grinned up from the snow.

"I don't know, Junior, but I do know that this is how to make those marks. It's a kid thing. It's what you do when you're nine years old and you ain't got nothin' else to do and the snow is pretty and you feel like thumbing your nose at the cold. They do it all the time, kids. Have for years. Give me a hand up— Heck, if you don't, I'll ruin it," the sheriff added plaintively. Kustovich extended big-gloved paws and waited.

Turner and his associate froze for a disconcerted moment. Then each extended a gloved hand and levered the sheriff upright. He turned to admire his handiwork.

"Not bad. Real nice, in fact. Haven't done that for—oh, shit . . . years." He yanked off a mitt and began flicking snow clods from inside his collar. "Whew, snow on your neck sure is cold. Forgot that. Now why do you suppose these perpetrators would want to fry your guys, then stop to make a snow angel? That's what's weird. What kind of hopheads we got here?"

"'We' have nothing here. The PID's work is classified." Turner moved back to the original snow angel. "Shoot it, close-up," he ordered. Camera-bearers swarmed forward.

A sudden scream whined into the clearing, rising and falling mechanically. One glaring red eye flickered through the black fence of bare tree trunks, following the now-deep tire tracks.

Shutters clicked relentlessly as Turner walked away, Kustovich behind him. The ambulance's white-painted sides looked dingy next to the fresh snow.

The driver, alerted, had stopped well beyond the roped-off area, but he left his emergency light on. It glinted hot pink through the snow flurries kissing past the charred car. Kustovich shivered in his warm winter woolens.

"We don't get many violent deaths up here," he admitted. "Oh, we get the fatal bar brawl now and again, or the occasional kid who wanders off and falls through the river ice. We don't even find that many dead rape victims. Too damn cold even for that. Now in one day I've got three stiffs for young Doc Moudry."

"Three?" For the first time that cold, clear noon Turner's voice betrayed interest.

"Three." Kustovich ticked off the morning's toll on his still-bare hand. "Your two here and that old lady found dead in her cabin. One of those north woods hermits. Probably croaked of a sick ticker. Old Lady Neumeier. Guess she used to be someone down in the Cities. Natural causes, though. Not like this."

Turner's face pinched tighter. Together the two men

12

watched as the scorched bodies were lifted from their grotesque positions and laid on stretchers in even more grotesque postures. For once Kustovich said nothing.

The attendants slammed the ambulance doors shut, mounted the cab and whined away with their spinning red light faint in the strong daylight. They reminded Turner more of clowns in some deep-freeze circus than angels of mercy.

Angels. The word—and the recent demonstration—made Turner's face sour. God knew the dossier was slim enough—a sketch of the woman, a smattering of medical records.

Of course, there was a lot more on the man. A whole lifetime's worth to sift through and enlarge under the microscopic eye that PID was so expert at exercising.

"A snow angel." Beside Turner, Kustovich mused into the distance, chuckling mildly. "Don't that beat everything? Who're you guys after, anyway, juvenile delinquents?"

Chapter Two

"You're sure they fit?" Kevin stared down at Jane's brand-new boots with something resembling parental anxiety.

Clumps of snow wedged under her heels were weeping onto the venerable wooden floorboards, but the boots were less than an hour old.

Jane stared down, too.

The boots were quilted nylon, down-filled mukluks, pale blue. Kevin supposed they looked stupid peeping out from under the luxuriously long hem of Jane's opossum coat, but he wasn't a fashion expert. Neither was Jane. And the boots were warm. The saleswoman at the Midnight Loon, down the street, had assured him of that when he'd ducked in solo to buy them.

"I remembered your size from that day in the dormitory," he told Jane, asking again, "They do fit?"

She nodded slowly, wearing the uncommitted dazed look she'd hugged shield-close since the . . . the bluff top. But who could emerge from an encounter that traumatic without a little shell shock? Not he, Kevin thought. He sighed and studied the relentlessly normal environs of an ersatz old-fashioned general store.

Around Kevin and Jane browsers ambled down aisles arrayed with post-Christmas markdowns and winter gift paraphernalia, ranging from soft-sculpture mallards to plush polar bears and cow-eyed baby harp seals. Sporting goods bristled along every wall; circular racks of winter outerwear formed islands in the stream of shoppers; crockery beribboned like pampered pets anchored a gift alcove.

And in the middle of it, Jane—wearing nothing more than her big fur coat and brand-new boots—stood dripping onto the hardwood floor.

The rural Minnesota town of Crow Wing counted on the tourist trade, even in the dead of winter. Shops like the Pine Cone lined a reclaimed Main Street to purvey trendy gewgaws to carloads of bored urbanites escaping the Twin Cities of Minneapolis and St. Paul.

"Oh, a sale. . . ." Jane's dazed eyes focused expertly on a rack of skiwear. She headed for it with a gleam.

Only Kevin's quick hand on her arm delayed her.

"No, no. Forget 'sales.' Staying in Willhelm Hall made you into a coed clone. We don't need that stuff. All we need is, uh . . ."

Kevin's face absorbed some of Jane's vacancy as he examined the consumer carousels around him. Nobody showed surprise at his bemusement, or noticed the mental fatigue graying his face.

He knew he looked completely unremarkable, thank God, a prime example of uncomplicated Minnesota manhood lost in a familiarly alien retail environment—early

14

thirties, clean-shaven, jeans-clad, confused. He could have been any typical husband or father out for a Sunday shopping spree, except that he was neither and he had never been typical.

And Jane could have been— He glanced at her and blanched. She was reaching out to finger a corduroy jacket sleeve, the damnable, inexpendable fur coat splitting slightly open on her torso. . . .

"Jesus Christ!" Kevin's hands jerked the coat edges shut. A woman shopper pawing through a rack behind Jane paused to lance him with a venomously reproving look. "You can't do that," he added softly. "If you see something you like, point it out and I'll pull it off the rack."

His crooked elbow soon bore a set of ladies' thermal long johns, jeans, turtleneck sweater, wool plaid shirt, and gloves. All they needed now was the jacket. . . . He looked around.

Jane's dark head was disappearing among the clotted clothes racks, bobbing toward something promising. He overtook her at a chrome carousel strung with Hudson Bay jackets, their characteristic red, green and yellow stripes screaming across the bland white wool fabric.

"This," suggested Jane.

He smiled. "North woods to the zipper teeth, but . . . too distinctive. Wearing one of these lollipops would be even worse than this." His hand tugged the sleeve of her fur coat.

"But . . . I like it."

"It's not right for where we're going," he insisted, gritting his teeth a little. Funny, he thought, how you never notice a headache until it's ready to eat you alive.

"It's right for where we've been!" she argued.

Kevin saw the glint of fine-edged anger sharpen her expression, and almost released his own exasperation. Once she'd been infatuated with him and he had forced himself not to see it. He could have used a little dumb, unquestioning adoration now, when so much was at stake.

He remembered that once he would have celebrated any tiny sign of autonomy in Jane as a personal triumph. Now it had become simply inconvenient. Risking everything to ensure Jane's independence, he now found himself the first to quash it. For her own good.

Kevin's free hand patted the front of Jane's coat as if he stroked a living thing. "I know it's tough to think of replacing . . . this, Jane, but we have to."

Jane's rebellious expression softened as it met the concern in his eyes. Childlike, she bowed her head and pulled the coat open to examine it. Kevin glimpsed a hand's-breadth of naked torso before he clamped the fur shut again.

"Keep it that way," he ordered, aware again of being an outsider in even the simplest matters. "We'd better get you into the inside stuff. No regular underwear sold here, I'm afraid," he noted, shrugging by racks with Jane in his wake. "You'll have to go New Wave this time."

Dressing rooms were impossible to spot in the rambling storescape. Kevin corralled a woman clerk and dumped the clothes into her arms.

"She"—he nodded at Jane—"wants to try these on." The clerk weighed the comforting bulk of a multi-item sale on her forearm and quickly led them to the establishment's rear, where tartan-plaid curtains masked two confessional-size dressing areas.

Jane docilely ducked under the uplifted curtain, her expression puzzled.

"Call me if you want anything, dear." The clerk crimped a brisk smile at Kevin and bustled away.

Kevin heard the mute motions of "trying on" behind the curtain.

"If it fits, keep it on," he hissed through the fabric, hoping Jane would know the correct order in which to install her new layered look.

She was out in a few minutes—booted, blue-jeaned, sweatered and shirted from toes to chin.

Kevin sighed real relief, his face losing five years of worry. Behind Jane in the tiny dressing room, the discarded fur coat overflowed a minuscule built-in bench to slump onto the floor like a dead thing.

Kevin collected the fur, then snagged a teal-colored down jacket for Jane on the way to the front cash register, and a cocoa-colored down jacket for himself. He began peeling hundred-dollar bills from his wallet, silently cursing the high denomination and Kandy's eccentric money habits, handy as they sometimes were.

"She'll take it all, and wear it," he told the clerk. "Have you got a bag for this?" He hefted the full-length fur onto the countertop.

Untidy iron-gray eyebrows visited the clerk's receding hairline. "I'll have to clip off the tags, sir," she complained, advancing on Jane with a formidable pair of shears.

"Fine; no problem," he said nervously, as much reassuring Jane as the clerk.

Scissor blades flashed around Jane's torso like a circus dagger-thrower's knives. Strands of thin white plastic fishline popped every which way as Jane's clothing was sheared of its sales tags.

Kevin tried to keep his booted foot from tapping the wooden floor as he and Jane dangled over the cash register for an eternity while the clerk computed each item.

"Three hundred and four dollars and eighty-five cents," she finally announced.

"Great!" The clerkish face expressed surprise.

Kevin could have kicked himself for thinking only of the many small, useful bills he'd get in change. Another mistake. Normal people don't relish spending hundreds of dollars at a whack. He wasn't going to be good at this, and he had to be.

"I thought we'd done more damage to the budget," he backpedaled, joking. "But you can't get around in this weather without the right gear."

"Absolutely, sir," trilled the clerk, carefully folding the fur coat into a large plastic bag into which it immediately and bonelessly collapsed. She wrung the bag's neck and secured it with a plastic twist, then slung it over the counter. "A coat like this really should be on a hanger, but this'll do until you folks get home again."

Home. The word hit Kevin in the sinuses right between the eyes, like Chinese mustard.

Everything familiar dropped away. He felt the weight of the coat, shrouded in something that was first cousin to a

17

garbage bag. He felt removed, as so many of his patients complained of feeling. He felt he stood on a hundred-year-old wooden floor that had turned into a hermit's pillar in some alien wasteland too vast to sense.

Something tugged at his arm. Jane's hand. Her dark eyes pierced his emptiness.

"I'll take it," she was saying, extending her other hand for the yellow sales slip and handful of bills the clerk was pushing at a momentarily nerveless Kevin. "We've got a long way to go," Jane added conversationally, apropos of nothing. And of everything.

She turned and led him out of the store to a beige '78 Chevy van waiting by a meter that read "Expired," as it always did on commercial Main Street, where no one had to pay for parking.

Nothing on earth approximated the silence of empty woods in winter. Nothing could be so vast and yet anonymous.

Kevin crouched beside the conspiratorial snowdrifts behind the van's rear bumper, pouring bottled spring water over the snow he had packed over the license plate.

Cold had crippled his leather driving gloves into claws. He slapped at the snow and continued the ritual. This roadside baptism didn't confer an identity—hopefully, it would disguise one. And they would be coming, he knew that. They had to keep coming. It was their job.

He looked up. Through the trees on his right, an occasional car hissed past on the plowed highway. This clearing that concealed the van while he performed his bizarre ablutions sat only fifty yards from Highway 61 outside of Crow Wing, Minnesota. Yet it seemed secure, probably because he wanted it to be. John Donne was wrong, Kevin mused bitterly. We are all islands, and safest when we are most set apart.

Jane was tramping around the clearing, her new boots driving footprints into the untouched snow, gloved hands swelling her jacket pockets, cheeks and nose rosy, thick dark hair riffling in the breeze.

Kevin paused to watch, tenderness and fear weaving a

18

saraband of frustration in his mind. He'd seen something once in a book when he was a kid—a kid's book—a painting of a small black pony against the snow, with a dark-haired girl in a muffler. And a small red apple offered across the blank canvas of the winter.

Right now Jane looked like that child, although she was well into her twenties. She even looked like she should be playing, although she never had.

"Done?" she shouted across the clearing.

He stopped himself from telling her to speak quietly and stood, dusting off cold-cracked leather palms. "Done."

"I like it here," Jane said, lifting her head to a bloodless blue sky marbled with insipid clouds.

"Me, too." Kevin stamped closer through the drifts, his feet long since having become leaden ice lumps in his boots.

"But we can't stay." Jane's eyes were level, very focused now.

He shook his head.

"Kevin, where are we going?"

"Away."

"Away?" she challenged. She had been challenging more lately.

"Somewhere."

"Why?"

"Because. . . ." The reasons didn't belong in this fir-pillared nave of snow. He spread his stiff hands in a wordless gesture.

She stared at him, into him, her eyes keener than kerosene. Then she mirrored his gesture, spreading her arms. Her lips parted with question and with cold, her eyes warming with intelligence, with understanding even.

Kevin wanted to kiss her. Before he could move, Jane sat down in the snowbanks, sinking from view like a drowning woman.

"That's what you did, in the woods," she said, laughing. She lay back in the snow, her figure a dark starfish beached on endless anonymity.

Her arms and legs—tentatively, slowly—began moving up and down, in and out. As if she were leaping off the

19

earth, or trying to. As if she were flying, or trying to. Around her, the snow shifted into the cookie cutter impression of an angel—a winged, full-skirted angel. A Christmas tree angel, as white and soft . . . and deadly . . . as fiberglass.

"Get up," Kevin said, his voice raw. "Get up!"

Bewildered, Jane stared at him, still smiling. "I saw you do it. In the woods. Last night. After . . . before. Why did you do it?"

"I—regression, I guess. Pointless regression. Get up." He waded into the fragile construction, his feet blurring its outlines, and pulled her up. His gloves beat lumps of snow off her back.

"You've ruined it," Jane lamented. "Kevin, why—?"

"Jane—" No more words came, just the name—the pseudonym—that they had both paid such an unfathomable price to retain.

Kevin enfolded her in a bearish embrace, his cheek pressing the cold softness of hers. It felt strange without the barrier of his beard between them. He missed it. Damn . . . needed to shave again. Didn't want to look like a vagrant, attract attention. Already he was tiring of the rules of the game, and it had just begun. . . .

"I don't know where to go," he confessed, more to himself than to her. He still viewed Jane as his charge—his precious, dangerous, two-edged charge. "I don't know where to take you. I only know that I have to do one thing at a time."

He broke their embrace to look back at the van, sitting bland and innocent in the snow.

"The license plates are taken care of," he said. "If that's enough. Those flashy C-notes of Kandy's have probably alerted every state trooper on Highway 61 by now. Or maybe *they* have to keep quiet about this. Maybe their hands are tied, too."

"Kevin, who? The men who followed us on the highway, the men in the woods who—?" She stopped, frowned, and looked into herself.

Kevin's rough gloves wrenched her naked face to his and kissed it away—the frown, the memory. Most of all the memory. Not many days before, his job—his only passion—had been helping Jane to remember.

She kissed him back with an ardor that always surprised him. He relaxed into that small inlet of warmth in this large ocean of cold called a world.

"We've got to keep moving," he said when their faces separated. Their breaths mingled into phantasmagoric traceries of vanishing frost. "Come on, we've got to dump the coat."

He turned back to the van, forced energy in his yard-long steps. Jane floundered behind him, gamboling like a pony. Her eyes brimmed curiosity as he pulled the yellow plastic bag from the back of the van, heaved it over his shoulder Santa-wise and forged across virgin snow to a ring of towering pine trees.

And like a dog, Jane tilted her head to watch as Kevin laid down the burden, then studied the area.

"Where, do you think? A good, out-of-the-way spot," he consulted her, trying to give her a role in their melodrama.

She looked around, then leveled her finger at a top-lofty, emerald-black fir tree.

Kevin grinned. "You don't have to keep pointing. Your coat's not going to fall open and reveal the Sally Rand of the Iron Range anymore. Okay, the tree it is. There's a good-size drift there anyway. Very Freudian, you know, to choose a 'fir' tree."

He crouched at the tree trunk, crouched and began pawing at the hip-high mound of snow driven under its branches. Jane joined him, laughing, snow spraying from her gloved hands, stars of glitter tangling in her eyelashes, her cheeks and lips red, red, and the snow so white, so light, so fresh, so cold.

"That's enough." Kevin sat back on his heels and slung the bag into the snowpit they'd made.

Jane's face stiffened as she finally realized what he was doing. He gave her a quick smile before pushing snow over the plastic, burying it in soft, silent handfuls.

It was quiet in the woods. And empty. Then Jane spoke.

"Zyunsinth," she said, her voice deep, so deep he turned to make sure it was Jane who had spoken.

21

Her eyes stared at the rumpled snow, and the crumpled plastic bag half-buried by it.

"Zyunsinth," she repeated, on a rising note of denial.

"Yes, I know, but it's . . . it's a dead giveaway, Jane. It's too easy to trace, an expensive, eye-catching coat like that. We can't afford to stand out."

"You're not . . . leaving . . . Zyunsinth here?"

"I have to. Jane—"

She hurled herself atop the sack, burrowed herself into the snow with it, her gloves tearing uselessly at the plastic. She wrenched them off and her bare fingers poked ragged holes in the material. Patches of fur pushed out. Jane's palms petted them feverishly while Kevin tried to stop her.

"Jane, we have to leave the coat! It's a hazard."

They tussled through his words. It was like interning at the state hospital again, Kevin thought, agrip with déjà vu. Like trying to subdue a schizophrenic. But he knew how to exert force in a crisis.

"It can hurt us, hurt you," he panted between efforts to confine her awesome energy. "I know how attached you are to the damn thing, but—"

Her eyes grew leaden with loss. She lay still under him at last, like a victim, her hair in her teeth, the snow in her hair, her cold white hands pinned to the death-pale earth.

Kevin shut his eyes and released her. When he looked again, she had sat up and was wiping a stream of tears from her face with icy palms. The tears frightened him more than the fury. He had never seen Jane cry before. Never.

"Jane. . . ." His hand didn't quite connect with any part of her, but hovered—nearby and irretrievably distant.

"Zyunsinth," she mourned, rocking.

"I know I can't begin to understand what . . . it . . . they . . . mean to you," he began, fighting for the cool control of a therapy session, fighting to become again the iceman in the white lab coat, if he had ever been that.

Her hands, twining, covered each other on her mouth. Her eyes were holes in the snow all around them, deep and dark.

"Home," she said.

He was silent.

Jane sat back on her heels, the tears still sliding down her cheeks reminding him of springwater icing a license plate. Kevin wanted to wipe them away and strip her of obscurity. Instead, he must act against his instincts, his profession, his ethics even. He had to help her to hide, even from herself, no matter what.

He turned and began piling snow atop the fur coat, speaking over his shoulder to her, to himself. She didn't try to stop him anymore.

"Your home is here, Jane," he said, hoping he would believe it, too. "With me. We're only . . . burying . . . Zyunsinth. See, you even picked a good tall tree to tell the site by. Maybe—someday—we can come back and . . . dig it up. When winter's over and everything's all right. Someday."

He wished he didn't sound as if he were speaking to a child. God knew she wasn't that. He wished he didn't sound as if he were fooling himself. God knew he couldn't afford to.

"Come back." Jane's eyes lightened. She watched the bag disappear under his tireless hands. "Someday. Yes, I think so. Someday they will come back."

He stared at her, inferring her meaning, chilled by the obvious truth of it, frozen for the moment beyond snow and pain.

Chapter Three

"He's our best lead."

Turner threw a photograph of a bearded man to the Formica desktop. It was one of those bland, smiling black-and-whites used in professional journals.

"It's the woman we want," Lindahl said, swiveling to study a gray January day. The office window was still dust-streaked with the past autumn's crop of falling leaves and rain.

Turner threw another image atop the man's—the pen-and-ink sketch of an unsmiling female face.

"We've got nothing in her file but this, and some medical reports. Blake's notes are nonexistent, or hidden or destroyed, though I don't think he's—"

"Smart enough to do it?"

Turner hesitated and twisted in his chair. Here in the Cities he wore a suit and a warm, inner-lined London Fog. Somehow, after the expedition north and what they had found—and lost—his city slicker garb rubbed him the wrong way.

"Oh, he's smart enough," Turner answered. "Harvard Med School, all those headline-grabbing cases. No, Dr. Blake is smart enough. He just isn't sneaky enough."

"He was sneaky enough to elude you in Duluth and evade your two men on the highway. To . . . incinerate two more."

Turner shook a weary head. "It doesn't track, Karl. I don't know the first who, what, why—or even how—on those deaths up there."

"We've got an all-points out on the van?"

"Sure. But we can't alert the locals to our interest, so it's just a phony moving violation offense we pumped into the computers. If the cops see it, they'll stop it. If they're looking hard enough. No, our best bet is still the people, not the vehicle."

Lindahl spun back, all bureaucratic melodrama, to face Turner. "Find them. Washington wants them bad."

"Washington." Turner came as close to swearing as he allowed himself. "Why? All we've got here is a rogue shrink and his patient on the run—and some rumored psi abilities that may not pan out. Why the federal case?"

"That's for me to know and you to not know."

"Okay. Fine. Pull all that upper-level clearance . . ." If he'd been about to say "crap," he didn't give Lindahl the satisfaction. ". . . mumbo-jumbo on me. You know those security levels exist mainly to give a bunch of bureaucrats a sense of self-importance. You spy guys would be nowhere without domestic operatives like me who know our turf. But I want bloodhounds on this one; the trail's too broad and too cold. You can't expect me to hunt blind."

"Sure I can," Lindahl said. "But what do you have in mind?"

"You ever see an old Hitchcock movie, *To Catch a Thief*?"

"Sure . . . I get it—"

"To catch a shrink, use a shrink to find him."

Lindahl picked up the industrial-strength stapler on his desk. "You're thinking of Nordstrom."

Turner nodded.

"He's been . . . useful, but—"

"He's a . . ."—Turner mentally deleted an expletive; it was a game he played, avoiding the obvious—"a cold fish," he finished forcefully. "But we can use him."

"I wish we had more on her." Lindahl indicated the sketch.

"We will." Turner rose and pulled his all-weather coat off the rack. "When we get him."

Lindahl's fist hit the empty stapler hard—a gesture all sound and frustration connecting nothing.

Outside, Turner paused to examine Fourth Street traffic. A day as innocuously gray as the granite five-story federal building itself swathed downtown Minneapolis. Two blocks down the street loomed the Victorian bulk of the Hennepin County Courthouse, its copper-roofed turrets poking green spearheads into the ragged winter clouds.

Dirty snowbanks hunched along the hidden curbs, thrown there by city plows after every snowfall worth calling that. Passersby minced along the icy sidewalks, heads lowered to shelter their faces from the chapping wind.

Turner kept his head erect as he walked to the dingy parking garage where his government-issue car sat on an upper level brutally open to the wind. It would be cold, but he was used to this godforsaken climate.

Vaguely distasteful assignments, like tracking naive psychiatrists and their patients, were nothing new, either.

Neither were distasteful deaths. Before this case was over, there would probably be more of them, Turner told himself.

Monica Chapman shifted slightly on the austere black leather psychoanalyst's couch, trying to pull her Perry Ellis wool skirt wrinkle-free beneath her.

She heard the tap of his Mark Cross pen against the spiral binding of his leatherbound yellow legal pad and froze. He watched everything. And he always occupied the traditional Freudian position behind her. Out of sight. Invisible but all-seeing. Like God.

Monica Chapman had long since stopped believing in God. Instead, she believed in—feared—her psychiatrist. *("For I am a jealous god and you will put no graven images before me. . . .")*

"You're fidgeting, Monica. A bad sign. Are you considering lying to me again?" His disembodied voice was low, resonant, baritone enough for a disc jockey and oily enough for a spa salesman.

She kept her eyes on all she could see from her supine point of view, on all he *let* her—or any other patient—see.

There was a wall of soberly framed degrees attesting to his credentials in semi-illegible hand-lettering; bookcases furnished in suites of identically bound volumes, so they seemed linked in some unreadable conspiracy of disinformation; the expensive German tape recording system with its showy, slow-motion oversized reels, so the patient was exquisitely aware of every word being engraved in its original tone for instant replay, again and again.

Why, why was she here? Why did it seem so impossible not to be here? The thoughts sank into a familiar track like a needle into an LP groove. Monica hardly felt the pain now, although she knew it must hurt—somewhere. She forced herself to look at things again, not thoughts. Things.

There was one framed photograph on the wall—black and white—of a ballerina. Gelsey Kirkland in *Swan Lake,* Monica thought, although she had never asked and he had never said. Frozen, the tulle-dolloped figure looked brittle and puppetlike, not human at all. Monica ruminated on the fact that Degas, the exquisite chronicler of the *danseuse*'s fragile ultrafeminine beauty, had hated women.

"You always fixate on my little dancer, Monica, why?"

"She's . . ." Afraid to irritate him, Monica lied, knowing it even as the word left her lips. ". . . beautiful."

"Yes. And you're envious."

Her long body in the designer suit jolted on the couch as if electroshocked ever so slightly. In the ensuing pause, Monica read his satisfaction at striking a nerve so soon in session. She would have glanced at the slim gold watch on her equally slim wristbone, but knew from experience that any sign of restiveness irritated him, made him . . . more demanding.

"I'm not envious—" she began.

"Of course you are. You know your self-hatred manifests itself in your drive to succeed in your career. And the more successful you are, the more you loathe yourself. And then you gorge—secretly, in your chic, narrow esophagus of an alley kitchen with all those stainless steel gadgets.

"Such things you gorge on, dear Monica, so tacky. Fish and chips, ice cream by the half gallon—and not even ice cream from some SoHo specialty shop, but common supermarket *lard*. You make quite a pig of yourself, Monica, in that high-rent apartment of yours. And then you come to me. For absolution."

She writhed under his expertly applied words, and ran her fingers nervously under the Perry Ellis waistband. Size six and already loosening. . . . It wasn't fair! She tried and tried until she was so tired and confused, until only an act of excess here, another there, would calm her, would ease the eternal inner ache.

"I won't describe how disgustingly you neutralize your excesses," he continued. "You would have made a fine Roman empress, Monica, purple-draped like some mountain grape, lying on your cushioned couch, waiting to have whole banquets delivered by some slave's hand to your lascivious little mouth. Pheasant . . . gravies by the tureen

. . . rich, thick puddings from ewers, all down, down your ravenous aristocratic maw. Then would follow the stately withdrawal to the vomitorium, where another slave would tickle your throat with the feather of a fresh-slaughtered emu and yet another slave would hold the golden bowl while you—"

"No, please!" Her throat was dry, raw, as if she'd been retching for hours.

"Instead you have your career and your privacy. Such has modern-day culture brought us. You have a white porcelain bowl to embrace—oh, pardon; I believe you told me your master bathroom has maroon fixtures. How decadent, Monica. How Roman of you."

"It's a disease," she said anxiously. "Bulimia is a disease."

"A most fashionable disease."

"And maybe I . . . retch . . . because of what my father and brothers did to me. I used to . . . throw up . . . every time, when they were done with me."

"But you stayed at home until you were eighteen. Why, Monica? You could have left, unless you had learned to like it."

"No!" But the accusation, like thousands of accusations rendered before: You always . . . you must . . . you need . . . you asked for it, drummed into her head until the voices echoed there of their own volition, accusing, accusing, until she would have crawled over shattered Baccarat to silence them. "No one would have wanted me," she muttered, "helped me."

"But I'm here now. To help you. You know you depend on me now. Monica, stand up."

She stiffened.

"I want to look at you."

"I haven't cheated! I didn't gorge all last week, honest, I didn't—well, only once, maybe, and then only on half a bag of Pecan Sandies. Please, Doctor, please."

"I must see you. Stand up. Now!"

Her slim calves slid together off the couch. Charles Jourdan heels hit the Berber carpeting in unison. Monica faced the windows now. Through the stiletto fence of open vertical blinds upper Manhattan drifted on the gray residue of a January afternoon.

She stood without making him say it again. It always took her breath away, facing him for the first time after the ceremony of the couch. He was such a little man, in his gray Brooks Brothers suit, gray like the day. He always seemed so much bigger than he looked.

Now he looked at her, through the rimless spectacles, studying her designer ensemble with perfect appreciation, although he himself could have been mistaken for an expensively clad ragpicker on the street. He had no style.

Monica didn't know what he saw, through those watery eyes of no color, through those thick glasses that refracted his expression into blank judgment. She had no image of herself at all. Except naked.

"No," she begged, her hands beginning to shake.

"Have you gained weight this week, Monica, is that it?"

"No!" she denied, telling the truth, the truth at last, as she could still glimpse it. She frowned her sudden confusion. "And I'm *supposed* to gain weight—the doctors say so."

"But you never do what you're supposed to." His voice, so in control, lowered and began to shake itself, with anger. "Take your clothes off, you silly cow, so I can see what a pig you've made of yourself."

"Can you . . . draw the blinds?"

"This is the fifty-ninth floor, Monica," he jeered openly, his voice lashing her, joining the voices in her head bursting into a chant of abuse. "No one can see you. No one would want to see you. Except me. Strip, you stupid bitch!"

Her hands jerked to the buttons of her jacket, her blouse. The supple, hundred-percent natural fabrics separated from each other with luxurious ease. Monica Chapman had not had a lover since . . . oh, years before, when she had thought "normal" was still something that could be bought like candy, or pursued like a degree, or earned like a promotion, or deserved like love.

29

All she had now was this, her psychiatrist, sitting there clothed and powerful, forcing her in ways even her brothers had not thought of. A dull spark of resistance flared from time to time in her brain, but the chorus in her head surged into a baroque mass of denial, and her own lone soprano always joined their blistering rhapsody of denigration.

"You love it," her psychiatrist said now, his baritone blending with the plainsong of her psyche. "Secret shame and guilt, my shabby empress, are your kingdom."

Her clothing lay at her feet, the peach silk French lingerie petaling around her ankles with her expensive panty hose.

If he had looked at her with lust, even the most cartoonish leer, it wouldn't have been so bad. His eyes held only contempt.

He got up and walked to his desk where the cold white daylight fell. The huge mahogany expanse was topped by a half-inch slab of crystal that shone green along the edge.

He swept the few items atop the desk aside and gestured to its glittering empty surface, so like his eyes. "Come here. I want to play the Game today."

She shivered, a painfully thin naked woman with painfully naked eyes.

"It's so cold," she protested, one last excuse for a life that itself seemed to have no excuse.

"You'll get used to it," he promised carelessly. "Haven't I proved again and again that you can get used to anything?"

Chapter Four

They slept beside each other fully dressed, like Hansel and Gretel in the woods.

Maybe part of that was Kevin's fear that they might have to move fast, have to flee the dinky motel outside the dinky town on the badly plowed county road.

Maybe it was part shyness, the awkwardness of the new selves he and Jane presented each other, dressed so atypically.

Maybe it was partly that they'd holed up so early, at five P.M.

Most of it was the cold. Despite the heating unit's hissing bravado, nothing much resembling warmth seeped across the mean indoor-outdoor carpeting to the old-fashioned double bed they lay in.

Jane had pressed herself into Kevin, showing a new dependence since the loss of Zyunsinth. He couldn't complain. Who, he had often thought, wants to compete with a satin-lined length of dead mammal skins?

He held Jane's sleeping form, feeling her breath collect against his chest and gradually swathe his naked throat with welcome warmth, and told himself that this was the woman he loved. She was and he did, but it wasn't as simple as that, if it had ever been as simple as that.

Why her? Why him? Why couldn't they be back at the University of Minnesota Hospitals, in his homely little office, playing doctor and patient, shrink and shrinkee? The campus would look desolate now, on the dirty selvage edge of winter, but students would bustle between the lordly buildings and cars would spatter down Sixteenth

31

Avenue and the ice-caught river would look like a faraway road through the stark trees. . . .

Bridget would brew her morning coffee strong for the Probe crew, then spike it with the Irish tease in her voice when Kevin passed her desk. Norbert Cross would hem and haw and crack the whip at the daily meetings, and Roger Matthews would evade and Carolyn Swanson would be her priggish, academic self and, God, he missed the security of everything he had once felt so free to despise. . . .

Jane burrowed against him, murmured.

"How can I love you?" he asked rhetorically. "I don't know you. You have no history; you don't even have a pretense of personality. You're an enigma, an empty slate, an experimental memory blank—"

She murmured again in her sleep. For lost Zyunsinth? Kevin clutched her closer. Jane murmuring, Jane burrowing, Jane acting downright human. Was that what he wanted, wanted to love? Was that Jane, even? He didn't know.

No bedside clock, not even a phone occupied the nightstand. Kevin had never traveled in such shabby circles, had never shorn himself so free of normal society. If he shifted to pull up his wrist and read the time on his solid gold Swiss watch—talk about something telltale he should have buried with Zyunsinth—he might wake Jane.

While he debated, she woke anyway.

There was no preliminary, no words, just her fingers pushing his clothes aside searching for his skin, her warm lips seeking the chill of his. Desire flared so suddenly that they both grappled like desperate teenagers overcoming a bundling board, exposing each other to the cold in inches.

Another man might have wondered if she'd been dreaming and wakened to take him in someone else's stead. Kevin had the luxury of knowing he was the first and only man to love her, for all her hungry skill. That iron-clad certainty alone made a potent aphrodisiac, a love potion, even in an icy motel room in Waukenabo, Minnesota.

Kevin needed it. For him, making love with Jane usually evolved into a ménage à trois, the everpresent ghost of his guilt joining in. Kevin had always been an ethically vainglorious shrink; he despised doctors who, sworn to help, exploited a patient's vulnerability.

That Jane was not victim, but partner; that he had fallen victim to love, not lust—the love he had admitted to a distraught Jane on the incriminating tape Dr. Cross had held over him—made it even worse. The only thing that pains a shrink more than being caught with your professional pants down is being nailed with your own renegade emotions in plain view.

Jane sensed his reticence and pulled him into the vortex of her urgency, the ebb and flow of her hands, mouth, body spinning him into co-conspiracy. Beyond her erotic motions he sensed the deeper, darker shadow dancers of her emotions—her isolation, her unique oneness. He felt again—for her—the Volkers' bruising rejection, the cold, dreary days of flight, the icy unremembered mysteries of the Crow Wing bluff.

Compassion flared into fresh passion. Their flesh warmed in conjunction. Feeling became incarnate. Penetration was his surrender, not hers. He moved into her, with her, forgetting everything, especially his regrets, his damnable responsibility.

Jane came first, stiffening in that stillness before the storm, then quivering her fulfillment. Despite the sexual high, Kevin couldn't stop himself from withdrawing before his own orgasm spilled into the funnel of her vagina.

He was an M.D., for God's sake; he knew such precautions were feeble protection. He denied himself anyway, letting the act's thunder dwindle and pulse away.

He felt green and foolish, and guilty again. Jane moaned sleepy satisfaction and drifted away, whispering his name, not Zyunsinth's. In aftermath, love built its own irrational erection within him. Whatever she was, whatever *he* was—and he was beginning to wonder—Kevin knew they belonged together.

He forced himself through a relaxation exercise, made his jumping skin, twitching muscles and overrevved mind slow one by one. Kevin drifted in the tingling, disconnected state between sleep and consciousness.

Suddenly, he knew what he would do. The psychiatrist in him had surfaced again. Tomorrow, when the sun rose and after they'd breakfasted at some hick coffee shop on some anonymous Main Street and he'd bought some fucking contraceptives in some faceless K-Mart corner, he'd take Jane home.

"Lost? Is this certain?"
"Unable to contact, certainly."
"But the control—"
"Dis . . . abled."
"Destroyed?"
"Dis . . . engaged."
"For what reason?"
"An . . . experiment."

Jane dreamed, hearing voices. Jane dreamed, not of other men, but of those other than men—or women, other than mankind, than humankind, than human.

The susurration lulled her—the "esses" of their speech. It was sound and pause between. Rasp and click, roll and hiss. She received it as English and rocked in the undulating ebb and flow of the sounds.

"Losssst. SSSSSertain/sssssertainly. Disssssssss . . . Disabled. Destroyed. Disengaged. Disssssssssssssss . . . exxxxssss. Experiment."

The words hummed down her veins, sparked from cell to cell, nucleus to nucleus. She heard them, saw them, smelled them, felt them . . . words throbbing through her with an almost sexual sense of possession. *Posssessssssion.* Esses,

34

exes, excuses, experiments. *Esss. Ssssss.* Hissing in the corner, under the window.

She sat up in the dark. The machine across the room hissed icily at her. Beside her, Kevin slept. She looked down at him, on his night-hidden features that she saw anyway in her indelible mind's eye. She touched the fingers of one hand to his face, feeling the roughness of his skin where new beard was trying to outgrow the scythe of his morning razor blade.

His skin was cold and the heating unit hissed and something in her hurt. Not her head, not her limbs. Not even the quiescent walls of her empty vagina.

She knew words. There had been words within her, to begin with, and then she had scanned the big, too-heavy book in the university and all the words in the world had rushed into her. Why should these most recent words, overheard in her own head, discomfort her?

She almost asked Kevin. She was used to asking Kevin, and he was nearby, which made her happy, which was a word she had never truly understood before. There were many such words, she sensed, and they made her afraid— another newly felt word.

But she paused. His cheek was warming to the presence of her fingertips. He was rough and quick and bewildering and so, so . . . separate. But he was sleeping and he didn't hear the hissing, as she did, and he would worry if he did. Or knew that she did.

Her fingers slipped away and she lay down, listening and trying not to listen. The buzzing came again, sawing at the edges of her awareness, endlessly gossiping.

"The over-others may disagree."
"It is small, this place. The unit can be traced and disconnected permanently."
"Obviously. But now there is no means of gleaning."
"Other means, like means, if they are used."
"Who gives the instructions?"
"All or none. It is the purpose."
"It is the necessity."

Incessant. Purpose. Necessity. Incessantly. If she was careful, and concentrated in strange, hidden ways, she could mute the sounds that surged through her. She let them ebb to a barely perceptible rasp along the pathways of her nerves.

By the window, the heating unit expelled a sputtered arpeggio, shaking her solitude. Jane turned her head to locate its featureless bulk against the faint light. Her calming ritual ran liquid through her, antennae of sensation feeling their way in the dark.

Jane's breath, misting in the icy room, sent tentative tendrils to the window. They gleamed blue-white like opaline fingers of gasflame in the dull light, then fisted and wrenched the heat control off.

The hissing died abruptly, within her and outside her, at once. The room grew colder in almost discernible stages from second to second.

Jane curled herself into the curve of Kevin and forgot it all.

*   *   *

He lay awake on the black leather couch and dreamed.

He always scheduled Monica Chapman as the day's last patient, so twilight was darkening his office as Manhattan's firmament of sky-high windows slowly sparkled into overtime life.

He let himself do what he seldom allowed his patients to do—relax on the psychiatric couch. The layman equated black leather with male potency, but he, being a psychiatrist, knew better. It represented female skin, the smoothness, the smell. Men liked it because it broadcast their masculine wants to the world; women because it attracted men.

He had always been attracted to other . . . things.

He let his eyes focus on the stark black-and-white photograph of the dancer, let them caress the shadows etched into her serene facial planes, into her attenuated neck, into the delicate ladder of chest bones descending from the sharp horizon of her collarbones to

36

the décolletage of her costume where no breasts over-flowed.

His breath caught at the splendid flatness of her form. Last, he fondly studied the fine shadow lines from elbow to wrist, ankle to knee, his perusal stripping her to the bones beneath the barely intervening skin.

Finally he sighed and let himself picture Monica Chapman naked. He mentally tallied her ribs, dwelled on the hollows of her hipbones, the bony geography of her knees and feet, hands and elbows. Almost enough for him, almost enough to assuage that bottomless gnaw that no analysis no matter how deep could reach.

It amused him to flirt with her chronic bulimia, lashing her into spasms of starvation, then flogging her into a more proper frame of mind only to unleash her abysmal lack of self-esteem and let her demons consume her for a time. He hated her sick complicity, and the fact that he dare not push her to the final self-consumption.

But she had her points; she was far, far too maladjusted to break free, to report him. And he kept her on the razor's edge of survival until she had come to expect it. Best of all was the complete submissive starvation in her eyes—that burning hopelessness, that numb painfulness that made her so vulnerable to his rather . . . unique . . . needs.

She was a good patient.

He came again, simply from dwelling on the ballerina's distance, on Monica Chapman's helplessness. It always helped, that removal from the source, the stimulus. He needed to fuck from afar, by proxy. His semen spurted neatly into one of the large white Irish linen handkerchiefs he ordered by the box from an exclusive men's shop on 57th Street. His initials occupied one corner. He would never taint his pleasure by emptying it into the charnel house of a woman's body. Not now.

He needed something else, he finally admitted in that somber New York dusk. He needed release of another kind, a job with no limits, something that would allow him to dig his fingers into the human psyche and knead it like the malleable dough it was.

37

The pressure was tightening around his skull, sucking him into the black hole that was the eye of his emotions. He knew he was sick. He knew he was dangerous. He needed to know that those attributes were needed—somewhere.

The phone rang and he turned his head slowly to it. His rimless glasses winked soberly in the twilight.

He needed a new assignment.

Chapter Five

Dirty winter roads unraveled beneath the van's balding tires.

Let them trace *these* tracks, Kevin thought. Sometimes the greatest safety can be found in a lack of safety. Beside him in the van's passenger seat, Jane hummed unmelodiously, as if eavesdropping on an atonal cosmic radio.

"Does 'home' mean those people?" she asked out of nowhere.

"They're called parents," he answered dryly.

"You said they *weren't* my parents," she reminded him.

"I was wrong. Don't look so surprised. The great Dr. Blake can be wrong. Look, I wanted to reject the Volkers even more than you did. They were interfering with my tidy little scenario for self-interest and your . . . independence. We were kinda rough on them, you and I. I knew you were more than just another amnesia patient, another Jane Doe for the newspapers to cluck over, but I didn't even begin to guess what you really were then—"

He saw anxieties rising in Jane's eyes that he wasn't ready to assuage. He cupped her face in the quieting warmth of his palm.

"I only knew that you were . . . special," he soothed. "Unique. I tried to deny any ordinary claims that had a right to you. Like parents, if their claims are ever ordinary. I was wrong. Don't you want to know how you came to be, Jane? Where exactly . . . you came from? Don't you remember anything of what happened on the bluff top this last time? Or the first, for that matter. You came into our world naked, do you want to live in it that way? Surely your amnesia must be ebbing a little now. Don't you remember anything of . . . *them*?"

Jane's face wrenched from his hand. She was staring out the window, but fields of white snow refused to mirror her reflection. In the sideview mirror, Kevin glimpsed only the tips of her eyelashes and a slice of uncompromising cheekbone.

"I remember . . . being brought to the hospital in the screaming ecnalubma. I remember you stopping by my room the first time—a little. And then I remember our sessions—everything about our sessions, about living with the student nurses in the dorm with Mrs. Bellingham. I remember you holding me. And I remember . . . the Volkers, coming and wanting to take me away, saying they'd seen my picture in the paper and that I was their lost daughter," Jane conceded at last. "They were . . . silly."

Kevin paused. "And you are still mired in adolescence. Cruel Jane. You can blow parents away with one word more effectively than any rebellious teenage punker safety-pinned from earlobe to belly button."

"You're angry with me?" Anxiety edged into her tone.

"That goes with the territory sometimes. With being human," he added with deliberate provocation. She ignored his challenge.

"I will . . . try to like them," she resolved fiercely, her hands fisting in her lap.

"Do you like anybody?" he asked, amused.

Startled, she considered. "No."

"Not even me?"

The length of her slow sum-uppance was disconcerting.

On occasion, Jane acted like an idiot savant—blissfully brilliant and aggravatingly dense.

"Sometimes I even dislike you," she confessed.

"You can still like me in-between."

"No. I love you in-between."

He felt strangely cheated. He began to ask himself honestly if he "liked" Jane, if it was possible to like anyone as unformed and yet inherently and totally herself as Jane.

"You're sure they are my parents?" She sounded anxious again.

"Biologically, yes."

"Before, you proved that they weren't and they went away."

"Yes."

She considered. "Everyone thought you were smart."

"I am. Too smart."

"What about her?"

"Who?"

"The . . . other one they found. Like me. Only dead."

For a moment he was lost. "My God, did you hear about that? I didn't know you knew the details. She was your . . . sister, I guess. That's where we all went wrong. We thought that you had to be the girl your parents raised, Lynn Volker, and that she had to be you. If Lynn Volker was proven dead beyond a doubt, you were not her, beyond a doubt. But there were *two* of you, products of the same ovum and semen, the same cell, maybe. So the Volkers didn't raise you, but they're still your parents. Your biological parents."

"And I am a clone."

"What?"

"You called me a 'coed clone' in the store. I know what *coed* means and I know what *clone* means. You think because I have not lived a word that I don't understand it."

His hands hit the steering wheel. "That was a figure of speech. I don't know for sure how or why—"

"I was only gleaning efficiently!" she flared. Tears brightened her eyes.

Gleaning. The word pinged alarm in his mind, as surely

as *Zyunsinth* did. Jane had used it repeatedly under hypnosis when he'd tried to unearth the secrets of her forgotten past.

His voice grew professional, which was to say, calm, interested and nonjudgmental. "When were you gleaning, Jane?"

"In the store! It is vital to glean efficiently—and, and all the girls in the dorm took pride in getting their clothes on sale—"

"The nurses in the dorm are twits!" he exploded. "Look, shopping is the opiate of the masses. It's a shallow, unimportant pastime meant to turn women into consummate consumers to fuel our incestuous national economy. Buying things on 'sale' is an illusion, the act of wringing value from a valueless pursuit. It doesn't really matter."

Jane was silent. "Perhaps it did once," she answered finally. "You took me to the big store downtown to shop, the place where I gleaned . . ." Her voice wavered. ". . . Zyunsinth. And now you said we needed new clothes after the light burned everything but Zyunsinth away. I don't understand."

"I just don't want you picking up the wrong values. Buying things for necessity's sake is different from buying them for amusement."

"You said I should like things, choose things. That they should reflect the I-ness of me."

"Ye-es. . . ." She had him. "But that was during your imitative stage. God, Jane. I don't know how to help you understand this crazy world of ours."

"Before, you said I was right to say the Volkers were nothing to do with me. Now you say—"

"I know, I know! I'm inconsistent. Now I think you might need—want—to know that someone, somewhere here on earth, has a legitimate claim on you. Besides the . . ." He sighed. ". . . the others."

She didn't answer. She didn't want to remember them any more than he did. That was why he had to pick at the memory still oozing beneath the scab.

"Jane, what do you remember of the bluff top when the light came down?"

41

"Brightness. Lightness. My . . . clothes melting away. Zyunsinth fallen in the snow. You . . . as far away and small as a snowflake. Many snowflakes of light. Cold, then heat, then nothing. And, and . . . being drawn within, my insides being pulled further inside. With . . . them."

"Do you remember them at all?"

Her head shook, violently. Jane suddenly scooted toward him, leaning across the dirty-floored gulf between their seats, her hands clutching his arm, her face buried in his sleeve.

"I believe it now. *They* are my parents. The Volkers. Kevin says so. I want . . . to see them again. I want to remember them . . . me. Please, Kevin, I must see the Volkers!"

"You will," he promised, fighting to keep the van from swerving at her tug on his arm.

Already the roadside signs had reduced the speed limit from fifty-five miles per hour to forty. He meticulously slowed the van to legal limits. Just ahead, the town of Crookston and the home of Adelle and Jack Volker loomed in the late-afternoon grayness.

The last—and first—time Kevin had driven these unassuming streets he had come clutching at a straw. Now he clutched the needle in the haystack in his hand, and only needed to locate the right thread. Maybe it would be the Volkers, he hoped, stopping the van in front of their simple frame house.

The street was quiet, deserted. Jane accompanied him up the walk with excited dread, fidgeting like a schoolgirl about to confront the couple who had accused her of stealing apples.

Volker himself answered the doorbell, looking lumberjack-solid in his plaid shirt. After flaring in surprise, his eyes grew relentlessly neutral, even when they rested on Jane.

"What are you doing here again, Dr. Blake?" he asked flatly.

"She wanted to come."

"*She* did?" Volker acted as if Jane were invisible. "Didn't want much to do with us when it really mattered."

42

"Maybe things are different now. Maybe she needs you." Maybe *he* needed the Volkers now, Kevin admitted to himself. "She changed her mind. That's kids for you," he added sympathetically.

Volker's face undammed like river ice. He stepped back and swung the door wide.

"Don't want Mother hurt again like the last time," he muttered. He followed Kevin and Jane through the icy, unheated porch into the front room.

The living room wasn't much warmer. In the kitchen archway, Kevin could see a mellow light beaming.

Jane walked in, circling the knotty pine cocktail table, memorizing the shabby sofa and carefully angled chairs. She walked finally to the opposite wall and paused before a photograph of herself—the standard out-of-focus high school graduation picture that looked as if the mists of time webbed its surface the moment its subject was captured.

Kevin edged closer, watching Jane absorb her own image in an alien environment. She had virtually no personal vanity—yet, but her eyes studied every detail of that photographic image: the Peter Pan collar, the curled hair, the barrette caught awkwardly near one temple.

The late Lynn Volker had been a fresh, attractive but unspectacular girl. Jane was her spitting image.

Kevin and Volker, linked by a begrudging, unspoken mutual awe, regarded Jane as raptly as she studied her own likeness. Jane stared so intently at the photo behind its shield of glass, within its cheap metallic frame, that Kevin feared it would melt, shatter, slip off the wall.

A crash made both men jump. Jane was unmoved. In the oblong of kitchen light, a shadow froze. Mrs. Volker stepped over the shattered water glass at her feet and edged into the room, her expression obscured by the light behind her.

"Jane-Lynn—?"

Jane's shoulders stiffened. Her profile tensed further, if that was possible. Kevin foresaw a repetition of her earlier rejection of the Volkers. He fumbled for some conversational double-talk to derail it, mask it, mute it.

43

Jane turned from the photograph before he could un-latch his tongue. She looked from woman to man, father to mother, from Volker to Volker, stranger to stranger.

Volker looked the same as when Jane had last seen him a few months ago, but his wife had faded—the permanent wave and color rinse had slipped from her once-meticulously done hair, leaving her ghost-gray.

"You must have been really dark-haired once." Jane addressed the woman, who seemed to need to stop and remember before nodding dazed agreement. "I have your coloring, but his features, if he were thinner."

Mrs. Volker gasped and pressed the corner of a cotton dishcloth to her mouth. Volker made an odd sound, half admission, half denial.

Kevin went to Jane. "Can we sit down?" he asked gently.

The Volkers' quick glances consulted each other.

"Adelle, I don't want your heart broken again . . . ," Volker began. "Remember what happened in the Cities."

"She's our girl, I always knew it," the woman pled.

"Our girl is dead. We know that now, thanks to all the publicity and those dental records from Montana. Our Lynn died on that camping trip in Montana years ago. I guess us being made the fools of the whole state for claiming this one at least got that much clear."

"Sit down," Mrs. Volker breathlessly urged Jane, ignoring her husband.

Kevin guided Jane to the sofa and sat with her. Mrs. Volker hesitated, then perched on the other side of Jane, her hands smoothing the print apron over her knees. Volker stood in the center of the room watching them.

"Would you . . . like something to eat, Jane-Lynn?" Mrs. Volker's voice was timorous.

Jane looked at Kevin.

"Some hot coffee would be great, Mrs. Volker. If you've got it on," he amended politely with a quick smile, thus ensuring that any motherly woman would make it anyway.

"Of course, Doctor. We're old-fashioned. Coffee's always on. Does she . . . drink coffee?"

"I don't know, Mrs. Volker. Let's find out."

"Jane . . . anything you want?"

"Bread," Jane blurted. "Zucchini bread; it was good."

"Oh." The older woman's face fell. She looked like the drawing of a conventional mother from a first-grade primer. Kevin expected Mrs. Volker to put up her hands and say, "Run, Spot, run." Instead, she apologized. "That was frozen from last summer's crop. We used it all up. What I brought you in the Cities last fall was the last loaf."

"Anything would be fine, Mrs. Volker," Kevin put in. "We've been on the road, eating at fast-food joints. Anything homemade would be an improvement."

The woman stood and practically backed away, unwilling to take her eyes off Jane. Volker didn't move to help his wife in the kitchen. Kevin's mouth quirked to think of the conventional parents fate had chosen for his wildly unconventional Jane.

"You been on the road," Volker repeated. "How come?"

"Tracing Jane's past. I think I've solved it. The what and why, anyway—if not the how."

"It help her any?"

"Maybe. I was hoping you would help her more."

He shrugged, the old man, and, wheezing, shuffled over to find his pipe. Jane was right, he could use a diet.

"We kind of gave up on her, Dr. Blake, for our own sakes, after that news story by that Bowman woman came out, about how deluded we were and our real daughter was so many bones and teeth out there in the wildwoods. It kind of took the heart out of us, the scandal and all. They still try to call us from those national rags, looking for a new angle—a new way to make fools of us on their front pages."

"People send us the clippings," Mrs. Volker said. She had paused in the doorway again, an enigmatic figure bearing a tray. "Like it was an honor."

"Why are you here?" Volker asked.

"To tell you that you weren't crazy," Kevin said, "to say that everything you thought happened to you years ago did happen."

This bombshell should have had both Volkers shouting

hallelujah and eating out of Kevin's hand. Instead, silence greeted his announcement.

"Well, that's something," Volker said at last. "A big Twin Cities psychiatrist saying we're not crazy. You acted like we weren't much better than slugs when we came down to the Cities to say"—he glanced at Jane—"she was our daughter. You just sat back and waited while everyone else proved we weren't—the reporters, the police. Now you show up again. Now we're her long-lost parents. What's the matter, Dr. Blake, you gone off your rocker?"

"Some people might say that, if I told them what I had seen two nights ago."

"Then keep your mouth shut," Volker advised tersely, "like we should have twenty-five years ago."

Mrs. Volker's hand had stolen across her lap to rest feather light on Jane's jacket sleeve. She tugged on the material. "Lynn, honey . . . Jane. You remember us any?"

"She can't, Mother!" Volker's voice held a twang of agony. "This one never saw us, never knew us, and even if she did, she's still got no memory worth worrying about. She's still an amnesiac, isn't that right, Doc? She doesn't know shit from shinola about anything—!"

Jane glanced to Kevin, confused. "Shinola?"

He shook his head. "That is Jane's particular . . . malady, Mr. Volker. She knows a lot of things she shouldn't, and doesn't know some rather simple things she should. Shinola's one of them."

"Don't cuss in front of the girl, Jack," Mrs. Volker put in by rote. Her hand slid down to take Jane's hand in her puckered palm and absently stroke it with her fingers.

Jane accepted the familiarity with taut tolerance, her eyes sliding first to the photograph of herself on the wall, then to Kevin.

"I know," Mrs. Volker mused to herself, "that if we let Lynn . . . let Jane . . . see her old room—Lynn's, that is—I *know* she'd remember something. Remember us. She can't look this much like Lynn and *not* remember."

Kevin's mouth opened to explain why Jane most certainly could, but Mrs. Volker's sad eyes pinned his lips shut before he could speak.

46

"You said you came back, you brought her back, because she really *is* our daughter, didn't you, Doctor?" Volker asked.

"Yes, she is, but—"

"Then let's do what Mother wants. Let's take her upstairs, show her where she grew up."

His wife didn't wait for agreement. "Come along, dear, I know you'll remember something if you only see—"

Docile, Jane allowed Mrs. Volker's hand to tug her to her feet.

"And take your jacket off—heavens, you're going to stay awhile. Make yourself to home."

Mrs. Volker's fingers unzipped the down jacket with maternal presumption. Kevin tensed, as he had when the clerk had gone snipping at Jane with scissors, but Jane seemed subdued, perhaps by her encounter with her own image on this unpretentious wall.

They stood awkwardly around the coffee table, four dark circles of untasted coffee steaming like a campfire in their midst. Gently, Mrs. Volker teased Jane toward the dining room, step by step. Kevin and her husband let themselves be drawn into the women's wake by default.

"She's not—" Kevin began, crossing glances with Volker, then subsided.

No one wanted to hear what he thought. All their emotions revolved around the centerpiece of Jane now. Around Jane, and what Jane would do, say, remember. Or not remember, Kevin reminded himself. She was good at not remembering.

The dark wood door at one side of a built-in dining room buffet opened on dim stairs suspended between plain, beige-painted walls. At the top a tiny window squeezed into the apex of the roof. A half wall topside kept anyone from falling down the stairwell.

It had been an attic originally, the space. Maybe fifteen years ago, Papa Volker or some local handyman had paneled it with walnut veneer and installed built-in bookshelves. Mrs. Volker had sprinkled the linoleum floor with rag rugs and festooned the undereave windows with yellow curtains. They'd installed a couple of single beds for girlish sleepovers, and a stereo, and called it a teenager's room.

Kevin turned around in the big, unheated space. A Rolling Stones poster on one wall brought a brief, rueful memory of the one in his office back at the University of Minnesota Hospitals, back at the Probe unit. Record albums kept packed company on the lowest bookshelves. Cheerleading pom-pons—orange and purple—decorated one wall like crossed swords. A slightly shabby chorus line of stuffed toys paraded along one bed pushed against the murky wall.

Mrs. Volker went to an undersized door and jerked it open. "She had plenty of closet space. I had Father build in lots of that under the eaves. Girls always need room for things. . . . Do you remember, honey? Do you remember any of this?"

God, I hope not, Kevin thought unkindly. Jane was silent.

"Maybe this was a mistake," Kevin admitted. "You don't understand, Mrs. Volker. I never said that Jane *lived* here with you, as your daughter. Only that she *was* your daughter."

"Ain't that the same thing?" Volker asked truculently.

"Not . . . in this case. Jane is . . . unique. I don't think you understand how unique—"

"Me!" Jane burst out. She pulled the closet door further open, drawing a mirror image of herself full-face into their midst.

It was as if a ghost of the dead girl—Lynn Elizabeth Volker—had materialized in the echoing room with them.

Mrs. Volker choked on a sob. Her husband pushed his hands deep into his pockets and turned to the window, leaving his broad, red-plaid back drawn on the rest of them like a shade.

Kevin felt an odd jolt of precognitive déjà vu, as if a scene never enacted in this room, and never to be enacted here, had laid its fuzzy outlines over an image from the past burned into the mirror.

Jane reached out to something wedged under a corner of

48

the full-length mirror—a faded prom memoir, a dance card dangling a tassel.

"Me?" Jane asked this time, less certain.

No one answered, and before anyone could try, Jane turned back to the room, studying it with a frowning intensity that brought new hope to Mrs. Volker's hopelessly ordinary features.

"Yes, it's yours, dear. You lived here. I sewed the curtains at the window with some material I ordered from Sears. We put the half bath in for you"—her eyes flickered to another door—"everything for you, even the music you liked to play so loud, that Father always complained about over his head—"

"I didn't complain. I just said it was loud, and it was. For God's sake, Mother, the girl isn't a saint just because she's dead!"

"She's not dead! She's here! Dr. Blake brought her back to us. She may not remember . . . oh, try, try," she begged Jane. "Try to remember."

A poignant silence dominated them all. Kevin Blake, psychiatrist, wished he were an honest exorcist capable of banishing all the ghosts called into this room—ghosts of what once was, what never was and what never would be.

"Try to remember," came a clear, plaintive soprano.

Music faint as a radiator hiss chimed into the room. Kevin jerked his head toward the stereo setup. The sound was too weak to pinpoint, but the familiar lyrics and music from *The Fantasticks,* typical teenage girl fare, unwound verse by cloying verse.

Jane was standing in the middle of the room, looking normal as north woods apple pie in her jeans and shirt and boots, her eyes closed, her head lifted, her arms and fingers spread slightly, as though she was contemplating engraving an upright snow angel on the air.

"Try to remember when—"

Mrs. Volker inhaled a hiccough of air and then folded her hands over her mouth. Volker had turned from the window and froze, watching Jane and listening.

"Try to remember—"

49

The repetition was beginning to wear on all of them.

"Where on earth—?" Volker began hoarsely, looking at Kevin.

Kevin stared at the stereo, then hurled himself to it, kneeling to the row of record albums. He kinked his head sideways and read through Steely Dan/Michael Jackson/Joni Mitchell/the Beach Boys to . . . *Cats!* and *Chorus Line* and—eureka!

"*The Fantasticks!*" he announced, pulling out the album and edging the record from the jacket. "'Try to Remember,'" he read off the label.

"It was . . . her favorite," Mrs. Volker said.

Kevin frowned at her, momentarily disconnected.

"Lynn's. Lynn's favorite song. They even mentioned it in the yearbook. The Crookston Excelsior. Under her picture. They listed all their favorite songs. That was Lynn's."

It still played in the room.

"The record's here," Kevin said, shaking it a little in his clammy hands. He glanced to the motionless turntable under its dust-blanketed smoke-colored Plexiglas cover. "It's impossible to hear it."

Nothing moved or spoke in the room. Only the music unspun regularly, and it came from nowhere. Was it real, Kevin wondered—or Memorex?

Then something caught Kevin's eye, a subtle, quick, mechanical movement, right where he should have looked for it. Close-up. The tape deck, of course. And the almost undetectable motion of a tiny cassette reeling past hidden heads, playing "Try to Remember."

"Jane," Kevin began.

"Me," sang Jane back. "Me, me, me."

He turned. She looked like an actress playing Helen Keller, head thrown back now, eyes closed, mouth open, limbs splayed as if they were principal sensors in her body.

"Jane, stop it!"

But she was deaf to him, blind to the Volkers. The room was pouring into her and she was funneling it back at itself. "Try to Remember" found its full volume, the plaintive song reverberating in the dead space.

Kevin pushed the Eject button. The mechanism jammed. He clawed at the thin plastic window. Behind it, the music, untouched, rolled on and on, trying to remember.

A new motion caught his eye. Above him, the record turntable noiselessly began spinning under its dust cover. He reached to stop it, but at his knees record albums began spilling from the shelf, spinning across the floor as if the linoleum were a giant turntable, spinning—and playing.

Rock beats, folk ballads, surf rhythms, blues—they all mingled, ghosting over each other, the slick album covers spinning at the same inexorable rate, perfectly, mechanically. Thirty-three and a third revolutions per minute.

"All me," Jane was announcing over the cacophony. "Me, me, me, meeeee!"

Dresser drawers slid open, strewing pieces of Lynn Volker's lost life across the rag rugs and matching chintz floral bedspreads—limp underwear and faded blue jeans, shapeless sweaters and socks, a red leather clutch purse, beads, a long-forgotten stack of wallet-size high school graduation photos—dead ringers for the portrait downstairs—unfurling like a pack of cards and stuttering across the floor in a ragged chorus line.

Mrs. Volker was screaming, her apron thrown over her head. Volker had spread-eagled himself against the window, as if defying anything to pass him.

Kevin forced himself upright amid a blizzard of clothes and stationery. A lead pencil made a pass at his left eye. Crepe paper swagged his arm. Lynn Volker's life—memorialized in this room—fell apart all around him.

There was no wind, nothing except the moving things and the motionless people and the raucous music. He skidded over the slick, spinning albums, tripping, losing his balance, then recapturing it, until he got to Jane.

Once there, he froze like the others. He'd seen mental illness take a lot of strange physical forms; he'd never seen anyone so transported as Jane.

"Is she . . . possessed?" Volker ground out over the screaming music.

Superstition snapped Kevin's awe. He reached out and

touched Jane's wrist. The flannel shirt puckered to her arm, as if infected with a massive shot of static. He felt his fingertips tingle, then reached to touch her other arm. This time the phenomenon didn't surprise him. Nothing would surprise him.

"Jane. Open your eyes. Your eyes—open them!"

Beneath her closed eyelids he could see the tremor of REMs, rapid eye movements that signal dreaming. She wasn't dreaming now, he knew, but perhaps her neurons were. "Wake up. Open your eyes!"

The dark eyelashes spasmed, but her eyes remained closed.

"Jane, it's Dr. Blake, and when I say the word, you'll open your eyes and your ears and your mind and you'll be in the room with me and the Volkers."

The confidence in his tone was pure reflex. He wasn't sure, but he was going to try to produce a waking state by resorting to a hypnosis-inducing codeword. An old word from their first sessions, before Jane had so much as repaired a broken fingernail with her telekinetic powers.

Psychiatry was his only religion, and its sacred words were his only weapon. It might work, that twentieth-century talisman of his, and it might not.

He leaned close to her ear, chilled by the unnatural warmth her body radiated, and whispered, repeated, shouted, "Ecnalubma . . . ecnalubma . . . ecnalubma" like a litany.

"Try to remember—Try to remember—Try to remember . . ."

The music died track by track until that last phrase rang sweet and low, repeating with stuck-needle stubbornness until it faded abruptly. Clothes slumped to the floor, rolling felt-tip pens rocked into stillness. Kevin's hands on Jane's wrists felt so cold he could have just retracted them from a deep freeze.

Jane's eyes were opening, slowly, the browns of her irises expanding into focus. She frowned at Kevin. "Me," she insisted. Something left her eyes, some fleeting, fleeing memory. "And . . . not me."

He nodded. "No. Not you."

52

Heat radiated from Jane up his arms, engulfing him with a welcome wave of warmth, then dissipating beyond him. She began shivering, violently. Kevin sank with her to the floor, held her teeth-chattering face against his shoulder, rocked her, warmed her, although he felt his own aftermath of chill.

Mrs. Volker had recovered enough to drop her apron. She was moving stiffly around the room, picking up the scattered belongings.

"I kept them," she explained wearily. "I kept it all just as it was when Lynn . . . went away. We thought she'd come back from that summer in Montana. And then, when she was reported missing, we never believed she was dead. We thought she'd come back. We knew she'd come back."

"You love her," Volker accused Kevin.

Kevin felt like a kid again, sitting on the floor of his messy room, confronting eternal adult charges.

"Somebody has to," he answered.

Mrs. Volker began disjointedly humming "Try to Remember" as she bent from the waist, in a way that was murder on an aging back, to pick up Lynn's strewn underwear.

Chapter Six

Jane's teeth chattered on the coffee cup rim.

Kevin steadied her hand until she took the first, bracing sip. Her eyes flashed him a rare shot of gratitude before widening in caffeine-struck surprise.

"Bitter," she commented.

No one commented back.

They all hugged their microwave-rewarmed coffee cups in silence, Jane and Kevin on the spavined sofa, the Volkers on their separate chairs. Who would have thought,

Kevin wondered, that the Volkers would have had a microwave? Life was chock full of surprises.

"Did . . . Lynn . . . ever demonstrate any exceptional abilities?" Kevin figured it wouldn't hurt to ask.

"Never! No. Lynn was a normal girl all the way," Volker said.

His wife picked at the pink seam tape binding her apron edge. "She had a gift for finding lost things."

"Coincidence," Volker spat. "First we're kooks who claim we saw a UFO a quarter century ago. Then we were nuts five years ago for believing Lynn hadn't really died in that wilderness she got lost in. Now Lynn's been proven dead and we're supposed to say our dead daughter was a weirdo—"

"What's a weirdo?" Jane asked Kevin.

Mrs. Volker's eyes rebuked her husband.

"Someone special." Kevin briefly pulled Jane's head to his shoulder. "Like you." He faced Volker again. "Look. You're not the only one who saw a UFO. I did, too, two nights ago. Maybe the same one, for all I know."

"You saw it?" Mrs. Volker sat forward on her maple rocking chair, stilling it.

"I saw it. Not as well as I should have. I was . . . worried about Jane."

"That's where she's from!" Volker was standing, his head partially obscuring the photo of his daughter on the wall.

"Oh, my God," said his wife, and pointed behind him.

He turned impatiently, his head shifting out of the way.

The photograph of Lynn Volker still hung where it had for seven years. Not even the glass had cracked, despite the telekinetic storm upstairs. But—

"Oh, my God, Jack—it's reversed!"

Kevin stood, too. He saw it but he didn't believe it. Lynn Elizabeth Volker was still smiling at the world—with empty white eyes and fiberglass hair, out of a shadowed face, wearing a black blouse . . .

Volker pointed to Jane like an Old Testament prophet confronting Pharaoh. "Get her out of here! Get her out of our house!"

"It's not her fault," Kevin said. "She's just . . . what she is."

"She's not ours! Never was." Volker was advancing, his sixtyish bulk more threatening because it seemed such an unlikely source of violence.

"Jack, Jack, please!" His wife was baby-stepping toward him, her face schizophrenic with mixed emotions.

"Please what, Adelle? I don't care what we saw, what *they* did to us in that thing all those years ago. I don't care what he saw two nights ago, or what they did to *her*! She ain't ours. She's an unnatural thing and I want her out of our house!"

"She's flesh of your flesh," Kevin struck back. "Your genes. That's how she was made—they took a cell from your wife, who must have been just pregnant at the time. Before even you or Mrs. Volker knew that—*they* knew. And that's all it takes, a single cell. Hell, even *we* can do it today. Test-tube babies. Genetic engineering. Don't you read the papers in Crookston? Baby Louise in England, dozens here at home. It's routine medical practice. If we can do it, why shouldn't they?"

"We dreamed it, do you hear me, Dr. Blake? It was . . . what did the psychiatrists try to call it twenty-five years ago?—small-scale mass hysteria. Delusion. We 'thought' we saw the ship. We 'thought' we saw those . . . things . . . on it. We 'thought' we were up in the damn thing.

"Well, we weren't crazy; we were wrong! We were dreamers, we were fools, and we aren't going to be nobody's fools anymore. We deny it. So what do you do with your precious Jane Doe now, who wasn't good enough for us to be her parents before? What do you do with her now? We don't want her. We got grief enough."

Volker's vehemence had left Jane cowering against Kevin's hip, like a puppy that knows only the fact of its misbehavior, not its specific sin. It left Kevin swallowing his own sour rage, his regret at having exposed Jane to this rejection, and his sudden personal sense of abandonment.

He remembered his own parents, whom he saw too seldom. He wondered if they would disown him when the newspapers made what they would of him, of their brilliant, never-understood only son, now on the run.

Mrs. Volker had crept up on Kevin during the outburst. Her hand on his arm nagged for his attention.

"Jane is . . . Lynn's sister, isn't she, Dr. Blake?"

"Not sister, exactly—"

"Twin? She's her twin?" Pathetic eagerness to grasp the unthinkable made Adelle Volker's face girlish in its uncertainty.

"More than twin—" Kevin hadn't thought it all out himself. He paused to phrase it accurately. "Jane is . . . Lynn's undeveloped self. The genetic raw material, unshaped by environmental factors. She's what your Lynn was when she was born—a baby, I guess. Only Jane's all grown up."

"She's nothing!" Volker pulled his wife away, over to his side. "Don't you go tryin' to make that creature into some helpless innocent to wring my wife's heart. If she's anybody's baby, she's your problem, Dr. Blake.

"You got a lot of guts comin' here again and upsettin' Mother 'n me and makin' us think there's any hope for our daughter. There never was. Lynn was an ordinary girl and she died. She died, and we know it now! She was just unlucky enough to have weirdo parents who may have been crazy once but they're not gonna do it again!"

In the ensuing silence, Kevin heard an old-fashioned clock ticking for the first time. He reflexively glanced around to see where it was kept, but his eyes snagged on the photo-reverse portrait of Lynn Volker and stopped. Maybe the old man was right; maybe what had once been positive —the Volkers' need for a daughter, Jane's late-found need to belong—had turned negative.

At his side, Jane spoke, her voice smaller than he'd ever heard it, like it came from a long way inside.

"Kevin. I want to go away."

He nodded at the Volkers. Mrs. Volker's face was frozen in distress. No one had consulted her, any more than they had when Lynn had vanished in Montana. He took Jane's hand and pulled her up beside him. He really was her only family now.

56

"I thought—" Kevin began . . . and ended. "I thought you folks could do her some good. Or the other way around. She's got a lot to figure out for herself."

"She's a freak," Volker answered harshly, his farmer's face hard-edged as a plow blade. "We never could have spawned her. Better to have our daughter dead and normal than like that."

Kevin turned Jane toward the door. "If anybody comes looking for us . . . her—"

"We never saw you. That's what we shoulda said twenty-five years ago. 'Sorry, never saw nothin'. . . .'"

"Dr. Blake—" Mrs. Volker stepped from the shadow of her husband, her hands working behind the screening curtain of her apron. "You'll . . . take care of her?"

"Yeah." He hadn't meant to sound so weary. "I'll get her . . . somewhere . . . safe and sound, Mrs. Volker. Home by midnight okay?" he couldn't help adding with something else he hadn't meant to sound—bitterness.

Adelle Volker just shook her grizzled, untended head and watched them leave through her tears. Kevin shut the door behind them, not waiting for those inside to make the final, excluding gesture.

"Cold out here," Kevin commented, looking down the snow-whitened street at all the snugly closed front doors in Crookston.

"They didn't like me," Jane noted quietly from the curve of his arm.

"Fair play. You didn't like them very much at first, either."

She frowned. "Everybody wants me. Why don't they?"

He couldn't help laughing. "Conceited, aren't you? Except that you're always so damn literal."

"You wanted to keep me away from them, away from the other doctors and Dr. Swanson, from those men. Even from—" She glanced up evocatively at the white-washed winter sky.

"From 'them,' I know. Yeah, I guess you are pretty popular, come to think of it. And it's gonna get worse."

"Is that because I'm a freak?"

"Probably."

"I know what 'freak' is; 'an abnormally formed organism; especially, a person or animal regarded as a curiosity or a monstrosity.' "

"Jane, shut up." He opened the van door and boosted her inside.

But when he got behind the wheel, she was waiting for him with unrelenting logic and her uncanny, emotionless perception.

"You wanted them to like me this time. I tried, but I couldn't help what happened upstairs. I'm . . ." She paused so long that Kevin found himself hanging on the next word, as if it might be as important as Zyunsinth. It was. "I'm . . . sorry," Jane said, her face puzzled. Perhaps she herself didn't understand why she felt compelled to say that for the first time in her life.

Kevin hugged her across the void between the seats. "I am, too. I am so damn sorry."

Over her shoulder, the blank face of the Volkers' ultraordinary white frame house stared impassively back at him. The town of Crookston didn't look one bit sorry at all.

*   *   *

Jane threw her third Baby Ruth wrapper on the floor. Kandy's van wasn't exactly pristine inside; Kevin twisted to survey the collection of brown paper grocery bags and newspapers piling atop Kandy's original debris in the space behind him.

The plowed winter highway unrolled like a silver Christmas ribbon tarnished gray after the holidays. Winter painted from a monochromatic palette—white fields, off-white sky, rough charcoal strokes for leaf-stripped trees and bushes fringing the overall shawl of snow.

The boring landscape numbed Kevin's survival instincts; driving didn't help him keep alert, but Jane, of course, couldn't spell him at the wheel. No driver's education taught in the great big High School in the Sky.

Kevin knew he shouldn't be heading south for the Twin Cities, but he didn't know where to go anymore and maybe "they"—whether police or G-men or extraterrestrials—

weren't following. The newspapers had said nothing, not even about anyone finding the two bodies north of Duluth. . . .

The van swerved as Kevin felt sleep buzz his brain with a kamikaze pass. Jane's big brown eyes immediately questioned him—a look he was beginning to read as accusing. Paranoia. Nice Greek root word. *Paranoos*—demented. A shrink of all people should be immune, he knew, but put anyone under enough stress and all the standard afflictions of the human personality come screaming out of Pandora's box.

"Put the wrappers in the empty bag," he instructed Jane. Maybe terminal tidiness would ensure normality. Another fancy phrase described *that* delusion, Kevin knew, but he was too fatigued to hunt for it. He glanced in the flat silver oval of the sideview mirror. Was that Jeep staying too close too long? Come on, either pass or get off the pot. . . . God, he was beginning to feel tired.

"Kevin?"

"Nothing. I was just watching the car behind us." Jane was growing hypersensitive to his moods now. The longer she spent with him, the more she seemed to know him, and there was something . . . freakish . . . about how perceptively she could tune in to the blips on his mental EKG.

"Are they following us?" Her jacket rasped as she twisted around to look.

"I don't know. Maybe I'll try to lose 'em." He sped up, the van hesitating until the gas took hold and shot them forward.

Behind them the Jeep, muffled with its winter canvas top, diminished into a squarish blob.

"All right!" Kevin congratulated himself. "Guess I was wrong."

"Want a candy bar?" Jane wondered next.

"God, no! Anything sweet right now would turn my stomach."

Her face fell at his refusal.

"Hey, it's okay. *You* can eat them. Maybe they'll keep you warm. This van is colder than a well-digger's designer shorts."

Jane signaled polite puzzlement, then bent to scrape up the wrappers and crush them into the bag behind her seat.

Kevin pulled a hand off the steering wheel and thrust it into his jacket pocket. A cold roll of bills curved into his palm, almost as comforting to him as steel balls to Captain Queeg. Money. With money they had a chance.

"Where are we going?" Jane asked.

Kevin couldn't bring himself to answer.

*   *   *

"They won't come back here." Turner was definite.

Nordstrom's face made the ridiculing little grimace that indicated mute disagreement.

"*They* might not. He will," Nordstrom said.

"Why?"

The imported psychiatrist threw his fur-lined leather coat over the plastic-shell chair, stationing his ostrich-skin briefcase by its splayed steel peg legs. The coat and case almost dwarfed Eric Nordstrom, a slight man whose air of neat effacement made him seem even smaller.

"Blake's an amateur," Nordstrom continued. "A rules player despite his surface disrespect for convention. He's too used to putting rats through mazes. He's forgotten how to be one. He'll come back here because he can't help himself."

Turner leaned into his molded plastic chair. Although small, the interview room in the federal building felt chilly, partly because national government policy demanded heat conservation—mostly because of the scalpel's edge of cold Nordstrom had brought in from the outside.

Turner disliked the man, but he didn't know why. Turner studied his vaguely unattractive features, muddy skin and thinning, badly cut hair, the affected rimless glasses. It was possible to imagine Nordstrom's mother disliking her new infant on sight; possible even to imagine Nordstrom born with a cold, winking monocle of glass propped up before each pale gimlet eye. . . .

"You'd like him better than you like me." Nordstrom hefted the briefcase to extract a fistful of manila folders.

"But it's me you have to work with, and him you have to catch."

"Who?" Turner sat up, wary.

"Blake. Young Dr. Blake. He and I attended Harvard together, did you know?"

No . . . kidding. Turner made himself smile cynically. "Oh? Old school ties going to get in your way, Doctor?"

The other man laughed, an oddly irritating sound. "We never got along, Blake and I. He was a nobody from the north woods with a few brains and a certain charm. Scholarship student."

The last two words reminded Turner that Nordstrom came from a wealthy New York family, that he didn't have to work for a living, and that he certainly didn't have to work for the government.

"Then this job should be a busman's holiday for you," Turner commented.

"Busman's holiday?" Was the man impervious to conversational clichés?

"You'll enjoy working on Blake, then?"

"Ah. You are a professional, aren't you, Mr. Turner? I forget that, sometimes. I won't be sorry, no, to interrogate Blake. But that makes it better, doesn't it, Mr. Turner? If you have to use a dirty tool, better it be suited for the job."

"I never said—"

"You don't have to like me. You just have to need me. Dr. Kevin Blake never did. But he will."

Nordstrom fanned the pale folders, each bearing a slim burden of papers. "I've got copies of his med school and residency records, his group therapy sessions. I've got as much on Dr. Kevin Blake as there is to find. Let me assure you, Mr. Turner, he'll come back." His hands, clean as a surgeon's, snapped the folders into a tidy pile. "Now, tell me, have you found the latest address on his parents?"

Turner reached to the notebook in his jacket pocket, feeling inexplicably reluctant.

Chapter Seven

"Jesus Christ!"

Martin Kandinsky, a wool cap jammed on his lowered head and his bare hands crammed into the pockets of an ancient wool jacket, backed away from the figure he'd collided with. He squinted into the five o'clock shadow of a winter's dusk. "Watch where you're goin', man!"

"I'm there already."

Kandinsky squinted harder, studying the stranger who'd confronted him. "Kevin! I didn't recognize you without the beard. Holy balls! What're you doing here?"

"Here" was the parking lot behind the Student Health Center on the University of Minnesota campus. Students streamed by, too bundled against the subzero temperatures to notice anyone crazy enough to stop and talk in the open air.

"I'm here to make a buy, what else?" Kevin joked.

"Don't kid about that, man." Kandy looked around with classic paranoia. "The cops have been on my case for the pot they found when they trashed my place."

"They trashed your place?"

Kandy shrugged. "It was trashed already, no big deal."

Kevin grinned briefly. He could picture the police turning Kandy's upside-down digs inside out. Kandy accumulated junk mail the way compulsive shoppers stockpile hotpads.

"I figured it'd be safer to catch you here," Kevin admitted. "I need to find out what's going on."

"You! You're what's going on! You weren't gone more than ten hours before the gestapo came around asking about you. They put your office under a microscope. I stashed your car in the Coffman Memorial ramp, but they impounded it."

"City cops or federal?"

"Who knows? They were kinda vague. You know how those storm troopers can get when they're on a rampage. They gave my joint—and I do mean joint—a good going-over. Promised me a stint in the cooler for possession if I didn't cooperate, but all they got was a few shreds. So . . . enough about me. How you been?"

Kevin clapped his friend on the shoulder. "How about I buy you dinner? Then you can sing for your supper."

Kandy followed Kevin to his own parked van, pausing to inspect it.

"Nice wheels." He wrenched open the side door and jumped inside, collapsing like Big Bird on gangly crossed legs. Belatedly, he leaned forward to examine the passenger in the front seat.

"Jane Doe, I presume." He glanced at Kevin. "I figured you'd have Wonder Woman with you. *Enchanté*," he greeted Jane in hopelessly oily French, detaching her cold bare hand from the seat back it clutched. He lifted it to his lips for an enthusiastic smack.

Jane watched Kandy with deep confusion while Kevin sprinted around to the driver's side and jammed himself back behind the wheel. He twisted to watch two opposite personalities on parade—Kandy ingratiatingly ugly and utterly impudent, as usual; Jane taking it all in with grave, miss-nothing eyes.

Kandy extended his hand for a conventional shake. "I see Kevin's got you all done up like Cathy Coed. Good thinking. My name's Martin Kandinsky, but they call me Kandy. I call you pretty cute."

Jane blinked and shook his hand. "Are . . . you one of Kevin's . . . other . . . patients?" she asked politely.

Kevin smiled. Jane was progressing; not long before she couldn't accept the idea that he had any patients besides her.

"Wounded," Kandy groaned, "a direct hit to the psyche. Naw, I'm a fellow shrink, Miss Doe. As sane as any shrink ever gets.

63

"Speaking of which . . ." Kandy turned his nearsighted eyes on Kevin. "I sure hope you don't harbor illusions of crashing at your old pad. The gestapo guys took your place to the dry cleaners; they went over it with everything but lighter fluid and a match. It's probably still staked out. Actually, oppression is an equal opportunity railroad now. Guy and gal. A female agent came along when they did my place. Maybe they want to use feminine psychology on Jane when they get her."

Kevin winced. First his car, then his condo. Was nothing sacred? "Where was Cross when all this was going on?"

"You do mean Dr. Cross, Norbert Cross, head of our esteemed Probe intensive psychiatric care unit?"

"Yeah. I know Cross was going to shovel Jane off on some government head-tank in Virginia, but Probe was his baby. He had too much pride to let some jokers take it apart."

"Maybe. But Cross is gone, Kev. So is Matthews and Swanson and even the Probe unit secretary. The offices are part of the neonatal unit now. Probe is el wipe-o. Gone away for to stay. As if it had never existed. So solly. Computer error. All gone."

"I've only been away myself for . . . seven, eight days! How can they—?"

"You've been away a lifetime, Kev, believe me."

In silence, Kevin revved the engine and guided the van into the dimming streets. The roadway was narrow, thanks to curbside piles of plowed snow and parked cars lining every avenue. The van crept along. Kevin headed for the nearest McDonald's, pulled into line and when his turn came bawled an order for them all into the speaker.

When the warm, bakery-white bags were thrust through the open window, he dumped them all on Kandy and headed for the lot's farthest parking space.

Kandy began cramming ketchup-bloodied fries into his mouth. Jane followed suit by tearing a ketchup bag open with her teeth and drenching her box of fries. Kevin took one bite of his first quarter-pounder and stopped, his appetite frozen by their innocent gusto.

"So where you been?" Kandy inquired genially.

"Outstate."

"Okay, I get it. None of my business. But, look, Kevin. This is Space Mountain. The big glide into nowhere. You're a non-persona now. And the chick, she's tomorrow's McNuggets. Those government types are serious. They want you nailed down and they don't care if they have to do it by the hands and feet. Why don't you turn yourselves in? Maybe they just want to give you a medal or something—first famous medical mystery solved by the great Kevin Blake. Maybe they're on the Side of Science."

"Kandy, there are dead bodies behind us."

Kandy whistled. "You?" When Kevin was silent he glanced to the watching Jane. "She really is something, isn't she? Far out. You find anything more out about her—how she comes by her, uh, talents?"

"Yeah. But I can't say. I can't prove it. Nobody'd believe me."

Kandy tsked consideringly. "That's what they all say before we haul them away. There's something you should know. Before the anti–A Team took over, I knew this cat—"

"Don't tell me they interrogated my cat?"

"No way, they left Blue Streak strictly alone. Besides, all cats look alike, especially Russian Blues. Anyway, I know this dude and he's a computer whiz, can really make those modems sit up and recite Deuteronomy and Numbers. So when they topsy-turvied my place, I had him go into your bank account pronto and whisk your money far, far away."

Kandy extended a Kinko Copies card with a name and account number scrawled on the back.

"That's you, fellah, if you want any dough. We must have done it before the G-whiz boys and girl got wise, 'cause the money's in the new account."

"Or maybe they let you *think* you got away with it and they've got the bank watching."

Kandy made calf-eyes at Jane and burst into the chorus of "I Wonder Who's Paranoid Now?"

"Me." Kevin snatched the card. "And you, too, if you're smart. I might try it. Thanks, Kandy. I'll repay you someday."

"Say no more." He stared at Kevin in the almost-dark. "You look terrible, man. Better eat that stuff. Then crash. Then get some bread from the bank."

"Yeah. Yeah. Yeah. I'll drop you by your car. Do me a last favor on the way? Pick up a *Strib* at a corner stand. I need to catch up on what's been happening around here."

The engine ignited faithfully. Dark had drifted over the day's encompassing whiteness. The van droned under streetlights, bars of alternating dark and light rippling its hood and windshield, mesmerizing Kevin. He paused to let Kandy get the newspaper, then drove on, finally pulling into the emptied campus parking lot and feeling much more noticeable.

Kandy cracked the side door, then hesitated, looking back at Kevin.

"Take it easy." He turned to Jane. "A pleasure, Miss Doe. 'Bye."

The door slammed shut, closing out Kandy, the cold and a lot of things Kevin had once cared about. Behind intermittent oblongs of lit windows, the university hummed into evening—students and professors working late, staying late, feeling secure and unthreatened. Kevin waited, watching while the yellow jelly-bean-body of Kandy's old VW chugged out of the lot onto the icy street.

He shouldn't have parked directly under a light, Kevin knew, but right now he needed something warm and yellow. He pulled off his gloves and unfolded the evening edition of the *Star and Tribune* that Kandy had bought.

The paper was stiff, cold. Kevin paged through it, ignoring Jane for once, hungry for the familiar black-and-white of the newspaper's type style.

He wasn't anywhere in it, nor was she. They weren't the apple of the public's eye, and maybe that was worse, maybe it meant they were in deeper trouble. They were anonymous fugitives, free to be plunged into cold storage so deep and frozen that even the sun wouldn't find them.

He scanned for mention of the deaths north of Duluth. As soon as Jane and he found a place to rest, he'd have to put her under hypnosis and recapture those lost minutes, find out what had really happened. He'd have to discover what powers remained to her, and why they'd manifested themselves so dramatically in the Volkers' upstairs bedroom. Eat. Crash. Get money. Jane was right; Kandy was nuts. Kevin had no time for any of that.

In a back section under an "Outstate News" heading, a word finally snagged his trolling eye. Kevin manipulated the paper, trying to illuminate the one-paragraph item. He read it without believing it. Then he looked over the paper's trembling rim.

Jane was watching him, as she so often did. He no longer felt flattered.

Yet who else could he talk to? He finally glimpsed how alone Jane must feel. He finally felt it, finally knew that no one *could* know . . . even as he most desperately wanted to share it with someone.

"Jane," he said, because she was the only one there. "Jane. Neumeier. Neumeier's . . . dead. She . . . died. It says of a heart attack. But they've killed Neumeier somehow. Up in her cabin. Natural causes! Bullshit."

Tears were gathering in his eyes in the dark, hot tears welling on the lip of chill flesh. "You remember Neumeier —we went to see her. And she helped us, put me on the right track about what you were. So they killed her, that great old lady. They killed her in the cold and the snow! Jane—you remember. Say you remember! She died for you—you must remember!"

Jane dropped her head. He could see only the crown of her hair, her dark, unconfiding hair. His shocked emotions were steadying now, and he knew he had been unfair, terribly unfair, but so was the world. He knew he should try to heal Jane, protect her as he had sworn, vowed, to do. He knew all that, and knew that he needed healing and protection more.

So he sat there, silent, lost in himself and in the insufficiency of that self, meeting the stranger he had become.

"I'm sorry," Jane said at last, looking up with sober, uncertain eyes. "I'm sorry."

Chapter Eight

Swashbuckling blue and green letters slashed across the white banners crowding the store's display window. Crimson neon spelling out L-I-Q-U-O-R washed the cars parked beneath it with an urgent, brake-light glow.

Jane huddled alone in the van. Kevin had parked, turned off the ignition and, promising not to be gone long, had locked the doors, after making Jane promise in turn not to leave.

So she scanned the screaming hieroglyphs of the hand-lettered signs, trying to recombine them into sense. "Gilbey's Gin. Fifth or Liter." Numbers reeled nonsensically to the back of her mind, but words began to merge under the rapid-fire strafing of her eyes. "Four Roses." "Smirnoff." "Two for $16.95!" "Bailey's Irish Cream for the Blue Nun." "Vermouth." Vermont? Or very mouth?

Jane's chin burrowed into her jacket collar as she absorbed the spectacle before her. Kevin considered *Zyunsinth* a strange word, she marveled, yet his world overflowed with even stranger words and no one noticed.

A tingling began worming around her fingertips and toes. Something in her subconscious knew it for subzero cold tentatively taking her by the hands and feet before assaulting the larger body.

Something else within her knew how to meet it, knew how to lull her acuity, her mind, her senses, her body itself to a level that required less heat. She downshifted easily into hypometabolism. Cold, that invisible incubus, bereft of easy warmth to steal, drifted elsewhere.

Jane drifted, too. The tingling migrated to her head and rasped there with the faint, rhythmic tenacity of a tree branch scraping the window outside her room in Willhelm Hall. She stared out the van's frost-etched window, scanning for landmarks. Some memories were dreams, Kevin had said. And some memories were not.

Memories. Jane's were jumbled. Her mind pawed the jigsaw puzzle pieces, trying to dovetail a coherent image from the ruins. For Roses. War of the Roses. A chaser for the Blue Nun. Chase. Chase her. Chaste. Run, Blue Nun, run. Blue with Cold Duck.

And always, above the words that cycled through her like ticker tape, were the lights, leaving her. Retrieving her. And re-leaving (relieving?) her again—odd lights, dispensing color but not warmth. Lights pulsing in the rhythm of delivery and birth. And rebirth. Pausing to withdraw from her the gleaning . . . again.

Jane moaned protest and stirred. A tiny light pricked the van's interior darkness. Some shred of sound scratched the quiet as if it were a screen.

Nothing moved, and the doors' rusted chrome button locks remained depressed.

Yet on the van's silenced radio, a firefly of light cruised the fine-line gradations, illuminated the tiny numbers one by one. Behind closed lids, Jane's eyes followed the light's advance and retreat up the scale of stations—no, Jane's eyes *led* the light up and down the horizontal FM ladder.

In the beginning was the light. Sound was an afterthought. A cacophony reminiscent of the massed spinning of Lynn Volker's slipcased record albums growled sotto voce in the van, echoed in Jane's mind. From Babel— meaning. Jane detected words again, English words spoken in un-English accents. The seeking fine red line in her mind automatically dialed them in. Words became voices, dancing phrases in the dark.

"If the lynx remain in place, surely the bonds can rejoin. We can—"

"We can nothing. The lynx are merely potential. This one unit is cast free of control, tumbling in the void."

"The liberation was an act of One."

"Of One, yes, called to by one not of its kind. It is most . . . unprecedented that those of us on deep extradition should revert so primitively."

"The One has been adjusted?"

"The One has submerged in All. And the mother-cell has sent another One to add to All, with new instructions."

"We have been . . . as we are . . . for some time."

"True. But we are All, and All wishes to make us more."

"We can grow. We have before."

"Still, the rogue probe is lost and we will not be complete until all our data-bearers are gathered again."

"What will the new one-in-all instruct?"

"That which serves the mother of us all—who is the child-cell."

"We have not completely severed the lynx."

"No. But we do not retain enough control to recall the probe."

"Does it sense us still, this rogue unit, do we think?"

"We think . . . but we do not sense much anymore. It is a sorrow that the old skills become so unnecessary."

"That way lies oneness."

"Which . . . one . . . of us moved to let the unit go?"

"We are assimilated now."

"Then it does not matter; we are repaired. Or are all of us suspect now?"

"Perhaps the voyager cell will know when we glean its message."

"Behold the imaging. It is pale, this world, and watery. The probe may mire itself in the swamp of it and sink beneath the weight of it."

"We have surrendered probes before."

"But never on their own initiative."

*　　　　　*　　　　　*

Jane's hand waved before her face as if to banish gnats. A grating crack echoed in the metal-walled van. She jerked upright, her eyes wide open.

"Sleepyhead," Kevin was accusing fondly, jamming himself into the van's newly lit interior with a wedge of cold and a brown paper bag. The door slammed shut, encasing them both in lurid red-lit dimness again.

"Hey, you got the radio going all by yourself? You're getting to be quite a techie. Jane, the Radio Wave Girl. Sorry to take so long; there was a line at the checkout counter."

He pulled off his gloves to wrench the dial and slide the bar of light from number to number. Voices and vocals Dopplered in and out of range. Country western whining blended with rock screeching and middle-of-the-road baying.

"Lynx," Jane said, sitting up and narrowing her eyes. Her bare hands hugged her upper arms as if she felt cold.

Kevin glanced her way. "What?"

"Lynx," she repeated with mournful certainty. "The lynx are gone."

He looked puzzled for a moment, his face leprosied with neon backwash. "Lynx? Still thinking about Zyunsinth in . . . cold storage, Jane? No more fur coats, thank God. No lynx, no opossum, not even a baby rabbit or two. I can't afford it, and neither can you. We'll get to a motel, and then we'll get warm."

"Why are the lynx gone?" Jane persisted with childlike monotony as Kevin backed the van out of the lot.

He was too weary to answer, but he did. "Endangered species, I guess. Getting extinct. Too many ladies with too few things to do wanting to buy dead animal skins."

Jane plucked at her jacket sleeve. "Down, you said, not like in 'up,' but like feathers. Did ducks die for my jacket?"

"Jane, I don't know how they get down—maybe they shear it like lambs' wool. Or harvest it by the handful. Maybe Santa's elves throw it from the sky. Or maybe people kill ducks and geese and take it."

"It's not good for things to die," she said.

"People don't *like* for things to die. But everything has to, sometime. It's when people or animals die . . . too soon, too painfully, too uselessly—or even sometimes too late—that we're sad about it."

A wail chainsawed through the cold throat of the night, a wail that wobbled up and down the minor scale.

Adrenaline hammered panic into Kevin's heartbeat, torched his mind with indecision. Reflex and second thought went one-on-one against each other.

A police siren. His foot tensed on the gas pedal, torn between slamming down or moving hard and fast to the brake. The whining howl grew shriller. Every good-citizen urge pounded into Kevin's skull was nudging his foot to the brake, teasing the steering wheel to the curb. Was it wiser to pull over, passive, and assume—hope—that the official vehicle would barrel on past? Wiser to bolt? Fight or flight or just belly-up give up?

Only split-hair seconds had elapsed while the macrocomputer of Kevin's mind ran its options. In the rearview mirror, he watched a weaving ball of crimson flash nearer. The van was still moving at normal street speed; he had done nothing at all.

Before he could change that, the oncoming vehicle loomed larger in the mirror—large, and white, with a word stenciled across its top in big, legible letters. A-m-b-u-l-a-n-c-e. Relief streamed to Kevin's farthest-flung nerve ends.

"Ecnalubma!" he announced jubilantly. "It's only an ecnalubma."

He twisted to watch the ambulance scream abreast while he edged the van to the curb. Rolling down the window, Kevin leaned out to read, head-on, the backwards letters meant to be seen only in rearview mirrors.

Once, months before, Jane had interpreted that careful gibberish as a real word. That was the August night when the ambulance had brought her wasted, naked body all the way from a rural Crow Wing bluff top to the University of Minnesota Hospitals in Minneapolis.

"Ecnalubma," Kevin repeated, letting his eyes revert the backwards consonants and vowels to their proper meaning.

He sighed as the shriek of the passing vehicle droned into the darkness. The person-long lump on the rear gurney had looked vague and anonymous. Heart attack victim? Bleeding ulcers? Some more abstruse malady? Dr. Blake was relieved to diagnose only one nonmedical fact: no ambulance was going to play pursuit vehicle for the CIA. He wondered how "paranoia" would read backwards, and painstakingly worked it out in his muddied mind. Aiona—para, para . . . aionarap.

Belatedly, he glanced to Jane.

"I shouldn't have shouted 'ecnalubma.' It didn't put you under, did it?" His hand gently rubbed her denimed knee.

"Under? No. The . . . ecnalubma screamed too loud."

"Ambulance, Jane," he corrected happily. She needed to know her world on its own terms now. "It was just an ambulance."

He steered the van down the dark, snow-churned street until it vanished into a stream of similar vehicles. It finally nosed onto the entry ramp to Highway 100, following the venerable north-south route until it joined Interstate 494, then peeled off onto an east-west access road.

"The wilds of Bloomington." Kevin surveyed the brightly lit, ruler-straight channel of freeway known as the Bloomington Strip. Bloomington claimed to be Minnesota's third-largest city, but it was a heartless community. Few ever saw its downtown. Instead, its soul resided along Interstate 494, beside a restless rhythm of passing cars and within an endless chain of upscale restaurants and singles bars, hotels and motels.

An hour later, Kevin, ensconced in one of the most downscale of the motels, was sitting on the edge of a double bed, watching Jane sleep in the bed across from him.

A strange world, he reflected, where a room for two had come to mean separate beds each big enough for two. It implied more togetherness—and more apartness—than he suspected the species could stand, no matter how nomadic it became.

The clubby motel glass he held seemed to grease his palm with the lingering oils of traveling salesmen and randy football players and giggling women desperate for what passed for a good time on the Strip.

But Chivas Regal slicked the inside of the glass. Why not? he'd thought in the liquor store while staring at the overlit rows of bottles. Why the hell not? The McDonald's bag lay on the bedspread beside him, bloated as a prostate patient's bladder, only with air.

He'd forced down the cold McDonald's burger as soon as he'd rammed the motel room night chain home, knowing he needed it. Warm booze—he didn't have the energy to find the ice machine—trickled through him, piping a relaxation so profound down his wrangled nerves that he could almost feel blood draining from his taut arteries in slow stages.

Risky, he knew. Risky to allow himself this small, calculated collapse at the lip of a glass. Risky to have registered, even under a pseudonym, at a motel.

But where was he supposed to go? What dive's water glass would he honor with his hoarded Chivas tomorrow night? Where would Jane lay her telekinetic head next?

"To aliens," Kevin toasted himself in the plain-Jane mirror above the Melamine-topped dresser. "And all good alienists."

The juxtaposition soothed him, as the Scotch had not. Who was better qualified to receive an alien visitation, to guide a human with alien talents through a too-familiar world, than an alienist? A shrink who saw his world shrinking under the enormity of one huge, artificial object in the sky over Crow Wing?

He looked at Jane again, and frowned.

Nothing answered him, except the raw silk whisper of the Chivas Regal he could not afford down his throat.

Chapter Nine

"I told you he'd head home!" Nordstrom crowed. "Instincts of a lemming. The man *wants* to be caught, to be crucified. A Savior complex, and a textbook example, if I ever saw one."

Turner didn't answer. Instead, he tapped his fingers on the Xerox of the university campus police report atop his desk. The Chevy van had been reported at the local McDonald's just last night. Its license plates had been described as "obscured," but the make and model were on target.

"We need his cooperation," Turner said slowly, "we don't need your latest techniques in search and retrieval, Dr. Nordstrom. I've done a little backgrounding of my own . . . on you."

Nordstrom's laugh was slightly self-deprecating.

"You're not even worried, are you?" Turner complained. "If a Senate investigative committee got their hands on what I dug up . . ."

"It's classified. All my work is." Nordstrom's smile hovered a whisker's width away from a smirk. "I'm surprised you wasted your time, Mr. Turner. I would have told you anything you needed to know."

"I wanted to know what you wouldn't tell me . . . or what you wouldn't let me read between the lines. Back at Harvard, you and Blake shared a lot of the same class rosters."

"They were large classes."

"Still, you knew him."

Nordstrom shrugged. "You knew that. Blake was one of those ingratiating fakers even crusty Harvard professors slobber over. Liberal, to a fault. Used to egg me into medical ethics debates—Blake was always trying to impress the impressionable. He didn't even know who I was. A most . . . disagreeable man. But it worked. I saw him win grades, win hearts and minds. . . ."

Nordstrom rose from his chair and paced away, shrugging. "Not mine." After a long pause he turned slowly to face Turner again. "I expect you to point out that I don't have one."

"One what?"

"Heart."

Turner spun a manila folder on his desk so Nordstrom could read the typed title. "The PID isn't noted for hiring heart. I see you were involved in that CIA scam to cool off the army's involuntary LSD guinea pigs from the sixties."

"Involved? I invented it."

"Those flashbacks you induced sent some of those guys back to the nuthouse."

"It kept them out of government claims court, didn't it?"

"How'd you do it? Induce flashbacks so destructive, I mean? Did you drop it in their brownies at a family picnic? Spike their Sunday afternoon beers? Even the guys' lawyers couldn't untangle what was LSD-echo and what was just plain craziness. Drove their cases out of court through sheer psychotic overkill. Was it some drug, some LSD derivative, something even I don't know about?"

"There are more drugs on heaven and earth, Horatio, than are dreamed of in your philosophy."

"Cut the . . . quotes, Nordstrom." Turner's shoulders shifted uneasily. "You work for me now. The job is simple: find the psychiatrist and his patient; persuade—repeat, persuade—the guy to work with her under our supervision. Failing that, you are to use your . . . skills, as needed . . . to debrief Jane Doe herself.

"That won't be easy. She's part wonder-worker and part time bomb, from what slim facts we've pieced together. Four dead men behind her, two of 'em the Crow Wing cops who found her, two of 'em mine. Even Dr. Swanson's paranormal experiments proved to be hard-won. We don't know exactly *what* Jane Doe is, and how hard it will be to find out."

Nordstrom smiled, showing Dentine-red gums. "I deliver the goods. And government imperatives allow me to push the human psyche to its limits—my own as much as anybody's. Everything that makes *Homo sapiens* civilized is useless when the ruling order requires a specific behavior. Useless to the victim, that is. Civilization has many uses for the hunter."

"Listen to me: The woman's mind is valuable, and the man is the key to her mind. That makes him valuable, too. No need to send him home in a mental body bag unless we have to."

Nordstrom's thumb and fingers rubbed together speculatively. "What if I produce a better key?"

"Prove it. What we don't want—what nobody wants—

76

is to blow this woman's abilities before we've had a chance to evaluate them. Blake's right about one thing: she shouldn't get into the wrong hands."

"Do some of those hands belong to our comrades across the sea?" Nordstrom sat down.

"Ask Baker. I'm just a front-line operative. A delivery boy."

"Then let me congratulate you." Nordstrom raised one eyebrow over the ground-glass rim of his spectacles. "From that report, it looks like it won't be long before the fugitives are in custody. Then I go to work."

Turner skimmed the page again. "We're looking for them in Minneapolis now; a big city makes a finer net than the boonies. You were right about him heading back here. Poor devil."

Nordstrom shrugged and flipped open a manila folder. The pen-and-ink sketch of Jane looked back at him. "Poor bitch," he parroted softly.

"Don't underestimate her," Turner warned. "Cracking that—from all reports—extraordinary . . . mind of hers will take skill, and maybe something Dr. Kevin Blake always had that you don't."

Nordstrom's face went livid. "What?" he demanded, a higher note scratching his voice's baritone sheen.

It was Turner's opportunity to smile coldly. "Heart."

*   *   *

"Jane?" Kevin shook her shoulder.

She sat up groggily in the semidark, murmuring "Dr. Neumeier—?"

"Were you dreaming?"

"No . . . I don't think so. But I thought I saw Dr. Neumeier—" Jane looked to the oblong of window where highway lights gleamed faintly through the drawn curtains.

"You couldn't have seen her. For God's sake, don't have nightmares that I can't analyze, Jane. We're not there anymore, in Neumeier's cabin in the north woods. Besides, Dr. Neumeier's dead, you know that. I told you myself just tonight."

"Then I . . . *heard* her." Conviction lifted Jane's voice to a single, repeated note. "She said that . . . 'They will always win.'"

Kevin was silent, recognizing the words of the canny old sociology professor, survivor of the Holocaust but not of the government's right to know in the Land of the Free.

He made himself confront the facts implicit in Neumeier's death.

They, the ones "who always win," the forces of official inquiry, must have reached Neumeier's wilderness cabin after Jane and he had left. Then they must have interrogated her—too harshly, triggering a fatal coronary.

Of course, Kevin himself had precipitated that by running to Neumeier in the first place, like a truant schoolboy hiding behind a favorite teacher. The lump of lifetime guilt Kevin collected somewhere at his center coiled up a few thousand more yards of secondhand string. . . .

Kevin made himself remember his patient. "Jane, what you overheard, that was said . . . days ago, nights ago. You're remembering conversational odds and ends—"

"I'm remembering," she challenged, a smile in her voice.

Now that she was fully awake and the light wouldn't shock her eyes, Kevin turned up the lamp on the bedside table between them. Even Edison's genius couldn't lighten the three A.M. blues. Kevin slouched on the edge of his bed. Jane curled up against her upholstered headboard.

"You want me to remember," she reminded him.

"You remember too much."

"And not enough."

"And not enough. Jane, I want—" Her eyes livened. "Not that. I want to put you under hypnosis again."

"Oh." She looked disappointed, then stretched impatiently. "I liked the chair in your office better. When you hypnotize me on a bed, my neck hurts afterwards."

"Simple cure." He tossed the pillows on his bed to Jane's. "Get comfy; then we'll put you under."

"Why?"

"I thought you didn't mind hypnosis."

"No . . . but there's so much in my mind now, every-

78

thing that's happened to me since I was found. I don't want to lose it."

"Jane, I don't want to lose any part of you, either. My God, that's my job, to find it. And so much is still lost. You're a miracle, you know that?"

"They didn't think so."

" 'They'? You mean the . . . guess I better find something to call them." Only euphemisms, cloyingly coy, surfaced in Kevin's mind. "The, uh, visitors?"

She shook her head. "Not *them*. Them! The Volkers. My . . . parents. If they thought I was a miracle, they would have wanted to keep me. Why did they have my photograph on their wall? And why did I look so different in it—the same, but different? Why do I feel . . . ?"

"Feel what?" he coached.

"Feel that I don't know what's happening to me anymore."

"That's not true!" He launched himself at her bed, tired springs squawling under his weight. "You know more than ever. *We* know more than ever. And forget the Volkers! I should never have taken you there. They're your parents by virtue of sheer dumb luck more than intention. They don't know the first thing about being parents except clinging to some illusion of a child. You're too real for them, too demanding.

"What you *should* want to know about is . . . those others, the visitors. The ones who took you from this earth in the form of a tiny cell twenty-five years ago and returned you as a grown woman. Do you know how many cells are in the human body? Sixty thousand billion. All those cells, growing, changing, encapsulating the information that makes you . . . you. And some of them were adulterated—had to be to give you the faculties, the powers you have. What about them? The ones who made you."

"They let me go! I remember that." Jane was shrinking into the piled pillows, as if to cushion herself against a lingering nightmare.

"Yes, yes," Kevin soothed. "But why? Why, when retrieving you and capturing all that information coursing along your neurons was their only purpose? Why let you go again? And with what attributes? Did they . . . empty your memory of what they wanted to know, or simply copy it onto their own records? Did they strip you of your telekinetic powers as painlessly as they stripped you of your clothes in the . . . uh . . . laser lift? Did they give you a message to give mankind—?"

"Humankind," Jane corrected.

Kevin waved his hand. "It's the same thing."

"It's not. Chauvinistic speech conventions are designed to reduce the role of women not only in history but in contemporary life as well."

He sighed his frustration. "This is hardly the moment for a women's lib speech—did you get that from the nursing students? I never should have sent you to stay with them in the dorm—it was like turning on a tape recorder in a disco."

"I . . . read that sentence. In a book. In the library."

"Then you *do* remember the information you . . . gleaned! That souped-up speed reading you did at the campus library stuck. So the . . . shit! . . . the aliens must've left your memory intact! That's why I need to pull out those latent memories so you can see them for yourself, so I can understand—"

"Understand!" She seemed panicked now. "You understand too much, and I not enough. Please, Kevin, I don't want to lose myself again! Never again. To let myself go like that."

"I'll bring you back, I promise."

"You can't bring Dr. Neumeier back."

Kevin's face froze as all persuasion drained from it, leaving bleak introspection.

"You're right. Neumeier's death is my fault. If I hadn't brought you to her, if we hadn't been tailed by whoever Washington sent, the good professor would still be alive."

Jane leaned forward and touched his hand with her fingertip. "There are places, Kevin, that *nobody* can bring you back from. I don't want to go to one of those. I've been there before, I think, and I can't come back too many times. If you make me go too far inside myself again, I may not be able to leave—ever."

"They left you here, turned you loose, with that kind of condition on it, you think?" He sounded horrified, and he was.

"Not they," Jane said gently. "You."

Her eyes radiated an awful honesty. Kevin searched himself, wondering who was the amnesiac, who the probe, who the tool of others' wishes.

"Maybe you should hypnotize me," he joked, gift-wrapping anxiety in humor. Such defense mechanisms were alien to Jane.

Silent, she watched him, the lamplight carving delicate arcs under her eyes, shadowing the skin beneath her lower lip, changing her—again—into something Kevin did not quite know.

His hand lighted on her hair. "I don't know how much time we'll have left to . . . work. There are things I need to know—for your sake as well as my own stubborn, self-serving curiosity. I won't . . . lose you. Not this time, not ever. Trust me."

She nodded soberly. He segued quickly into the hypnotic ritual before she could change her mysterious mind. He told her that she was relaxed, that she was safe, that she would be all right. And then he whispered the word. Ecnalubma.

Jane went under like a perfect pupil, into perfect peace. Kevin envied her that induced serenity for an instant before he kicked his professional mindset into gear and began asking his questions. Then he began listening. And watching.

Chapter Ten

At three o'clock in the morning, Nordstrom was staring at a Milky Way of stars—headlights streaming on the freeway beyond his Registry Hotel suite window along the Bloomington Strip.

He savored his position of height, of aloofness, a habit of his New York City upbringing. He liked the night and its anonymity—that, too, a residue of urban jungle infighting.

This flat, open suburban wasteland, with its hints of cold vastness lurking just beyond the last snake of illuminated freeway, repelled him.

Of course, the January cold—the primitive January cold—justified his fur-lined storm coat more than any piddling snowfall that could swirl into the glass canyons of Manhattan.

Nordstrom had tossed the coat on an overstuffed chair, open lining fur-side out. He paused, vodka glass in hand, to admire the mink's rusty black sheen in the incandescent lamplight.

That's how Nordstrom liked to wear his status symbols —close to the vest. Concealed. A teasing presence that tantalized the less blessed.

He eyed the manila folders sprawled across the king-size bed, adding a random pattern to the bedspread's neat geometric print.

Nordstrom liked addling order with a random element, too, especially someone else's mental order. Now the subject of his disorder was Kevin Blake.

Where was he? Nordstrom mused deliciously at the window. Someplace warm and comfortable, like this? At peace with the thought of new work about to begin?

No, Blake would be out of his element—in the dark and the cold, in whatever corner of it he could buy, beg or steal. He would be desperate to belong again to the common herd of the law-abiding. He was a herd animal who didn't know it, Nordstrom thought, cut loose by circumstances from the security of the mindless masses. Blake would bolt, would run himself into the ground and would give up, sniveling, ultimately.

Then Nordstrom would go to work. He anticipated matching wits with a fellow psychiatrist, he admitted to himself. Particularly this one. His knuckles whitened on the glass with its bloodless white liquid. Odd that it should come down to this, he and Blake, after all the gulfs between them.

Nordstrom had manipulated his own life from birth. With his first breath, wealth and its expectations were his. Unfortunately, he never grew beyond that first gangling adolescent spurt that promises much more. He never outgrew his infant unattractiveness—too much head and eyes. Eventually, there came the teeth, also too much, despite the costly machinations of a Park Avenue orthodontist.

So despite the money, Eric Nordstrom grew into the kind of ill-assembled man on whom trousers always sagged and custom-tailored shirts invariably wrinkled, and whose high-priced 57th Street haircuts immediately turned into something Walter Mondale would sport.

Such details had not bothered his obsessively intelligent mind, though he recognized them with a kind of icy dislike. He had been a solitary, driven child—more adult than most of the grown-ups around him.

He hadn't minded until Harvard. And Julie Symons. Nordstrom sipped his vodka and changed hands on the glass to warm one and cool the other. Julie Symons's father was a top cosmetic surgeon, her mother begotten in money and married to someone who could beget more of it. First they begot Julie, a tall, fragile girl with the darting shyness of a hummingbird.

Tall. Nordstrom even hated the look of the word. But

Julie had spoken to him, as if Eric Nordstrom weren't a worm who'd oozed up onto the sidewalk into her path. Julie Symons—a born dancer with the kind of brownette coloring that looked exquisite in pink, and Nordstrom hated pink.

She was dead now.

Nordstrom went to the bed, flipping open the strewn folders, one by one, until the photograph of Kevin Blake jumped into his vision.

Julie had spoken to Eric Nordstrom.

But she had screwed Kevin Blake. Filthy.

The phone rang—not an abrupt, old-fashioned buzz, but an up-to-date electronic two-note wail. Nordstrom, expecting it, took his time answering. He checked the crocodile-banded Piaget under his French cuff before lifting the receiver. Eight-fifteen exactly, as arranged.

"You required a consultation?" the voice demanded without preamble. It quavered in the artificial tone that indicated it was deliberately garbled, that the call itself was scrambled.

In nine years, Nordstrom had saluted five different voices with the receiver and had never known the name of one of them, other than a terse code word. He used the latest silly monicker now.

"Overseer?"

"Affirmative. You requested contact. What is your situation? You are not to contact Overseer unless it's an emergency."

"It is. The local authorities aren't helping catch the fugitives—"

"That's usual. We don't want them to get too curious. Our agents will find the subjects."

"That's just it. Your agents—agent—may have a stake in not finding them."

"You mean Turner?"

"Turner, and maybe others. But Turner's the—key. I think his . . . heart . . . isn't in this. He's gone soft. He found out about assignment Angel Dust."

"It's possible he has clearance for that. We can check."

84

"It's his attitude. He doesn't want to catch this pair. He's . . . protective of them."

"So are we. In our way."

"He's got it all wrong. He wants the psychiatrist and the woman handled with kid gloves. That treatment will never break down the doctor-patient relationship. He wants me to waste time trying to convert Blake to our side.

"I say, forget him! Get to her; she's the vulnerable one. Blake'll never help. He's a fringe type—liberal big mouth. He'll scream civil liberties so loud it'll raise the dead. I went to school with him. I know. The guy's practically a fucking Commie. Turner's . . . insane to think we can work with him."

"You can do wonders with anyone."

"Not if your men won't let me."

"Anyone else besides Turner oppose you?"

"Not . . . directly. You know my specialty. I work best alone, with a blank check. Everybody in this iceberg town could screw up this operation. They're unsophisticated hicks when it comes to a sensitive operation. I need complete authority—"

"You've always worked through channels."

"Channels will bury us this time! I need control. Otherwise, I won't be responsible. You think this is your usual drip-dry brainwash job? Hell, no. These things have to be handled delicately. Turner, whatever his problem, wants to wade right in and hack around.

"Trust me. I know my man—and I will know my woman. Give me carte blanche and then watch the telekinetic toasters fly. I'll give you some stuff that'll really curl your oak leaves—"

Silence on the phone, not even the sound of breathing. For one panicked, gasping moment, Nordstrom wondered if he'd been cut off—if he'd never been speaking to anyone at all—or if it was all a plot, a figment, a paranoid delusion. . . .

"We'll consider your request."

A dial tone hummed into Nordstrom's ear, faintly dismissive. He hung up as slowly as he had answered and returned to the bed. Kevin Blake's face still lay grinning up at him with that too-too Freudian beard and that public relations smile.

Nordstrom remembered watching with sour, envious satisfaction as Blake had watched Julie inexorably succumb to anorexia nervosa. That's when Blake's post–med school specialty had firmed, surprising all but Nordstrom, who had watched. Psychiatry.

That's when Nordstrom had declared his own specialty. Also psychiatry.

Oh, nobody knew about his secret fixation. He hadn't even gone to the funeral. Fiancée, that's what Julie was to Blake, officially, but everybody knew that old man Symons had no patience for Julie's infatuation with a penniless nobody. Fiancée. That was frozen in time now, that travesty, with Julie.

Nordstrom's eyes narrowed.

A closed coffin. That's what the fine-print obituary in the *New York Times* had promised; that's what the visitation delivered to all comers, including the great Dr. Blake.

Even then, Nordstrom had his ways. He was a medical student, after all, and he was obsessed. He got into the mortuary, his palms sweating as he anticipated his pretext crumbling under the first question. But no one cared; no one asked. Maybe he looked like a funeral director.

He saw her, as Kevin Blake never had, dressed in something pink and soft that sank into the exposed cradle of her bones like rotting flesh already. They'd done her up completely, probably for old lady Symons—the hollow, painted face, elegant as an ivory skull polished here and there with fever; the buffed fingernails and sculpted hands; the carefully done hair wearing a permanence of form it never aspired to in life.

At first it enraged him, the notion of anonymous fingers handling Julie's paper-thin form so intimately. The final indignity, the cliché went, and everyone touching her but him, even at the end. Then it fevered him. He began to imagine himself with the sharp-pointed shears and the hair spray, himself arranging and manipulating the clothes, the limbs.

In that roomful of closed coffins, he stared at Julie Symons laid like a princess on a cream-colored satin bed and then kissed her thin, painted lips. They were quite, quite cold.

Nordstrom stared down at the tasteful hotel bedspread, his heart hammering. Kevin Blake smiled up at him, the bastard! Nordstrom's trembling hand flipped the photo into the dark of the folder.

He opened the last blank manila file, the one with the pathetically few papers and the sketch of another dark-haired woman. Jane Doe. His lips curled as his mind pronounced the lumpish nonname.

Another nobody, just like Kevin Blake, he decided. But unlike Julie, alive. And Kevin Blake cared about this one, too, or he wouldn't be playing fugitive from one godforsaken end of Minnesota to the other. Nordstrom smiled into his vodka.

Blake, unlike Julie, had hardly noticed that Nordstrom was alive. Yet somehow in school, Blake and Nordstrom always ended up on opposite sides.

They had again, only this time Nordstrom ran the class and established the rules. This time, Nordstrom would win.

Chapter Eleven

Jane felt herself lifted off the earth—her body hovering as high and light as thin air.

No. . . . Her mind refined the impression. She was actually *sinking*—so deep it made her feel she occupied another altitude. Whether high or low, she always felt light when Kevin hypnotized her. She wasn't one to imagine things—her alien upbringing had stunted that facility—but at times like this, Jane fancied she felt like a dolphin cruising far below sun-dappled waves, making intelligent blips in the depths.

Kevin's voice came to her, a lifeline of bubble-garbled rumble she somehow understood; she followed its wavering filaments through the fathoms of her weightlessness.

"I might as well get the lurid stuff over with first. Tell me about the visitors, Jane." Kevin's voice came now, not so much demanding as inquiring, not so much to be obeyed as to be pleased. "Tell me what happened when their light beam lifted you into their ship. I saw you assumed into their presence, like some undressed saint. You must have seen them. Inside the ship. What were they—are they—like?"

Jane swiveled ponderously amid the aquamarine murk of her awareness, the psychic shift tattooing sensation across her memory like fanning seaweed.

"Snow angels," she finally said.

"Snow angels." A long silence swirled around her. In another state, Jane had learned to anticipate, to read, to react to the tone of that voice. She would explain. Or defend. Or deny.

Here, nothing was required but the slow, sure drag of memory along the foggy bottom of her internal sea.

"Snow angels," Jane repeated dreamily. "I like the look of snow, but it's cold. They—those beings, my keepers— were like snow—so many, so massed. Cold but light. They sparkled as their mind turned. It would be easy to sink into them—down, down upon the table, under the bright beam above, floating on them, drifting through the stars with them, seed and sowing bound together, mindless, memoryless.

"They made not-being seem better. Normal. Others drifted in their care, as I must have, too, orphans of other worlds. Unplugged, that is what we were in that state. Disconnected. Prongs no longer probing to the center but drawn away. Untouching.

"What were they like? They were like mist in the mind. I felt them moving upon my memory—cold, white steps that sank into nothingness. Lifting here, sinking there. Leaving no traces. Footless footprints. They melt away.

They leave me melted. That is what they're like. Like melted snow angels."

"Okay." The word's bluntness somehow didn't shatter Jane's reverie. " 'Snow angels' it is. That'll look great in Project Blue Book along with the other wacko entries. . . . Did you get a chance to . . . communicate with them?"

"Oh, yes. They spoke English. They had plugged the words into me to begin with. I spoke to one and all. I . . . argued for maintaining my me-ness. Some . . . one listened. So I was returned, the ground cold on my feet, but me not caring. No one caring but Kevin, who bought me Zyunsinth and brought me Zyunsinth again, and then buried Zyunsinth—!"

"Jane, hush. It had to be. That coat isn't Zyunsinth, only the memory of Zyunsinth. Zyunsinth are the people . . . creatures . . . of another world like ours. Did your—they —say why they released you? Once they removed the information you had gained by living among us, once you were empty again, surely they planned to take you away and leave you to gather data from another, similar place?"

"I don't know what they planned. They were . . . intrigued by my me-ness. They seemed like doctors."

"Doctors?"

"All gathered around in white, looking and asking but not seeing or telling. I was returned. They didn't say why. I didn't ask. I was not aware until I stood on the bluff and knew that I was outside the homeplace, that I was no longer on the scanning table—"

"They . . . operated on you?"

"What is 'operated'? They asked me to put myself in their control again."

"Did you?" The voice grated with concern.

"I . . . don't remember. I stood before them and asked for myself back. Then I stood in the dark and the cold— and they were only faceless metal hovering over me and a pitiless eye of light. Snow angels. Light and cold, fleeting but eternal. Unforgiving."

"Did they have hands, feet? When the Volkers had their close encounter, they mentioned slitted eyes."

Jane felt her head nod as slowly as a manatee's bumping

noses with an underwater rock. "All that. They had all that. They were like us, but different. Different among themselves. But the same. As we are. I . . . I did not belong with them."

"Of course not! You belong here. You were human conceived, if not reared. And now you've lived among your own kind for several months."

Kevin's voice was swelling into a distant roar, as it often did when it feared the undertow would take her. Jane remained serene, drifting beneath a latticework of light and shadow, skimming along the fibers of her own nervous system, hearing herself humming.

"Jane. Jane!"

"Yes?"

"Not so . . . deep. Remember, you're here with me in the motel room, that's all."

"There's more here than that."

"What?" Again, the burr of panic thickened the voice.

Jane made her own words calm, calming. "Memory. Memory we have with us always."

Quiet filtered through the opaque current of memory. A long quiet. Then, words again.

"All right. Let's go back before the bluff top. Before the aliens came to retrieve you. Let's go back to the woods between Dr. Neumeier's cabin and Duluth. Let's remember when the cars had the van sandwiched between them on Highway 61, and I turned onto the side road. Then I drove the van into the drifts until it stopped and got out, leaving you in the front seat—"

Jane felt seaweed coil her limbs, sensed a sudden smothering immensity to the water around her. Tendrils of her breath wreathed the coral, coiling into a shape like DNA. She climbed the double helix like a diver scaling an umbilical cord of air to the surface. Shadowy shapes buffeted her. She no longer breathed. Her senses darkened, even as she felt herself being lifted, lifted. . . .

The DNA spirals—half coral and half medical textbook drawing, both impressions superimposed on each other by her retentive, image-scavenging mind—grew faces and elongated into flames. She felt no heat, only herself dwindling into the depths far below her and the click of her altered cells reorganizing her body until she seemed to be one raging, singing autonomous cell that gathered and gave back—

"Jane!"

The word came swinging down toward her like a vine, offering an alternative safety.

"Jane, relax! Nothing is hurting you. You're safe—"

"No!" Her own voice sprayed air into the water all around her, surrounding her and the DNA in a snowstorm of bubbles. *"I* am hurting *something!* Too close, they come too close. I must guard what I have gleaned. It will not be permitted for my self to be compromised—self must survive for the gleaning's sake. I see now! The other power speaks from the man's mouth, it oozes around coils, into neutrons and electrons trapped in boxes. My body makes them dance, the bits of being, so fast that they burn, they boil, they . . . expire. The machine wraps itself in its own shroud of suicidal particles and rolls away, far away, down into the dark."

"That's not the woods! That's Matusek, Jane! You're reliving Matusek's squad car blowing up and rolling off the Crow Wing bluff the night he found you. You caused that, didn't you, Jane?"

"Jane? Jane was not Jane then."

"No, you hadn't been officially tagged a Jane Doe quite yet, but, Christ, even if it was some defensive mechanism the aliens had genetically engineered into you—Matusek was just a country cop. He was calling for an ambulance, why blast him?"

"The machine . . . competes."

"The squad car radio? That explains the tape recorders you got into telekinetic wrestling matches with later. You're at war with household appliances? God, when they program a glitch, your snow angels do a damn good job of it. Wait. Rest now. Let me . . . Just calm down. You. And me."

Jane waited, dangling in half water, half air. Breathing

91

both. She remembered the holding tank and drifting in its artificial atmosphere. She remembered the chill familiarity of half-being.

Kevin's voice came again in the old lulling singsong.

"What about Kellehay?"

"Kellehay?"

"The other cop who found you that August night. The man who was with you when Matusek died, who rode back with you in the am—in the ecnalubma . . . to the hospital in Minneapolis. The young guy who died—the day after."

Jane felt her head shake leadenly, felt a warm grasp on her wet, chilled forearm. It threatened her grip on the DNA rope ladder.

"Jane, you must remember! My God, he went through the window of your hospital room—backwards, from the way the glass cut him—and you were semiconscious by then."

"Someone came," she remembered unhappily, her mind twisting, twisting to elude the images that came flashing up the rope. "At night. Alone. He . . . talked a lot. To himself, I think. He pressed the pillow over my mouth and pushed me down, down . . . down again—"

Jane gasped as she felt her self slip and spiral down the endless filaments. . . .

"There was, there was . . . that within me then that would not allow my existence to end. The cells bring forth. The cells repel. He fell back, but came again, I think. I'm not sure. He came so close, and the I of me was so far away. He pushed, and was pushed away. From me. Toward himself. His self poked a hole in the night and went shattering into sharp little pieces. I never knew he had a name."

"We all have names. We just don't know them sometimes." Jane cocked her head to the deep resignation in Kevin's voice. She pulled herself up along the DNA rope again, listening.

"Then it was self-defense, at least," he was saying, more to himself than to her. She could barely comprehend his words. "Kellehay had cracked, not hard to see why. He'd seen your built-in . . . defenses . . . kill his partner, but no one would listen when he said you were dangerous, especially his shrink for a day. Chalk up another one for the whiz kid. . . . All right."

A sigh of air brushed Jane's cheek. Her consciousness sensed a new location. She seemed to be floating now, on the surface, twined in weedy chains of DNA.

"All right," Kevin repeated. His voice no longer bubbled with distortion, as if he, too, had come back from someplace dark and deep. "We're back in the woods I asked you about in the first place. It's night. Dark. I've left you in the van to see what the men in the car behind us want. I guess I know. They're after you—government errand boys out to deliver one missing piece of merchandise . . . slightly reused in a few other worlds, but your basic telekinetic human model, after all.

"And I do my Custer's Last Stand bit, and the two guys pretty much cream me. They're pros. My head makes a good gong on the van doors. I wake up in the snow to find their car torched, the guys spread like . . . like goddamn strips of Sizzlean over the hood. How did that happen, Jane? Are you some preprogrammable Rambo? Did your built-in defenses take over again? This is the one they'll burn us for. What the hell happened?"

She turned her head too quickly. It hit something she couldn't see, a black impenetrable barrier, like a box floating on the water. An oblong black box that didn't mean anything to her.

"Don't fade on me now," Kevin's voice urged. "I know it hurts. It hurts me, too. That's the price of being human. Be human now. Tell me! Tell me how—why—you killed those two men."

Jane's hands clenched on masses of soggy DNA, wringing them taut. The bright blue balls that formed it floated alongside, buoying her.

"Remember, Jane. You can remember anything you want to if you try hard enough. Try! It's important. I have to know why you did it. I think I know why you forgot it—the first thing that happened to you in your own world that you blocked out. I think you don't want to be a killing machine anymore. You want to take your risks like the rest

93

of us. Maybe the aliens disarmed you when they let you go. Maybe you can't do whatever you did anymore. It's not your fault. It's never been your fault. But I have to know. Tell me, please—"

She sighed, and let the weeds enfold her, let herself float on their surrounding mass. From far above, a spotlight of sunshine dissected her in its rays. Her skin seemed pinned back. Exposed, her memory expanded like a ripe melon in the sun.

At its exact center, white and dead and cold, a scene was tacked to her inner eye: the drilling yellow headlight eyes of the idling car behind the van; two hulking figures black against the light. As she saw, she spoke, feeling her lips move, but hearing nothing. Seeing only, Jane moved into her memory.

She saw the black of night held back only by a dark fence of bare trees. The humpbacked silhouette of the car. The men waddling through the snowdrifts toward her. And there, another midnight spot—the lump of Kevin collapsed at the rear of the van.

Dead, she thought. Gone, she thought. Thought became feeling. They came toward her, the two vague figures, came to take her—again—to somewhere else. Came to rend her memory from her—again—and give it to something else. Some machine. Came to take Kevin, who was so quiet and still, almost as still as the woods and the night.

Were these men those who had a right to take? For a moment she was confused. And then she heard Kevin's voice and he seemed to be saying that no one—no one at all—had a right to take . . . to take her. To take him. To take anyone against their I-ness.

And so she stood there half-blinded by the headlights but seeing more efficiently than ever before. She remained, even as the defensive forces bunched in her body, leaving her little room. She remained this time, and decided. When the men came close enough to touch her, touch him, she refused them. She felt the strength pushing at the fringes of her mind, and gathered her awesome energy into a fine-honed flare of power.

It seized her and flowed through her and spit out from

her in breath and the heat of being, wind and fire propelling, repelling.

She saw—this time she saw, clearly—how her internal energies consumed the men. She saw their thick winterwear crackle and vanish, heard bone crunching on metal, smelled ash and flesh in the clearing.

When it was still, she looked to the form at her feet. It remained as motionless as the others. Emotion opened up its empty lungs and screamed. Memory would look no further. Jane released the rope, plunging down through every element within her, as she had then turned and fled into the endless winter woods.

At last the defensive programming found an opening and rushed inward to flood and uphold the organism, to crush a cold compress of forgetfulness over the inner eyes. Jane sank into her self, and the survival instincts she had been engineered to follow finally took her.

The recaptured moments of consciously wielded power turned screwlike in her brain, slowly seating themselves. She felt herself sink again, under the weight of too many memories. Kevin, she thought, might call it humanity, but she was not sure she could claim that condition.

"Jane. I'm bringing you out. Now! Hang on. Just listen to my voice. When I count to three, you'll be in your normal consciousness. You'll be back. One."

She was leagues deep by then, spinning into seclusion.

"You're coming up. Hang on! Two. For God's sake, Jane—three! Three."

Three.

The word hung between two worlds, between inhale and exhale. Between then and now.

"Jane . . . ?"

Something shook her, bubbles bursting and propelling her to the surface again. She sputtered, blinked her eyes to rid them of water. . . . She opened them to utter dryness, her mouth too sand-gritted to speak. Jane stared into the blue of Kevin's eyes and mistook them for sky. His expression clouded.

He shook her again, desperately. "Jane? Okay?"

Her tongue wet her lips.

"You should remember everything now. I can make you forget if it's too painful—"

"No!" This time the drowning panic beat along her pulses. "If I forget what hurts, how will I remember what doesn't?"

His anxious face sagged into relief. He drew her hard into his arms. "Welcome to the human race," he said, laughing and not laughing.

Over his shoulder, Jane regarded the closed curtains of the window. "I'm not very . . . human, am I?"

Kevin laughed again, ruefully, pushing her away to stare into her face. "No, but you're getting better. Or should I say, worse. I understand now. Your genes were programmed to defend you without discrimination. You killed Matusek by mistake, by reflex, without even thinking about it.

"When Kellehay came to your hospital room, he was attacking you. Your powers automatically pushed him out the window when he became lethal, but you were already developing a sense of good and bad, of necessity and impulse. You knew on a subconscious level that you *had* to use the powers. You were defending yourself against a real attacker, God help the poor fool. And that night in the woods, with the two government men—"

She looked away, lost again in an elliptical orbit around herself.

"Jane, look at me." Kevin pulled hard on all the easy-come-by persuasion in him. Jane had to see that herself and her acts were justified. So did he.

"That's what bothered me most," he admitted. "The cold-blooded way you torched those men, bad guys or not. The way you forgot it again. It smelled of regression. Only, now I see . . . it's *pro*gression!

"You were defending *me*, in a way, weren't you? That's what set you off. You thought I was dead. So instead of fading and letting reflex take over, you controlled your powers to defend someone else as well as yourself. Me. You're beginning to know better. I only hope they don't hang you for being what you were made to be."

"Hang," Jane repeated. " 'To fasten from above with no

support from below.' That's how I feel when you hypnotize me. That's how I felt when they . . . kept me dormant."

"Don't try your dictionary declensions on 'hanging,' Jane. Here's the best application of the word: something—someone—to *hang* onto. Let's you and me hang onto each other. Sanity can wait."

"Was I wrong?" she asked, her mouth muffled against his neck.

"About what?"

"To let . . . it . . . take those men?"

"It was either them . . . or us. And I don't want them to get you." Kevin pushed her away to look hard into her eyes. "If the men come again, if they get me—don't think about anything. I can take care of myself. You just . . . run. Get away from me fast. Use what you have to stay free, to stay yourself. I wish your powers came in a sliding scale, with something this side of lethal, but don't feel guilty about what you are, were.

"You're so lucky. You were born free, guiltless. No original sin on your soul. If you only knew how the theys in our world can use you with guilt! That's the real original sin. I bet that's something your aliens haven't even begun to learn from us yet. . . .

"So promise me. From now on, it's Jane first. Jane free."

She nodded, as Jane always did, very seriously.

Chapter Twelve

"Son of a bitch!"

Kevin stared at himself in the motel mirror.

Blood welled profusely from the jagged nick his so-called safety razor had gouged in his neck about two whiskers away from his jugular vein.

He stopped the flow with a corner torn from the in-wall

Kleenex dispenser, which seemed incapable of disgorging an entire sheet at one tug, and swore again.

Behind him in the mirror, Jane's face popped into view. "I liked your beard better," she commented with customary—and at the moment irritating—dispassion.

"So did I, but any photos of me the police care to circulate are bound to be bearded." Something occurred to him and his eyes netted hers in the mirror. "Did they show any facial hair—your aliens?"

"They are not mine. If anything, I am theirs. And no, they didn't, not at all—!" Her eyes lit up. "Kevin, do you realize? Since you hypnotized me, I can remember my last time with them on the, the—"

"Don't be shy. The improbable is hard to articulate; the impossible should be easy. Spit it out: the spaceship. Star cruiser. Pick up any paperback space opera at the book-store. Some inventive brain has thought up something different to call an interstellar vessel. Be imaginative."

"The . . . ship," Jane decided upon demurely. "And they had no hair."

"Not even on their heads?"

"No . . . but maybe they were wearing . . . caps." Jane frowned as she boosted herself atop the sink cabinet beside him. "I really didn't pay much attention. Why are you laughing?"

"God, what the government, the people at SETI, what *Chariots of the Gods* addicts would give their red corpuscles to know, *you* didn't pay attention to! I hope they goddamn catch us! It would almost be worth it to have a front seat at the government think-tankers trying to debrief you. . . ."

Jane reached out to pull the bit of tissue from his neck and replace it with a new piece. "When the student nurses taught me to shave my legs, I cut myself. Once."

"Never again?"

"No. I learned how to avoid it. It's very simple, if you know how. Why do so many humans do things that make them bleed?"

"First of all, not every human is a klutz. Second, a little bleeding does us good. Reminds us we're vulnerable.

Third, our kind is basically inconsistent, which you'll discover when you spend more time with real people."

"You aren't real?"

"Yes, but . . . we've been existing in a pressure cooker, Jane. You've been thrust from one abnormal environment into another—hospital, university dormitory, motel rooms. Someday, I hope, you'll get a chance to lead a normal life—to sleep in the same bed night after night, buy a Coney Island, read the Sunday morning comics. . . ."

Panic surfaced in her eyes. "I don't know what any of that is, except for the bed."

"That's okay. It's basically unimportant stuff that becomes important when you can't have it anymore, that's all."

Jane pensively leaned her head on Kevin's shoulder. He froze as if upholding something ponderously fragile.

"Kevin, will you ever stop having to know about me?"

"No." He wished sometimes he could. "It's my job, my nature. And you were made to be demystified."

"Sometimes I wish—"

"Wishes are the stuff of humanity, Jane," he teased, uneasy at the plaintive note in her voice. "Watch out or some Blue Fairy will pop out from behind the shower curtain and you'll become a real girl in no time."

"Ah." She glittered with knowledge received, recognized and catalogued. "That's from *Pinocchio*. I could do that," she added.

"Do what?" he asked, not paying much attention. Jane wore only her thermal underwear. Kevin, responding to their loose but long embrace, began pressing her closer, losing himself in her scent and accommodating softness. . . .

"The thing with the nose."

The moment was definitely gone. "What!?"

"It would take time, of course." Jane examined the ceiling to consider. "Maybe . . . overnight. But I don't think it would happen only if I lied. I could do it even when I told the truth."

"You always tell the truth."

"Yes, but I might need to lie if they catch us. Maybe I should practice."

"Jane!"

"You didn't like it when I made my fingernails grow overnight, though." Reconsideration made her mournful. "You probably wouldn't like a longer nose, either."

"For God's sake. I don't know whether to laugh or commit hara-kiri. Jane, when you made your fingernails grow out overnight that time, it wasn't that I didn't . . . admire . . . your, uh, talent. What I really didn't like about your telescopic talons was that they proved the incontestable . . . otherness of you."

"You don't like me!"

"No, I do. I'm beginning to like you almost as much as I love you, which puts me in *real* trouble. I had forgotten that fingernail incident. I guess you could alter your nose, if you set your inalienable mind to it, but I wish you wouldn't. I like it the way it is. And I'm confused enough as it is."

He finished by pecking the tip of her nose. Jane giggled, then plucked the tissue off his neck. He winced as the now-caked blood pulled away a bit of epidermis.

"I'm glad I don't have to shave my face," Jane said.

"Me, too."

Kevin busied himself rinsing off the razor and the faucets, thinking ahead to making sure the rooms were clean of any trace when they left.

Jane's fingers toyed along his forearms, riffling through the curling hairs; sometimes he felt that he was merely a Zyunsinth substitute—furry little humanoids, they must have been. Give Jane a blow-up King Kong and she'd probably be equally content.

"If they won't find us because you *did* have a beard," she was ruminating idly, "and *don't* have one now, maybe *I* should grow a beard as a disguise."

He turned. Because she sat atop the sink cabinet, their faces were on the same level. Her eyes, as usual, were quite serious.

"You . . . could . . . really do that, couldn't you?"

Jane nodded. "You're making me remember, Kevin, not

only what, but how. I don't think I was ever meant to know these things. I was made to glean, to store, to release. But never to . . . modify."

He put his fingertips to her cheek, drew his thumb against the grain of the almost-invisible downy hairs at her jawline. Every woman, even the fairest haired, hid a shadow of the man in her, and vice versa. In fact, maleness itself was a piece of inborn genetic engineering—an intra-uterine modification performed upon the wholly female fetus every human being begins as.

"I suppose the blueprint is there," he admitted. "It's merely a matter of adjusting the hormones. You're trying to tell me something that I don't want to see, aren't you, Jane? You're telling me that . . . they didn't just make you different. When they released you again on the Crow Wing bluff as an independent being, they opened the gates to your learning to manipulate yourself."

"Not them, Kevin. You."

He stiffened. "You keep saying that! *They* made you, not me."

"You are unmaking me, Kevin. When we make love, you like me to have orgasms—"

"You like it, too!" he countercharged, horrified by the implications he saw yawning before him.

"Oh, yes. It is very pleasant. But I learned that, how to do it whenever I wanted to, from the library books. I don't know why so many women have difficulty; it's all in the books and so simple . . . like growing fingernails. I learned it before I knew what it felt like because I wanted you to . . . like me."

"God." He pushed her hands away. A tic spasmed underneath his eye. "You make me feel like some Svengali, some cheap tin manipulator. Jane, I always wanted you to be what you could be, not what I needed you to be. Never that. Better you'd gone with them."

"Maybe," she said, looking into the mirror yet seeing neither of them. "But now I need you so that I can be what I can be, and therefore, I must be what you need."

He shook his head. "Give me a break; that's what I need. You'll confound 'em in the temple, believe me. Look, we gotta blow this joint. We'll talk the metaphysics of being another time."

"Okay." She hopped off the countertop, unannoyed.

They dressed in placid silence in the other room. Jane seemed over her whimsical impulse to grow a beard. Kevin smiled as he picked up his watch from the nightstand and slid it on his wrist, putting himself back into the time stream, armoring himself to think like a fugitive.

The timepiece's rich gold glinted a reminder of the life he'd left—not wealthy, but well enough off compared to being on the run. The watch also, belatedly, reminded him of his parents, whose extraordinary gift it had been on his graduation from med school. His dad had never owned more than a Timex, and his mom kept her one good watch for special occasions, an ancient Lady Elgin with a tiny low-grade ruby inset into the winding stem. . . .

Bearded ladies and gold watches . . . Kevin caught himself; he was getting wacko—should retire from the shrink game permanently. It might be a forced retirement.

"If I had some of that," said a fully dressed Jane, "I would buy you a new razor."

"Thanks for the thought." Kevin glanced at the shrinking roll of hundred-dollar bills he was about to stuff in his wallet.

Jane reached for a bill and he handed her one.

"If"—she looked up eloquently—"if they didn't know better, they might think these were the most vital life form here. Everyone guards them so carefully. Can I have one?"

"Not on your life. It's dangerous to have something everybody else wants—and you already have a head start on that score, my Lady Jane. I'll keep it. Less chance of losing it, and we need every penny now. In fact, I'm going to live dangerously and try—" Kevin pulled the tattered business card Kandy had given him from his jacket pocket. "Try being 'James Anderson' for a day and get some of my old money out of the new bank. 'Jim Anderson'—God, that's *Father Knows Best!* Trust Kandy to go for some crazy juxtaposition."

"What's *Father Knows Best?*" Jane asked dutifully as she trotted out the motel room behind him.

"History, my dear," Kevin said, letting the heavy door slam shut. "Ancient history."

*   *   *

Daylight is never so relentless as on a white-washed winter day. The flat off-white ground and sky joined forces to glare at Kevin. He wished for sunglasses, then decided they weren't important enough to risk discovery by buying. So many little things in life seemed hopelessly distant now.

He supposed he should dump the van and find some other wheels, but the enormity of buying—stealing? Oh, come on, get serious, Blake . . . you, steal a car? You'd leave a trail a mile wide—the enormity of changing vehicles confounded him.

The nice part about the van, and maybe the only nice part, was its very blandness. At first glance it looked like a delivery truck—bakery or diaper service, name your cover. Dirty melting snow had spattered the wheel wells and added a chic black-dotted veil to the adulterated license plates, further obscuring them.

Nobody'd look twice at the van. Kevin ducked to face himself in the side mirror before mounting the front seat. Nobody'd look twice at him now, either, he thought, a little miffed by how easy it was to become a complete nonentity when one's usual props were stripped away.

And Jane . . . he smiled at her across the way. In her standard winter duds, she looked a hundred percent, apple pie, Minnesota-wholesome normal, God bless her rosy cheeks.

Maybe they would make it, he thought. Maybe they just would bloody well make it.

Chapter Thirteen

Kevin cased the Upper Midwest Savings & Loan building from the parked van, feeling like Clyde Barrow in a lifted Ford.

He'd gone in and out of banks a hundred times without even noticing the obligatory guard stationed near the main doors, but now the guy with the holstered gun looked seven feet tall.

Retired guys, potbellied and farsighted, that's who they got for bank guards, he reassured himself.

"Is that where the money is?" his Bonnie asked with utter innocence.

"Yup."

"They need a big place for it."

"All that room is for the *people* who watch the money. Now listen, when we go in, stick with me. Don't look at anybody, don't talk to anybody. And if anything goes wrong—"

"Wrong?"

"If an alarm goes off, or the guard comes running, or the cashier hits me in the face with a lemon meringue pie. . . ." Jane absorbed all his worst-case scenarios with equal seriousness, her eyes nine-year-old round. "If anything seems wrong—just get away from me. Don't get caught."

"It would be like going back to them?"

"Worse. The aliens would only take your memory; these geeks would rip out your soul."

"A soul doesn't exist."

"Yeah, it does, only it's a little hard to pin down."

"Like a memory?"

"Exactly like a memory."

Kevin cracked the van door, checked for oncoming

traffic and slid out. The street squeezed dirty slush up to his anklebones. He squeegeed around the van to let Jane out and together they walked up the badly shoveled sidewalk. Where the S&L building began, the snow miraculously vanished, revealing only wet concrete sidewalk.

"Something must have landed here," Jane speculated.

"Yeah. Under-sidewalk heating. Old Upper Midwest S&L must be doing all right." Kevin took her arm, although there was no danger of slipping now. "I don't know why I'm so nervous; it's *my* fucking money. . . ."

People brushed past in the noon-hour rush. Good cover, Kevin congratulated himself. He glanced back at the van. It looked as legitimate as any other vehicle drawn up to the row of parking meters, lined up like dull silver soldiers to infinity. . . . Parking meters, holy shit!

"Jane! Wait here! Don't move."

Kevin parked her against the institution's windows and sprinted back to the van, clawing for change in his jeans.

Some criminal mind, he jibed himself . . . planning to snatch his worldly funds from under the feds' noses and he forgets to plug the friggin' parking meter—!

He tore off and jammed the hampering gloves inside his jacket. His bare fingers instantly stiffened in the wind chill. Only nickels and dimes and pennies squeezed out of his jeans pockets. For want of a quarter . . . He finally found one and crammed it into the meter slot. The red line popped into position: fifteen minutes. He vacillated. What if something went wrong? A nickel made it twenty-five. Reassured, he could afford to worry again about something else.

Jane! He whirled, his eyes paging back to where he'd parked her—right behind the bus stop sign . . . gone. Gone. Ohmigod. . . . Should have dragged her along, even if it made a spectacle, should've something!

Kevin started back up the street, his eyes raking passing figures like a pickpocket's. Everybody wore down jackets. All the women were dark-haired and just-so tall. He crammed cold hands into jacket pockets to hide his fists and lurched toward the S&L's grandiose glass entry. Maybe she'd gone in to get out of the cold.

A fat man in a furred Russian hat stepped into his path as a bus arrived. Kevin smelled diesel fumes swirling behind him, heard the brakes grind. Even now Jane could be stepping up the black rubberized stairs, wandering God knows where, whisked away as surely by the Metropolitan Transit Commission as by any otherworldly aliens. . . .

The fat man tried to belly-brush Kevin aside. Kevin turned, savage. "Watch the hell where you're going—!"

At the bank's window-wall, obscured by the fat man until he had moved, Jane was standing with her nose pressed against plate glass. Kevin joined her, anger still flaring under his relief.

"I told you to stay where I left you."

"Some people came and pushed me down."

He glanced along the stone-and-glass facade. Waiting bus riders were strung out like birds on a wire, each hugging the debatable shelter of the building's skirts. Jane had been edged three windows down. He squeezed her arm.

"Sorry. Guess I panicked. What's so fascinating inside?"

"Them."

Kevin looked, feeling foolish. A hallmark of urban sophistication was being able to walk by everything without noticing anything.

The S&L's first floor was carpeted in Kelly green. Walnut-veneer desks at regular intervals, each wearing a visitor's chair like a motorcycle its sidecar, made a giant hound's-tooth pattern on the vivid background. Crisply feminine workers—all young, impeccably groomed, skirted and bloused and bowed at the collar or dripping tasteful gobs of gold and sterling silver jewelry—minced across the carpet on soundless high heels.

"These are the people who watch the money?" Jane wanted to know.

"Some of them."

"They remind me . . ."

"Yes?"

"Of them. The ones on the ship."

"You're kidding!"

"Kidding?" she inquired politely.

"I mean, you don't mean it!"

106

"Why would I say something I don't mean?" Jane turned again to regard the unstill life beyond the window glass. "They remind me of them. So many, so busy, so alike."

Kevin digested the comparison. Watching bank employees through a plate glass window was indeed a rather alien experience, if you thought about it. Who were these people, and what were they all doing here? If you didn't *know* . . .

Sobered, he took Jane's arm and guided her through the big glass doors into the vaulted marble lobby where the guard with the huge black leather holster stood watch near the mid-sized parlour palm in the large ceramic pot.

Another guard patrolled the cashiers' domain, where travertine check-writing stations sprouted like stone mushrooms. Kevin and Jane paused at an unoccupied island while he worried out Kandy's card.

"Stay here." He reluctantly ordered a change of plan, eyeing the line before the nearest cashier. Jane was too unpredictable; he couldn't risk her saying something outré to the cashier. "I'm gonna have to get some blank checks. Remember, if there's any trouble—if anybody . . . talks too much to me, or if that guard there comes toward me, just run for it. Hey, it won't happen. This'll be a piece of cake, a shoo-in, a—"

Jane was looking more disoriented by the instant. Kevin patted her cheek, still chilly from the outside cold, gave her a look that lasted long enough to mean good-bye, even though he didn't believe it, and affixed himself to the line behind a man smoking a pipe.

The fancy travertine floor wept as winter-decked people stood there in their snow-heavy boots. Kevin eyed the black panning boxes that housed the videotape cameras, then ducked his head.

The line trudged forward, a baby step at a time. The pipe fumes ahead of him smelled of ripe berries, mixing uneasily in his nostrils with the bus's vile after-stink. Already the heated air was turning his down jacket into an oven; something itched on his throat. When he scratched it, his fingernail came away bloody. He remembered too late the shaving nick of the morning.

He looked behind him again. Jane still stood where he'd

107

left her, doodling with the chained ballpoint pen on one of the forms. Kevin hoped it wasn't anything too incriminating. . . .

The line lurched a silly little millimeter forward. Kevin followed, pushing up his jacket sleeve to read his watchface. Ten minutes into his hard-bought twenty-five. Yeah, they'd make it. He peered around the pipe smoker to count how many preceded him. Only four. They'd make it, just as he'd promised Jane. He stopped fidgeting and started mentally rehearsing the spiel he'd give when he got to the head of the line.

*   *   *

Jane looked up. Pillars of brass-trimmed beige marble soared above her. She'd worked off her gloves to play with the pen and now ran her palm over the cool, stainless steel core bisecting the marble table. It was nice and high, she thought, the table—just right to stand at, lean on. But cold. Everything here was cold, although it was inside and seemed well heated—shiny and hard and cold.

And the people . . . Jane turned full circle for a panoramic view of the lobby. She'd never seen so many people walking inside a building before, not even on the university campus. The hard floor rang to the click of their boots and shoes. The sounds echoed up and up to the highest pillar top.

Jane glanced to where Kevin had been standing. Somebody else stood there now. An odd, disquieting feeling exploded in her, like a pull on an internal, invisible string. She edged sideways and peered harder. She saw a lady in a plaid coat, and the outline of a cocked pipe farther ahead . . . but—

She released the marble pedestal to which she'd clung since Kevin had left her. She stepped away, feeling as if the earth had been scooped away from her feet until she had only the cold square foot of marble upon which she now stood.

Kevin had kept warning her something might happen. What if *nothing* had happened? How was she to act then? What if he was simply . . . gone?

Jane turned around, so fast her head felt funny, but then her head was beginning to feel even funnier—closed, cluttered and muffled. People's voices echoed against the brazen sky, making no sense. Footsteps neared and washed away. Kevin had vanished, swallowed by the crowded emptiness. . . .

Jane's eyes began darting from place to place, clicking images into focus, burning them into her brain in rapid succession. They were all meaningless. Then—

She saw it. She fixed on one small strand of sanity in the melee. Sound softened, words unwound and made fleeting sense again. "—and then I go, 'If that's the way you feel,' and he goes—" . . . "—selling at forty-nine and seven-eighths, not bad considering—" . . . "—she'd be a much better manager if she'd come to terms with her marriage; that man—"

Jane smiled and let the noise peel past her. She moved toward what she saw, toward what would save her.

Chapter Fourteen

Kevin saw the pipe smoker's broad gray tweed back melt before him. He stepped up to the decorative grate and grinned at the clerk.

"Just, uh, opened a new account. I need some temporary checks while I'm waiting for my personalized ones. You know the U.S. mails."

She laughed on cue. "I'm surprised you weren't given some when you opened the account."

"Well, I was. But I lost 'em. Christmas and all." Kevin tried to remember what his most charming, truth-telling, social smile felt like. It'd been so long since he'd used it, two whole weeks maybe.

"If you've got your account number?"

"Sure. Um . . . 67334989—dash—08. Gosh, these things are long."

The clerk flashed an automatic smile. Her long lacquered nails clicked the sequence into the computer keyboard. She nodded and, eyes still glued to the unseen screen, asked, "Address is 1708 Dupont Avenue South, Mr. Anderson?"

"Right." At least the Anderson part was right, Kevin consoled himself, ignoring his ignorance of the rest. "And I want some cash now, too."

The clerk didn't bat a mascara-gobbed eyelash, but slapped a checkbook holder and a slim batch of blank checks down on the hard cold marble. "I'll have to run a statement for you. It might take a while to get the computer."

"Oh, sure. . . ." He glanced to the central computer station, where two clerks were already fidgeting. His cashier joined the procession to see the Great God Microchip.

Kevin twisted to glance back—six people behind him, all staggered to watch the front of the line and therefore arranged into an impossible barrier. He couldn't even see the station at which he'd left Jane, much less Jane.

Above him, the high-tech eye in the internal sky panned past him. He spotted a tiny TV set and recognized himself on the third pass. He looked furtive. Minutes had elapsed. Maybe he should vanish right now. The clerk was still waiting for the console, her nails drumming the travertine. She didn't seem to be pressing any red buttons or calling up any artillery.

Someone behind him in line pushed closer. Kevin eased forward. Nobody liked his personal space infringed upon in public, not even when layers of outerwear made the contact purely a formality. The pressure didn't let up. Kevin shifted position again and turned to do his average citizen cold glare.

An unaverage citizen stared back. Kevin read law enforcement in one summing glance. Two nondescript men —both six feet, both wearing expressions of utter control —bracketed him, pinned him to the cashier's cage.

"Just come with us, Doctor. No theatrics," one advised in a practiced undertone.

Kevin shrugged. His cashier suddenly moved away from the computer station. He wondered if she knew what he was wanted for. Of course not. But it hadn't stopped her from doing her duty. The account had been watched, as simple as that.

The men nudged Kevin out of line and back into the ebb and flow of the lobby. One let a leatherette case flower in his palm. Kevin glimpsed a photograph that could have been any middle-aged, short-haired, hard-faced man, some print and an official-looking seal.

"Where did you leave your patient, Dr. Blake?" the man asked politely.

"Not here," Kevin said quickly. So they hadn't noticed Jane yet. Elation thrummed through his despair.

They were bustling him out of the lobby, out past the station where he was sure he'd left Jane. The imposing clatter of their triple footsteps made a dark-haired woman in a down jacket look up as they passed. Not Jane, he realized, with a dreadful double dose of relief and frantic worry. Where *had* he left her, then?

"We'll check the area anyway, not that we have any reason—yet—to disbelieve you, Doctor."

"Who are you guys?"

"I showed you identification."

"How many crooks can read that fine print? We've got an aging population, you know."

The man actually smiled, tightly. "You've never heard of us."

"Then why advertise?"

"That's for us, to let us know we're real." An iron grip on Kevin's arm stopped the trio. The man looked at his so-far-silent partner, then nodded. "We're going to sit this one out, Doctor, in the car, while my men finish looking in here. Then we'll go someplace warm and cozy and you can tell me all about it."

"And if I don't come peacefully?" Who was he kidding? These guys had probably done this a hundred times. But where was Jane? Why hadn't they spotted her already, if they were pros?

"We'd rather not cuff you. We'd rather not make a scene. Maybe you wouldn't either."

He considered. The more ruckus he raised, the more cop types involved, the more likelihood Jane would be found. She couldn't have gone far. . . . He forced himself not to look around, and nodded once.

The man relaxed a very little. "My name is Turner," he said, "and so far you're a law-abiding citizen. Keep it that way."

They gave him the low-key, undercover bum's rush out. Kevin let them, hating his own complicity, but not once, ever, looking back for Jane.

*　　　　*　　　　*

Jane stood in line, inching forward with the rest of her line mates, oblivious to everything but the delicate brush of fur against her palm.

A whole, gorgeous golden wall of Zyunsinth loomed ahead of her, slung over the shoulders of a tall, gilt-haired woman wearing a leopardskin hat and high-heeled leopardskin boots.

Jane thought she was wonderful, and happily inhaled some exotic scent that made her want to sneeze but was so *rich* in a strangely artificial way.

Keeping her light grip on the back of the coat, Jane looked around for Kevin now that she felt anchored again. She was only four lines over from where he had been—or was it three? Her mind backflashed for the precise image. Four. Her memory had been accurate. He should be right . . . there.

But he wasn't. Nor was he waiting at the station where he had left her. Zyunsinth pulled out of her grasp and she shuffled forward to keep in contact with it. Jane's eyes began systematically panning the lobby—like one of the watching cameras—scanning for height, hair color, clothing, even a flash of blue iris.

Nothing. She repeated the procedure, letting her concentration run bone deep. She knew if Kevin was there, and if she really looked for him, she would see him.

Zyunsinth lurched ahead again, then a brassy voice challenged, "Miss! Do you *mind!*"

Jane did. Her fingers tightened possessively on the fur. Its hackles raised. Long hairs fanned up like porcupine quills all the way from Jane's fist to the collar. The woman's square jaw dropped.

"How did you—?"

Jane released the coat, rejected the coat. Her need suddenly felt hollow in the face of a greater loss. This golden fluff wasn't Zyunsinth. Zyunsinth was dead and buried. Kevin would have said Zyunsinth had only been a symbol of something else anyway. As the woman flounced ahead, the man behind Jane neatly closed the gap, flashing Jane a look both surprised and smug.

The lobby's din had risen to a discordant buzz again. Jane stepped into its distance, paused, stepped again. People milled around her. No one looked at her. She cocked her head and listened. Nothing. She waited. Nothing at all.

At the marble pedestal, three strangers huddled, passing the chained ballpoint pen among themselves. Jane joined them, but they ignored her. She picked up a discarded form, the one that she had scrawled upon. The letters—some printed backwards, although she knew better now—drilled into her brain. AMBU⅃AИCE—the first word she had written, for Kevin in his office with the comfortable chair and the funny poster of dancing tongues dangling behind the door. . . . The door. Jane turned. She saw the door to the street. Maybe Kevin was there. Or in the van. She began walking briskly to the exit, joining the flow of people, melding with them in their haste and their anonymity.

The van, Jane told herself, turning left at the door and striding down the sidewalk. The van.

Jane stopped.

The van was coughing at the curb, its breath huffing out of its rear tail pipe in tired bursts. Someone—not Kevin—was at the wheel, behind the windshield, turning the van away from the curb into the traffic.

Jane gasped as a passerby bumped her.

"Sorry," the young man mumbled, not sounding it at all.

Jane retreated against the building. Behind her the efficient girls in high heels rushed to and fro on a soft velvet-green carpet. Outside, other people had lined up against the building, too. Jane wondered what they had lost.

The hole left by the van stayed vacant. Jane watched it faithfully. She even jumped when the little red marker clicked against the left side of the curved window and a bright red fan snapped into position. It read "Expired."

A slush-spattered bus, once red but now mostly brown, shouldered to the curb ahead of where the van had been. While Jane watched, several people waiting along the building shuffled forward to mount the bus. She saw them stuff things into a box at the vehicle's front and heard the mechanism chortle as it swallowed small silver circles.

Jane pushed her gloved hands into her empty pockets, but they felt no warmer. She looked up, at pillars of high-rise buildings arrowing toward a slate-gray ceiling of sky. The street echoed, too, with shards of meaningless sound.

"Kevin," Jane tried saying quietly, but that seemed to be just another meaningless sound in a world already over-stocked with them.

She retreated to utter silence.

People came, and waited by the wall, and filed into the buses that arrived, and paused, and drove on. No matter how many people left, more seemed to come, and there always seemed to be another bus if they waited long enough.

Gradually, it got dark.

The Sifting
January 12

*　　　　　　*　　　　　　*

"...the ague of the skeleton...."

—T. S. Eliot
"Whispers of Immortality"

Chapter Fifteen

"God, don't you think I'd tell you if I knew?"

Kevin stared pensively at the limp roll of hundred-dollar bills on Turner's desk. "She has no money, no place to go, no shelter from the cold—I never thought we'd get separated."

Turner had turned out to be a gentleman, Kevin found, or at least it suited him to masquerade as one. It had been a genteel snatch.

Only a half hour after being pinched in the S&L lobby, Kevin sat in a drab room in some gray government building downtown. He'd been searched, of course—the usual patting down and pocket emptying—but no booking, no fingerprinting, no cell. Just talk. So far.

The contents of his pockets—wallet, Kandy's van keys, loose change—littered Turner's desk.

"Can I see that ID again?" Kevin asked. "Now that I'm sitting down and can read it?"

Turner produced the small case and slid it across the desktop.

Kevin opened it gingerly. "PID. What does that stand for?"

"What did Probe stand for?"

Kevin flashed Turner a reappraising look. "Yeah. I hear that the past tense is appropriate. The Probe unit is gone with the wind. You guys—whatever you are—can shut things down fast."

Turner waited.

"Probe didn't stand for anything, I guess, except what it did. No acronym. It only meant that our small psychiatric

117

team dealt with unusual patients in radical ways. Multiple personalities, cult deprogrammings, the criminally insane. It was a license to cut corners and red tape, to fly a little."

"So's the PID. And that *is* an acronym." Turner leaned forward. "Paranormal Intelligence Division."

Kevin whistled. "Of what?"

"That's . . . not for publication."

"You mean the *government* actually takes that Mind Wars stuff seriously?"

"Don't you?"

Kevin shrugged, then smiled wryly. "Remote viewing, telepathy, psychic hocus-pocus, no. But I take lots of things more seriously than I used to, including myself."

Turner grew even graver. "You should, Dr. Blake, take things very seriously right now. We want Jane Doe. Washington has decided that her abilities, if genuine, could be vital. Mainstream scientists are very interested in paranormal abilities. Targ and Puthoff had remarkable remote viewing results with ordinary subjects. Imagine what might happen with someone like Jane Doe. And her telekinetic abilities are largely unexplored."

"Do you hear yourself? You want to set Jane up and make her perform! The Targ experiments were back in the seventies—nothing more has come of them. Why use a human mind as a long-distance voyeur when the skies are crammed with spy satellites and we have cameras that can pick up a license plate from space? As for telekinesis— nobody believes in Uri Geller and his spoon-bending routine anymore."

"Freud was interested in the paranormal—"

"And was ambivalent. The human mind can play many tricks, I know. What might strike the layman as psi phenomena could be a childish omnipotence fantasy. So-called powers could be an unconscious regression to some vestigial evolutionary mode of communication—the appendix of the mind, and as useless."

Turner smiled. "You argue like a conservative, Doctor. So much for 'dealing with unusual patients in radical ways.' Besides, what you think doesn't matter anymore.

What does is that Jane Doe is no longer your private property. The cat's out of the bag. Help us find her and we can overlook the . . . irregularities that occurred in your misguided flight from the authorities."

"How could I flee the authorities when I didn't even know any authorities were after me?"

"Why did you take Jane Doe and run?"

"I didn't. It was therapy."

"Therapy? In the bridal suite of the Duluth Radisson? The desk clerk and bellman have identified your pictures. I've read Dr. Cross's report on you, heard the tape of your last session with her—"

Kevin fought to maintain his distance, but Turner's words had raked a razor across his Achilles' heel—his sexual relationship with Jane.

"Tell me about the bridal suite therapy, Dr. Blake," Turner prodded ruthlessly.

If labeled an ass, might as well act the part, Kevin concluded. "I told you I was a radical shrink. I wanted to take her around the state, see if any place rang a bell with her."

"Did the woods in Duluth ring a bell? Was that 'therapy,' too?" Turner's affability faded as anger leaked into his eyes. "I lost two men there, under brutal—and mysterious— circumstances."

"What about Professor Neumeier's cabin?" Kevin challenged back. "Did you perform your own kind of therapy on that old woman? Dead of a heart attack, come on! She survived Auschwitz but not you guys."

Another kind of pain briefly seized Turner's eyes. "She was . . . terribly old. It shouldn't have happened. A routine interrogation. We never touched her. She was more fragile than she looked."

"Oh, great. And that's why you want Jane, to interrogate her! You really expect me to smile and stand aside while you people probe my patient's delicate brain with an elephant gun?"

"We're not inhuman, Blake, just doing our jobs, as you were doing yours. I'm no judge and jury. I don't care about

119

your libido or hers. Jane Doe apparently has extraordinary abilities. They could be useful to science, to the future, to our government, yes. You have no right to play dog in the manger. Cooperate, and you can help her, assure yourself that no damage is done—"

"Sure, I baby-sit syringes while your government shrinks narcoanalyze Jane with battery acid. If you bully boys realized what fiendish drugs have come out of the biological warfare and Cold War spy labs, you wouldn't inject them into the cockroach who ate your sister, believe me."

"That's not my job. It's my job to find Jane Doe—and you—and get her into the proper hands."

Kevin snorted at the final phrase, and Turner's face darkened.

"Who gave you a God license, Blake? You don't own Jane Doe just because she happened to fall into your lap. Nobody does. Thanks principally to your own efforts, the kooks from Crookston were debunked. Even if you got the Volkers to raise h— . . . a hue and cry about the government taking Jane, they have no legal power over her. Neither do you."

"Is everything a matter of legality to you?"

Turner grunted. "Morality. I knew you'd come to that. I'm just the man on the street. I do my job. If I can persuade you to cooperate, you'll come out of this with only your pride bruised. Otherwise—"

"Now the threats tiptoe out."

"Take this one seriously, Dr. Blake." Turner's tired eyes pinned Kevin to his own weariness; even now his backbone was turning to rubber. "It's not up to me what happens to you. If we're unable to persuade you to tell us where Jane Doe is—"

"I don't know. Goddammit, I honestly lost her!" Like most people, Kevin lied best when he was telling the truth.

Turner smiled. "Maybe you did lose her. We don't honestly care. We just want to find her. If you help, things will go well for you. You'll walk out of here with the keys to your condo and your car, with your life in pretty much one piece. You'll need a job, but you'll get very fine references. From Dr. Cross—"

"That bastard was willing to hang me out to dry! Poor old Norbert, I used to respect him once."

"Apparently it was reciprocal. Yeah, I hear you could have had an important career. Why not save that? You're on treacherous ground ethically anyway. I'm no therapist, but maybe you need to get away from Jane Doe, let her get free. Sure, you'll feel a little tragic, but you've lost girlfriends before, I'm sure—"

"Fuck off! Find some other house shrink." His degree of anger reflected his degree of temptation. Kevin was so tired, and the offer seemed so damn reasonable. If Turner hadn't reminded him of losing Julie . . .

"We already have." Turner rose and shrugged. "I'll be sorry to turn you over to him." He paused at the closed door, then looked back. "You know, Dr. Blake, you may be right. Jane Doe may not have any exploitable psychic talents. Tests may simply prove her unessential. She could be released again very shortly."

"You work for the PID. What do you think? Do you believe in this psi stuff?"

"Frankly? No. No more than I believe in the Volkers' close encounter story."

"Yet you'd hand Jane over—whatever she is, she's a traumatized human being, an amnesiac who's been chased from pillar to post—knowing your cold warriors would poke around inside her head with a meat hook looking for something that's very likely not there?"

"It's my job," Turner said. "I lost two men chasing her—and you. I'd rather we found something that made all that worthwhile."

"You're something else," Kevin accused, letting anger and contempt—and impotence—ooze into his voice and eyes.

"Maybe. But just sit tight here and hang on hard. You haven't met *our* shrink yet."

*   *   *

Jane bent to the bottom of the bus stop pole. An oblong of green paper had been wind-wrapped around its metal base. She unpeeled it.

It looked almost like money, except that the paper was too flimsy and the writing was all wrong. But she'd seen people exchange this slip for a bus ride.

She glanced around the darkened streets. The sodium iodide lamps, flickering on, had pocked the snow with pools the color of Mercurochrome.

Fewer and fewer people waited for buses now, and the buses came less and less often. The girls behind the glass window had gone long before, slipcasing their typewriters and dimming the green glows of their computer screens.

Parking spaces along the street stayed empty when they were vacated now.

Kevin, Jane knew—as surely as she knew things like how far away the sun is and the speed of light—wasn't coming back.

When the next gear-grinding red behemoth lumbered to the curb and snapped open its double doors, Jane followed an old woman with a shopping bag into the inviting yellow light.

The driver took her paper without glancing to her face. Jane perched on the long bench seat near the stairs and twisted to watch the Upper Midwest Savings & Loan, a neon-red emblem looming above its entryway now, slip behind her.

She tried to observe the passing streets, but someone stared back at her from the dark, and the little old lady across from her on the bus peered over her shoulder. It took a moment for Jane to realize that she was sandwiched by reflections—her own and the lady's.

Jane pressed her face to the window, putting gloved hands to her eyes as blinders, and began reading street signs as the bus jolted past them without stopping. Fourth Street. Then Fifth, Sixth. The bus stopped at Seventh and three people got on. Eighth and Ninth ground by, a patchwork of sparsely lit buildings sprinkled with pedestrians.

At least the bus was going in the right direction, Jane thought. She would get off—her mind zoomed into focus on the street map of Minneapolis she'd once seen. The gridwork of black lines and tiny type tightened into perfect focus. She'd get off at Franklin Avenue and walk the rest of the way.

Kevin had been angry with her once before when she'd walked alone at night to his place—angry and then, unaccountably, pleased.

Jane remembered how he'd held her, Zyunsinth spread over them both, how they'd slept together on his sofa as warm and kitten-content as that soft, silly creature of his. There had been no sex between them that night, but Jane didn't mind. For one thing, she really hadn't known how to do it yet. For another, some things were even better than sex. Sometimes.

She smiled and cradled her face on her hands, swaying to the bus's melancholy motion. Kevin had tried to take her home not long ago; maybe he had gone there now, too.

Chapter Sixteen

Turner's office boasted only one oversized window, and night had finally faded it to black, like a TV tube that gives up the ghost. Kevin waited under the humming fluorescent lights, staring out the window and knowing that there was nothing to see beyond it, nothing but his own reflection, murky and evasive.

He knew, too, that the wait was meant to unnerve him. It did. At last he got up and paced the chilly room. They'd hung his jacket in the outer office, as if he were just a regular visitor and could leave whenever he liked. But he figured that he had become an official enemy of the state—an obstruction, really, not important enough to rank as an enemy. A bureaucratic impediment.

He gave an infinitesimal tweak to the brushed chrome

doorknob. It seemed to have contracted lockjaw. Okay, Turner, he told himself with comic-book bravado. Maybe I've got lockjaw, too.

Unluckily, his mind hadn't locked. It revved, that numb, overtaxed brain of his. It conjured gruesome scenarios of Jane lost, frozen, raped, run over. The worst one remained the thought of Jane captured. She was on her own now. Where would she go? Kevin couldn't say, but they wouldn't believe that.

The door cracked open walnut-neat. Turner hovered behind some incoming figure.

"I'll alert the stakeout at the condo; maybe she'll head there," Turner was telling someone else behind him.

No! Kevin's mind revolted at the fiendishly apt logic of that idea. It hadn't occurred to him. No, Jane, no! Don't go there. Stay . . . lost.

The stranger on the threshold resolved into a smallish man with an army of manila folders marshaled under his elbow. He turned to shut the door behind him, shutting Turner up—and out.

A fur-lined leather coat that would have looked good on George Hamilton draped his shoulders. An expensive ostrich skin briefcase dangled from his free hand. He took Turner's place at the desk, opening the case and eyeing its contents hungrily. One by one he laid out the folders, like cards in a tarot deck, dealing from others hidden in the case. He paused now and again to regard Kevin over the sinister circles of his thick, rimless glasses.

None of it scared Kevin, none of it—stranger, silent treatment, stupid props—until the man lifted a hinged black plastic case from the bowels of the briefcase. It opened with a click. Kevin could guess what lay inside.

The case's raised cover shielded its contents from Kevin, but the man seemed to gloat over them, his hands moving to caress certain objects within.

"When does Sydney Greenstreet get here?" Kevin asked abruptly.

"You always had a smart mouth." The man didn't look up.

Move and countermove. Kevin contemplated the balding spot crowning the man's bowed head. Now he was supposed to get unglued trying to place the bastard. He chose silence. Any reply would have weakened his position.

Folder after folder was shifted, straightened, flipped tantalizingly open and then snapped shut again. The oblong black case remained open—too small to contain a firearm, too large to house false hope for Kevin.

The man finally looked up, directly at Kevin. The overhead bank of fluorescents poured light the color of bile down on them both. One lamp, failing, sizzled with faint blue lightning. Kevin wondered if that was deliberate, then dismissed the idea as paranoia. They could pull a lot more effective tricks if they wanted to.

"So, Dr. Blake," the man began. Kevin still couldn't place the voice, the face. "How long," he went on pleasantly, "have you been screwing your patients?"

A blood-red bull of rage charged through Kevin, herding all the adrenaline in his body before it. He dammed the reaction before it became just what the doctor across him had ordered. Now Kevin recognized the man—the manner of attack.

"At least I don't screw up their heads, Dr. Nordstrom." Nordstrom smiled. "I'm flattered."

"No, just unforgettable, like a posthypnotic suggestion."

"Speaking of hypnosis, I'm surprised you used it on Jane Doe. I thought you considered yourself more adventuresome. That's a . . . milquetoast method—out-of-date and overrated."

Kevin quashed the impulse to answer that he'd done pretty well with it; that's exactly what Nordstrom wanted to know. "Look, Aaron, let's cut out the cat and mouse—"

"Eric," Nordstrom seethed, his face whitening against the shiny black square of night behind it.

"It's been a while," Kevin agreed. "I didn't know you got your kicks from government cases nowadays."

"I have a private practice as well, in Manhattan. Quite lucrative." He opened a manila folder. "I was surprised, too, to find you . . . subsisting . . . on a university salary. You would have done better in private practice."

"Money's not everything, as you oughta know," Kevin

shot back, wincing anyway at the sight of Nordstrom flipping through the particulars of his life. Letting an antagonist see your salary was almost worse than letting him observe your sex life.

"Of course you had your headlines," Nordstrom mused, cracking another folder, one obviously older than the others. Kevin glimpsed tatters of yellowed newsprint, even recognized the still-white, slick page with the old item from *Time*. . . . How had the PID managed to unearth this creep? he wondered. Probably the same way Probe had found Kevin.

Nordstrom decisively shut the folder. "I have no headlines, but I've had interesting work, too, all these years. My consultation cases. As you know, the government and the universities don't pay that well. But they offer other advantages. I too have 'ridden the cutting edge of current psychiatric practice,' Blake. Smarts, sometimes, doesn't it?"

Kevin recognized the line from the *Time* article, and shrugged. Offhand gestures had always nettled Nordstrom's sense of formality.

Nordstrom opened a new folder, its front flap slapping the desktop, all business. "Your Jane Doe is an intriguing case."

"I thought so, too . . . at first."

"You apparently thought other things later. I'm eager to meet her, the woman who pulled you off your pedestal."

"She's just an . . . interesting case—"

"Your eyelids widen slightly when you lie, the way William F. Buckley's do when he's going for the jugular, did you know that, Blake? It's almost as if you have to force yourself to watch yourself do it. You'll never last in this game without lying."

"I'll practice," Kevin promised sharply.

Nordstrom nodded, his manicured hand cupping his mouth but not quite concealing a slightly crooked smile. Kevin's memories of the man came trickling back. Nordstrom had been too unlikable to dwell on, but he'd been bright enough, in his self-effacing way, and rich enough. And sly enough.

"I've been thinking." Nordstrom steepled his hands. As his suit sleeves drew up, Kevin saw the glint of a watch far richer than his own. His watch lay on the desk, with the other possessions Turner had taken from his pockets. Kevin's body remained free, but his person had been stripped of his things, his accessories.

As if a mind reader, Nordstrom picked up the timepiece, letting the fine-jointed gold band lie snake-supple across his small, manicured hand.

"I've spoken to your parents. . . ."

"My parents?" Kevin kept his voice cold, polite, like Nordstrom's.

"Nice people." The watch still draped his palm, on the verge of slipping to the desktop.

Kevin didn't care, he told himself, but he projected his parents into the watch they had given him anyway.

"Nice people," Nordstrom repeated. "Ordinary people. Proud of you. And puzzled, of course."

"What did you talk to them about?"

"You."

"And what did they talk to you about?"

"You."

"They don't know who you are—"

"I told them. I'm assigned to a special government unit, I said. 'Oh, like our son,' they said." Nordstrom smiled. "Your mother got on the extension. She was so excited to hear about you. Doesn't get too many long-distance calls. Been a bit busy lately, Doctor? Forget your familial duties?"

"It isn't a duty, but then you wouldn't understand that."

"Don't worry, I didn't tell them what hot water you're in. I simply sowed a few seeds. Said there was a case I needed to question you about. One of your female patients. That you were missing, you were . . . both missing and we . . . were concerned. I said that some people thought you had run away with your patient, so to speak. They are old-fashioned folk, aren't they, your parents? It was better to speak in such terms, wasn't it?"

"You contemptible bastard," Kevin said without feeling.

Feeling wouldn't help him now. "Yeah, they're real easy. It must have given you a kick to manipulate people like that. They live in a town so small they think everyone who rings the doorbell or the phone needs something, and deserves it."

"They gave me what I needed." Nordstrom put the watch down, nudging it so it lay straight. "Oh, their Kevin wouldn't do anything wrong like that, no. Elope with a patient, never. Violate his professional ethics, heavens no. It was rather touching. Too bad they were wrong."

"Parents often are wrong about their children, particularly the grown ones. Weren't yours about you?"

Nordstrom's lips screwed a millimeter tighter. "Your parents defended you to the ditches, you'll be gratified to hear. Told me all about you and your early days—your grades, your girlfriends, your track medals, your civic spirit—such a paragon, such an all-American boy. They finished up with your scholarship to Harvard."

"That should have got you up-to-date."

"Odd, though, that's when I discovered *I* knew more about you, from that point on. They didn't even know about Julie Symons."

Kevin shrugged the shrug that had infuriated Turner. He hoped it would do the same for Nordstrom. "Maybe Julie Symons wasn't that important." It did.

"She was!" Nordstrom's fist hit the desk, folders twitching at the blow. "You . . . lying—" His face smoothed. "She was," he repeated more coldly.

"I didn't think you even knew her."

"You didn't think a lot of things you should have then."

Kevin shrugged again. "So you got my parents all worried about me—about where I might be, about what I might have done. I don't like it, but they're parents. Parents have worried for a long, long time. They'll get over it."

"Still, it's bound to be distressing. They'll call the Probe unit first—and find it . . . gone. They'll call your apartment . . . and get no answer. They'll start to look for your friends, and realize that they don't know who they are. Or maybe that you don't have that many—"

"I'm particular."

"You don't need anyone!" Nordstrom charged. "How long since you've seen your parents—those nice, gray-haired old people in Elk River?"

"Six months, so sue me."

"They're very worried about you, Kevin." Nordstrom's eyes grew soulful as he assumed the role of guilt-applying authority. Kevin could see that the man would have a certain force with his patients if they were unsophisticated or damaged enough.

"Yeah, well, I'm pretty worried about me, too," Kevin said wryly. His frankness momentarily disarmed Nordstrom.

"You should be. I'm nobody to trifle with."

" 'Trifle with.' Come on, Nordstrom, no wonder nobody takes you seriously. You want to talk no friends, take a look at your own social calendar. How *could* I remember you off the bat? You weren't very memorable, except as something unpleasant people have to take sometimes, like castor oil. Pursuing degrees instead of humanity. You want to talk maladjusted, let me put *my* cards on the table—I'm a pretty good analyst, you know."

"Shut up!" The man's voice sank to a whisper. "Shut up. I had connections, who needs friends? And Julie was my friend—didn't know that, did you, Dr. Hotshot? Julie Symons wasn't yours alone; she was mine, too."

"That's sick, Nordstrom." Kevin's contempt was deeply genuine now, so real he couldn't look at the man.

Manila folders rustled. Kevin used the pause to reassess his opponent, to figure out what Nordstrom really wanted, what Nordstrom really was. He didn't like the possibilities that were clarifying in his mind.

"She was mine!" Nordstrom's intensity of tone implied spittle. Kevin was glad he was sitting six feet away. He looked back at the man, because he had to.

Nordstrom's fist whitened in the chilly room; it clenched, crushed something shiny and black and white. Kevin felt his face melt like a Salvador Dali clock as he realized what it was.

He was up and leaning over the desk, manila folders scattering, the briefcase lid banging down, Nordstrom's Ivy

League tie knot in his hand, his other hand crushing wool suiting material.

"How the fucking hell did you get a hold of that, you twisted son of a bitch—?"

Kevin didn't recognize his own voice. It sounded raw, as if he'd been shouting himself hoarse at a basketball game. The room buzzed. It seemed crowded with light and color and sound. His hands knew they could tear Nordstrom apart. He wanted to let them.

Nordstrom's glasses had jolted crooked on his bland, ugly face. Kevin could have squeezed, shaken, throttled, except that Nordstrom's eyes flicked significantly away, down and to the left. He repeated the gesture, quick and slick as a snake's tongue sniffing the air for scent. Kevin followed the glance.

At last, now, leaning over Nordstrom across the desk, Kevin could see into the black case.

He saw what he had been afraid he'd see—a glistening row of syringes cradled in notched velveteen, fine white lines scribing their sides to the fifty-milligram mark. Chemical abbreviations for the clear liquid contents were scrawled on the adhesive tape wound around them. Kevin recognized sodium pentothal and amytal sodium, a hypnotic drug, but three more syringes lay there, unidentified foreign substances filling their familiar shining tubes.

"At my discretion, Blake," Nordstrom enunciated. "My discretion. It suits me to interview you in an unaltered state now. But if you don't control yourself, I'll go to these sooner rather than later."

That clinical array iced Kevin's rage. He eased back into his chair, brooding on the drugs. Such things were useful in the practice of psychiatry, had helped many patients and irretrievably harmed a few. He didn't like them, but someone like Nordstrom would say that was because he liked to hog all the glory with his technique in session. Kevin would say that the human mind, given half a chance, could produce more wonders than a battalion of injected chemical wonder-workers.

"Nice work if you can get it." Kevin stretched out his legs and laced his fingers over his stomach. The posture

130

would irritate Nordstrom for its studied insouciance, but it was also physically unthreatening. Nordstrom, Kevin realized now, was far too dangerous to threaten.

The man was smoothing the wrinkles in the stolen photograph. Kevin had kept the picture under glass for ten years—the only surviving likeness of Julie. Watching Nordstrom's fingers crush and then caress the slick paper image made his guts clench until they hurt, but he knew Nordstrom wanted it to hurt. In any psychiatrist-patient encounter, the one who hurts less will emerge the stronger.

A prick of fear, like a needle delicately encroaching on Kevin's skin, burned into the base of his neck.

"You had no right to take it." Kevin nodded at the photo. "It has nothing to do with anything now."

"It has everything to do with it!" Nordstrom glanced up, his glasses still low on his nose so the unfocused fever of his eyes—mud-brown—drove into Kevin's. "It's the key to you, Doctor—to your delusion about this amnesia patient, to your obsession with her. . . ."

"*My* obsession!" Kevin laughed. "At least my obsession lives." It was a cheap shot, cheaply intended. Nordstrom's pupils contracted to pinpricks and Kevin felt a throb of new hope.

"But . . . Julie was always special," Kevin began again, not sure exactly where to lead Nordstrom, yet aware that now—for the moment—he could do it. "Julie was one of a kind. I can see that . . . anyone would hate to lose her."

Kevin hated exhuming Julie and exposing her—and himself—to this particular postmortem.

"Beautiful," Nordstrom crooned to the photo. "Beautiful."

Kevin nodded. Julie had once been beautiful to him, too, and sometimes silence makes the best crowbar.

Nordstrom continued to stroke the ragged white lines his fist had etched into the photograph. Kevin abstracted himself from the sight. Julie . . . maybe Dr. Cross had been right to call her death the turning point in Kevin's life, his career. But Kevin knew that Julie was dead. He knew the difference between memory and reality. Nordstrom didn't seem to—or care.

131

"You better get used to me having this, holding this."
Nordstrom brandished the photo again. "You don't understand yet, do you, Blake? I'm the government's most useful
headhunter. I have total discretion to pry into any corner
of your life that intrigues me, to probe every nook and
cranny of your mind. I can make any disposition of your
body that I deem necessary, including pumping you so full
of my magic potions you would babble your soul to me for
a season pass to the Buffalo Bills."

"Truth serums are a lie," Kevin said calmly. "You know
that. They rely on environmental factors as much as any
inherent power. They hang on the gullibility of the subject,
the skill of the questioner. Sure, they knock inhibitions for
a loop, but I know that it's *believing* that truth serums work
that makes victims vulnerable. It's hard to hoodwink an
educated consumer, Nordstrom."

"Still, you'd find it . . . unpleasant to be out of control,
to know that I was rummaging around in your subconscious." Nordstrom elevated the photo of Julie. "Still
beautiful, isn't she?"

Wrinkles radiated through the paper, making it look as if
glass had shattered across the photographic face. Kevin no
longer considered Julie's emaciated ballerina's look beautiful, but a badge of pain and deprivation, of the distorted
push for perfection that had driven Julie to the slow, dying
fall of anorexia nervosa.

"Yes," he told Nordstrom, keeping his eyes steady, "she
was beautiful." Then it hit him, the really wacko thing
about Nordstrom's fixation on Julie—not that it existed,
but that it existed still. "Eric, what was Julie to you? What
is she to you?"

"She is . . ." Nordstrom's eyes radiated not lust, not
even love beyond living with, but ingrown obsession. "—mine now, as she was never yours. You threw her
away, all of you. I kept her. I was even the last to see
her."

"You? The hospital didn't allow any visitors at the end,
except her parents and brother. And me."

"I didn't see her there. It . . . irritated me, Julie sick and
lying there, and me not allowed to see her; Julie literally

shrinking and me not seeing it. The last I'd seen of Julie had been that fall—on campus—running across it, her pink dancing tights showing between her boots and her skirt hem. Julie swathed in scarves and jackets and thick wool skirts so I couldn't see her. And all the time, shrinking, dwindling, melting—"

"A lot of us didn't see it at first," Kevin interjected roughly. "Is that it? So you blame yourself, Eric, for not noticing Julie's illness, for not being able to help her? That's very understandable—"

"Oh, if I had noticed . . . I would have been her dresser." Nordstrom's eyes grew dreamy. "I would have been content to stand in the wings and watch her on stage, pale tights clinging to every bone and hollow, the satin bodice so flat and stiff, her arms ladders of light—baby pink spotlights above—and the deep shadows, her face more dark with night than bright. Her eyes, lost. I would have waited in the wings, counting the vertebrae on her back as they etched sharper and sharper into the shadow. I would have waited in the shadows for her to sink into shadow, until her skin had worn as thin as her toe shoes, thinner than a withered leaf in the fall, that fall, and I would touch it and find my fingertips on the bone. . . ."

"Did you love Julie, Eric, or did you—do you—love death?"

"Julie *is* death, Kevin." Tears glazed Nordstrom's eyes.

Kevin sat silent. He had learned more than he had wanted to. Despite his horror of Nordstrom, the professional fever pulsed in him—what a classic case the man was! What a challenge to delve the chronic alienation and envy that had formed the current sociopathic personality. What a . . . triumph to help, heal, so diseased a mind. It would take a sensibility that was healthy to the extent that Nordstrom was ill.

Kevin relinquished the fantasy for what it was.

"When did you see Julie last?" Kevin asked quietly, not because he could use the answer, but because, having descended into a loved one's grave with a ghoul, he needed to exhume his own guilt.

"At the funeral home. Julie was at home to guests . . .

133

dancing *Sleeping Beauty*. I wakened her with a kiss. She's been with me ever since. I've been wanting to tell you ever since."

"Is it making you happy?"

"Yes! Happier than standing ignored on campus, watching you and Julie play your own private version of *Love Story*. So sad, so tragic," Nordstrom mocked. "Poor Kevin, going on without Julie. But you weren't worthy of her." Nordstrom waited for Kevin's denial or anger. There was neither. He jabbed harder. "You were unfaithful to her. Look at you, forgetting Julie for this—"

He jerked open another folder and tossed the sketch of Jane down beside Julie's photograph. Kevin tensed. It was one thing to psych yourself into letting an enemy manhandle your past; quite another to see him mess with your present.

"I've treated a lot of patients since Julie; I've had a lot of women since Julie." Kevin was deliberately crude to depersonalize the subject.

Nordstrom leaned intently forward, his fingers gathering both images toward himself. "True enough. But have you ever really loved again, since Julie. And"—Nordstrom's icy eyes warmed—"and lost? Again."

Chapter Seventeen

"Excuse me, miss, do you have the time?"

Jane stared at the woman in horn-rimmed glasses who'd laid a mittened hand on her arm. The woman clutched several packages under her other arm and seemed worried.

"No one *has* time," Jane answered scrupulously. "Time is a myth of sorts. An appearance. Time is our own motions named and numbered. It really is a metaphysical problem. I read once—"

"No, no. I meant, a watch." The woman spoke even more slowly than Jane, enunciating every word. "Are you wearing a watch? Can you tell me what *time* it is?"

"Oh." Jane lifted her wrist, as Kevin used to do, and paused. "No, I'm not wearing a watch." She thought a moment. "But it's . . . six thirty-eight—"

"Thank you." The woman turned, but Jane's hand reached out to delay her.

"Eighteen thirty-eight oh-one-dot-eighty, exactly," Jane finished.

"Fine! Jeez, sorry I asked. You could have just said no!" The woman huffed away, rattling her packages.

"I'm not sorry," Jane said after her.

Alone, she hugged new self-knowledge to herself. No one had ever told Jane she knew the time automatically, internally. She would have liked to ask Kevin about it, but of course, she couldn't. That disappointed her. It made the cold seem more efficient at slipping up her jacket sleeves and down its collar. It made the distance she had to go seem a little longer. Jane had never felt tired before.

She remained standing by the bus stop sign along with the other waiting people. She had just gotten off the last bus and had no intention of taking the next, but Jane liked the presence of this clot of people near the snowy street corner.

There was something cozy about their silent congregation, something almost conspiratorial. The dark evening and the hushed, falling snow felt like their voices. And their comings and goings intrigued her.

A bus snorted up to the curb. Its huge headlights spotlighted dancing snow flurries. Jane stepped politely back while people surged past her into the bus's packed interior. She had discovered she liked to guess who would embark and who would wait for the next bus. Three stayed she had thought would go, and two went she had thought would stay. Her estimates were getting closer.

She sighed and looked up at the streetlamps. Snowflakes flirted around the globes of light, thick as, as . . . falling dandruff. Pleased with her comparison, Jane turned and trudged alone down Franklin Avenue.

Kevin's place was twelve blocks away, her inboard map

told her. The distance was nothing like the three miles she had walked once before to get there. She kept her gloved hands in her empty pockets, lowered her face to the tickle of the wind-blown snowflakes, and kept walking.

Franklin Avenue was faced with two- and three-story buildings on either side. Some were decaying apartment buildings, most were storefronts housing wholesalers, old-clothes dealers and basement gemologists.

By the time Jane turned from Franklin's glare to the dark, curved residential streets south of Loring Park, her internal clock chimed half past seven. And she was hungry.

She'd never felt this kind of urgent hunger before, either, and wondered if she had to, or simply expected to. She lifted her face to the night and let snowflakes melt on her tongue. At least she wouldn't be thirsty, she thought.

Kevin's building finally hulked before her; she recognized it immediately. His apartment was on the third floor, reached by the wooden stairs lacing the building's rear. Jane loitered among the trees bordering the parking area. Her eyes accurately picked Kevin's from the patchwork of doors dotting the three stories, then raked across the windows that should be his.

One oozed a subtle incandescent glow through closed vertical blinds. Thin stripes of soft light cast a pattern like golden bars onto the night-darkened glass.

A strange feeling clasped Jane in its alien arms: it was composed equally of excitement and peace. She searched herself for the proper word and found it—not in the clearinghouse of her retentive memory dictionary, but in something she had absorbed in her sessions of white-lightning reading. This sense of aching familiarity, Jane thought, might resemble . . . coming home.

She started across the parking lot, her mind already resurrecting the rooms she had seen only once—three white-painted walls, one of age-dusted brick, bookcases, a stereo setup, the little kitchen, the big sofa. . . .

Two men stepped from a parked van and stamped their feet. Near them, Jane sensed the eternal scan of electrical impulses, the watchdog machines that made her hackles rise.

136

Jane paused, caught in a pink-gold sodium iodide circle. She didn't move. She didn't move at all, not even to let air lift her lungs and then let them collapse. Instead, she listened. Her blood surged thickly in her ears. She slowed it to a meander through her veins.

"Crazy to check it out again!" one man grumbled. "Colder out than the balls on a brass monkey, and we've been cooling our heels all shift. We'd have seen somebody come. Why do we always get the dead-end stakeouts?"

"Ass-numbing is right," the other answered, laughing. "Shut up and climb. We got all night. Might as well look busy."

The men lumbered up the semilit stairs, dark forms as faceless as the men in the north woods, as any of the men Kevin had warned her against.

When they passed beyond even her acute earshot, she let her breath ease warmly into the snow swirling before her face. She skittered across the lot to shelter under the shadowed stairs at mid-building. Not long after, the clump of descending feet sifted snow like flour through the cracks in the stairs. Words sifted down, too.

"—wild goose chase, I told yah. Nobody's comin' back to that hole."

"Hey, not a bad place!"

"Don't like all that modern crap, though. Too empty."

"Got a coffin nail?"

A small flame spit into life between the two men as they paused at ground level. Jane jumped as she saw it, then uncurled her fingers. The men walked on, talking. Jane no longer listened.

Later, much later, when falling snow had veiled the rear window of the men's van, Jane slipped up the steps, treading carefully in their footprints. Kevin hadn't liked leaving traces.

He had left the imprint of his snow angel in the north woods, Jane thought incongruously. She remembered her spell of amnesia in the woods, remembered beginning to feel real again and not lost in some remote part of her own body.

Then Kevin had appeared before her refocusing eyes—a dark blot on the snow, but moving as he lay there supine,

137

sweeping his arms and legs in and out. He reminded her of a bundled, flailing infant she'd seen a woman on the bus lay on its back and fuss with. Did Kevin sometimes feel his self falling away, too? she wondered.

Jane confronted the door at the top, familiar from her previous visit, but locked. She stripped off a glove and touched a finger to the brass circle that had swallowed the key. She relived standing here with Kevin, remembering him talking and turning the key, remembering—if she thought hard enough, deep enough—remembering the nearly subsonic sound of the lock's tumblers twisting to the lever of his key.

The sound's recalled rhythm erected a physical model of the action in her mind. Her fingernail pressed into the tiny slot, adapting to its internal jigs. Jane poured into that empty mold with her mind, with something more than her mind, with something corporeal growing from her mind.

Her finger turned. Right—no, left. Her finger twisted left until the lock wrenched it. She heard the subsonic click in proper sequence. Her other hand turned the knob and pushed the door ajar. Jane slipped through.

The rooms were unlit except for the pale beam of a brass floor lamp near one window. Near another lay a pile of disheveled books. The brick-supported bookshelves themselves lurched against the wall—empty, sagging.

The long maroon sofa covered with a velvety stuff that Jane somehow remembered was called mohair looked as if it had erupted, spitting cushions to the floor. Perhaps Kevin's kitten had played here, Jane thought, for long, ragged rents ripped the vintage upholstery. On the crowded floor, where fallen cushions didn't lie, more discarded books did.

Jane waded through the tented volumes, some fallen agape with pages creased at random angles. Other refugees from the emptied bookcases peppered the chaos. No item had consciously claimed Jane's attention when she'd spent her one night here, but each rang a note of recognition with some deeper sense as she saw it displaced now.

A glass cat lay whiskers-down on the rug, its severed tail a half foot away. A small bronze bust of a bearded man had fallen faceup to gaze sightlessly at the bland ceiling. Something glinted coin-bright in the wreckage. Jane instinctively bent to gather it.

"Oh." She stared at a fresh ruby of blood on her forefinger, then pressed the cut shut with her thumb. All that glittered wasn't gold, as the book had said. This glimmer was only glass, broken glass.

Jane found another gleam, one less edged, and picked up an empty brass picture frame. One like it had surrounded the photograph of her . . . other . . . self on the Volkers' living room wall. Her memory couldn't place this object in the room. She frowned, crouching over it, the vacant rectangle framing an abstract of blue-denimed knees.

Jane stared at the denim within the gold as if making a thread count. Some glint echoed in her memory, a faint, hidden glimmer among the books. . . . Kevin would have called it a beacon from the subconscious. She glanced up to empty shelves, to a position her memory populated with— with . . . Jane stood, excited, cradling the empty frame to her chest.

Kevin would be so proud of her, so pleased with her memory now! She visualized the photograph her conscious mind had never really seen. Her mind's eye focused so clearly that she could draw it if she had to: a half-obscured image of a long-necked woman with swept-back hair and an expression of haughty passion riding her angular face.

Jane didn't like her, but then, perhaps people didn't like the girl in the photograph the Volkers kept on their wall. Kevin had always cautioned Jane to be fair-minded.

Jane liked the portrait's absence less, nor did she like the cold cutting presence of the empty frame in her arms. She didn't like the broken-backed books on the floor or the scattered cushions, either. She had never disliked so much before. That she could remember.

Jane walked into the kitchen. The kitten's stainless steel dishes lay there, empty. A rubbery ring of dried milk circled the bottom of one. She remembered the Zyunsinth-like feel of the tiny furred creature, its blue-gray sheen and the pricking, sudden surprise of claws striking from the heart of its softness.

"Blue Streak," Jane called, and listened to the silence.

She went down the hall, peering into rooms she had never seen, had never imagined were there. Somehow, it had never occurred to her that there was more beyond what she saw at the moment. The bathroom was sleek, white and had a skylight. Jane liked it. She used it. The bedroom was painted white, too, the bed on a low base, paperback books marching across the wide headboard shelf.

A phone sat on the nightstand. Jane rested her palm on it. She had never talked on a phone, although she'd seen Kevin and the girls in Willhelm Hall do it often. Numbers snaked across her mind, all the phone numbers she had ever seen—printed on the dial at the hospital and dorm, or written on the official sheet where she'd glimpsed Kevin's home address once by accident.

Jane plucked that number from the endlessly repeating string and picked up the receiver. She pressed the proper buttons in turn, comforted by the phone's obedient chatter as she dialed. It sounded like one of the ground squirrels that chittered across campus and begged for candy bars.

She dialed Kevin and waited hopefully for him to answer. There came instead a sound—a raw, whining sound, like the siren of the ecnalubma . . . ambulance, Kevin said she should say now.

A harsh, impersonal voice told Jane that it was sorry, but that her call could not be completed as dialed. It told her to check the number and try again, or to remain on the line for operator assistance.

Did operators operate? she wondered. She turned to regard the white bureau's sagging drawers and the strewn clothes that dotted the room's order. It looked like Lynn Volker's bedroom after she had visited it. Jane felt that somehow, she had caused this, too.

She wandered back to the main room, pausing in the kitchen to open the refrigerator. The small light inside illuminated empty wire shelves. Three long-necked bottles of beer huddled at the back. A circle of leather-dry lunch meat reposed in an open cellophane package next to some small containers of yogurt under the meat tray.

Jane picked up the dried salami and the yogurt and a

140

bottle of beer. She laid them on the coffee table and pushed the cushions back into place, then sat to twist open the beer, gnaw on the meat. She unlidded the yogurt last. The package said it was plain, but blueberry-sized circles of green blotched the snowy surface. Jane dipped in the spoon she'd found on the drainboard and ate it all.

The clock on the floor still ticked. It showed just past nine, but Jane already knew that. Once she'd found her time sense, it flashed into her mind uncalled for, whenever she thought of time.

So did Kevin. She curled into the corner of the sofa. His scent was here but there was no comfort in it. It was wrong, all wrong. She felt as if she'd been stripped of all but the husk of her memories.

Jane supposed she should sleep, that Kevin would tell her to sleep, but she got up, and slowly, item by item, began restoring the shelves to their proper order—every book, every trinket claiming its rightful place from the intricate unconscious map of her memory.

She wished she could put Kevin back into place as easily.

*   *   *

"Is it working?"

"So many new pathways to follow . . . we cannot know. So much has altered spontaneously."

"This probe is no longer a tacit collector, then. It is no longer a properly programmed tool."

"Rogue is the word of this world's dominant language for it. A creature that deviates from the predetermined rule of its nature."

"Its nature is what we made of it."

"Then it is true now neither to itself nor to us. We may need to abandon it."

"We have never abandoned so valuable a property before. Could it not be recalled and reconstituted? Some of the alterations are . . . unique."

"Tainted is the word of this planet for such willful redirection. This 'I-ness' the probe professes is unpredictable."

"So are the creatures of this place, and all the creatures we

have found. So were our mother-cells before we harnessed them."

"It was an ill time when we found we could reach beyond ourselves. We exist in a vast whirlwind of random entities unlike ourselves."

"Their 'I-ness' is random. Consider the pattern. They are more like each other, more like ourselves, than they know."

"Their records indicate that this has occurred to them, but they persist in believing in something, anything, other than the sameness."

"They are at least . . . interesting."

"Our own rogue member has been reabsorbed, yet we hear among us random words. Who speaks?"

"We all speak, as we always have, from our hard-bought oneness."

"These lesser creatures do not strive for oneness."

"Why do we study them, then?"

"A good question for us to meditate upon. Perhaps the voyager cell, with its newness, can contribute to the thought process."

"It is possible that all could become so much One that we could no longer act."

"Acting may be the curse of any kind; our best course may be to withdraw."

"Still, we would not know."

"There are many things we do not know. What would we lose in this instance?"

"Perhaps we would not know how not to know the next time, if we act and there is a next occasion."

"We grow . . . divisive."

"So does the simplest cell in any world."

"We must recall the probe. It was an aberration on our part to release it again."

"It is part of us, this tool of ours. Sometimes we can hear it singing in the distance."

"Not our tune."

"No."

"Disquieting, to have set a song in motion and hear it compose itself, to speak in the terms of this place."

"We must write a new tune now, in the same key."

142

"We grow . . . overfond of the creatures of this planet."

"They do what we once did. Perhaps the mother-cell remembers."

"The mother-cell remembers all. It is for us to forget."

     *   *   *

The doorbell rang.

Jane jumped awake, popping herself out of the warm sofa corner. Her ears and extremities tingled. Unseen daylight from beyond the closed blinds bathed the living room in a subaquatic glow.

The doorbell rang again. Jane followed the last ring through the living room to a hall and then to a door she'd never noticed before. She opened it on a dim hallway. Two people stood there, staring at her.

"Thank God!" The woman's face wore the same numbly pained look Mrs. Volker's had. "We thought, when we couldn't get through *anywhere*—!"

"Where's Kevin?" the man interrupted.

"I don't know," Jane said.

"It's all right to let us in," the woman said. "We're Kevin's parents."

"Oh." Jane stepped back. "Kevin doesn't seem to think much of parents."

A silence held the threshold, then the man stepped over it.

"Look here, young lady, we haven't been able to reach our son and there's something disturbing going on. We don't care who or what you are—" The woman's hand pressed warning into his arm. "We just want to talk to Kevin."

Jane stepped back and let them precede her into the living room. They walked directly to the sofa and sat, as if they knew the room's arrangement well.

"He's not here," Jane explained, following them.

"We don't mean to . . . disturb you," the woman repeated. She eyed the empty beer bottle and yogurt carton on the coffee table. "It's none of our business what—who —Kevin is involved with. Do you . . . date him?"

"No."

"Don't be so dainty, Clare. You know the young woman sleeps with him, and probably lives with him."

"Sometimes," Jane said, "but I don't live here."

"Where is he?" the man demanded anxiously. He was a narrower man than Mr. Volker, with iron-gray hair and a nervous inflexibility.

"He's not much like you," Jane noted, looking from one to the other.

"He's . . . our son."

"I'm not much like the Volkers, either, but I think I will be someday."

"The Volkers?"

For the first time in her remembered life, Jane felt a stab of pity. "It's all right. We don't understand it all either."

"Aren't you worried about Kevin, if you don't know where he is?"

"Worried. That's a faraway word. I don't worry much, about anything."

"Young people today!" Mr. Blake ground out under his breath.

"But there are things I don't like," Jane said, her voice hardening. "More and more, there are things I don't like." She smiled suddenly, her face radiant with memory. "I like Kevin. Most of the time."

Jane moved to the newly discovered front door, pulling her gloves from her jacket pocket.

"Wait!" the man called nervously. "You've—you've got to tell us what's become of Kevin. We don't give a damn about you, about what part you play in his life—just tell us what's going on. He's our son!"

"He's lost," Jane said. "I think he's just lost."

She closed the door noiselessly behind her as she left.

Chapter Eighteen

"I wish to Hades you'd taken him to a safe house for this."

"You said we didn't have much time."

"Still, if he's damaged, I'd rather it didn't happen in a federal building."

"And you accuse me of having no heart. . . ."

The voices came in stereo—badly connected, fuzzy stereo, too distorted for Kevin to identify.

Even the words remained disassociated . . . a collection of sounds, of sibilants and fricatives and barely breathed vowels. Were they whispering? Or was Kevin hanging somewhere between a trance and drowning?

He didn't care. Too many punching bags of cotton wool hung between him and them. He doubted he could beat his way out, even with his brain. Wait, some instinct told him. Just hang in there, don't fight it. You'll come back and maybe—maybe you're hearing something you don't want to miss.

He sensed motion occurring around himself—the odd footfall, a rustle of clothing light-years away. Light itself was seeping between his closed eyelids, his shut-down senses. He had a fleeting impression that he was encased to his neck in an emerald-green block of ice, being rolled back into a morgue drawer . . . and struggled to escape the bizarre delusion.

"He's coming out," a voice was saying indifferently.

"And you got nothing."

"I got everything."

A door slammed. Or maybe a piece of paper just hit a desk. Things sounded magnified or muffled in turn. Kevin's hands wanted to accost the sounds, wring some sense out of them. His mind strained to get a grip on his sensations, to mug reality. Reality played hard to get, as usual, boogying at the edge of the limbo he inhabited.

"Did it have to take all night?"

"You could have left. You didn't have to wait."

"Yes, I did. Poor . . . devil."

"He'll live, but we don't need him anymore. Stash him somewhere for a few days until I get her."

"This is America, Nordstrom. He's got some rights."

"Dump him. Out of the way. And be quiet. He's coming around."

"Not moving any."

"The mind moves. The mind always moves first."

Kevin rode a stainless steel elevator to the top of his head. He stopped on the thirteenth floor. Sleek doors sliced open. Kevin walked down a hall ablaze with white light. He walked into a room, sat down in a chair, leaned back.

His eyes opened. A blank-windowed limestone building filled the windowframe opposite with hyperrealistic architectural detail. Daylight made his eyes wince. Turner stood to his left, his face ashen and eyes empty. Another man sat on the corner of the desk. Nordstrom.

Kevin struggled to sit upright. His feet, numbed from hours in the chilly room, buckled at the ankles. "What—?"

Kevin automatically pressed the fingers of his left hand to the pain in his right arm and flexed it. His shirt sleeve was rolled up past his elbow, tight enough to play tourniquet. He pulled away his fingers. Old blood had pooled purple under the pale skin of his inner elbow, flooding and concealing the blue roadmaps of his veins.

Empty syringes twinkled glassily on the desktop. Unanchored memories tumbled through the vacant corridors of his mind.

"Nice trip?" Nordstrom didn't even look up from repacking his equipment.

"I've had better." Everything was in retrograde now. Kevin wondered how much of himself was being stacked away behind ostrich skin barriers. He made himself relax. No point in trying to force recall.

Had those syringes really been emptied into his veins, or

just a convenient trashbin? Even Nordstrom wouldn't overmedicate a patient without emergency resuscitation nearby. Psychiatry was often a game of blindman's buff, and the patient was always It.

Turner cleared his throat. "You feel okay, Doctor?"

"Are you asking me or him, Turner?" Kevin wondered.

Irritation twisted across the man's bleak face. "Believe it or not, I feel some responsibility for the people in my custody."

"I believe it. I used to feel that way myself—*if* I've got a self left, and Dr. Nordstrom didn't drain it all into some secret soul bank he keeps hidden in that briefcase."

Nordstrom quirked a smile in Kevin's direction. He clicked his drug case and briefcase shut in turn. "I'll want to confer with you, Mr. Turner, in private." He strode for the closed door, the heavy coat swagging from his shoulders.

Kevin watched him go. He'd hoped for more time to evaluate Nordstrom's demeanor. Then he could psych out what he'd told the man—if he'd told the man anything.

"You'll be all right," Turner was saying again, sinking wearily into the chair behind his own desk.

Kevin nodded. The room vibrated out of focus until he shut his eyes.

"You still won't cooperate? Help us debrief Jane Doe?"

"'Debrief' Jane. You make her sound like one of Nordstrom's ostrich attachés . . . and you haven't got her yet."

"We'll have her. Just as we've got you. If you won't help, I'll have to take measures—" Turner warned.

"Take measures." Kevin let his head roll back on his shoulders and studied the patterns on the inside of his eyelids. They were . . . distracting, a moving paisley print of light and color and oblivion.

He must have temporarily dropped out. He awakened again to voices—gruff, droning voices in the outer office. His eyes opened with the door and Turner came in.

"Get your stuff."

Kevin shoved himself to his feet. His head stayed attached, no small achievement. At the desk he methodi-

147

cally stuffed his belongings in all the right pockets, another victory. He paused before buckling on the watch again, remembering how its gleam had oiled Nordstrom's neat, possessive hands. Then he noticed the time.

Kevin's body jerked slightly, as if shocked awake on the brink of sleep. Something slid serpentinely through his brain, some worm of self-doubt Nordstrom had planted there—or a postdrug suggestion? Who knew what Kevin had done and said in the past ten hours? . . . Only Nordstrom, and he wasn't talking.

"Ready?" It was Turner at the door like a tired host ushering out the last guest.

Kevin ambled into the anteroom, beginning to congratulate himself on getting his sea legs, on his clearing mind.

Two uniformed police officers waited, their insulated navy jackets and holster-bristling forms filling the little room.

"Thanks for the door-to-door service," Turner told them.

"Bauer in Narcotics says we owe you guys on that Lake Street drug bust," said one cop, turning a professionally indifferent face to Kevin. "Okay, hands on the wall."

"Wait a minute! What's the charge?" Kevin had just time to shoot Turner a burning look before the cops took matters—him—into their own hands.

They jolted him up against the wall, spreading his hands, his feet, before he could register their intentions.

"Measures, Doctor," Turner said, vanishing into his office.

The traditional TV cop-show pat-down followed, quick but humiliating, then Kevin's arms were wrested behind his back. Cold steel clipped onto his wrists and cinched tight.

"Hey—you can't just arrest me! What are the charges?"

The policemen roughly pivoted Kevin and pushed him to the door.

"I've got a right to know the charges," he insisted, feeling like an irate citizen. "What are you arresting me for?"

"Probable cause," one cop said tersely.

"Of what?"

148

"Of murder."

That shut Kevin up. The cops nudged him out the door, walked him down the hall, pushed him through the gaping elevator doors. They weren't brutal, but they didn't take it easy, either. With his hands confined behind his back, Kevin was a clumsy piece of goods they maneuvered with pitiless efficiency.

In the elevator, Kevin studied their faces—about his age, professional in their street-hardened way. He might like to sit next to them in a bar, share some beers and bullshit. Talk about life on the streets, about the stresses of being a cop.

Right now, he worried more about the stress of being in the custody of a cop.

Outside, winter air buffeted Kevin in the face with the additional ignominy of being seen. People stared as he was hustled to the curb, their faces blank slates of hostile curiosity. The squad car would have been snow white if so much mud hadn't spattered it. License plates reading "Police" made sure no one would miss it.

The cops jerked Kevin to the rear door, the cuffs grinding into his thin-skinned wristbones. It hurt and he didn't say so, couldn't say so, wouldn't say so, already expecting gratuitous abuse, already knowing that complaint generated only more abuse.

They didn't shove his head down as he was pushed into the back seat, like TV cops—actors with an actor's way of solving a blocking problem—always do. With his hands behind his back, it was tough to bend enough to avoid banging his skull on the doortop. Kevin did, but he knocked his anklebone on the door rim instead.

He huddled in the back seat, a steel grid between him and the cops up front. On the dashboard, a small computer screen ran meaningless statistics. Through the car's side windows, he could watch people bending down and twisting their heads to see him.

"What about my Miranda rights?" Kevin asked suddenly. "You didn't read me my rights!"

He realized then that glass as well as wire separated him from the cops. The glass was smudged, and the inside of

149

the squad car had that hacked-out feeling you get in cabs, like a lot of people you wouldn't care to know had ridden there before you.

Maybe the cops were psychic—or they read lips. They turned in unison over their navy shoulders to gift Kevin with a knowing grin before the driver put the car in gear.

The tires swerved into the mid-street slush, kicking up a spittle of muddy spray against the rear windows. Kevin stared at the passing normal world through a leprosy of filth.

Jane, he thought, isolated in his cell of fear and anger and impotence. If only Jane doesn't have to come to this. Where *is* she?

*　　　　　　*　　　　　　*

"Got a nickel, dearie? Just one nickel for an old lady."

Jane turned from the display window of Dayton's department store. Beyond the chill glass, frozen-faced mannequins posed, draped with an assortment of furs.

"What?" Jane stared down at the squat, bulky figure beside her. It was wrapped in layers of unmatched clothing. A seamed, squirrelish face peered up at Jane from under a tower of overlapping hats. Between them, a mittened palm was poised as if to receive a tray.

"Money, honey. A few coins for an old lady. I haven't eaten since yesterday."

"Neither have I," Jane said, "and I don't have any money."

The old woman reared back. She reminded Jane of Neumeier in some unlikely way, just as shrewd and just as careful.

Her quick eyes took stock of Jane. "No purse," she noted.

Jane spread her empty gloved hands. "No purse."

The old woman's eyes flicked to Jane's pristinely ordinary clothing. "You got money. How're you gonna eat without money?"

"I don't know."

"Oh . . . you are in trouble, dearie. Forget the nickel."

She waddled off down the street, shaking her snarled

head, dragging an overstuffed shopping bag after her like a dog.

Jane shrugged and turned back to the store window. She couldn't think of anyplace else to go, except the hospital. Kevin wouldn't like that, she guessed. Besides, she didn't want to go there.

A burst of excited exclamations down the street made passersby pause and look back. Jane finally did, too. The old woman was returning, her lips pinned back over pointed teeth into a grin.

"Look here, girlie! A fin." She waved a green bill under Jane's chin. "Come on, I'll treat you to lunch on me. You better get street-smart if you're gonna walk around here with no money."

The call of Zyunsinth drew Jane's eyes to the window again. The old woman tugged on Jane's sleeve.

"You shouldn't go around in this cold with nothin' on your head. You could catch pneumonia. Here." She doffed the highest of her hats and stretched to install it on Jane's head.

Jane twisted to see her reflection in the window. An impressive spiral of maroon felt with a winking rhinestone butterfly poised atop her hair.

"It all goes out the top of your head, dearie—the heat. Just blows it off like a tea kettle if you don't wear a hat. Now, come on. My name's Panama Hattie. There'll be a lunch line already, but maybe we can stop off first for a spot of . . ." Panama Hattie smoothed the tattered five-dollar bill in her ragged mittens. "—tea, sweetie, we'll have a small spot of tea."

*　　　　　　　*　　　　　　　*

"You didn't order tea," Jane complained, staring into a murky mahogany liquid in her glass.

"Tea I call it, tea it is, though men be thick about it sometimes and you have to call it blackberry wine to their faces."

Panama Hattie glared at the bartender before leaning back into the booth. Jane heard the woman's heels drum the bench bottom beneath the table. She was so small her feet didn't reach the floor. She raised the wineglass to her lips, sipped, then smacked appreciatively. "Aaaah."

Jane eyed the place, certain that Kevin would not approve. The sign outside had said "The Brass Rail," but there was no rich glint of brass within, only the glimmer of glasses and eye whites in the semidark.

Air crowded close, weaving a tangle of smells—tobacco, vomit, beer, whisky, sweat and mold, and mostly . . . men. The unshaven, red-faced men along the bar stared at Jane. She stared back.

If the street was cold, the Brass Rail was hot in an unhealthy way that made sweat trickle down Jane's overbundled body.

"Drink up! That's a treat there—Jane, you say it is. A rare treat. I don't come by fivers that often. You're my lucky charm. I meet you and, presto!—five in the palm of my hand, and I don't mean fingers. I don't often drink tea in a place like this. We coulda had a whole bottle to ourselves from Skelly's, for the price of these two bitty glasses. But when I'm out with a lady friend, I like to put on the dog."

Hattie stuck her red, runny nose in the air and tilted back the glass. Jane swallowed from her own glass. Sweet, thin fiery liquid surged down her throat. Hattie's fingernails were dirty, she noticed, her hands twisted and horny. Jane suddenly wished she had used the shower at Kevin's place.

"All right, my lady. It's off to lunch. If you're not going to finish that—" Hattie's disreputable hand whipped across the scratched tabletop for Jane's glass. More "tea" gurgled down her wattled throat.

Jane watched, not wanting to contradict the first person to have taken her in hand the way Kevin had. It was nice to be told what to do again, to not have to decide anything. When Panama Hattie wriggled down the bench and dropped to the floor, Jane rose and followed her. Like Kevin, Panama Hattie seemed to know where she was going.

Chapter Nineteen

Kevin must have driven by the Hennepin County Court House a thousand times. Everybody in Minneapolis knew it—a massive, turreted gray granite building that looked like the Bastille.

This time they drove him right up to it, right up to the main Fourth Street door. He couldn't figure out why they had bothered to drive; the trip was only two short city blocks and the cops seemed to take deliberate pleasure in parading him in handcuffs.

Squad cars were double-parked along the whole south side of Fourth Street, empty or idling, all ready to roll. Kevin's cops pulled him roughly from the car. People on the sidewalk stopped to stare.

The cops propelled him in front of his audience to the main doors and through an unheated entry.

Inside, the gray court house stones echoed like a cathedral's, and its vaulted rotunda ceiling glowed reverently with stained glass. A mammoth time-grayed marble statue of a naked, bearded man—Neptune, it looked like, but Kevin knew that it represented the Mississippi River—reclined before a grandiose stairway.

The cops spared Kevin an ascent up the opera house stairs. Instead, they bustled him around the side to a row of up-to-date elevators.

A waifish woman poured into a cheap leather miniskirt—a spindly, feral Lolita in her late thirties, probably a hooker—sprinted down the echoing corridor in high-heeled boots. She obviously knew her way around these intimidating halls. On the street, Kevin wouldn't have glanced at her; here and now, he envied the woman her edge.

They took him to a fourth-floor waiting room painted deep orange. The lettering on the wall read "Adult Detention Center." That didn't sound so bad, Kevin reflected, until you remembered it still meant "jail."

People sat at the rim of the circular space—the passive, disinterested kind of people you find waiting for buses in a seedy part of town.

Beyond a glass partition, beige-uniformed Sheriff's Department personnel hovered over hot computers in a command center.

They allowed Kevin through a door marked "Authorized Personnel Only." The two city cops peeled off and Kevin was suddenly being herded through a drab, efficient entrail of official processing by Sheriff's Department officers.

At every painted metal door, he was jerked to a stop until a buzzer sounded. Then the cop opened the door and pushed him through. Behind them, the door ground shut with a clank of internal locks.

Hand-lettered signs littered the pale yellow walls like Sunday school graffiti. "Jail Intake" in red, with an arrow. "Authorized Personnel Only." Beyond glass barriers, the authorized personnel watched. Kevin glimpsed himself in the glass in passing—a shadow man in a shadow mirror, wavy and distorted.

In one cul-de-sac between two locked doors, Kevin had to spread his hands against the wall and submit to another search. The cop in charge donned see-through plastic gloves before touching him, and ran his fingers through Kevin's hair before checking his torso and limbs—twice and thoroughly. The hand-sweep along his crotch was impersonal but probing. It took all of Kevin's self-discipline to keep from bucking his body away.

"Clean," the examiner noted. "No cuts, no wounds. Guess we can keep him," he added sardonically.

Kevin's escort nodded. "We better. Come on."

Kevin was jerked to the closed door opposite the one they'd entered, then jerked to a stop while the uniformed woman behind the glass hit the lock release. Kevin glanced at her curiously. Her beige sheriff's outfit made her look grandmother-petite, but the black leather holster on her narrow hip looked more than standard size—huge.

Down more fingerprinted halls they went, these lined with castoff church pews—or courtroom benches, Kevin supposed. They passed a neglected water fountain, the stainless steel caked with white mineral deposits. A dry spasm in Kevin's throat resurrected memory of his recent drugging.

"Water?" he asked.

"Later," the cop answered, his eyes indifferent.

In the intake area they finally unlocked the cuffs. Kevin's shoulders sagged into normal alignment, aching in protest, his wrists throbbing.

They made him take off his shoes and wristwatch, and empty his pockets again. The gold watch met the same impassive disinterest. Kevin was beginning to hate the way he had to surrender it—first to Turner, now here.

They showed him around a corner, and in a cinder-block cubicle he peeled off his clothes, as told. A new cop stepped in and conducted a strip search with cold, plastic-gloved hands. By then Kevin had steeled himself for the inevitable, the rough, quick fingers in the open mouth, even the scrupulous passes across his groin and buttocks. Like going to the doctor, he told himself, lying through gritted teeth.

But lower body cavities were excluded from indignity. Kevin gratefully pulled on the shapeless pants and shirt they handed him. The damned things were cut and colored like surgeon's greens. Slipperlike laceless tennis shoes on his feet made him feel an invalid, eased him into a familiar hospital mode, soothed his wildly fluctuating anxiety.

Outside the cubicle, he signed a receipt and watched his clothes dumped into a wire basket atop stained items that smelled of a county hospital detoxification ward.

Kevin last glimpsed his gold watch as a clerk shut it into a manila envelope with his cash and keys.

He began to feel like a kid enrolling for school for the first time. They stood him against a wall and shot his photo with a big Polaroid. They weighed and measured him. They booked him in a glass booth. He filled out a long

155

medical screening admission form, with questions ranging from "Have you ever been in jail before?" to "Do you feel suicidal now?" One no, one maybe.

He wrote his name—last, first and middle—and stared perplexed at the next blank, "DOB," until he translated it. Date of birth. Under the "charges" section, Kevin checked off PC—probable cause. The others were MIS—misdemeanor?—and DOM—domestic? Where it said "Alias" he almost wrote "Judas Goat," but figured that, like the IRS and Mother Nature, official copdom was nothing to fool with.

Some might take heart that the authorities cared enough to inquire into his physical and mental state. Kevin knew better; the form legally absolved them of responsibility if he happened to hang himself with a spaghetti noodle by morning.

Next they slapped his finger and palm prints on the back of the booking sheet, using printer's ink that spurted a strong, chemical odor into his nostrils like smelling salts. They wiped his messy hands afterward with ink remover and handed him a bar of green Lava soap to use in the sink.

Encouraged by these domestic touches, Kevin sized up the cop who still escorted him. "Say, can I use the bathroom?" He couldn't remember his last leak. The drugs had overridden natural functions, but now his bladder was burning from an uncustomary combination of nerves and neglect.

"Later."

"I really gotta go—"

"Later!"

The cop commandeered Kevin's arm, steering him down another dingy hall where two wall phones—one black and one fingerprint-smudged beige—were bolted side by side.

"My . . . call?" Kevin asked.

"Your call," the cop said magnanimously.

Kevin stared at the phones, not knowing who the hell to dial. A sign listed the jail address: "Room 36, Old Courthouse, 300 South 4th St." for those confused enough not to know where they were. "Located in the Old Clock Tower

Building," the lettering added—a Chamber of Commerce touch Kevin figured must be lost on the mislaid souls confronting these phones.

"Just one call?" he wondered.

"One call."

"I don't have a lawyer—"

"Look, call or forget it. I don't care who you call—your mother, the mayor. . . ."

"What . . . charges am I being held under anyway? You haven't even read me my rights."

"No charges, fellah. We have thirty-six hours to hold you before filing formal charges. We got you on probable cause, murder. That's all, right now. And that's enough."

"When . . . can I get out?"

"When we let you out."

"Come on, there's bail. And thirty-six hours . . . Today's Friday, so—"

"Your arithmetic won't cut it in here." The cop kept a poker face. "Today's Friday. The thirteenth."

Kevin blinked at the impersonal triumph in the man's voice. Maybe he was really a nice guy off duty; maybe it was just his job to make everybody feel scared and guilty and like scum. It worked.

"Day of arrest doesn't count," the cop added.

"So . . . midnight Friday to Saturday. I should be out noon Sunday."

"'Cept Saturday don't count."

Kevin was beginning to get the message carved in the stone face before him. "And Sunday?—"

"Don't count."

"My thirty-six hours don't begin until midnight *Sunday*?"

"Not exactly." The cop smiled this time. A little. "You had the bad luck to get picked up on a holiday weekend—"

Kevin saw it coming and resented it. "Holiday! What the hell—this is January! There's no national holiday in January!"

The cop shook his head. "How soon they forget." He was enjoying this. "Martin. Luther. King's. Birthday. January

157

fifteenth. This is Friday, January thirteenth. The holiday falls on a Sunday and gets moved to a Monday—" He shrugged.

"So the soonest I can get out—?"

"Noon Wednesday . . . maybe. *If* you make bail. If I was you, I'd make some kind of call, buddy. Come on, I can't wait all day. You're not askin' for a date."

Kevin picked up the phone.

*   *   *

"Hiya, Boomer."

Panama Hattie beamed into a wrinkled old face blessed with a white stubble of beard and a nose as bulbous and empurpled as a turnip.

"Yer late. They're gonna run out."

"Nah." Hattie cast an expert glance at the line fringing the side of the blond brick building. Jane had read a large sign up front that said "House of Charity." "They always save some for me."

Boomer's rheumy eyes slid to Jane. "Who's the social worker?"

"Hell, this ain't no social worker. This here's Jane. She's a street baby. Orphan-like. I took her under my wing."

Boomer eyed the hat atop Jane's head, and nodded. "I hear the Salvation Army's full up nights now."

"Where you been crashin', then?" Hattie asked anxiously.

Boomer jerked a shoulder behind him. "By the tracks."

"Don't the cops come by and roust you?"

"Sometimes, but it's so cold nights nowadays, they don't bother us much. I got together a real nice place there. Can't you go to the women's shelter tonight?"

"They're full, too. And this one makes it two. . . ."

"Hattie, you know you kin always hang your hats at my place. Not a lotta room for an extra, though—"

Hattie's torn mitten rested on Jane's shoulder. "She's a nice girl, real quiet. She don't belong on the streets. Somebody gotta look out for her."

"Somebody oughta look out for you—nearly lost a few toes last winter, sleepin' out. My place is better, though."

"Thanks, Boomer."

The line shuffled forward. Jane looked around. It wasn't much different from the bank—people mindlessly waiting for some mysterious transaction to occur somewhere at the front of the line far away.

This line waited in the raw wind and endless cold, though. Jane stamped her boots, feeling numbness stealing over her toes again.

"Keep hoppin', dearie. It's the only way. We'll be inside and nice and warm soon enough."

Hattie's prediction was nine-tenths optimism and one-tenth truth. Jane's infallible internal clock told her it took exactly forty-eight minutes and sixteen seconds and twelve milliseconds before the glass door finally swung open to admit her and Hattie and the old man known as Boomer.

Inside, the room was crowded and the line remained, eeling its way to a far steam table. The congestion stewed the rich human scents that the outside cold had masked into a heady brew of sweat, dirt, urine and old vomit. The smell had sent more than one do-gooder directly out the door of the House of Charity.

Not Jane. The overwhelming closeness touched deep memories of huddling together with a circle of hairy humanoid bodies, with smell so thick it had a heft to it, with warmth and . . . safety. Safety from the dark and cold of night and the distant icy silver sun that she had last felt among the creatures she remembered—just barely—as Zyunsinth.

Memory flashed cue cards in front of her eyes—shards of scenes Kevin would have given his last hundred-dollar bill to have tapped. The drift of simmering stew merged in Jane's flaring nostrils with a familiar, untended animal smell. For the first time since she had awakened without a memory and with only Kevin to guide her, Jane felt at home.

Shuffling past the steam table, Jane accepted the brown mess ladled into her bowl and shoved her tray on down the stainless steel track, Hattie behind her clucking encouragement.

"Not much meat, but the gravy's good. Take some bread.

Plenty of bread. Keep you warm. Oh, thank you so much, Mrs. Mendez. . . ." Hattie squirreled the Sunkist orange meant for her alone into a layer of her garb, then winked at Jane. "They treat regular customers right here, Janey!"

Shoulder to shoulder, Jane sat with the ragged and the old and the feebleminded at one long table among many. Here for once she didn't have to premeditate her table manners, or debate which implement accompanied which food item.

The people all around her ate as they felt like, fingers swiping pieces of bread through gravy or sweeping escaping tidbits onto forks. Jane began to see why Kevin and the other doctors at Probe had marveled over the perfection of her unfilled teeth; people here seemed mostly toothless, but they smiled at each other anyway.

"Ahhh." Panama Hattie pushed her tray away and intertwined her fingers on the tabletop. "It's only midday, and I don't feel like walking that cold street again so soon, no sir, I surely don't. Maybe we can figger a way to stay a spell—how about we see if the Painting Lady wants a new face to look at?"

Jane, appreciating her full stomach, nodded. Hattie ushered her over to a corner of the crowded room. A woman in a bright red smock, her dark hair tied with a green bow at the base of her neck, sat at an easel flecking color onto a canvas.

Jane stared, entranced. The bits of color resolved into a face, a portrait like Lynn Volker's—only much more interesting. Jane's eyes narrowed as the impressionistic image coalesced in her vision.

It was a young man the woman painted—there were very few young people at the House of Charity; he must have been—with Jane—one of the youngest. He wore a funny plaid scarf and a too-big wool jacket. Jane tilted her head, studying the painting over the woman's scarlet shoulder. He had brown hair, the man, and a beard and blue eyes. And he was handsome, Jane perceived that quality in its essence for the first time. For an instant she had thought he might be Kevin, but he was much hand-

160

somer than Kevin, with a distance and sadness in his eyes that made Jane frown in wonder.

"Don't she do a good job, the Painting Lady? She's done me, you know," Hattie crowed, "and she's makin' a real masterpiece of Gentleman Jimmy."

Jane glanced where Hattie's head had nodded. A man sat on a battered old church pew in the exact pose as the man in the portrait. Jane found herself looking into the same beautiful sad eyes that the Painting Lady had erected on canvas. Then Gentleman Jimmy smiled, revealing a mouthful of gaping, crooked teeth.

Jane jerked her eyes back to the painting. It had not smiled as she had expected.

"Oh, don't Jimmy look handsome—can you do the same for Janey here? My friend Jane? She's just new, you know."

The woman glanced over her cheery shoulder. Jane liked her face—handsome and strong, lined in all the right places, and her smile showed lots of teeth. Little gold-and-diamond earrings twinkled in her ears and a big gold-and-diamond ring sparkled on the left hand that held the palette.

"New, I guess!" the woman said, looking Jane over carefully. Her expression softened. "I'd like to paint her, Hattie, but . . . she hasn't got the face I'm after. She hasn't *lived* enough, if you know what I mean. She doesn't even look like she belongs here."

Hattie was silent a moment. "Maybe none of us looked like we belonged here once, Mrs. Myerson. Maybe you might want to paint a 'before' instead of an 'after.'"

"Hattie, I'm sorry." Distress etched the woman's eyes. "I don't mean to exploit you and your friends, really. All *my* friends think I'm crazy to come down here—but I've never been happier than when I'm finding my 'faces.' Sit down on the pew, dear, next to Jimmy." She nodded Jane over to the bench. "I haven't time to do a full portrait, but I'll manage a charcoal sketch, how's that?"

"Oh, a sketch . . . that's very artistic, Janey," Hattie cooed.

"Yes. . . ." The woman picked up a large white tablet and a dark pencil and began dashing lines onto the drawing paper. "Several of my paintings are going on display in the Senior Citizens' Center window this afternoon—that's why I was rushing to finish up Jimmy. Maybe, if your sketch turns out good enough, it'll be in the show, too. I'll call it *Girl in a Hand-me-down Hat.*"

Jane smiled tentatively.

"My, what gorgeous teeth you have—Hattie's right, you *are* new to the streets. But you don't have to smile for the sketch—most of my subjects don't smile."

"I want to," said Jane, remembering Lynn Volker's photograph. "I want to smile."

The Painting Lady shrugged her gaudy shoulders and made the pencil rasp across the pebbled paper.

"It's your face . . . Jane, is it? And it's pretty interesting, after all. You look like you lost something and you haven't discovered what it is yet."

"Ain't she a marvel?" Hattie set her shopping bag down and scraped a folding chair across the floor so she could sit and watch the sketch take form.

"Oh, Hattie—!" The woman laughed, an assured, tinkling sound like diamonds looked, Jane thought. "I just do my paintings, that's all."

The sketch was finished within an hour. Jane came to stand politely behind Mrs. Myerson's shoulder and approve it. But she was disappointed. It wasn't in color like Gentleman Jimmy's, and Jane thought the hat looked a little silly. And her smile, although it was wide and showed tooth after perfect tooth, didn't match the sunny confidence that had stretched Lynn Volker's lips in the photograph on her parents' walls.

She and Hattie watched the artist pack up her works and hurry out with a good-bye wave.

"It smells here, I guess," Hattie ruminated after she'd gone. "She didn't say so, being polite, but her friends think she's crazy to come here. I guess because we smell bad. I don't notice it no more, but I guess we do."

"You do," Jane said. "It does smell. And some of it's

nice, and some of it's not so nice. But all of it's . . ." Jane frowned, looking as if she'd lost something and she didn't know what yet. "—it's . . . real. I feel like I've been here before."

Jane gazed around the simple, thronging, reeking place and smiled happily. "Zyunsinth," Jane greeted the heedless mob. "Zyunsinth."

Hattie grinned back at her. "It's not so bad, is it, dearie? You get used to it. And it's better than being cooped up somewhere official-like."

Chapter Twenty

The cop stopped Kevin at another big metal door.

"Emergency buttons ring the perimeter, but don't hit one unless you're damn sure you really need to."

"My . . . cell—?" he began.

Then the door swung open with that angry, grating sound and Kevin was shoved through.

Cell, hell. . . . Plenty of hell.

Kevin met the slow gathering stares of eight pair of eyes—bloodshot eyes in yellowed whites and Sanka-dark faces. Unfocused eyes; nervous, flickering eyes in broken pasty white faces. Yet . . . dead eyes, every last pair of them.

Kevin moved into their midst, sensing that clinging to the door's metal safety would only incite his . . . cellmates.

The term was new; the turf alien. But he was there and had better make the best of it. If not, they'd see he got the worst of it.

"Look what they threw us now."

He didn't even try to identify the speaker, instead easing over to one of the brown-painted metal tables bolted to the floor. The seats were attached to the table's central post, so there was no chance of hefting one to brain a fellow inmate.

Kevin knew he walked wrong, talked wrong, carried himself wrong. He was the wrong race, the wrong class, the wrong everything. Innocent. Now he knew what the word really meant.

Both tables were empty, but he sat in a chair, claiming a place among them. He didn't dare choose one of the matching brown metal bunk beds yet. Men lay in some; others were unoccupied. He'd claim his narrow slab of space later, after his predecessors had revealed their choices.

A prisoner shuffled over the concrete floor in his cotton slippers to give Kevin a contemptuous once-over.

"What you doin' in here—skinny little white boy with a fifteen-dollah haircut?"

Kevin wasn't short and he wasn't skinny and his haircuts cost twenty dollars.

"Yeah, what'd they get you on, DWI?" another man demanded.

They were all moving now, toward him, slow as sharks; cruising behind him, circling, smelling new blood in old waters.

Three other white guys shared the cell. One slumped on an upper bunk it must have been a sight to see him scale—an overweight hacked-out man on the wrong end of his fifties. He watched Kevin with apologetic, terrified eyes.

"Is that who they put in here, DWIs?" Kevin asked.

A stocky Hispanic man muscled like Arnold Schwarzenegger smirked. "Only if they ain't got room. This is a high-security cell, man. You musta skipped school or somethin'. You don't belong in here."

"Does *he*?" Kevin indicated the middle-class fat man on the bunk. Better him than Kevin.

They all turned on cue to eye the other guy. "Nah. Harry's a DWI wimp, ain't that right, insurance sales- man?" one taunted. "But he dances real good to the right music." Sweat trickled down Harry's cheek.

"What're you, white boy?" another black guy asked. If

164

the prisoners didn't come big, Kevin concluded, they came mean.

Kevin shrugged. "Nothin' much."

"Don't put yourself down, my man." The biggest black guy sat on the lip of Kevin's table, his massive long thigh muscles bulging out even the loose jailhouse pants. "You're in here with us. You must be one bad dude. What'cha in for?"

"Murder," Kevin tried. Maybe the rap would intimidate them.

"Murder."

A big black hand crimped into the wimpy cotton of his shirtfront. Kevin felt impending physical force as he had not felt it for years, not since being a little kid and some irate adult had hovered to give him a smack. Even the cops' rough custody seemed benign by contrast. Thunder hovered in the cell's arid atmosphere, in the black man's basso rumble. "Maybe we don't want to sleep with no murderer around."

"Hey . . . it's only PC." Kevin tried to sound inured to Probable Causes and Misdemeanors and Domestics.

The fingers uncurled as the man straightened and ambled to the other table, still eyeing Kevin. On the farthest bunk against the wall, Kevin noticed a figure rocking. The man was ageless, shapeless, classless. His features twisted into the thin-lipped grin and the slant-eyed grimace of the mental defective.

"What's he doing in here, if this is a high-risk cell?" Kevin had to ask under the prod of professional concern. "Guy like that shouldn't even be on the street."

"Right on." The big black guy turned slow as Leviathan to study the isolated figure. "Old Waldo's looney-tunes. But the nuthouses are crowded, just like the jails. That's why we's all packed in here like sardines, even skinny little new fish like you."

Kevin ignored the taunt and rose, moving to an archway. Beyond it stretched a cinder-block maze of shower cubicles, sinks, a toilet and urinal. Graffiti even decorated these inside walls, though what the inmates used to write with Kevin couldn't guess.

165

He hated to do it—back to them, pecker to the hilt in porcelain—but he needed to piss so bad it was going to come out his ears if he didn't. He stationed himself so he could glimpse the archway in the meager slice of polished metal mirror over the sink and studied the obscenities interlarded with phone numbers defacing the faceless wall.

"That must be some big thing, white boy, you gotta take that long to piss."

"Fuck off," Kevin threw over his shoulder. His body tensed for a physical attack even as his mind forced himself to relax and flaunt the awesome hiss of his long-dammed urine. But no attack came. He rejoined the others in the main room without incident or further comment. More men sprawled on the bunks now that the mild excitement of a new arrival had faded. They still watched every move he made.

Old Waldo huddled in his corner, chewing his loose lower lip, a tear of drool caught in the corner of his wide, foolish mouth.

Harry the drunk looked soberer than a man should have to, and watched Kevin relentlessly. Kevin could read his mind. Maybe they'll pick on *you* instead, Harry was thinking, hoping—and sober enough now to loathe himself for it.

Harry was stuck, Kevin realized, just like he was, stuck in jail for the long, holiday weekend. Martin Luther King's birthday. The ironies boggled even a psychiatrist's mind.

Kevin boosted himself atop the far bunk above Waldo; he figured no one would claim that spot. He was right.

Kevin lay back, slowly, arms behind his head so he could lift his elbows and conceal his expression while still checking the others out.

There was nothing in the room to watch except a television high on the wall opposite. A rerun of *Gomer Pyle* droned into their midst; Kevin's ears finally registered the incredible reality of it. The laugh track tittered on cue. Kevin's stomach tried to give hunger a stab, then hit a solid wall of drug hangover and gave up.

Nordstrom had given Kevin something, no doubt about

that; what had Kevin given Nordstrom? He lay on the brown wool blanket and let his mind unwind, pushing away all worries of his arrest—such as what murder he was charged with, and what if they could make it stick?

The important thing was, what had he told Nordstrom that could help the PID catch Jane? He let his consciousness sink into self-hypnosis, inducing calm. It could be dangerous to make a sitting duck of himself in a place like this, but Jane might be in a tighter place, he told himself.

Foggy memories steamed up from the rock bottom of his subconscious. He had an impression of Nordstrom asking, always asking, prying. Nordstrom wanting to know. About Jane . . . about Julie. Kevin shuddered involuntarily as a memory took shape on his mental TV screen—him and Julie making love on the Symonses' wine leather Chesterfield library sofa. Shit! Talk about unremembered reruns . . . he hadn't thought about that, about making love with Julie at all, for years. Nordstrom, sick bastard, must have used his opportunity to feed his own delusions.

Kevin's guts recoiled at imagining the details the psychiatrist must have gleaned in those stolen hours of uninterrupted mind-fucking. Still . . . maybe Nordstrom's obsession had its uses. Better that Julie, long dead, should be sacrificed now than Jane. Jane still had her integrity, her blossoming personality intact. None of the foggy memories Kevin resurrected from his interrogation seemed to focus on Jane.

His relief drove so deep that he must have violated every instinct of self-preservation and let his long-delayed sleep take him.

A determined rattling woke him—Kevin lay disoriented, wide eyes staring at a plain white ceiling. Below him, the men lined up at a stainless steel cart to take food trays.

Kevin jumped off the bunk and cast a look at Waldo, still playing with his face in the corner—the man looked like every pathetic case Kevin had treated at State all those years ago. Inside, Kevin raged at the system that released such people to the untender mercies of life on the street. When he got out of here, he vowed, he'd look into it. For now, there was nothing he could do but slide into an empty spot at the table next to Harry.

Jail food tasted okay if you liked recycled library paste, Kevin found; the company was less appetizing. But it didn't matter, he was too hungry to abstain. Kevin joined the others in shoveling the stuff into their mouths with baby-blunt spoons.

"What—what *is* your line?" Harry, the insurance salesman, asked under his breath between bites.

"I'm kinda a . . . salesman, too," Kevin answered evasively.

"Who are you supposed to have murdered? Wife? Girlfriend?"

Kevin heard a weary laugh—his own. "They haven't said yet. Cops, I guess. Maybe feds."

"One tough dude," the black across the table mouthed, meatloaf flecking his big white teeth.

Kevin remained silent, knowing nothing had been settled yet. Maybe he had a lot more to worry about—Nordstrom's incursions, Jane, whatever charges he faced. Right now, he worried most about making it through the night.

*   *   *

Twilight made the semaphores on downtown Minneapolis streets twinkle red and green like leftover Christmas tree lights.

People gathered on corners, coins clutched in mittens and gloves, to take packed buses home.

Jane, Hattie and Boomer straggled down the emptying streets, letting the buses roar by.

"How far is it, Boomer?" Hattie would holler every half block, stopping to puff and lean against a storefront. "It's these bum pins, dearie," she'd complain to Jane. "Old Jack Frost nipped 'em last winter. Get's so I can't feel where I'm walkin'—"

Jane considered her own feet. They felt fine, but that was because Kevin had bought her nice new boots in Crow Wing—and because whenever she felt the numbness over-

168

taking her toes, she . . . sent . . . her blood rushing back into them.

"Jest a few more blocks. Come on, girls. I gotta treat." Boomer flourished his brown paper bag.

Hattie pushed herself off the brick wall. "Gotta stay someplace. 'Sides, you're seein' the toney side of town, Jane. You ever been in Butler Square?"

Jane looked up at the big brick building and shook her head.

"This all used to be old warehouses. Then the rich folks turned it into shopping centers, and that's why we have to hoof it so far to find a spot to call our own."

Boomer was waiting for them to catch up. Cold had reddened his empurpled nose, painting it to match the sunset that was spilling over the horizon of treetops ahead of them.

"What d'you think of our town?" Boomer, never having seen Jane before, just assumed she was from someplace else.

"It's . . . big."

"Where you come from, sister?"

Jane seemed perplexed. "From a cell."

"Oh. You been in stir. That's bad. A young thing like you. 'Course, I get arrested every now and then." Boomer's head shook, making his flap-eared storm cap look like it was attempting to fly. "Warm there, though. They make you take showers and eat lots of hot food. Not a bad place, I guess, once you're used to it. My place is better, though."

"Am I?" Jane asked, trotting after Boomer with curiosity.

"Are you what?"

"Your sister?"

"Sister? Noooo. That's jest what I call all the ladies. Had a sister. Had four of 'em. Bitches, every last goddamn one. Glad to never see 'em no more. Years it's been. 'Course, maybe, they're jest as glad not to see me." He dug an elbow into Jane's side.

She stepped farther away and persisted. "I had a . . . sister once. Maybe. I never met her, though."

169

"Busted family, huh?" Hattie had caught up and pulled on Boomer's arm, stopping him. "Boomer, give us a sip. It's damn cold."

"Won't be cold at my place," he boasted, pulling his brown paper bag closer. "You're taking liberties, Hattie."

"I put a buck in for that bottle!"

"Cost three," Boomer taunted, turning and stomping away on oversized boots.

Hattie hurried after, but Jane paused to look back.

The tall downtown buildings were aglow, their glass walls reflecting the lurid red-orange sunset. The wind made Jane's eyes water—or something did. She thought of Kevin and the bank building lobby they had stood in together only hours earlier . . . twenty-eight hours and thirty-seven minutes and three seconds and one millisecond earlier.

Time, she realized, was strange, because it didn't feel like that long ago. It felt like she and Kevin had been together only instants before, as if he would come around the corner and say, "Jane, what are you doing way over here by yourself? Come on"—and she would say, "I'm not by myself, Kevin, I'm with Boomer and Hattie, and Boomer's my brother only he doesn't like sisters and Hattie's so nice, just like Mrs. Bellingham at the dorm, and I was in a place that felt like Zyunsinth—you know, Kevin, Zyunsinth, the place I was that I forgot, only I remembered it for just a moment, and it was nice there—close and warm and not, not lonely. . . ."

Jane stood and stared at the alien city, in the descending dark, in the cold and the wind. She ripped off her gloves and wiped the water from her eyes to see the skyline better, to see it clearer—hard-edged and distant.

"Janey," Hattie called from behind, as if the old woman knew her, had always been calling her name.

"Come on, sister, get movin'; gotta keep movin'," Boomer shouted. Jane got moving.

Chapter Twenty-one

They came for Kevin after dinner sometime, he couldn't tell exactly when. They had his watch.

"Come on, Blake," they said, and he went. Happily.

The last thing he noticed in the cell was Harry's pale eyes turning lighter in panic. It amused Kevin, bitterly, that his presence there could seem protection to anyone.

"Where are you taking me?" Kevin asked as politely— or maybe just as neutrally—as he could manage. It was their world; treat them rudely and you would get it back in spades.

"Questioning," one cop gruffed back.

In another anonymous cinder-block hall painted some pastel shade so bland it melted from the memory instantly, the cops deposited Kevin outside a door inset with window glass, one of many lining the hall.

One cop opened the door and escorted Kevin into an official interrogation room—or half of one. What began as a small square room had lost ground where a sharp angle of intersecting hall wall cut across one whole corner.

Beyond the stark table and plastic molded chairs, the walls arrowed toward a vanishing point, stopped by an end wall maybe eight inches wide. The trapezoidal shape lent the room a skewed perspective. Kevin felt like a swollen Alice in Wonderland crammed into a room grown far too small.

Was the room's claustrophobic shape intended, he wondered, to increase the prisoner's anxiety? Or was it just a fact of overcrowded life in the Big City Jail, where corners were quite literally cut? Or was he all too easily turning paranoid? When the cop nudged his shoulder, he sat at the table, back to the door. A pair of metal ashtrays overflowing with cigarette butts kept formal company along the wall, like salt and pepper shakers in a perverse cafe.

The door opened. Kevin forced himself to stare into the vanishing angle of the room. At last a face—homely, world-weary and familiar—lowered itself into the opposite chair.

"Detective . . . Smith, isn't it?"

"Dr. Blake, I presume." Smith's leaden features flickered a smile. He pulled a crushed cigarette pack from his coat pocket and offered Kevin one.

Kevin automatically glanced at the full ashtrays before shaking his head.

"I know." Smith rasped his battered Zippo to life against the dark end of his Camel filtertip. "You warned me once to stop smoking. I guess I warned you then, too."

"Yeah, you did."

"So." Smith regarded Kevin closely. "Greens become you, Doctor. Beard gone. Look like a surgeon. You don't look like the scum in here, that's for sure."

"I *am* the scum in here."

"Who would have thought it?"

"You, for one," Kevin returned. "I don't think you buy anybody at face value. Must be a professional failing."

Smith inhaled so long on his cigarette that Kevin thought he was going to swallow it. The detective spit out smoke, coughed delicately and opened a manila folder.

"Anyone read you your rights?"

"No, and isn't that illegal? I've been in custody since morning—"

"Nobody has to read your rights unless we interrogate you. Anybody interrogate you yet?"

"No. . . ."

Smith sighed. "You have the right to remain silent. If you give up the right to remain silent, you have the right to have an attorney present . . ." On he went, reciting the formula with bored familiarity.

"You got a lawyer?" he asked when he'd finished.

"No."

"Who'd you call?"

"A friend."

"And . . . ?"

"I don't know. He's looking into it."

"Call anybody else?"

"They only let me have one call."

Smith's eyes rolled. "They really have it in for you, don't they? You're gonna have a tough time in here."

"What do you mean? One call's all that's allowed, isn't it?"

"TV stuff." Smith waved the smoke away from his face toward Kevin's. "You get up to three, at the officer's discretion, of course."

"Apparently I didn't get the benefit of any discretion," Kevin said bleakly. "So I *could* have called a lawyer—"

"Lawyer won't help you." Smith crushed his already smoked fag into the piled ashtray. A stink of smoldering filters wafted into Kevin's nostrils. "You're in for the duration. Damn unlucky to have hit a holiday weekend. You don't have to talk to me, of course."

"Maybe I won't."

Smith's eyes narrowed. He leaned across the table. "You know, I'm not surprised to see you here, Doctor. I knew something weird was going on at the University Hospitals, with that cop from Crow Wing jumping out the window and that patient of yours, that girl he found, all curled up in her bed comatose, you said."

"Is that what I was arrested for—Kellehay's death?"

"Maybe. Maybe Matusek's, too—"

"Come on! That was up in Crow Wing. I wasn't even there!"

"And a couple of detectives are coming down from Duluth after the holiday. Those two . . . deer hunters . . . that died in a questionable car crash—you were in the vicinity then. They want to question you. Also, an old lady—an ex-professor of yours named Neumeier—"

"Neumeier! Jesus Christ, what else are they going to hang me for—Jimmy Hoffa?"

"Don't kid, son. North woods would've made a nice place to bury him."

"Look, Smith, I'm not even talking to you. No lawyer, no talk. All right? You've got me here for five days anyway."

173

"Okay. This is off the record." Kevin eyed the manila folder suspiciously. Smith cracked it open. "Window dressing, Doctor. I guess you know a little about that." The folder was empty. Smith watched Kevin register that and smiled. "I guess you know a little about shaving regulations, too. One-man band at that Probe unit, weren't you? Only you finally got ahold of something too hot to handle. Her."

Kevin kept silent.

Smith shook out another cigarette, lit it, sat back. "See, I never bought that she was what you said she was. I never figured she was . . . normal. It never added up that someone as smart as you would dance so hard to protect someone who didn't really need it.

"So now they've got you on warrants for probable cause in maybe . . . three, four unexplained deaths. *You* kill someone? Tell me to clap for Tinkerbell, and I'll believe that first. No, not you. Her."

Kevin's muscles tensed from the top of his scalp on down.

"Never forget the first time I saw her," Smith mused over wisps of cigarette smoke, "lying in that white hospital bed looking like something from someplace they liberated in Germany after the war. Thin, her hair more butchered than cut. Asleep, you said. No, Doctor, she wasn't asleep that night; she was faking it, faking it good. You know that as well as I do."

Kevin looked away, to the butt-glutted ashtrays.

"So some people are dead now. You're here. And she's scot-free. Look, if she isn't responsible for her acts—if you can get somebody a little less involved than you to testify to that—the courts can't hurt her. You're a different matter."

"Why the hell do you care?" Kevin blazed.

"I do my job, just like you thought you were doing yours. I want to solve Kellehay's murder. And I smell a frame. 'The feds found you.' Hell, do you know the last time the feds went out of their way to help the locals on a bust? Oh, sure, everything's cosy-rosy on the drug stuff lately, but on anything else, it's the same old cold shoulder."

"You warned me," Kevin interjected, fearing that Smith was ruminating too close to the bone now. The detective went on talking.

"So I wondered, why would the feds put you on ice on a bunch of PCs that any semismart lawyer could crack you out of in no time? Pressure? Sure. Get you out of the way, even surer. I want whoever killed Kellehay. That's my case, my jurisdiction. I don't give a flying crap about Matusek or the two gentlemen outside Duluth—"

"Government men," Kevin put in.

Smith smiled. "That's mighty fine gold-leaf they're wrapping around your frame. The records show the men were just average citizens. Tourists, you might say—"

"Nothing will stop me from protecting my patient," Kevin interrupted.

"What d'you think you are—a priest? Maybe . . . and I just say maybe . . . God's on their side, but nobody's on yours, Doctor. Nobody. Not even your Jane Doe. You think she needs you. What about you needing her? Where is she? If she's so tough cops jump out of windows to get away from her, why doesn't she help you now?"

"She's helpless," Kevin ground out between his teeth, pushed against the wall of his own guilt for having failed Jane. "Damn it, don't you see? She's helpless!"

Smith dropped his cigarette to the concrete floor and ground it out under his size-twelve shoe. He gave Kevin a look more resigned than angry.

"No, Doctor. You don't see. Jane Doe's not helpless at all. Never was. You are."

*   *   *

"Here we are, snug as the three Billy Goats Gruff."

Boomer grandly indicated an overturned dumpster under the Northern Pacific Railway bridge.

"You're an old goat, all right," Panama Hattie grumbled good-naturedly, setting down her overloaded shopping bag.

In the deep twilight, the downtown Minneapolis skyline lurked black against fading burnt-peach clouds. Jane

175

turned to the west, where the trees laid bare their midnight veins against the sunset. The snow all around gleamed faintly pink, and railroad tracks thick as ganglia bristled through the deserted river flats.

Boomer's "home" was the abandoned dumpster he'd managed to jam under the root of the railroad bridge. On its side it made a three-walled lean-to. Old blankets fluttered at its open mouth.

"It's warmer than they got." Boomer waved at the shadowy figures crouched elsewhere on the inhospitable snowfields around sparks of fire.

"And what keeps 'em out of it?" Hattie wanted to know.

"A pickax blade I found." Boomer wheezed rather than laughed. "And they know I found this dumpster, hell, some of 'em helped me drag it over here. They know it's mine. Rule of the road. I let whoever there's room for come in, 'course. Never entertained two ladies before, though."

"Better be warmer," Hattie warned, dragging her bag into the dumpster's lee, "or we won't be ladies."

"It will be." Boomer hoisted his brown paper bag by way of a promise.

"Come on," Hattie told Jane. "Get in before your tail freezes."

Jane started to move, then stopped. "I don't have a tail."

"You will if you don't get in here."

Jane shrugged and joined them inside, sitting cross-legged beside Hattie while Boomer stretched up to pull down the tattered blankets.

Before he shut out the last of the light, he lit a match to a pile of sticks and newspapers piled in a cast-iron skillet at their feet. The fire crackled into life, dancing in the convex mirrors of their eyes.

"Keep-fire," Jane said suddenly, kneeling to extend her bare hands over it.

"Sure, I keep it going," Boomer said. "Long as I can scrounge somethin' that'll burn."

"Stay away from my bag," Hattie warned.

She doffed her two upper hats, leaving only a dingy, sequined turban on her head. She was busy emptying the

176

varied contents of her bag, producing a white mug announcing that "Living Well Is the Best Revenge" and a chipped china cup. These she lovingly wiped on her sagging sweater pocket and offered to Boomer.

In moments he had filled them with a clear stream from the lip of his brown paper bag. While Hattie passed the dainty cup to Jane, Boomer swigged directly from the bag.

"Nothin's warmer than South Dakota Everclear, Janey. A hundred and fifty proof. Even ole Jack Frost warms up to South Dakota Everclear." Boomer's lips smacked appreciatively.

"Right good stuff," Hattie agreed, allowing her seamed face to split even further into a smile.

"Kevin gave me something like this to drink once," Jane said.

"Only *once*? A babe in arms jest like you said, Hattie."

"Who's Kevin, honey? Your boyfriend?"

"Oh, yes. . . ." Jane liked the idea. All the girls at Willhelm Hall had boyfriends—or wished they did. Jane sipped again from the burning clear liquid, feeling the flames lick warmly at the edges of her chilled body.

"Where is he? How come he lets you wander around alone without any money? Bad things happen to girls who do that. Some boyfriend."

"No, Hattie. He was with me, then—" The fire's rhythmic leap hypnotized Jane. Her eyelids fluttered. "I think the, the police came for him."

Boomer snorted. "Lucky him. Warmer in jail."

"Jail?" Jane asked.

"County jail, little lady. That big mean-lookin' gray building with all the towers over and back from House of Charity. If you want to visit your boyfriend, we'll show you where tomorrow."

"I could see Kevin?"

"If he's in jail, sure."

"Tomorrow?"

"Sure."

Jane thought. "Tonight?"

"Naw, not tonight. Even jail closes down at night.

177

Tomorrow. Say, this is good stuff. Want some more, Hattie?"

While Boomer refilled Hattie's mug, Jane crept to the blanketed opening and lifted a corner. Dark had claimed even the whiteness of the snow; it reflected nothing now but the night.

Jane stared up. Looming in the east against a sky nearly as dark hung the basalt towers; one must be the county jail. Tomorrow.

Above her, snagged like one of the sequins in Hattie's turban, a full moon shone down on the bottomless black of the earth below. Jane had never noticed a full moon before. It broadcast the bright, chill light of something that she *had* seen before.

"The silver sun . . ." she whispered. "Zyunsinth."

A scene flashed into her memory, complete and yet more remote than a photograph in a history book. Jane remembered the cold world where the well-haired creatures she knew as Zyunsinth fed their keep-fires and stared up at the silver sun, toward the basalt towers.

She remembered, her impressions colliding and falling into place like something that had broken and then defied nature to reassemble itself.

She saw it as she had seen the University of Minnesota campus all the previous fall, the Volkers' house in Crookston a few days before, the Upper Midwest Savings & Loan building only yesterday.

Jane's naked fingers clutched the chill blanket, her mind pasting image after recalled image into its rapidly turning pages, her thoughts leaping ahead to blanks where only raw possibility waited. Kevin, she thought, would want to know, would be so glad to know that she finally was remembering events that had happened in real time—

"Shut that drape, Janey! We're freezin'."

"Oh. I'm sorry. I was thinking."

"Think in here where it's warm. Ain't it cozy? Boomer's right, he's got a real nice place here."

Jane let Hattie pull her back into place between the two of them. She liked the pungent warmth of this metal cave,

178

the crude familiarity of Boomer and Hattie's faces, the acrid scent of tongues of flame licking away all the afternoon's overbearing odors. . . .

Hattie and Boomer were swaying a little around the fire, their eyes glistening happily.

"A-way in a man-ger no crib for His bed—" Boomer began singing.

"The lit-tle Lord Je-sus lay down His sweet head," Hattie joined in.

Jane stared, then smiled and swayed with them, shoulder to shoulder.

A buzzing was beginning in her ears. It had started when she drank Boomer's South Dakota Everclear. It had intensified in the cold night air when Zyunsinth had flowered in her brain—Zyunsinth as it had been, probably still was and likely would be.

Now the hum enveloped her, as if memories were congregating in her body, were milling through her arterial and nervous systems, swarming in her brain cells, looking for a home.

The voices came again—partly the strange recalled sounds of the Zyunsinth around their keep-fires, partly words from her recent, easily remembered past as Jane Doe here, partly the disembodied voices of those others that she sometimes heard sliding in and out of focus in the space behind her eyes.

*   *   *

"The lynx return. We are almost able to locate the probe."

"The lynx were lost. Broken. Disconnected."

"They mend."

"Not through our manipulation."

"No, through spontaneous regeneration."

"The probe repairs itself?"

"The probe betrays itself. It replays data that we hold. Data call to data. And probe to probe."

"The voyager cell has emerged."

"And merged. We speak as One."

"And say—?"

"We must retract this errant probe. We must recall it."

"It no longer answers our cell summons. Even with the lynx reweaving, it remains uncontrollable."

"There is one summons it cannot resist, one source it cannot refuse."

"The mother-cell means nothing to this creation of another species."

"There is a mother-cell within it. There is that it cannot resist, especially since it has taken control into its own hands."

"What is this invisible leash we hold—a tracer gene? A dormant molecule of DNA? What does this renegade probe have that would be strong enough to betray it now that it has gone beyond us?"

"Itself."

*   *   *

Jane blinked. The lynx . . . no, the *links*! She was beginning to feel the *links* reforging in her body—to understand who, and how . . .

Before her eyes, so little time had passed that Boomer was still leaning, laughing, singing across the fire.

"It's past Christmas," Hattie put in.

"Still a good song," Boomer answered, resuming. *"The little Lord Je-sus a-sleep in the hay—"*

Boomer leaned farther over the flames, his brown bag tilted into the white mouth of Hattie's cup that announced "the Best Revenge" through her mittened fingers.

The bottle slipped, whipping a lash of liquid over the fire. The flames fought back, snapping high into Boomer's face. He reared away, shouting something that wasn't a song.

Hattie screamed.

Jane watched.

The flames sprinted for the dangling blanket edges and quickened, shooting like bright gold embroidery over the fabric. Thickening smoke dimmed the vision of a writhing wall of orange-gold heat sealing the three people into the dumpster's heavy metal insides.

"Oh my God, oh my God. . . ."

Jane couldn't tell who called—Boomer, Hattie, or the voices in her head. She felt their bodies press her against the dumpster's back, felt hot wind singe her cheeks and smoke stopper her eyes, ears, nose, mouth. . . .

It stunned her, this force she had once generated without even thinking about it, as Kevin had helped her remember under hypnotism. It was savage, swift, pitiless.

She heard only coughs around her now, racked and faint. Jane realized that she had not inhaled in some moments, that the air in her lungs remained clean. Some self-preserving instinct let it seep into her system in cunningly husbanded amounts.

Someone nearby was clutching her arm. Someone far away was drumming on the dumpster's metal skin. Jane stood, feeling the dumpster ceiling brush the top of her borrowed hat. There was nothing here to contest, no electric pulse that found a sister echo in her neurons. There was nothing here to defend against but the hunger of the fire.

Jane felt force gather in an inner depth, then come spilling out, flinging itself to her extremities, to her finger-tips and the stiff, outflung ends of the hair on her head. Panama Hattie's hat popped off as an electrical storm of psychic force stiffened Jane's hair into a corona of energy.

Everything in her—the force, her intentions—flung outward and upward. The dumpster cracked free from its skirts of snow, tipping a slice of cold fresh air into the contained space. Its movement tilted the three occupants onto the snow-covered earth—Jane stepped off the metal lip as it moved, Boomer and Hattie tumbling sideways to the snow.

Fresh air fed the flames, but the dumpster was inverting, then lifting straight up, as inexorably, as awkwardly as a helicopter. Inch by inch it rose, drawing the dangling flaming curtain up past the people crouched behind it.

Boomer and Hattie lay on the fire-scorched earth, sobbing through shut eyes, their eyebrows seared, their coughs relentless. A semicircle of awed onlookers—shadowy winos, bag ladies, bums—gathered around the fire site, the flames' yellow flickers scrubbing their faces cleaner than water had recently.

Wondering, silent, they watched the dumpster levitate until it hung well above Jane's head. Then it catapulted backward, like a circus clown's handspring, and thundered to earth in a sheet of flying sparks.

It lay charred, mouth upward, flames still spitting from its darkened cavity into the darker night.

Jane stood alone in the ring of melted snow. She inhaled deeply. Hattie's waning sobs crooned like a lullaby.

"A miracle," said a voice from the dark.

"My God, it's a miracle."

They were gathering closer—vague, undifferentiated figures with vacant eyes and pitted faces and mutilated hands clutching empty bottles.

One reached out to touch the hem of Jane's jacket.

A spark snapped at the night, a tiny comet of energy winking itself out. Jane's hair fell strand by strand to her shoulders.

Jane looked at them, then up at the full round moon hanging like a silver coin over them all.

She turned and walked into the dark, across the tracks, toward the basalt towers. Court House. The words sizzled into a black blot on a map laid out on her brain as carefully as any congerie of cells.

She walked the thin black lines in her mind, not waiting until tomorrow.

Chapter Twenty-two

Kevin paused on the threshold to the cell, his return making himself the eternal newcomer.

He wanted to be alone. He wanted to think over what Smith had said. He wanted to remember Jane.

Despite appearances, a jail cell did not allow for solitude, for thinking, or for remembering anything other than the law of survival.

On his bunk again, suspended over the crooning moan of Waldo the wacko, Kevin let his mind unravel into self-flagellating filaments of worry and guilt.

How could he have been so stupid? He had managed to strand Jane in an alien cityscape—without money, without food, without the slightest survival skills.

Smith insisted Jane wasn't as helpless as Kevin thought. And she was powerful, even he had to admit that, powerful in ways that defied speculation. Yet . . . his conscience writhed. Did only he see her vulnerability?

Kellehay hadn't. Kellehay had wanted to kill Jane. And had been killed. Carolyn Swanson hadn't. Swanson had done her parapsychology tests on Jane, pushed Jane, and got results at too high a price. Only Kevin had respected Jane's selfhood, her unique heritage. And his reward was discreditation, imprisonment, self-delusion, maybe. . . .

Lights-out was coming. The men began to file listlessly into the shower area, eyeing Kevin until he jumped off the upper bunk and joined them. Even Waldo waddled in.

The hiss of communal running water lulled Kevin's anxiety with its deceptively friendly sound, heard in a hundred locker rooms and summer camps. Kevin stripped off his insubstantial greens, turned on the water until the cold ran hot and stepped under the relaxing stream.

Running water gradually cranked off in cubicles around him, until only the patter of his showerhead rang on the concrete floor. He reached to shut off the controls. Before he could, Jesús, the muscle-bound Hispanic, had jerked back the curtain and was barring the exit from his stall.

"Hey . . . okay, man." Jesús flashed a grin that had nothing to do with smiling. "You real pretty bare-assed. How about you and me make a date?"

The others, leering, had gathered behind Jesús, a wall of peer group pressure personified. They weren't necessarily queer, they just needed an edge—any edge—against anyone.

Kevin's body froze, his mind churning in overdrive. God knew a track career—going for the distance, the solitary, head-bound distance—didn't count as physical education in self-defense. God knew playing God over a psychiatric couch didn't engender street smarts. On a purely personal level, Kevin just knew he had better defend his honor or forget it for good.

Jesús had dressed in a hurry, his greens bleeding quarter-sized wet spots, using another crude psychological edge, the clothed versus the naked. But Kevin had an advantage only the effete could employ. A college education—and then some. He decided to use it.

His hands fisted into the loose fabric of Jesús's shirt. Kevin's rage toward Nordstrom erupted into action as he slammed Jesús hard against the shower wall.

Muscles and brain pulled in concord, his adrenaline pumped madly, his sense of nicety abandoned ship. His attack rammed Jesús's back against the chrome shower controls, pounded his kidneys into the hot and cold faucets, even tilted the man's torso as he hit to allow for the fact that the right kidney was lower. Premed Anatomy I.

Breath was still hissing out of Jesús like air from a flat tire when Kevin smashed the man's head against the concrete shower wall and pinned it there with his forearm, the built-in curved club of his radius bone pressed murderously against the man's windpipe.

"Lay off, motherfucker, unless you want to kiss your asshole hello."

184

Bluff hung in the balance. Jesús hurt bad right now in all the right places, he knew, but five other men with something to prove hovered somewhere at Kevin's back.

Then a voice keened into the tense silence.

"Ow, Owwww, Owwwww."

Everyone turned to look.

Wacko Waldo was banging his head against the concrete walls, screaming his "Ows" in rhythmic reaction.

"Shut up!" they hissed, advancing on Waldo.

Harry, his face white as Wonder bread, faded around a corner. Kevin kept Jesús pinned until his eyewhites rolled up, then let him slide to the shower floor.

"Shut up, you crazy creep," the men were hissing at Waldo, their dark hands reaching for him.

Kevin, his mind and muscles temporarily liquid, pulled on his clothes. Oh, Jesus, he thought, aware of the expression's irony, he couldn't just stand by and let them beat on a sad head case like Waldo. Win one, then lose it all. . . . He started toward the men, who were banging Waldo's head against the wall for him now.

A screaming buzzer went off.

Kevin jumped. So did five other startled men.

"Who the shit hit that?"

Rollo, the industrial-strength black, turned to glare at Kevin, then jerked his eyes to the outer room. "That fuckhead Harry—!"

The overhead mike demanded explanation. Nobody answered it. Then the cops rushed in. Everybody eased back against the nearest wall.

"Who hit the alarm?" a cop demanded.

Silence. Harry, peering over the cop's shoulder into the shower area, cleared his throat, but kept still.

The cops cruised the showers, finding Jesús soon enough. One knelt to examine the semiconscious man for injuries.

"He fell," Rollo said abruptly. "Old Waldo started his howlin' act, then Jesús musta got scared, and slipped in the shower."

"He's dressed," noted a cop.

"He was gettin' out. We didn't do nothin', 'cept try to shut up Crazy Waldo. Why is this wacko in here, anyway?"

185

"He doesn't belong in here," Kevin put in.

The cop's expression tightened. "You all belong in here, or you wouldn't be here. If Waldo sings too much for your taste—tough." He rose and prowled into the main area, where his partner waited.

"The Mexican's got no external injuries. We don't check you goldbricks into County General unless you got cuts. So either the guy fell—or somebody in here knows how to throw his weight around without showing." They holstered their sticks and passed Harry on the way out.

"I guess we don't have to tell you how sorry you'll be for hitting that panic button," one told Harry. The cop's head jerked over his shoulder to the gathered prisoners. "They will."

The big brown metal door clanged shut again. Someone outside flipped back the spy door and peered through the smudged glass before shutting the cover.

The black guys glanced at Kevin, then at Jesús, still on the wet stall floor. Their eyes flicked away from both men, from Waldo even, who had sunk to the concrete, boneless as a kitten.

"Keep it shut," Rollo growled in farewell. He fronted out into the main room. The others followed.

Kevin bent to help Waldo up.

"It's okay, Doc, ain't it? You were real nice to me in State. I 'member that, yes, I do."

Kevin stared at the foolish face, at the eyes that never quite stopped roving. They all looked alike, after a while, the mentally defective, even the ones you might have been nice to once, years ago.

But the man remembered, my God, the man had remembered him.

"It's okay," Kevin answered. "Thanks. But—"

"Oh, I don't know you. No, sir. I don't know nothin'. I been on the streets a long time. Long time. I know some things."

Kevin helped the man back to the bunk. He didn't have to worry about appearing soft-hearted; the cops had just done him the unwitting service of declaring him dangerous. In here, that was a supreme defense.

Harry was edging along the far wall, his gut quivering against his distended shirtfront. Kevin eyed the emergency buttons strung at regular intervals along the walls. So close, yet so far. Harry got within a couple feet of one and froze. The men watched. Rollo sprang panther-quick, cutting Harry off from the button.

The insurance salesman grimaced a sick smile, then crabbed along the wall in the opposite direction. As he neared a new button, another man intercepted him. Everything was tacit—the game of cat and mouse, the threat. Only the outcome was obvious. Harry would pay for having squealed.

Kevin lay Waldo down in his bunk. He didn't seem hurt, just pleased with himself. His parting gesture was a finger over his lips and a long, conspiratorial "Shhhhhh."

Kevin boosted himself into the bunk above, sorry for the man edging ratlike along the walls, but too tired, too damn worn down to worry about it.

"Hey, Blake," big Rollo yelled, "we could use you."

"Fuck yourselves," Kevin growled back with schooled indifference. The worst part was that he was beginning to feel it.

Someone at some outside control console turned off the lights. Kevin lay in the dark and covered his eyes with his forearm. His radius ached a little and his ears heard too much. What he heard last was the soft, repeated, sympathetic "Ow, owwww owwww's" of Waldo rocking and rolling in the bunk below.

*   *   *

Away from the fire, it got dark. And cold.

Jane shivered and walked on, aware suddenly that she was no longer sure where she was going. The glittering towers ahead seemed farther away. Dark pooled into an impassable obsidian moat between Here and There.

Jane stopped. Words were sizzling along her synapses. Images in her mind shattered and scattered. A map broke into dotted lines that disintegrated into unconnected dots.

The words/voices in her bloodstream boiled into cacophony, part insect-buzz, part radio-dial-static. The voices were neither male nor female; neither brute nor human. They just were.

"Closer. Closer. Tuning in station Kay-Jay-N-Eeeee. Data call to data. Data recall data. Data call . . . Dada call. . . . Overload. Reload. Ready to disperse. And tired, tired, tired. So tired. . . . Site certain, depositing same. Blue Nuns for White Roses. Kevin Tarzan, Jane . . . tired, not thinking, slipping away . . . The same, but different—Kevin gone, Jane missing. Recall. To recall, to be recalled. Something recalling Jane. Something probing. . . . And then—contact! One will go and one will come. One will become None. One will—"

Jane gasped, feeling her mind and her memory shrinking from the sides of her skull. Her feet dragged through the snowdrifts.

Out of the darkness came embodied darkness, striking her, surrounding her retreating self. Two forms collided with hers, emitting words that no longer made sense. Force exploded against the side of her head, shaking all the voices she had ever heard loose, including her own. Alien hands began pawing at her body. Her mind, withdrawing into a cold white night, recorded them even as it declined to interpret them.

"Hurry! Before anybody comes!"

"Was that a light I saw?"

"Where?"

"Over by the River Road?"

"Headlights. Or some fool's campfire. Quick, roll her into the brush."

Jane, feeling almost weightless, felt herself plummet, touch bottom and bounce softly—over and over against the sides of the . . . the holding tank.

Air came to her from far away, absorbed without being breathed. Air by osmosis. Sounds vibrated the glass cocoon, stirred the unnamed ether surrounding her. Voices became meaningless data, eaten but not digested.

"Say, good gloves . . . !"

"The jacket's mine!"

"And boots."

188

"Shut up. They're makin' a fuss across the tracks—"

"Damn stupid fools always make a fuss—no money! Not a goddamn penny!"

"She's not breathing."

"Sure, she is. Roll her back in the brush. Let her sleep it off. Must've been some party over there."

"Good gloves."

"We can use 'em. She's not feeling a thing. . . ."

Jane floated, all memory twisted into a single thread dangling just beyond reach. She could feel nothing, hear nothing. Not even the buzzing voices.

Janeness drifted away, finally. And I-ness. There was only floating, only withdrawal, only retreat into a past that refused to be remembered.

Chapter Twenty-three

"It was done yesterday." Turner lay the second sketch of Jane Doe beside the one on his desk.

"Where?" Nordstrom hovered over the two sketches, his oversized head twisted to view them right side up from the wrong side of the desk.

"House of Charity." Turner laughed as Nordstrom's eyes grew bigger behind the miniaturizing lenses. "It's a soup kitchen for transients. A do-gooder painter sets up her easel there regularly, looking for 'life studies.'"

"How'd you find it so fast?"

"Got copies of the old police sketch to all the beat cops in town. I don't know why the locals went with a police sketch instead of the standard Identi-Kit workup, but it helped us a lot."

Turner's hands weighed the two images of Jane Doe while he studied them. "The original sketch isn't artsy-fartsy, but it sure made the new portrait sit up and sing for the patrolman who saw it displayed in a window at the Senior Citizens' Center. Part of an exhibition." He put down the police sketch and studied the newer one. "That Myerson woman isn't a bad portraitist—and there's something arresting about the subject. That's why it made the window—the only black-and-white piece. So it was like every lead—half routine investigative work, half gift."

Nordstrom plucked the canvasboard from Turner's hands. "Fenced in by a few strokes of charcoal, our elusive Jane Doe. What was she doing at a soup kitchen?"

"Maybe she was hungry."

"She does have a lean and hungry look."

"You're hallucinating, Doctor." Turner spun away to wrestle his overcoat off the office rack. "She looks much better in the soup kitchen sketch—more substantial, and more alive. I wish—"

"Yes, Mr. Turner? Wishes are healthier expressed."

Turner jammed himself into his London Fog and brushed past Nordstrom on his way out. "I wish Blake had agreed to work with us—to work with her *for* us," he said brusquely. "All right, let's go see what we can turn up."

Nordstrom dropped the portrait back on the desk and trailed Turner out, smiling.

His smile faded at the House of Charity. The dead eyes winding around the corner watched indifferently as Turner and Nordstrom shouldered past the line into the building. Forced-air heated the soup kitchen's diverse odors of food and filth into an exquisite communal reek. Nordstrom fished an initialed white linen handkerchief from his suit pocket and pinched it over his cold-reddened nostrils.

Turner reacted to neither sight nor smell, brushing past tattered wrecks of humanity as if he were merely moving onto a crowded elevator at Dayton's department store. He headed straight for the red-smocked back in a far corner and wafted a newspaper clipping of Jane Doe's original police sketch onto the easel.

"Mrs. Myerson? You sketched this woman yesterday. Do you know where we can find her today?"

"Of course . . . Jane, wasn't it?" The woman glanced

190

over her half-frames to Turner. "Yes, I did it yesterday . . . but how did you—?"

"The manager at the Senior Citizens' Center said you mentioned the sketch was fresh."

"I see." The woman tilted back her raven-haired head and stared at Nordstrom. "Why do you gentlemen—?"

Turner flipped out his ID, watching the lines on the artist's handsome face deepen. Her short, red-lacquered fingernail rapped the leatherette case before he retracted it.

"These people trust me. I can't be responsible for identifying them. They've come here because they want to be forgotten, even by family."

"I'm not family."

The woman shook her head, resisting.

"She's schizophrenic, Mrs. Myerson," Nordstrom lied smoothly, his voice deep and sincere. "She needs medication desperately. You know how many of these people have been deinstitutionalized over the past few years."

"Do I ever! It's a tragedy. They're no more fit to cope by themselves than lost puppies. Jane . . . didn't seem like one of them. She was a bit shy, a bit remote maybe—"

"She's ill, Mrs. Myerson, and young enough so that we can treat it. You're right. She doesn't belong on the streets."

Nordstrom fixed his eyes on hers until the woman glanced down at the newspaper sketch. She traced the lines of Jane's newsprint face with an articulate fingernail.

"She came in with Hattie," she capitulated, looking at Turner again as she spoke. "Panama Hattie."

"Local character?" Turner asked.

"Very."

"Where does she hang out?"

"Where do they all hang out? In caves, crevices, corners, over heating grates, under bridges. But Jimmy—" When both men looked confused, she nodded to a young and ragged Robert Redford huddled over a nearby food tray. "Gentleman Jimmy said Hattie stayed by the railroad tracks last night. Apparently, there was some . . . unpleasantness."

"City police?"

"No, among themselves. Hattie hasn't come in yet today. She usually does at noon."

"Description?" Turner poised his gnawed Venus Velvet pencil over a tiny notebook.

The artist smiled, scarlet lips showcasing white teeth, and quickly sketched a face onto her drawing pad. "You'll know Panama Hattie, Mr. Turner. She looks like every other bag lady you've ever seen—pure Central Casting, except she stockpiles hats on her head, all on top of one another. The most fantastic, Salvation Army hats! That's what made me decide to draw Jane, that mad little hat Panama Hattie gave her. Otherwise, her clothes were perfectly ordinary and her face was—"

"Was what?"

"Oddly blank. It had no character, no pain lines. Of course, she's young. . . ."

Turner nodded, pocketing his pencil.

"Hurry," Nordstrom urged in his ear. "I don't want to lose her."

"Yeah, this is your moment, isn't it? Don't worry. I've got a feeling that this time we've got her for sure."

*   *   *

"God. Where the hell's the meat wagon?"

Officer Joe O'Connor rose from inspecting the body of a naked young woman in the snow. He fought an unheard of urge to drape her with the blanket from the squad car's trunk, crime scene or not. Instead, he stripped off a glove and wiped his runny nose. "The slimeballs didn't leave her a stitch."

"What'd you expect down here?" His partner pointed to a semicircle of silently watching indigents. "Where's the old broad with the hats? She seemed to know something about it."

Panama Hattie was sitting on a fallen branch, her hats and eyebrows singed. O'Connor lumbered over to take a statement. The ballpoint pen felt like an icicle in his big, bare fingers.

"You know the deceased?" he began.

"Jane. That's all I know. Just Jane."

"She live on the streets?"

"Guess so. That's where I found her. Had no money."

"When did you find her?"

"Oh . . ." Hattie had to think about it. "Yesterday, it was. Before lunch. Before teatime even. Early."

"How'd she end up here?"

"Me and Boomer brought her back. Boomer made a snug place for the night. We had a party . . . and then— then it gets all confused—"

"Just tell me one thing at a time."

"Boomer's fire goes up, real hot and high. Caught on something—blankets maybe. It was amazing. . . . " Hattie stared into the distance until Officer O'Connor spoke again.

"Then what?"

"Oh, we all almost burned up. But . . . Jane got us out, she surely did. She didn't seem afraid of the fire."

"Body doesn't look burned."

"I told you. Janey got us out. Her and Boomer and me. It was amazing."

"Then what? Ma'am?"

Hattie opened her mouth to speak, then shut it firmly. "Then . . . Jane left."

"She say where she was going?"

"No."

"You didn't ask?"

"No."

"You know what time this was?"

"No."

O'Connor sighed. "You see anything, see anybody that might've rolled her?"

"She didn't have any money, I told you."

"She musta had clothes, lady."

"Oh, clothes." Panama Hattie winced. "My best wine felt cloche with the sparkly pin. It's gone, too. Yeah, Janey had clothes, nice clothes. That's what I noticed about her. Her nice new clothes. But she didn't have no money, no sirree." A tear wavered down Hattie's grimy face. "That's how I'm gonna remember her, like she was last night. Not like what's left."

"That's fine. Anybody else know anything about this?"

Panama Hattie looked over her shoulder at the gathered transients. Their sad faces stayed as blank as ever. Hattie's deadened, too. "No, we don't know nothin'. We just happened to be here, is all."

The rattle of a car jolting over the rough snowy ground made O'Connor turn hopefully. He shoved his notepad inside his jacket—damn ballpoint didn't write in the cold, anyway—and pulled on heavy leather gloves. Then he saw it was an ordinary passenger car.

"Tourists! Where the hell's the damn wagon and the detectives?"

The men from the car moved to meet O'Connor as eagerly as he stalked them. One flashed a government ID.

"What's going on here?" the newcomer asked.

"Nothin' now. Party been killed. The ME hasn't showed yet. You hear it on the radio?"

Nordstrom was going to say no, but Turner spoke first. "We heard about it. What've you got?"

"Caucasian female, early twenties maybe. No visible identifying marks. No visible marks of violence. No clothes. Could be rape, but I don't think so."

O'Connor was leading them to the thin line of under-brush that fringed a crease in the white terrain. "One of the bums called it in, can you believe it? What's your angle?"

"Confidential."

"What about him?" O'Connor's fat glove indicated Nordstrom. "He confidential, too? Detectives'll skin me alive letting civilians mess up a crime scene."

"He's a government consultant."

O'Connor shrugged and shifted his big, navy blue bulk. The motion revealed the crime scene, revealed the body lying naked in the snow.

"Shit," Turner said.

No one noticed, not even Nordstrom.

They all stared at Jane Doe, her skin snow white in the bright winter daylight, her arms and legs radiating out like spokes. Only the dark patches of her head and pubic hair jolted the marble coldness of the image.

"She must have been alive when she . . . fell here, or was

thrown," Turner finally said. "Snow's melted around her body."

"Lot of snow melted around here," O'Connor put in. "These crazy winos are always lighting campfires—sometimes they light themselves afire. Had a close call just last night again. Guess she pulled a couple of 'em outa the fire—"

"So she died a heroine," Nordstrom put in ironically.

"Any guesses?" Turner wanted to know.

O'Connor shrugged, his nylon jacket screeching. "Not my department. But her clothes are gone. She was rolled for 'em by some drunked-out winos. She was walking back toward town, alone, when last seen."

Tires squeaked across packed snow behind them.

"Here's the coroner now, and the detectives." O'Connor's relief came as palpably as his frosty breath. "Good, maybe we can get this show on the road. Kinda makes you cold, just to look at her like that."

Turner pulled off a glove to rub his wind-scrubbed face in a bare, warm palm, then stepped back to let the police team record the death scene as his own men had done near Duluth not many days before.

The officials surged past Nordstrom, too. He didn't move, but stood staring into the shallow gully. Something about the psychiatrist's carrion intensity irritated Turner. He wheeled and stalked through the snow to the watching winos.

What bothered him was that untouchably dead body, yet another bizarre image in a case that was stacked with wild card images. First his men, fried up north. Now her, iced down here.

"You Panama Hattie?"

He had stopped before the stooped little woman, her head hanging under the weight of her hats. A grimy white turban wrapped her shrunken cheeks and temples like a swami's headdress.

"Can't you tell?"

"Sure. About her—?"

Pain stirred in the old woman's guarded eyes. Turner was surprised to feel an echo of it in his own.

195

"Tell me what you can," he added more gently. "I need to know what happened to her."

"It's what *didn't* happen to us." An old man had stepped forward, a baggy-pants emissary of every bum Turner had ever seen—or tried not to see—on any street corner.

"She saved us, Jane did," the wino said. "She jest made that dumpster rare back and get outa the way. Otherwise we would've been burnt bacon, Hattie and me, and Jane."

"Dumpster?"

The old man turned and shuffled through the snow. Turner glanced back to see cameras pressed to faces like binoculars. No one watched as he followed the old man and Panama Hattie across the fretwork of tracks to the black span of a railroad bridge.

A plague of dead fire sites had pocked the snow everywhere—the largest surrounded a charred dumpster not far from the hill where the bridge began. The wind whipped the fire-singed blanket pennants streaming from the dumpster's gaping mouth.

"This was my place," the old guy said, smiling with his tongue tip parked in the notch of an absent tooth. "Real nice. Jammed it sideways up under the bridge there. Lean-to like.

"We was sittin' in it—Hattie and me and this Jane Hattie picked up somewhere. We was bendin' an elbow or two and some of the stuff slopped into this little fire I had goin' in a frypan—hell, the stuff they sell nowadays would start a fire in an asbestos factory. Anyway, we were goners, for sure, with the blankets over the mouth of the dumpster aburnin' like there was no tomorrow—"

"The dumpster was on its side, is that right, so the only way out was through the burning blankets?"

"I wasn't gonna go through that!" Panama Hattie shivered until her hat feathers shook. "Boomer 'n me was done for, all choked up so we couldn't see. But Jane, Jane just stood up, and then . . . well, we all tumbled out of the dumpster onto the ground. And it jest picked itself off of us and flew up in the sky and then it was gone and there was like a meteor shower—"

"Hold it." Turner prowled around the dumpster, peered

into its empty, charcoal-dark maw. "You're saying that *Jane* caused this thing—it must weigh a ton or so—to lift in the air—*she* lifted it?"

"She didn't lift nothin' but herself," the old-timer called Boomer said. "It lifted itself. Then we lifted ourselves right outa there, you better believe it!" The old man grinned, his beard stubble snow white against his grimy skin.

Turner shook his head as if to clear it. Remarkable powers, they'd said in Washington. The Russians would give their cherry-red asses to have a subject with that kind of psi potential. And now she was dead. Kaput, her and all her works.

"You just let her go, after that?" Turner demanded.

"We was shook up, sick," Hattie answered defensively. "We didn't know what to make of it, what to think. And Janey was like that anyway—she'd get a notion and off she'd go. Maybe she wanted to see that boyfriend of hers in county jail—"

"Boyfriend?"

"Kevin, name was, she said. Some boyfriend, left her with no dough, not a nickel—I know, I tried to hit her for a crummy nickel and she didn't have one. Then the next lady I hit on fishes out a fiver—Jane was lucky, you know? I don't run across much luck. Guess she was luckier than I knew. 'Cept for herself. . . ." Hattie tugged her turban lower around her ears, managing to dislodge a tear with the gesture.

"If you tell the police about what Jane did—"

"Tell them? Tell a uniform?" Hattie hooted. "They don't believe us. Never believe us. You can't imagine what a job it was to try and get someone to come and fetch Janey." She turned and eyed the mute transients behind her. "'Sides, these drunken fools got it all wrong. They got as many stories as they got toes between 'em—though that ain't many in this climate."

Hattie spat daintily in their direction, but Turner plodded over to them anyway. The fresh, icy air sanitized the annunciation of odor that clung to their kind. They seemed merely worn, torn rag dolls of people, rather than the unkempt outcasts passersby shied from on streets.

"My name's Turner," he told them. "Last night—when the fire broke out—did you see anything unusual?"

Eyes studied the drift tops, gazed over Turner's head, met his with steady vacancy. He had expected that.

"I saw it," finally keened one pipecleaner-thin black man. "A big dark dumpster in the sky—flying like a bird. Like a crow. It made the stars shrink, yessir. It made ever'thin' colder. It jest hung there, with a light pretty as a treetop angel, all lilac-like. A light like the Wise Men saw in the Promised Land."

"I'm talking about the burning dumpster."

"Yessir. I know what you're talkin' about. I'm talkin' about it, too. It was big up there and it hung and hung there for a long time. A long time. I don't think that little girl did it . . . no, I don't. A heav-en-ly vis-i-ta-tion, that's what it was. We got people saved from the flamin' furnace here. We blessed."

Turner sighed and began trudging back to the distant group of policemen in his own tracks. Nordstrom's small avid figure still hovered over the gully edge, lenses twinkling in the relentless sunlight. Turner knew a moment's perverse satisfaction that the man's quarry had eluded him so utterly.

"It was dark last night, mister," the old black man was crooning at Turner's retreating back. "Real dark. Then we saw the light, and all our woes are over."

Shaking his head, Turner rejoined those whose indifference he understood. An ambulance, siren muted for the dead, rolled across the scarred snowscape, adding its tire tracks to the melee.

Two attendants slid down the staked-out bank and loaded Jane Doe's body onto a stretcher. She had died recently enough that her limbs were still pliant despite the cold. Her slight body sagged in the attendants' grip for a few sickening seconds before the flat stretcher claimed her, shaping her to its own stiffness. By so little time they had missed her.

At last the rough brown blanket was draped over her nakedness. Dead, Jane Doe seemed as fragile as Patty Hearst on her capture, and something shameful in the chase,

Turner reflected. Someone sighed relief behind him. Turner twisted to see the first cop on the scene, tension lines around his eyes finally relaxing.

Turner contemplated the depression Jane Doe's body had made in the drift. Where she lay the snow had melted away to bare ground. Stones, dried leaves and broken sticks formed the dark silhouette of a figure. Its posture reminded Turner of a snow angel that had sunk too fast to earth. There was nothing pretty in it, only emptiness.

He started back to his car, then remembered Nordstrom. The guy was trotting like a fox terrier alongside the stretcher, lifting the blanket and pressing his bare hands to the body. Fingering it—throat, hands, even the feet.

Nordstrom looked up and caught whatever expression was grabbing hold of Turner's face and twisting. His own was ecstatic.

"She's still alive, Mr. Turner! By God, she's still alive! I've got a faint peripheral pulse over her anklebone. She might be in hypothermia, but at the proper facilities—"

Faces fell in disbelief all around Nordstrom. The attendants almost dropped the stretcher. One folded back the blanket top to reveal Jane Doe's bloodlessly calm, madonna-like face. Only the dead get complete privacy.

Turner swore out loud for the second time that morning, softly, to himself.

"Poor bitch," he murmured. "Poor unlucky bitch."

The Gleaning
January 14

*   *   *

"No contact possible to flesh. . . ."

—T. S. Eliot
"Whispers of Immortality"

Chapter Twenty-four

Jane awoke.

A man was leaning over her, staring.

Jane stared back. She saw herself reflected, small as a figure in a snapshot, on the shiny lenses of his glasses.

"Hello. I'm Dr. Nordstrom. I'm here to take care of you."

Jane blinked to wash her reflection away. When her eyes opened again, they saw straight through Dr. Nordstrom's magnifying lenses into his eyes. They shone as hard and reflectively as his spectacles.

"Déjà vu." Jane sampled the words. She'd never said them aloud before, but her French accent was impeccable.

The man withdrew a little, a very little. "What?"

"Déjà vu. 'An inexplicable feeling of familiarity.' But you aren't familiar."

"Then perhaps the situation is." Dr. Nordstrom's deep voice eased into her consciousness. "Think back."

Jane did, remembering only cold and confusion and the slow, deep process of awakening. She knew suddenly that she had forgotten something. Because she had forgotten it, she couldn't say what it was.

She turned her head on the pillow. Each appropriate word popped into her head as needed. *Bed. IV. Hospital room.* Oh, yes, hospital. . . . No wonder it all seemed so familiar.

"I'm at the University of Minnesota Hospitals?"

"Something like that." The deep voice came slower now, as if it talked to a child a long distance away. "You've been a very . . . ill young woman."

"Ill. Is that what I feel?"

"Gravely ill," the voice repeated, dwelling on the words in a way Jane didn't like. This man dwelled on everything —with his eyes, his voice. His mind.

Jane's thoughts jerked into another gear. "Clothes. I don't have clothes. The light took my clothes—"

"We'll get you other clothes. Later."

"Who is we?"

"The people who are here to take care of you. The nurses and doctors. Myself. You've been ill before. You know what that means."

"I don't like it." Jane tried to sit up, but found her limbs too weak to support her.

Dr. Nordstrom pushed her back, his hand pressing on her chest. It stayed there, cold through the thin fabric of her hospital gown. He seemed to be measuring her heartbeat.

"Don't be alarmed," he urged, his voice reassuring but his eyes still the same, still opaque.

Jane sat up again, this time against the force of his restraining hand. "Kevin," she said, articulating another word that had spurted into her mind. An image, and an emotion, followed obediently, as if leashed.

"He's . . . away." Dr. Nordstrom's expression hadn't changed, but somehow he had. "Lie back. Lie back and you'll get better sooner and can have anything you want."

"No one can have anything they want."

Dr. Nordstrom smiled. It reminded Jane that Kevin's smile was much nicer. "Some of us can, dear."

Lying down again, she studied the ceiling. It was covered in tiles with rows of dark dots punched through. Acoustic, her mind coached. So sound wouldn't carry. Another memory spun into place. Dr. Swanson's lab in the basement of Whittington Hall. Rooms with locked doors with windows in them. Acoustic tile everywhere—ceiling and walls. Kevin hadn't liked that place at all. Kevin hadn't liked Jane being there.

"I've got to go," she said.

"No." Dr. Nordstrom's voice softened with certainty. Another emotion underlay it, one Jane had never perceived or experienced before. She cocked her head. His smile returned. "You'll need to stay here awhile. You and I are going to work together. We're going to . . . explore . . . what will make you well. We'll look into your memory, into those powers of yours—"

"I want to leave," Jane insisted.

"You can't." He sounded quite final now. "Your physical condition is too tenuous. You're a very sick young woman. Somehow you lost weight again. Why, you're nothing but skin and bones. They very nearly took you away for dead."

His hands shaped her form outside the sheet, clasping her wrists, knees, elbows, hips in turn. He touched her a bit like Kevin had touched her later, when he no longer had medical reason to touch her body. He had never touched her like this in the hospital.

Jane considered, her reactions hamstrung between responding to a familiar stimulus, and the unwelcome source. She decided to think it over. So much was confused. She felt cold to her bones. What she was experiencing in this hospital room was only a shadow overlaid on what she really knew deep in her brain: snow and cold and dark of night. And the ship.

The ship formed in her mind, a huge, hovering bat of darkness with one lurid eye calling to her. The ship. But that must have been days and days ago, maybe . . . a week . . . since the ship.

Something more—so much more—had happened since. Hadn't it? She couldn't recall anything beyond being returned naked to her Mother Earth, to Kevin, but knew no panic. Maybe this Dr. Nordstrom would help her remember, as Kevin had.

Jane matched his perpetual stare with her own. Dr. Nordstrom was here to help her, but she would only tell Kevin about the ship that she didn't . . . quite . . . remember.

*   *   *

"Where are you taking me?" Kevin wanted to know.

The cop finally gruffed out, "Visitors."

Kevin felt like a pariah as he was hustled through the halls. The uniformed men and women with holstered hips walking these workaday halls ignored him as they passed.

He was looking forward to seeing someone who would recognize him, accept him—probably Kandy and his lawyer. The cop had said "visitors," plural.

A long Plexiglas panel divided the room into "Home" and "Visitors," into "us" and "them." Kevin was ushered to a cubicle with a phone. Two people sat on the other side of the Plex, and they weren't Kandy and some lawyer. Kevin almost wished the cops *would* drag him away screaming, à la the movie cliché. Instead, he faced a new kind of confinement.

"Hi, Mom," he found himself mouthing like a football hero on TV. "Dad."

Grant Wood could have painted this portrait of sober parental shock. His mother looked cast in wax—the careful details of her Elk River–modish outfit seemed picked out in wire armature. His father looked as Kevin had never seen him, worried white.

Kevin picked up the phone and sank onto the molded plastic chair. "Who told you?" Pen strokes scarred the tabletop in front of him, inarticulate doodles from the terminally self-conscious.

"Is it safe to speak?" his mother wondered.

"Good question, but what can it hurt?"

She nodded sorrowfully, but his dad took the receiver to answer.

"That . . . Kandinsky fellow told us. We asked at the university and someone said he was a friend—"

"He is."

"Kevin, what the hell's going on?" His father was recovering enough to assume the mantle of parental outrage as if he'd personally loomed it. "They said that you were booked on a *murder* charge!"

"I am, I guess. They haven't bothered telling me."

"Good God, why didn't you call, son?"

"They don't let you do long-distance in jail, Dad. Besides, I didn't want to upset you and Mom—"

His mother, listening in cheek to cheek with his father, swallowed a sob, masking it with her gloved hand.

She wore those fuzzy wool gloves with black leather palms that always reminded Kevin of an ape. He could see why she kept her gloves on; it was cold in the visitors' room. Besides, someone like Kevin's mom only took off her gloves in places where she was staying for a while. She wasn't ready to accept this mean, compartmentalized room as more than a place of passage for herself—and Kevin.

"Look," Kevin said. "It's absurd, the charges. But they've got me locked up over a long holiday weekend—"

"Holiday?"

Kevin smiled wearily at his dad. "I guess they don't close down much in Elk River on Martin Luther King's birthday yet. But the mail doesn't come, remember?"

"Oh, yeah. Hard to keep track of a new holiday." Arthur Blake frowned vaguely.

"How was Christmas at the store?" Kevin asked.

His dad shrugged, and Kevin suddenly knew where he'd gotten the gesture. "So-so. Folks are still pretty tight, even at Christmas."

"Thanks for the presents," his mother put in. "Those special candies—"

"Truffles."

"—whatever, were real good. I'm on a diet now, though." Her smile was as modest as ever. Clare Blake had always done what was expected of her, at the proper time and in the proper season. January was for diets. And Christmas, Christmas was for . . . guilt trips. "You look so much nicer without the beard," she couldn't resist putting in now.

"Sorry I didn't get up for the holidays, Mom. I had this critical case—"

"All your cases seem to be critical. You should have gone into hardware," his dad joked—or perhaps *didn't* joke. "Nothing's critical there except maybe plumbing supplies."

"I'm not in hardware, Dad; I'm in software. Human head stuff. Psychiatric treatment doesn't follow a schedule. I had this case—"

"Is that . . . she . . . the one you went off with?" His mother's faded blue eyes held the grave, tell-the-truth-now look Kevin hadn't seen for years.

207

"I didn't 'go off' with her. It's too complicated to explain—"

"All your cases are that way," his father put in.

Kevin found reflex forming the words, "You don't understand." They didn't, but he didn't say it. Again.

"My cases are demanding," he said instead. "This one especially."

"Who was that man who called?" his mother wanted to know. "I . . . didn't like the way he put things, like he needed to know that he knew something we didn't. I didn't like *him*."

Kevin grinned at her. "Very perceptive, Mom. You'd make a good shrink."

"Women's intuition," she returned, pleased.

"There's something to that . . . maybe. But the guy who called was just trying to scare me by putting a scare in you. It must have worked, if you two drove down here from Elk River."

"Finding out you were in jail put a worse scare in us," his father said. "Kevin, how can you sit here—you have never been in jail a day in your life—and take it like it's nothing? We'll find a lawyer; we'll get you out."

"Not until Wednesday. By then it'll be too late maybe. It's Jane they really want. My patient."

"We met her." His mother put her ear back to the receiver after dropping this bombshell, the ape-gloves folded primly on the clasp of her go-to-church real leather purse.

Kevin sat to attention. "Jane?" He whispered automatically despite the phone—half from shock, half from caution. "Where? No—don't say."

"She's an awfully odd girl, Kevin. Are you really . . . serious . . . about her?"

He just shook his head. Explaining Jane and himself to anyone—even, or especially, his parents—seemed futile. "Can you . . . hint . . . where you saw her?"

His mother leaned into the Plexiglas, breathing confessionally into the receiver. "Your condominium. We went there looking for you."

"When?"

"Oh—" Her eyes sought her husband's. "Thursday."

"Thursday. And this is Saturday, right?"

His father nodded. "We closed the store Wednesday night and drove down early Thursday. Now I guess we can tell customers it was for the holiday weekend."

"Did my place . . . look all right?" The feds must have tossed it, too, Kevin guessed.

"Fine. Perfect. Your decorating is a little barren for my taste—," his mother added scrupulously.

"Was . . . anyone else there?" Government men.

"Just her." His mother's face tightened. "She was right at home."

"She wants to know does this Jane person live there," his father put in man-to-man.

"No, Mom. Jane doesn't live with me. She was only at my place once."

"Oh. Well, she made herself right to home yesterday morning. Ate some food from the refrigerator. An empty bottle of beer was on the coffee table." Distaste flavored her tone. In Clare Blake's book, nice girls didn't drink beer and certainly not from the bottle. "Maybe *you* had it," she added hopefully. Real men, on the other hand, did drink beer. From the bottle. Only.

Kevin smiled, warmed despite himself by the soft, familiar slings and arrows exchanged between the generations, between country parents and city sons. They felt far less lethal than the projectiles the cold, cruel world of strangers had hurled his way recently.

"I'm glad Jane found some chow," Kevin said. "You don't know how I've worried about her—"

"What about you? What about us?" Arthur Blake grabbed the receiver solo, swinging into full parental mode again. "It's always been your work. Your work first and foremost."

"I'm sorry. I never would have brought you into this."

"That's just it, Kevin!" His mother was hissing into the mouthpiece, agitated. "You leave us out of everything— your life here, your work. You never tell us anything."

"I can't tell you what's really behind this, either."

"Why?" his father demanded.

"Because it's worse than even you think."

Their faces fell in tandem, a side effect of thirty-eight years of textbook marriage.

"Go back to Elk River," Kevin urged his parents in the same quieting tone he found effective with patients. "There's nothing you can do—nothing they'll let you do, except get hurt. Just . . . don't believe everything you hear about me," he added. Having their only son in jail was no picnic for his parents. He had to warn them that it could get worse.

The cop had opened the door behind him.

"We'll . . . talk to that Kandinsky fellow again," his father suggested. "If he's getting a lawyer—"

The cop had Kevin by the arm, pulling him up from the table. Kevin had already accepted the way of the world in jail, but his mother didn't have to.

She rose with him and pressed against the clear plastic. Kevin touched fingers with her through the barrier, half convinced he could sniff the faint aroma of a recent home permanent. Next he would be smelling gingerbread cookies and seeing the old kitchen linoleum in his dreams—regressing to the peaceful past that had never been as tranquil as it seemed in retrospect.

You of all people, Blake, should know better, he told himself as the cop closed the door, framing his parents' worried faces behind a sheet of smeared glass.

He'd botched it again, as he always did, with his parents, in the name of sparing them, sparing himself.

A white-attired trusty wheeled a cart of supper trays down the hall as Kevin was hustled past. No gingerbread men lurked in the tray's shallow food wells. He looked.

So Jane had still been free as recently as Thursday night—free and raiding his refrigerator. Triumph did a loop-de-loop in Kevin's arterial system. Jane was free! That was what he was fighting for, keeping quiet for, getting dumped on for. That made everything worth it.

Kevin laughed suddenly to himself. Aloud.

The cop glanced suspiciously in his direction.

Kevin laughed even louder.

Chapter Twenty-five

Jane Doe lay sleeping in her hospital bed. A rack beside her trailed thin plastic tubing to her arm, silently dripping some clear substance into her veins. Her arms lay at her sides, the fingers loosely curled into her palms.

A large mirror on the opposite wall reflected a white-uniformed nurse who fussed at the other side of the bed, but Jane didn't stir. Her eyes were almost closed, and her rough-cut hair fanned on the pillow, looking as coarse as a horse's trimmed mane.

Silence occupied the room with her, and a sense of waiting, a certain somber anticipation usually found in funeral homes and hospitals. The only prop missing was the obligatory vase of flowers.

Turner stared down at her for a minute more, basking in the satisfaction of the successful hunter, then left the room.

The hall beyond was quiet, too. No public address system rasped out summonses. No one paged Drs. Kildare, Casey, Welby or Craig. No one paged any doctors, because there was only one doctor to page, and no one at all to do it.

Turner cracked a nondescript door next to the one he'd left and stepped into a room. Through a glass darkly, he glimpsed Jane Doe still lying in the same position, still . . . dormant. It was an odd word to use, but that was how he thought of her now.

Hunched over on a folding chair the color of tepid cocoa, Dr. Eric Nordstrom sat drawn up to the looking glass that was a window for him, a reflection for anyone in Jane Doe's room. The rooms had been prepared—Turner almost thought of it as setting a stage—to Nordstrom's exact specifications days before. No one had ever doubted that Jane Doe would be found.

Turner waited, struck by the scene's unconscious symbolic power: Nordstrom—a watchful human eyepiece of an inhuman microscope focusing all its faculties on the room beyond.

So Nordstrom hoped to probe the brain of the woman in the bed. So he hoped to steal from chamber to chamber and up the spiral staircase of her memory and oversee the unfolding of her reputed abilities. The man was an earwig, Turner suddenly perceived, drilling through the brain on a relentlessly linear path, razor-straight from ear to ear.

"Have a chair, Mr. Turner; the show hasn't started yet."

Turner grunted and went to stand over Nordstrom. "We don't have a lot of time."

"Why not?"

"Blake can't be kept on ice forever."

"Blake! He's redundant—and knows it."

"Washington waits for no man."

"It'll wait for this. You can't rush . . . certain things."

"What do you plan to do?" Turner asked at last, roweled by curiosity.

Nordstrom braced an elbow on his knee and tapped his lips with his fingers. "Watch. Wait. Manipulate."

"Is her condition that serious that you have to wait?"

"Her condition? Her condition is marvelous. So . . . fresh. You'd think she was a slab of salmon just dropped by air from Scotland. The moment I got her body-wrapped in blankets, her temperature began to rise—steadily—to a perfect ninety-eight-point-six. Her vital signs are textbook —on the nose for her age and weight."

"Odd about her weight—"

"What do you mean?"

"She looks drastically thinner than I expected from the Myerson sketch. How on earth could she have lost so much weight in just a day or so on her own?"

Nordstrom shrugged. "Water retention and depletion, maybe. Women lose weight easily."

"Not to hear my wife tell it."

Nordstrom squinted over his shoulder at Turner. "You have a wife. How interesting. I never associate you government types with such accouterments."

212

"I don't have a dog," Turner said, tightening his jaw, "so don't get your hopes up. What does she weigh exactly?"

In the ensuing pause, Turner observed the quarter-sized bald spot at the center of Nordstrom's skull. He wondered what he would find if he drilled right through that spot into the psychiatrist's skull. Probably dry ice.

"What does she weigh?" he repeated.

"A hundred-something." Nordstrom shrugged.

"So do I."

"A hundred-and-two and three-quarter pounds, all right?"

"That's about what she weighed when she was first found. Blake's records indicated he didn't much like that weight. She was up to a hundred and twenty-five when she left the hospital."

"Blake has proletarian tastes," Nordstrom sneered. "Blowsy, bloated females. She's perfectly healthy, believe me. You should be so lucky—no fillings, no visual impairment—"

Nordstrom's strange indifference to his patient's physical frailty irritated Turner enough to unloose a taunt. "And no hymen anymore, I'd guess, from reading between the lines of her and Blake's little odyssey. Or didn't you check that out?"

Nordstrom's shoulders stiffened. "That . . . intimate an examination wasn't necessary. What do you take me for?"

"I don't know. I imagine I'll find out. I'm your official baby-sitter."

"I don't need anybody!"

"Liaison. This is a top-security, top-secret government site, Dr. Nordstrom. Any personnel on duty here have been checked out from birth to the next solar eclipse. We are very careful whom we let in. And out."

"Where are we, anyway?"

"You don't have to know."

"It's hardly top secret. We drove for two or three hours, northwest I'd say. We're in rural Minnesota, somewhere. And this building—" Nordstrom looked up, as if envisioning much more than he saw. "It was dark when we arrived, but the structure was huge, rambling. Almost . . . Gothic,

were one inclined to a romantic turn of thought. Therefore
—it's some . . . factory, I'd say. Some deserted factory.
You must have set up this hospital stuff in a small corner of
it."

"Not bad. I thought you were all wrapped up in your
patient back in the ambulance, but you didn't miss much."

"I generally don't. You don't like this assignment."

"I don't like most of my assignments."

"Duty-driven. Obsessive-compulsive. A lot of self-hate.
Authoritarian father, but you need it. Hence, Uncle Sam."

"I never asked you for a *self*-analysis, Nordstrom."
Turner remained amused while the shrink scraped his chair
closer to the two-way glass. He ignored the jibe.

"We don't have a lot of time," Turner repeated. Then he
left.

Nordstrom's figure remained hummocked near the window. He moved finally, furtively in the empty room. His
briefcase sat by his feet. He lifted it to his knees, tipped it
open. More manila folders fanned agape inside. Satisfied
they were there, he put down the briefcase and went into
the room next door.

The "nurse"—and so she had been, at one time—had
long gone.

Nordstrom checked the IV. The clear thin liquid dripped
implacably. Turner, he thought, like most laymen, probably took the substance for some kind of sustenance—sugar
water. In this case it was saline solution only. Pure unadul-
terated salt water.

Nordstrom looked down at Jane Doe's flat form. She'd
undoubtedly . . . perform . . . better on an empty stomach. His fingers twitched. Turner's jibe rubbed like a burr
at the base of his skull. Suddenly he was breathing heavily,
furiously. He stripped the top sheet off Jane Doe.

Her deep, shallow respiration continued unaltered. A
fragment of overhead light glimmered in the slits of her
eyes. Nordstrom's left hand reached out and his fingers
clenched the hem of her short hospital gown. His eyes
studied her knees—marvels of articulated bone.

Donne had been right, Nordstrom thought, what did it

come down to—always—but "a bracelet of bright hair about the bone." And what Eliot had said of Donne was right on, too: "He knew the anguish of the marrow/The ague of the skeleton; No contact possible to flesh/Allayed the fever of the bone."

No one saw such things anymore. No one knew how to be metaphysical. A crude line of prose flashed across the poetry of Nordstrom's thoughts. Turner and his insinuations! His obscene insinuations. *Insinuation* was too fine a word for it.

Nordstrom's eyelids flickered. His fingers clenched and unclenched on the rolled gown hem. The fabric's texture reminded Nordstrom of the coarse, thin and invariably white dishcloths the maids in his parents' house had used. In time, the towels became spotted with faint clots of yellow, remnants of forgotten stains. Nordstrom had sickened at the sight, at seeing the dusky-skinned maids wiping—laughing and chattering in alien tongues—and wiping the dishes the family ate their food from with cloths caked with old stains.

Soon he had grown too old to wander into the kitchen, but he never forgot the stains. Now, Turner had spoiled the surgical precision of his preparations by mentioning the unmentionable.

His fingers jerked up the gown, brushed a nimbus of yet unseen fleece. Should he check? Prove Turner a liar? Or prove that once again the sheets were soiled, the dishcloths filthy, the linens sticky and warm. . . .

No, he would not debase himself to rut and probe like the rawest schoolboy. He had never debased himself. He would assume the best. Jane Doe was a blank slate, and he held the chalky bone to write upon it with. His fingers trembled and released the gown. Wrinkled, it fell back over the lean lines of her thighs.

Nordstrom checked her eyes—finding his heart pounding again like a guilty schoolboy's. They remained the same . . . all but shut, a pearly bone-white glimmer shining through the thick hairs of her dark lashes. The coarseness of these features—ocular matter, flesh, hair—disgusted him, and he left the room, shutting the door very carefully, as if someone might hear him.

Someone did.

*   *   *

Jane's eyes flick open on his departure—wide, alarmed. She has been . . . dreaming. Her thoughts hover over the word, the concept. *Dreaming.* She somehow knows what that means, but has never associated that particular state with herself. At least not consciously.

She blinks. In that instant, it is as if the camera that is her eyes has frozen every detail of the place on some undeveloped film behind her eyes. For an instant light and dark reverse in her mind. The bed is black, as are the walls, her skin. . . .

The window—she glances to the mirror and peers into another room—the window is wider than it is tall, just as it had been in the other hospital room where she had wakened once before. For the first time.

She sits up and gets out of bed. Alongside her, something jolts, then comes jerking after, as if a leash has been pulled. Jane does not recognize leashes. She feels the tape pulling at the fine hairs on the outside of her elbow but ignores it and goes to the window.

So does the other room's occupant, pulling closer. Jane pushes her face to the glass, feels the cold surface flatten the tip of her nose, sees her vision cross. She backs away. So does her . . . her reflection.

Jane touches a hand to her face. She seems different than before. Shrunken. Colder to the touch. Was this how she had looked in the University of Minnesota Hospitals? Kevin had said she was gaining weight, later. He'd sounded pleased, and had let her look in a mirror.

She steps away from the startled image of herself. Kevin had said. . . . But it is confused. *She* is confused. Why is she back in the hospital again? Where is Kevin? What had been the last thing she remembered, besides dark and cold and something very large pressing down upon her . . . ? And voices, buzzing.

Jane glances at the mirror. Her troubled self still stands

there, and suddenly, from some distorted corner of her mind, an image flies into the picture like a glossy black crow cawing for attention.

A man. There is a man in the mirror with her—behind the mirror! Jane steps back as the man's image grows more concrete. The crow spreads rustling wings. Its caws come soft and certain, like the ticking of a clock: A shadow forms behind the Jane in the mirror, engulfs her, walks out of the mirror.

Jane retreats, hearing the distant rattle of something falling, feeling a quick, burning pull at her elbow. She sits back on the bed, one foot folded under her. Beside her the IV tower crashes to the floor.

And then . . . then she is reliving it all again. The past, or a dream, or something she had been told had happened and now did.

The man is coming at her, spewing words, anger. Matusek, he is shouting hoarsely. How did you get Matusek? Jane can't discern his features, but his voice is perfectly familiar, and her brain even produces a name for him. Kellehay. She has seen him before, just like this. But—

The onrushing image is armed with a soft white shield it presses against her face, against her wildly disoriented brain. Déjà vu, Jane thinks, falling back on the bed. The girls in the dorm TV lounge had called such things a "rerun." "Oh, they running that old thing again?"

This rerun of Kellehay looks and sounds and seems as real as the unremembered original. Jane feels she dangles upside down with a pillow as cold as snow pressed over her face, sucking the breath from her mouth and nostrils.

Then she *is* lying on an ice-cold bed of drifts. Gasping for breath, for memory, Jane feels herself lifted off the snowy sheets, feels her body lighten and rise like a bubble. Inside a buoyant translucent cocoon of self-distance, Jane gazes down on . . . herself.

This self is stripped, naked. She looks colder than the snow surrounding her bloodless body. Her eyes are shut, her lips slightly parted on a pearly bone-white glimmer. Snow drifts over her limbs, washing watered silk patterns

217

across the alabaster skin, patterns that change even as Jane watches.

Jane there, Jane . . . dead. Jane here . . . Jane alive but . . . disconnected from herself. Or connected to someone, something else? The past—or present? A memory, like Kellehay, made flesh? Or an unforgettable episode of amnesia?

Then Jane is plummeting into that frozen image of herself, her senses merging with its senseless form. Ice numbs her brain and runs cold talons down her nervous system. Snow, light and lethal as a feather pillow, shifts over her mind, her body, smothering, smothering—silent, soft smothering. . . . In the distance, she hears voices.

Jane screams at the enveloping blankness of her brain and pushes off reality in shadow form. No, no, no!

The whiteness evaporates. A shadow is catapulting backward, away from her, growing smaller and dimmer. It is still large enough to crash right through the mirror/window. Glass shatters with the shriek of wind chimes. The silver ice of its surface blackens to jagged starshapes made by something falling through. Kellehay is gone. The pillow of cold death is gone. Her helpless vision of herself is gone. Only Jane remains.

Jane huddles on the bed, her feet ice-cold, her fingers numb. The last time a similar shock had disoriented her, she had retreated into the warm inner circle of herself. Now she isn't sure that self is to be trusted.

Now she doesn't retreat.

Jane rises, slowly, and patters barefoot over the floor to the hole in the mirror. Her reflection does not advance to meet her this time. She peers through the cavity into a darkened room occupied only by an empty folding chair.

Chapter Twenty-six

"God, Kandy, I wish you'd sent my folks back home to Elk River instead of here," Kevin said.

"What was I going to do? Lie? I have enough trouble lying to my *own* parents." Martin Kandinsky shaped his elastic form to the molded chair's rigid curves and eyed the "contact" visitors' room.

"Boy, they sure don't go upscale on decor around here. You catch that *orange* they painted the waiting room walls? Guaranteed to induce severe psychosis in a catatonic. Haven't these folks ever heard of Nonaggressive Pink paint?"

"You should see where they keep me," Kevin answered. "Makes a Kafka film set look like Palm Beach moderne."

"You have a private cell?" Alvin Ruderman asked.

Kevin glanced to the earnest-looking guy in a T-shirt sitting beside his friend. Like Kandy, Ruderman sported enough long curly hair to coif an Assyrian king. But Kandy's lawyer knew the territory. He'd gotten Kandy in for a "contact" visit—no Plexiglas barrier, no phone—by calling him a paralegal.

"Dormitory," Kevin said.

Ruderman winced. "Ouch. Can't be fun for a guy like you."

"I'm okay. What I'm worried about is Jane."

"Your . . . missing client," Ruderman put in.

Kevin glanced at Kandy, then started laughing.

"My missing client. Delicately put. You could say that." He slid his elbows across the table and lowered his voice. "I've, uh, had some good news today. From my parents."

"See?" Kandy beamed. "It wasn't a total loss."

Kevin quieted him with a glance and spoke even more

softly. "They saw Jane Thursday night. At my place. My . . . old place, I guess you'd say. Anyway, at least I know that she hasn't been caught yet. That makes all this worth it."

Kandy scratched his scraggly sideburns.

"What's the matter?"

"Your place. I tool on by every now and then—okay, I'm curious. The thing is, Kevin, I've seen this big van parked there—brand-new and all enclosed. No funny little bubble windows and not a speck of custom paint. It's there all the time. Smells like the feds are watching your place."

"My parents came and went okay!"

"Your parents aren't important, apparently," Ruderman said. "To anyone except you."

"But Jane was all right! My parents saw her there. From what they said, she was fine."

"Thursday night." Ruderman proved himself a realist. "This is Saturday. They could have picked her up as she left, and your parents would have known nothing about it."

"Shit!"

"Sorry, man." Kandy looked it. Even his woolly queue seemed to droop down his back.

"They could have missed her, too." Ruderman pushed his black-framed glasses over the pimple perching on the bridge of his nose. "It's possible. If they *did* get her, there'd be no police record, though, not like yours. Clandestine, that's how the buggers would handle it."

Kevin washed his face with his palms. Worry made his skin feel like corrugated cardboard—and his fingers were cold, a sign of anxiety.

"I'd . . . hoped she'd be okay until I got out of here—"

"She might be, man." Ruderman shrugged. "Look, I'm saying they *could* have got her. Doesn't mean they did. They're not gonna tell *us,* that's for sure."

Kevin nodded dully, visualizing the calendar. Friday the thirteenth. Then today and Sunday. Then Monday the sixteenth, the holiday; Tuesday, Wednesday . . . God, he'd go wacko waiting in here that long! He looked hopefully at Ruderman, who was shaking his head.

"No way. They got you good. There's no way to shorten your thirty-six hours when the first four days don't count."

"What does count?" Kevin wondered.

"Keeping a low profile." Ruderman almost hissed his intensity. "Don't give these cops any lip. No name-calling, nothing. They'll Simonize the floor with you. Just keep your nose clean and wait. Besides, we're only assuming they're filing you away to teach you a lesson. They could get serious and arraign you. You could be facing a whole lotta years in places much worse than this. Stillwater Prison, for instance."

"Hey, Kev, worry about your own skin for a while," Kandy put in. "I bet Miss Doe is doin' okay. That girl always did have unsuspected resources."

"Yeah. Thanks, Kandy. Ruderman."

Kevin tried to give the lawyer a parting handshake, but a hand descended firmly to Kevin's shoulder. He tightened, then steadied himself. A cop hovered as he rose and shrugged at the two men. Then the cop wordlessly escorted him back to the dorm cell, back to the routine of idle incarceration.

Jail was all routine, Kevin began to see, for the cops and for the prisoners, if not for him. His cellmates slumped on their bunks, acknowledging his return with leaden-eyed curiosity.

Big black Rollo—a knife artist, it turned out, and the cell's natural leader—had accepted Kevin as an old-timer. His successful "tangle" with Jesús haloed him with lingering macho glory, just as the stigma of caving in would have dogged him.

The morose DWI, Harry, huddled against the wall, mulling the lesson his cellmates had punched home just last night. Wacko Waldo, slumped on a chair, was in for the duration, too. Nobody wanted him anywhere else.

Kevin could only lie on his bunk and watch TV—a rerun of *The Beverly Hillbillies*. Most of the men were leering dispiritedly at the buxom blonde in the cast. She was probably a grandmother by now.

He stared at the ceiling and listened to the laugh track,

clocking the guffaw that came regular as a pendulum. He hoped Jane was somewhere warm and safe right now. He just hoped that she—somehow—was somewhere safe in good hands.

*   *   *

"Where is she now?"

Turner bent to pluck a dagger of shattered glass from the floor. On the other side of the wall, he could see the men fitting a new sheet of two-way mirror to the frame.

"Down the hall," Nordstrom answered. "In another room. I didn't think she'd turn this volatile. Rushton's with her."

Turner nodded. "The nurse."

"Ex-nurse."

"Ex-nurse." Turner's lifted foot swept some mirror shards from the seat of the folding chair. "You know, Nordstrom . . ." Turner managed to smile pleasantly. "If you'd been sitting in that chair"—Nordstrom's glasses flashed in the dimness as he looked where Turner pointed —"that shattered glass might have nailed you."

"But I wasn't sitting there. Will you stop nursemaiding me?"

Turner smiled. Nordstrom was antsy to get the window repaired and Jane back to her "hospital" room without realizing that the mirror was a large-scale peephole.

"Besides," the psychiatrist was adding icily, "Jane Doe had no idea about the existence of this room—how could she? She just panicked in the night, got disoriented, thrashed around her room, and knocked something into the mirror."

"What?"

"How do I know what? The IV. It was torn loose."

"The impact must have come lower than that, from the glass splinter pattern. Looks like a bullet came right through it—not just a neat one-holer, but a shot that sent out shock waves, like in a pond when you throw a stone in. Look, you can see the spiderweb effect edging the old mirror."

Even as Turner spoke, workmen pulled the remaining glass free.

"You're saying that she did it deliberately—threw a tantrum, threw something at it and broke the glass."

"You sure are slow on the uptake for a shrink, Nordstrom. I'm saying that she did it *by herself.* Without using any intermediary. Any tool. Any *thing.*"

Nordstrom bit his lower lip, gnawing what was already raw and cracked white. "You mean her . . . powers. You're saying she's already demonstrated them. Here and now. Then, good! That's . . . more progress than I'd hoped for."

"Congratulations," Turner said so slowly that Nordstrom searched his face in vain for irony.

Turner pussyfooted around the broken glass, then bent to claim another shard of glass. "Weird. Even the tint seems to have burned off. I'll have my boys play jigsaw puzzle with this mess. Might be instructive."

Turner cracked the door open on a well-lit slice of hall, making himself into a shadow man against it. He paused before leaving for a last word.

"By the way, Dr. Nordstrom, whatever Jane Doe did last night—and however she did it—she did indeed rip the IV loose. It was dripping that clear stuff you're pumping into her all over the floor. I figured it was sugar water." Turner waited, then made his point. "Then I tasted it. Doctor."

Turner shut the door, leaving Nordstrom alone in the windowless room's eternal dusk, dead center of a bouquet of splintered glass, staring though a hole in the wall.

Chapter Twenty-seven

She is lost.

The room to which they returned her is the same she awoke in. It should not be.

The shadow named Kellehay has evaporated, but so has the broken glass that banished him.

So the room is the same, but it is not the same.

Dr. Nordstrom connects her again to the plastic tubing through which clear liquid flickers. He seems to be waiting for something, watching her and waiting.

Jane is indifferent. She has been linked to a similar apparatus before, she remembers, when she first came. It is as unnecessary now as it was then.

Across from her the mirror reflects the upper third of the room, its most characterless portions—ceiling and wall joints. Cobwebs.

Jane reflects, too—upon events. She knows firsthand now, from her own relived experience, that she expelled Kellehay out of the hospital window. She doesn't think to the inevitable end of that action. She only knows that Kellehay is gone now, forever, and it is her doing.

What she remembers most is the *feeling* of Kellehay falling out of her life into his death. She recalls how the power had welled in her and overflowed until it simply crowded Kellehay out of reality as he knew it.

She has never thought about her power before, never seen it as something separate. A tool. She would like to hold it, her power. Turn it this way and that. Weigh it. Study it. It doesn't seem to be that kind of thing.

She can only think it, dream it. It is flowering in her mind now, petal by petal. Its roots probe deep within her

224

very nature, relentlessly fueling the pattern of her body's biochemistry.

Some strands of it bear such labels as "instinct" and "reflex." Others modify themselves, adapt. Still others respond to outside forces. One such force enters the room now.

Dr. Nordstrom is smiling, as he always seems to be when she sees him. He bears a tray. Dishes rattle as he pulls a blond wood hospital table over her bed, pinning Jane beneath the bland overshadowing arm. The position invariably makes her feel slightly trapped.

"Some dinner, Jane," he says, grinning—but she remembers that they always grin in hospitals when they produce food, as perhaps they do when they produce babies.

"Soft foods," he croons, foolish as a nurse, any nurse. He picks up the spoon—there is only a spoon, no fork, no knife—and prods at puddles of soup and egg custard and other pale, gelatinous things in saucers.

Some of it is hot. Scents tickle Jane's nostrils, triggering physical responses and more . . . memories.

"Sit up, Jane. Here, against the pillows, so you can see yourself in the mirror. You look much better already."

Jane cocks her head at herself. She looks the same. She looks as she looked before Kevin put her in Willhelm Hall. Before she . . . adapted to the student nurses' ways. Jane lifts a hand to her dark hair. It just brushes her shoulders and could use a combing.

Dr. Nordstrom is lying. Jane knows she looks awful. Gaunt. Pale. Dazed. She remembers the student nurses pushing small plastic trays of colored powders at her, banishing her pallor with small pointed sponges. Alarm vibrates through her consciousness. How did she come to look so dreadful again? And so quickly?

But she can't remember. It's becoming a habit. She remembers nothing of where she's been, or with whom, or for how long. She remembers nothing since those who had created her returned her to the place that had created her kind. Jane knows what to label this strange lack of continu-

225

ity. Amnesia . . . a medical term, but it would make a pretty name. It is as if her life—or what passes for it—has been a chain, and every other link is invisible.

Dr. Nordstrom is leaning so near that Jane can see a pale comma of eyelash pressed to the inside of one eyeglass lens. He is pushing a small bowl of pungent heat under her chin.

"Try some," he's saying, smiling, his eyes mirthless and shrunken. "It'll bring back your strength. You must eat."

Saliva pools in Jane's mouth. Reflex again. The smell, the idea of eating provokes a string of memories. Breakfast in Kevin's condo the morning after the night she went to find him; late-night Chee-tos parties in Melanie's room at the dorm. "Food" means nothing to Jane. Memories of certain foods at certain times have their own associative power. Her stomach yawns and stirs.

Jane reaches for the shiny silver spoon Dr. Nordstrom has poised at the lip of her mouth.

"But perhaps it's too soon." He jerks the spoon and bowl away, shoves the table toward the bed's foot and takes its place. "You probably don't even feel hunger yet, do you?" He smiles.

Jane's appetite, roused, subsides with a subterranean growl. Dr. Nordstrom pats her flat abdomen. "You'll get food soon enough. Soon enough to grow fat on it. Perhaps we should work on food for thought, first."

There is no perhaps in his tone. Memories of food shift into flashing visions of the people the foods were eaten with—chattering girls, Kevin . . . and raw, dripping food rendered over a fire. They are all sitting in a circle in the cold, wearing fur coats, clawing hunks of venison into their mouths. They? Who? That's not what Dr. Nordstrom is asking in that deep, narcotic voice of his.

"What word did Blake use to hypnotize you, Jane?" he is saying. "His notes are unclear on that."

"Word?"

"Word." The smile congeals on the surface of Dr. Nordstrom's face, just as the chicken fat skins the soup cooling on the tablearm just beyond reach.

Jane hoards the notion, then spits out the first word in her mind. "Zyunsinth."

226

"Zyun—sinth?"

Jane nods.

"That's Blake, always has to be different. I'm going to try hypnotizing you, all right?"

He doesn't wait for Jane's affirmative, but begins droning in his narcoleptic voice. "You are very tired, Jane. Very sleepy. You are relaxed and sleepy. Your eyes grow heavy, too heavy to keep open. You hear only my voice, give only my voice all that you know. . . ."

Like the food, the words strike some chord in her suggestive center. Jane floats on a cold sea of white linen, clinging to the surface.

"Zyunsinth," Dr. Nordstrom says, sounding embarrassed.

Jane enjoys hearing the familiar syllables; experiencing the familiar circumstances. If only Kevin were here! She smiles. In the gray haze beyond heavy eyelids, Dr. Nordstrom is no longer smiling.

"Jane! You do hear me, don't you?"

She wishes Dr. Nordstrom would keep quiet; the ritual of hypnotism has sparked many warm memories that Jane had been carrying like cold seeds inside her skull. They scatter now, take root and stretch, shoot up past the soil line in her head into the sunlight on her hair.

"Jane, answer me!"

Jane opens her eyes. "Yes, Dr. Nordstrom?"

"Are you hypnotized or not?" His smile has wrung itself tight, like a cleaning rag.

Jane considers it. Seriously. "I . . . don't think so, Dr. Nordstrom."

"Why not? I used the word you gave me."

"Yes. . . ."

"Well?"

"I don't know. I liked hearing the word. It's *my* word. And I feel very rested. But I don't think you took me to the place Kevin did. It's all too much 'here' yet." She looks at him limpidly. "Kevin would find that very interesting."

Nordstrom's arm backhands the food tray off the table onto the floor. Jane blinks. The presence of the food had

227

agitated hunger. Its absence stirs another instinct into action. She feels her body float down the metabolic dial until it rests on "empty." So she is and so she shall remain.

"There'll be no more of that until you cooperate," Dr. Nordstrom promises.

"I don't understand. I'm doing what you tell me. What else can I do?"

He leans in, over her. He is like an ice-cold iron coming down on an ironing board.

"Tap your powers for me, Jane. Show me what you can do. You broke that glass last night—"

She glances to her image in the mirror. "It's not broken—"

"We fixed it. Don't play stupid. You *will* show me how you make things move."

"I—I don't always know."

"You do it. You know. If you won't unlock your subconscious, I'll have to batter down your consciousness. That takes longer. And it hurts, Jane. There'll be no more food until you produce results."

"I'm not hungry now," Jane protests logically.

"That's the first symptom of starvation, Jane. You don't have much to hang on by. Only a filament. I can keep you on the edge of life for a long time." His eyes glitter behind the glasses.

"You are not like Kevin," she accuses.

"No. I won't coddle that arbitrary psyche of yours. I play hardball."

Jane looks blank. Dr. Nordstrom pulls away. His teeth are sawing at his lower lip and a droplet of blood suddenly bursts into bloom on his mouth. He rubs his hand across it, spreading the crimson to his fingers. Jane watches, then speaks.

"Marlene at the dorm used to get cold sores all the time, Dr. Nordstrom. She used Blistex. She was really mad when she got them just before a date—"

"Shut up!" Dr. Nordstrom says in a way Kevin never would. Jane feels her face sadden. She misses Kevin. He

228

would never let her be so confused. Why can't she remember him clearly? Why does the bright colored light make everything around it fade to black? If only she could remember. Kevin always said it was important to remember. . . .

Dr. Nordstrom has risen and is backing away from the bed. He pulls long canvas straps from below the mattress, begins buckling Jane immobile upon it.

"You want to eat, I know you do! Damn sluts always want to eat and ruin it. All right. You'll use your powers."

He points to the dishes on the floor, toppled but not broken—made of thick creamy restaurant-grade pottery too heavy to break. Stepping-stone puddles of chicken noodle soup splatter the beige vinyl tile. Egg custard has broken into spittle-shaped globs.

"You want food," Dr. Nordstrom says with a challenge in his voice. "Pick it up. Levitate it to your mouth, stuff yourself with the damn dishes, for all I care! Blake got somewhere with you, and I will, too. My way. It won't be pleasant."

Jane lifts her head from the pillow to study the scattered food. It doesn't look very appetizing anymore. Neither does Dr. Nordstrom. His eyes seem hollower than hers and the stubble Kevin complained of after he razored off his beard is beginning to freckle Dr. Nordstrom's narrow lower jaw. Melanie at the dorm, Jane remembers, was crazy about Don Johnson on *Miami Vice*. Dr. Nordstrom is no Don Johnson, Jane decides. She knows that much.

"Either way, I'll be happy in the morning," he is telling her, telling himself. "If the food's still there, I know you'll be weaker by that much. If not, I'll know how to force you to use your powers."

Something occurs to her.

"What if I need to go to the bathroom?" she wonders. With the IV trickling endlessly into her arm, she feels a constant burn in her bladder.

Dr. Nordstrom finally smiles again. "Dirty yourself."

He leaves without saying good-bye.

229

Jane lies in bed, the big straps tight across her chest and thighs, the little ones tight around her ankles and wrists. She finds Dr. Nordstrom highly inconsistent.

*   *   *

Wacko Waldo is crooning "Melancholy Baby" to himself in a decent imitation of a kazoo. He has perfect pitch.

The cell is dark except for the unearthly glow of light from the shower area. Kevin stares at the cinder-block wall where the light bathes it. He feels like a kid at camp. Maybe, if he visualizes what he wants hard enough and long enough, he can make it happen.

What he's visualizing is a bit of heavenly intervention. In his mind, a figure darkens against the pale background.

It is vague and tall, and wearing one helluva big fur coat. There's just enough light to reveal the glimmer of slitted eyes. It's sort of a cross between a pimp and King Kong and it's the only thing keeping Kevin sane as he listens to the snoring and the humming and the sound of his own brain quietly cannibalizing itself.

Zyunsinth lurks there, in person, ready to come in—level everybody, pull out an Uzi and bust Kevin out of jail.

Then where? he wonders. His inner self is irritatingly answerless. It is probably three in the morning by now, he figures, that classic hour for nocturnal angst.

Chances are that even Nordstrom sleeps. Or does he? He could easily be insomniac. Even now he could be slipping the narrow silver eyes of his array of needles into Jane's veins, pumping the same sinister drugs into her body and brain that he used on Kevin.

He shuts his eyes. The retinal afterimage remains—a dark furry figure burned onto a dirty white wall. Staring, Kevin sees the tiny likeness resolve into perfect focus, drifting in the dark of his eyes. It exists, the damn thing exists—a monster of the id, the ego, the embattled subconscious. He watches it grow.

His eyes peel open. Something shapeless is shambling against the ill-lit shower wall. Kevin's heart quickens with a contradictory blend of alarm and Frankensteinian hu-

230

bris. Jane has proven the mind capable of extraordinary feats. Maybe he can . . .

The figure sways from foot to foot and begins humming "Good Night, Ladies" in flawless kazoolike tones.

Chapter Twenty-eight

"Suddenly everybody wants to see me," Kevin complained. "I wish you folks could stagger your visits over the next few days. It's gonna get lonely in here and it's only Monday morning. Nice of you government types to visit on Martin Luther King's birthday, though. I thought you'd take the day off."

"I hear you have adequate company in your cell," Turner said.

Kevin dropped the false cheer. He was surprised to see Turner here, especially so early Monday morning. "I didn't know you worked the dawn patrol."

"I work when it's needed."

"So . . . what can I do for you?"

"Treat Jane Doe."

"That easy? Sure. When I get out. When I find her."

"You can get out when I say so. And you don't need to find her."

Kevin struggled to keep his face blank. Turner was putting on an act, he told himself. Turner was doing what he was paid to do: applying a calculated amount of pressure to a predictable reactor—Kevin.

"You claim you've got her, then?"

"I'm tired." Turner leaned back in his chair and let his face show it. "I don't need a last dance with you. We've got her. Actually, Nordstrom's got her."

"You sonofabitch." Dull jailhouse rage choked Kevin. He knew better than to attack Turner, but he also knew that he wanted to. He wanted to attack them all, and he was too damn smart to do it.

Turner gave Kevin's rote obscenity a nod of recognition. "Too tired for that, too. If you'd agree to work with her, help her, I could get you out in a minute—well, a couple hours, anyway. They cling to their paperwork around here, even when cutting red tape."

"It's a lie. A bluff. Psychological warfare. You don't have Jane. You think I don't see that this whole place, this whole detention system, is designed to soften me up?

"Why was I paraded in the front door? All the other guys came through the underground garage, nice and private and more secure. No, I get civilians gawking at me all the way in. Everybody else gets two or three phone calls. I get one. They hoped the bastards in the dorm cell would nail me to the wall, but it didn't work that way. You think I haven't figured that out?"

"I always said you were smart. Think it over. Why would I lie about having Jane Doe? What would I get out of a bluff?"

"I might . . . drop my guard. Say something. Give you a clue to where she really is."

"I'll tell you where she is." Turner stood and leaned over the table. The higher he loomed over Kevin the lower his voice got. Kevin had to admire his psychology.

"At this moment your Jane Doe is in an abandoned plant somewhere in mid-state. She's lying in a room made to look like a hospital, with a big mirror on the wall and a little shrink sitting on the other side watching everything she does.

"He's 'feeding' her on saline IVs, Blake, making notes in his manila folders and getting ready to take her brain apart like a Tinkertoy.

"She's way thinner than her sketches. Some bums found her lying naked in the snow near the railroad tracks in downtown Minneapolis. She'd been mugged, stripped and left for dead. The meat wagon almost took her away Saturday morning, but Nordstrom saved her. Found a pulse in her foot. Inventive, our Dr. Nordstrom. I guess we both should be grateful."

232

Kevin's head was in his hands. "No."

"Treat her. That's all you have to do. Take her where you would have taken her anyway—to her outer and inner limits. It's your job, Blake. Nobody can do it better."

"No."

"Don't trust *me*. Trust your instincts. She's confused. And weak. And dangerous, I think."

"No."

Turner straightened slowly, as if it hurt.

Kevin heard the rustle of Turner's raincoat. It sounded like someone opening a box of crackers—the rectangular old-fashioned kind with the dark blue wrapper that he hadn't seen in years. For a moment he felt young and small and wished he could hide in somebody's kitchen all night and sneak out to eat soda crackers and Kool-Aid and they'd never find him and they would be very, very sorry. . . .

"What'll you do?" he asked Turner.

"My job."

"It's a lousy thing to do."

"Sometimes. I'm sorry," Turner said before leaving.

Kevin was sorry, too. So damned sorry.

A flashbulb smashed into the shattered glass.

The retinas of every man in the room exploded with small novas of light. Turner was the first to step to the worktable paved with a jigsaw of broken mirror. His fingertips glided over the reflecting pool of puzzle, looking like a kid's finger-spiders. They crawled cautiously over the sharp fissures dividing the segments.

Nordstrom broke the spell.

"I suppose you want a medal?" he asked, his weak eyes still watering from the flashbulb. "Well?"

Turner's fingers lifted—reluctantly. "The image burned straight through the glass, almost as if on film. It completely altered the molecular composition of the mirror."

"You must have laboratories squirreled all over this barn." Nordstrom looked to the echoing ceiling, where pipe-hung lights glimmered in faint constellations against the grimy concrete vault.

233

"The only thing we have here that's your business is Jane Doe."

"'Thing.' That's the spirit, Mr. Turner. I was afraid you were turning sentimentalist on me."

"The letters don't mean anything to you?" Turner persisted.

"Letters is stretching it . . . more like graffiti by blow-torch."

"K." Turner pointed. "E-L-L-E-H-A-Y. The shaping is primitive, almost . . . primordial. I'm no shrink, but it's as if they came from a very primitive brain, an under-brain—"

"You're no shrink. You should see what sophisticated adults can draw during therapy. We're all a cell's breadth from the animal in our ancestry. So . . . she formed these letters in the glass before breaking it."

"No." Turner picked up a shard, turned the dark jagged edge to the light. "My tech people say it's as if the letters formed in the glass *as* it was breaking, as if the letters are what broke it. The molecular alteration doesn't extend all the way to the surface—or even to the broken edges, for that matter. It was an . . . interrupted . . . process."

Nordstrom took the sliver from Turner. "Clever of you to have spotted a message in all that wreckage, but hardly what we're looking for, Mr. Turner. It smacks of fraud, to my mind, of psychic hocus-pocus. Of theatrics. Wouldn't it be amusing if that's all you had here, if the great Dr. Blake had blown his whole career for a fake? Besides, what's a . . . Kellehay?"

"I thought you had pored over the Jane Doe files. He was one of the two police officers who found her on that Crow Wing bluff. He went to the hospital with her and later plunged out the window of her room to his death."

"Ah. I'd forgotten. Odd name. But this case is cluttered with bizarre names. And words. Blake even hypnotized her with a piece of gobbledegook." When Turner looked sufficiently curious, Nordstrom snapped out the word. "Zyunsinth."

Turner chuckled wearily. "Sounds like one of those code

names they love at headquarters. So that puts her bye-bye, huh?"

"Not . . . yet. Apparently Blake said it differently. Or he may have given her a posthypnotic suggestion to refuse to respond to anyone else."

"You can't hypnotize her? That's serious, Nordstrom. With unexplained physical evidence mounting up"— Turner's hand swept across its own reflection in the patchwork mirror—"we need to deliver more than more questions. We need answers. Might as well prove her a fraud and be done with it."

"Perhaps that's just what I will do. You don't really care, do you?"

"Oh, I care."

Nordstrom turned from the mirror-topped table. "I'll really get down to work with her today. She should be softened up by now. If I still can't hypnotize her, I can always go to narcoanalysis."

"Maybe you got the wrong word."

"You want Blake back in on this," Nordstrom accused. "Where did you go so early this morning? I wouldn't try it, if I were you. I get along too well with your superiors."

Turner shrugged and turned his back on Nordstrom.

*   *   *

Letters are tumbling down the corridors of Jane's consciousness in Morse code, stringing after one another like the lighted dots she'd seen in a photograph of a Times Square billboard.

Letters and words and names. Symbols and representations and codes. Figures shadow-box at the fringe of the display. Some are the furred creatures she had known as Zyunsinth.

Others are hairless, white, clothed—ambulance attendants she remembers, two sets, each face etched on her subconscious in photographic detail. There is the man with the Adam's apple; the one with the hairs inside his nose iced over; another with a fan-shaped purple blotch on his wrist beneath the cuff of his white jacket. . . .

And she sees women in white—white slips and white bras and white panty hose, women in white all the way through, so they seemed transparent. And other figures wearing white—vaguer, sexless, sizeless. Memories of whiteness swarm around Jane, flurried and congregated, humming and buzzing.

At first the buzz echoes the drone of the wall-unit heater in her room. Then the sound swells into one with the blankness and begins pulsing into her understanding.

"Contact missed badly."

"Not by very much."

"Still, the damage is not repaired. The links are not completely severed."

"We were precisely aimed at the moment of deposit."

"Some random element . . . overcame the connection."

"The probe remains operative."

"The probe remains rogue."

"Perhaps we must intervene again."

"We come only to wait and watch."

"Their probes came to us first."

"Only to our edges. And their probes have always been innocuous."

"To our examinations."

"What will our probe appear like to them?"

"Less innocuous. Ours are altered to survive hostile environments intact."

"So are theirs. They do not hazard genetic material to the deeper Void."

"So precious they hold it. A peculiar concept. All things biological are the end product of expendability. If we did not slough the extraneous cells, the mother-cell would not remain ever-new."

"They are much enamored of sameness though they espouse individual differences. A most intriguing notion. They remain the most complicated of the species we have surveyed."

"Will contact be possible ever, do we think?"

"Unlikely. Crude and volatile. Still, tenacious for all that. They would not adapt well to the concept of existence

236

extension through assimilation. They wish always to stand apart."

"As does the rogue probe. How could we release it again at its request?"

"It surprised us. A weak cell responded to its novelty. Even we cell-mates are not beyond the failing of curiosity, for all we know of variant biological forms."

"And in these beings are our own roots?"

"Of course. Though they will not last so long as we."

"We will last as long as light."

"As long as light."

"And they?"

"Less long than the light of their little sun—even the last of them."

"We could feel pity."

"It is possible that they will live long enough to touch upon our metamorphosis."

"Their world will change so much."

"Only if they do."

"We learn much of what we are not. Sometimes we long to learn of likeness rather than dissimilarity."

"We are like none in our Oneness. We will collect our data, our probes and withdraw. They will hardly mark our passage, except as rumor."

"Or . . . religion."

"Very true. All creatures seek that larger than themselves."

"We find it. Within ourselves. Soon we shall no longer reach out, no longer glean the chaff of other worlds. We shall be content within our own world. We shall be Still."

"Yet . . . we remain curious. The patterns these beings scribe fit so well into the destiny of the universe, yet they themselves only see destiny on the palms of their hands."

"Wait until they have no hands, then they will see destiny in the stars."

Chapter Twenty-nine

Nordstrom opened the door to Jane's room and looked first at the floor. The dishes still lay there. Food blotches had hardened to scabs on the vinyl tile.

Jane still lay bound in her bed.

"Awake? Or never asleep?" he wanted to know.

"I rested," she said calmly, opening her eyes.

"And fasted. Too bad, in some ways you're an ideal patient for me. You have a self-discipline I don't find in many females."

He had begun unbuckling the restraints. Jane lay perfectly still, ignoring even the brush of his hands. He lifted the adhesive tape at her elbow and disconnected the IV.

"You can visit the bathroom now, if you like," he mocked, ripping off the top sheet as if to expose some secret.

Jane rose and went into the small adjacent bathroom, leaving Nordstrom staring at pristine bed linens.

"You held your urine all night?" he demanded, following her. He would have opened the closed bathroom door, but she had locked it. He eavesdropped, listening through the hollow-core door. He heard only the faucet pouring water into the sink and, finally, the flush of a toilet.

"Jane, let me in!"

"Not until I come out."

"Why did you lock the door?"

"I wanted you on the other side of it."

"I can have it broken down."

The door opened suddenly. Jane was standing before him in the white hospital shift that made her look so childlike, staring at him with her deep-set unchildlike eyes. She was almost exactly his height.

Nordstrom blinked. He wasn't used to seeing patients eye to eye. He was always seated when they entered, and he always had them lie down before he began. He was used to looking down on them. "Don't lock yourself in again; I can have it broken open," he repeated.

"So can I," said Jane, returning to the bed.

"You've already missed breakfast. I can cancel lunch, too."

She sat on the bed, slightly propped against the pillow, and folded her narrow hands over her abdomen.

"Doesn't that disturb you?" He advanced on her cautiously now. She was behaving abnormally—abnormally calm, abnormally docile.

"I'm not hungry."

"I told you, that's a sign of starvation."

Jane smiled. "Yes, but you think in extremes—no food or all food. That's what the girls were saying at the dorm all the time—'I'm starving!' But they weren't starving at all. They were eating potato chips and Hostess Twinkies and nachos—I think that there is something in-between, Dr. Nordstrom, don't you?"

"No!" He pulled a chair over and sat, ignoring the fact that Jane was propped up in her bed above him like an ailing queen. "Life, our minds are nothing but polarities, nothing but extremes—love/hate, life/death, satiety/hunger. . . ."

"Strength/weakness," Jane added to the toll.

"My strength is your weakness."

"Your weakness is my strength," she replied.

"What do you know of strength? You're a memory-impaired Raggedy Ann, moving from the hands of one man to another, one shrink to the next. You'll obey whoever your new master is."

"I obey . . . myself."

"Who told you that drivel?"

"Kevin."

"He was wrong. You always obeyed Kevin. Now you obey me."

Jane frowned. "Kevin said—"

"Kevin is gone now."

"I saw him, standing outside. I was drawn inside. I couldn't stop myself. Nothing could stop me."

"Nothing can stop you from doing as I wish."

"Kevin said the I-ness of me was sovereign. I remember that now, Kevin——"

"Kevin screwed you!"

She smiled. "Yes! I know that word. That's what the nurses said in Willhelm Hall. They talked a great deal about screwing. The books don't mention it. The books are much more technical. Are you technical, Dr. Nordstrom?" Jane cocked her head. "Do you want to do what Kevin did with me?"

He retreated. "No! What he did was . . . a violation. Of his profession. Of his self."

"One can't violate what refuses to be violated," Jane said. "I don't like you, Dr. Nordstrom. I think liking is a prerequisite to screwing, although sometimes disliking is. It is very confusing. I love Kevin. He loves me. You don't like me. I don't like you. You are . . . arbitrary. I don't think Kevin would like you, either."

"Like has nothing to do with it."

"I think it has everything to do with it. I don't like this room, this tube in my arm, this funny white gown with the strings up the back——"

Nordstrom was flailing for the constraints, pulling canvas webbing taut and buckling Jane into it.

"I don't like these straps, the food you don't let me eat, I don't like——"

He was cinching her into place, drawing the webbing so tight it cut grooves in the meager flesh of her arms and thighs.

"—these straps."

"Life is full of things we don't like."

"I don't like people who say 'we.' I like 'I.'"

Sweat seeped from Nordstrom's brow and leaked down into the wells of his eyeglasses.

"I like 'I' too," he taunted back. "And *I* am in control. You will do as I say. You will starve and soil yourself and waste away doing what I say! That's all there is to it. You are . . . programmable. You will use your powers because

240

to not use them is to perish. You don't want to die, Jane Doe. You don't want to cease to be. After all, you love Kevin. You don't want to lose him. If you lose yourself, you lose him. Forever."

Nordstrom paused at the stainless steel water carafe on Jane's nightstand. He poured himself a glass of water.

"That tube you hate is your lifeline, Jane. Look at it drip on the floor. You disconnected it yourself. You disconnected yourself. You are trying to play suicidal games, but you don't want to go all the way. You can't fool me. Make the tube rise. Play a snake charmer's tune and pipe it back into your arm. It's your only salvation. In the meantime, lie there and think about it. I want a verifiable demonstration of your powers, or you will die of your own individuality. Think about it."

He left the room.

*　　　　　　*　　　　　　*

Jane doesn't think of death, but rather of herself, her life.

Calm beyond feigning, she lies still in her bonds, slowing her body's furnace to a glow instead of its normal burning. This confinement is not so different in its way from existence in the holding tanks of the alien vessel.

What memories she retains of that experience parade through her mind. She had been far less sentient than this in the aliens' hands, in their cold scientific storage—her senses muted, subnormal, her metabolism dormant. She suspects she had spent years in that semisuspended state.

Dr. Nordstrom is threatening her with mere hours.

Some of that suspended animation must have regulated her body in the hours—days even—after the aliens had deposited her atop the Crow Wing bluff.

Like any newborn thing, she had lain helpless yet protected by the very muted metabolism that made her oblivious to her surroundings. She had been like a hibernating mammal—sheltered from hunger and cold by her laggard circulation, her numbed brain.

No wonder her weight had been low; less bulk meant less energy to support life. Of course, had she not been found, she would have . . . dwindled in time. She would have been

241

lost, surrendered to the earth that had spawned her kind. No doubt others of their probes had suffered just such a fate, never to be found. . . .

Even now a tingling along her limbs—perhaps caused by the tight straps, perhaps not—fills her with an electric sense of self-communion. She sees herself reflected in a shadow box of mirrors, duplicating to infinity.

The image of herself marooned in the cold and snow— Dr. Nordstrom insisted that was how she had been found this time, saying that only his dedicated examination had located the telltale pulse to show she lived—no longer frightens her or seems to challenge her own existence.

For cold can be overcome. Her extremities buzz with possibilities, as if even now the blood is stirring in veins and then capillaries, as if blood were catching fire and life and surging through the body's frozen wastes like life-giving lava. . . .

Even without Dr. Nordstrom, Jane sees, she could have saved herself. She *can* save herself. She is not one, fragile disposable being but a resurrectable chain of selves. If the aliens can empty her, she can fill herself again. If the snow can freeze her, she can accept it—and ultimately reject it.

She feels it thaw around her, the cold. She feels some remote stiffness loosen, as if physiological bonds were breaking. She feels her eyes open (although they are open already), her mouth part in an ah of surprise as air/ oxygen/breath suffuses her being (although her mouth is closed). She feels her mind swell, like music, and scale an endless empty expanse of cold into the warmer upper air (although it should be colder there).

She feels herself draw together, as if she is watching someone else—some other stronger/weaker self—accomplish it. She feels herself sitting bolt upright in the lonely cold that surrounds her, rising from the dead. Now *that* would impress Dr. Nordstrom. . . .

Jane wants to sit up as revelation opens a window on her mind. The darkening room seems illuminated with a honeycomb of new corners, all producing a multiplicity of angles, all leading someplace new. . . . In some odd way, she feels her body—or the distant pale white ghost of her body—levitate like Lazarus (she had read of him some-where, once).

Her bonds hold her supine, but the thoughts will not be restricted. Perhaps. Perhaps *she,* Lynn Elizabeth Volker, the one Jane was supposed to have been and was not . . . perhaps she had been a probe, too. A probe that had failed, that had died and lain under snow and summer wind in the Montana wilds before she could be retrieved after twenty-one years of silent, secret gleaning.

Jane lets her limbs relax against the tight straps. Kevin would be so interested to know that. Kevin would be sorry to know that Jane sometimes thought better without him there. When he was with her, somehow he became the quester of her fate, her past. Alone, she posed and answered her own questions, confronted her own selves.

Kevin. The name produces the same fondness as Zyunsinth did, and the same vagueness. For a brief moment, Jane senses the irresistible call of him stirring her being. She must rise and go now, and see Kevin, find Kevin. No, it is mere memory she feels, pseudofeeling. Kevin remains something she knows she liked, without quite remembering why.

Time may have passed. While she had been thinking, dreaming, someone had extinguished the lights in her room, perhaps from a distance. She had heard no one come or go, had heard nothing but the crack of her ice-bound thoughts breaking free, so slowly they seemed motionless.

Time had passed, for the door to her room opens now. Jane's eyes, closed, refuse to open in response. She is deep, deep in her own inner seas, free of the voices that some-times come, free of everything.

"Julie. . . ."

The name echoes hers enough to buffet her free-floating consciousness. She ignores it.

"Julie."

The voice is only a whisper, but it hovers too close. Her glorious sense of immortality, of self-extension, shrivels. She feels dead again. Ghosts pluck at her winding sheet. Ghouls tug at her cerements. Her mind spins, revolves, her body seeming to roll with it as she feels the brush of

243

disembodied hands on her limbs, feels the creep and crawl of hidden things clinging to her skin and bones.

Jane's lethargic consciousness stirs. It battles its way to the surface of the sensate world, drags her up, up toward light and clarity and feeling.

It is dark when she at last breaks contact with her inner self, dark when she comes to herself in the dark room, alone. She had not been alone until just recently, some instinct sharper than memory told her. Dr. Nordstrom had been in the room, while she had absented herself in her self. He had . . . touched her.

Jane's skin crawls with goose bumps, as if every hair follicle shrinks at the idea. She has never experienced such physical revulsion, such emotional upheaval. Her muscles gather against the taut restraints even as her mind unerringly finds and follows a line of electromagnetic energy—the disturbed air where Nordstrom had recently passed.

A band of the same energy coils around her temples and squeezes hard, until she feels her dormant blood pounding through her veins as if it has just awakened. She shuts her eyes. Upon the darkness energy scribes its shadow forms. Atoms swarm like insects as her vision passes through layers of separating walls. The corporeal disintegrates into a veil of a billion flyspots, then fades. As her instincts hone on her object, an image seesaws into focus—a room, a bed, a figure upon it surrounded by hand-sized leaves . . . no, by *papers.* Photographs.

Everything is etched in lines of black and shades of gray, like a bad black-and-white snapshot. The figure on the bed is an unarticulated lump emitting an aura of living, breathing energy. It is not restrained.

For a moment, Jane's outreaching consciousness becomes self-bound again. She senses the straps confining her. Her energies poise to snake the canvas tongues back through their stainless steel buckles. She knows how to do it, knows that she can do it. She can do anything.

But what does she *want* to do? Kevin, distant byword that he is now, had always said it was important to find out and do what she herself wished, not what others expected of her.

In this instance, Jane decides, she wishes to do exactly what Dr. Nordstrom has asked her to do. He has demanded an exhibition of her powers, as Dr. Swanson had also required in her own coercive way.

Jane will oblige under his terms—without freeing herself in any way but the psychological. Dr. Nordstrom will find his wishes fulfilled beyond his wildest dreams. . . .

*   *   *

Kevin wanted to wake up, and he couldn't. The door to dreamland was bolted tight. Behind it, he was copulating endlessly.

Anonymous women rushed him like enemies in a war zone. He received them with ritual thrusts, businesslike as bayonet strokes. They fell away and were replaced in turn. Each one engendered a successor, each woman wore a hymen like a shield.

Aghast, feeling overwhelmed, he took them murderously. Only tearing through the hymen freed him—then only long enough for a new virgin to spring up in the former one's place.

The hymens got tougher, the job more distasteful. He was losing the battle. He seemed to thrust against fleshless bone now; skeletons hurled at him, engaging him in an endless dream of death.

He wanted to wake up more than anything in the world. He didn't.

Chapter Thirty

Eric Nordstrom lay alone in his room. It seemed he had always been alone in his room.

This room was borrowed, inadequate. The furnishings were exquisitely anonymous—home rent-a-care and hospital practical. Nobody but institutional business managers bought bureaus like the chest-high example on one wall. Stained anemic maple, it upheld a solitary box of Kleenex.

And the bed . . . Nordstrom tossed atop coarse sheets and pillowcases. The springs didn't give at all and the pillows gave too much, at the slightest pressure, like some of his patients.

For a reading light, he had the glaring ceiling fixture. For nightstand amenities, he had a stainless steel pitcher of water and a squat glass tumbler.

It was more than Jane Doe had this night, Nordstrom reminded himself. He checked his watch, a Piaget with a lizard strap. Five o'clock in the morning. Usually when he couldn't sleep—which was often—he played solitaire and studied certain of his collection of books. He wondered why he bothered to wait up and watch so long, do nothing, but he knew.

She would crack, soon and massively. He didn't want to miss it. She would split her seams, spill her guts, shatter her selfhood and sink into his control.

Not that Nordstrom expected to uncover any astounding powers in Jane Doe. She was all hype and no go, typical of a Blake project. Flash up front and vacancy behind. It would be a pleasure to expose her as a pathetic fraud . . . to dispose of her and leave the wreckage for Blake to piece back together. If he could.

Nordstrom rose and went into the small adjacent bathroom, his kidskin slippers whispering over the tiles. All the rooms on this hall were arranged in classic hospital style— spare, clean and possessed of an empty feeling whether occupied or not.

It amused him to picture these mock rooms from a bird's-eye distance—from above they would resemble cell after cell of stage settings, parading like model rooms in some vast department store of government duplicity.

There were rooms here Nordstrom had not seen: where Turner and his staff slept, probably a crude dormitory except for private accommodations for the few women; where the labs and communications centers were installed; empty chambers where the building's original function had once taken place. Nordstrom wondered briefly what that was, then forgot about it. People were so much more interesting than places and things. People reacted. Places merely . . . witnessed.

He leaned over the extradeep bathtub and started a stream of water pounding into the shiny porcelain. In a small medicine cabinet mirror—the like of which he hadn't confronted in years—he saw himself lit harshly from above. Shadows dripped down the furrows of his face from his eye sockets. He looked ghoulish, dangerous. Even criminal.

Blake had looked like this, he reminded himself—still did on some police blotter. Such a comedown for the mighty doctor. A police record. Thanks to Nordstrom. A shattered patient. Thanks to Nordstrom. Nights of no sleep. Thanks to Nordstrom. Nordstrom hardly ever slept.

He opened the mirrored door and took his electric razor from the metal shelf. Everything in the room seemed to be either black or white—white for walls, fixtures, floor; black for the objects Nordstrom had imported—shaver, hair- brush of European boar bristles, eelskin eyeglass case.

His insomnia had improved of late. He had actually drifted off between midnight and four A.M. He attributed his newfound serenity to an interesting case load. First Monica Chapman, coming along so nicely. And now Jane Doe. If Blake's credibility was decimated, as Nordstrom hoped, perhaps Jane Doe would be assigned to Nordstrom

247

for rehabilitation when the government was done with her. . . .

He plugged the shaver into a chrome-covered outlet, the reflection of his hand flashing across the shiny surface. A blue spark discharged into the air. Something buzzed like an angry bee.

Nordstrom retracted the plug to study the prongs. Everything seemed all right. He plugged it in again and sent the shaverhead buzzing across his jaw.

This night should have done it, he congratulated himself. She'd be seriously dehydrated by now—not enough to harm but enough to hurt. That was always the key. Gratuitous harm was stupid—and it seldom accomplished anything. Hurt, though . . .

It reminded him of a hotel, this sparse bathroom filled with the whine of his electric shaver. Nordstrom liked hotel rooms. He liked the whispers of passing lives and secret sins that hotel rooms buffeted between themselves and the grinding elevators in the hallways beyond the rooms. He liked imagining the train of events rattling from room to room, an endless stream of cattle cars full-up with the stacked ghosts of every room's collated occupants. Hurry up, please, it's time.

The reverie had distracted him. The shaver hit his chinbone and ricocheted off. Nordstrom huffed out his disapproval of himself. He was invariably neat to the point of tidiness, and prided himself on the trait.

Beside the sink, the toilet seat, tidily shut, recoiled against the porcelain tank with a bang. Somehow the water had backed up. Feces swam in a soup of urine.

Nordstrom stared into the mirror. In his hand, the shaver lurched. It buzzed his cheek, ploughing a new furrow across his skin. Tiny flowers of blood sprouted in neat rows from every hair follicle.

He dropped the shaver. It plunged into the filthy toilet bowl and began lashing back and forth on the end of its black cord, spewing contaminated water.

Nordstrom reached for the plug, then froze. It could electrocute him—or at least transmit a nasty shock. . . . He looked to the mirror again, just in time to see its shiny chrome edge swinging sharply toward his face, like a slap. Foreseeing the impact didn't blunt it. The cabinet door hit Nordstrom so hard he felt his cheekbone crush the mirror like an eggshell.

Pain needled into his sinuses as shattered glass ground into his face. The door never rebounded from the blow, but remained pressed to his cheek. His hands grasped the unbroken edge and tried to push it away. Nothing gave. It was as if a concrete wall had grown behind it.

Nordstrom used his hands, shaking now, to push himself off the medicine cabinet door. At the side, he heard a familiar sound—the flush of a toilet. He glanced down to see the small chrome handle jerking back upright, to watch the water in the bowl whirling around and the shaver bobbing on the maelstrom's surface like a boat. The place smelled like a sewage treatment plant.

"Crazy!" Nordstrom backed out of the room, slamming the door shut just in time to dodge his eyeglass case as it came hurtling toward him.

The other room was undisturbed. Nordstrom paused at the bureau to snatch tissues from the box and dab at his raw face.

A series of sudden, disabling blows to his torso and legs drove him back on the bed before he could determine what had done it. He stared. Across from him, bureau drawers gaped open, their swaying metal pulls chiming against the brass backplates.

Nordstrom gasped, trying to pull his breath back up from his feet, where it seemed to have retreated. His ribs screamed their agony. As he rolled sideways to relieve the pressure of gravity, the manila folders spread across the bed began flying at his head, sharp pasteboard edges slashing into his exposed face and neck. He lifted his arms but the folders fell into him like bats—a blind force flapping into any barrier.

"Stop it!" he shouted. "Stop it, you controlling bitch!"

The bed jerked out from under him. He collapsed to the floor, then looked up to see the mattress and metal frame separating as they fell toward him in concert.

Nordstrom scrambled across the vinyl tile, keeping his

upper body free of the falling bed. A metal edge ground its teeth into his calf. Reality blurred. Color drained from his cognition.

He dug the heels of his hands into the floor, seeking purchase. The tiles lifted—lifted, one by one, under his hands and floated there, a few inches above the floor. Nordstrom stared at the tarry black adhesive beds they had torn loose from.

All the tiles were lifting in dominolike sequence, lifting and falling like waves, so the entire room seemed aswim. Nordstrom's stomach lilted with the illusion—it had to be an illusion—and spewed the contents of his stomach into a salmon-pink puddle on the lurching floor.

The bed shifted on his back, flattening him. Nordstrom's face pressed the floor. His own vomit smeared his features, its odor poured back down his burning nasal passages.

"Stop it!" he screamed. "I'll do anything—anything!"

The room's motions suspended. Uprooted tiles hovered in the air—absolutely still.

"What do you want?" he asked, lifting spattered lenses to the light high above.

There was no answer, but somehow Nordstrom knew. He was sure he heard the answer articulated clearly in his brain.

Sobbing, he gathered himself to his knees and, using his hands, began scooping the vomit back into his mouth.

Chapter Thirty-one

Even Kevin's jeans were wrinkled.

He reclaimed them Wednesday afternoon with the rest of his clothes. They all lay at the bottom of the basket he'd dropped them into five days earlier.

"Go on, put them on," the cop ordered.

Kevin returned to the cinder-block cubicle and exchanged his jail uniform—like a doctor who's done for the day he dumped his used greens into a laundry basket—for what amounted to his personal uniform, his blues.

It felt like he was dragging his own skin back on after someone had been on a six-day binge in it. His nose identified odors forgotten since his internship—urine and vomit, stale smoke and beer. In Massachusetts General Hospital he could always walk away from the transient stench. Here, this reek had infiltrated his clothes until it became a personal exhalation, like bad breath.

He was led down a blue-carpeted corridor. Getting out of jail took as much paperwork as it did to get in—and more waiting. They checked his age again, and his next of kin. They even double-checked that the thumbprints on his record were his, as if he could have somehow slipped skins while inside.

Two hours later Kevin stood again in the orange-walled waiting room, dressed in his own clothes, however nauseous, a free man again, however conditionally.

Everyone was waiting for him—father, mother, Kandy, everyone but the lawyer, who'd said the release would be routine. It was. Apparently nobody wanted Kevin anymore.

"Hey, stay back," he ordered as they rushed forward like he'd won the bonus round on *Wheel of Fortune*. It didn't work, at least not with his mother, whose embrace enfolded him in a whiff of permanent wave.

"Kevin," she rebuked, "I smelled a lot worse on you when you were a baby."

Parents invariably made the kind of jolly reminder that would plunge any adult offspring into serious depression. Kevin shrugged it off, shook hands with his father—another grave, silently rebuking ritual—and slapped Kandy on the arm.

"I owe you."

"No sweat."

"They gave me the money back—and my watch." Kevin

251

flourished his wrist at his parents. "All safe and sound. If they're not pressing charges, like Ruderman says, I should have access to my bank account again."

"Sure, but it's under another name, remember?" Kandy objected. "More red tape."

Kevin's parents blinked politely at the non sequiturs passing between their jailbird son and his hippie friend.

"You know what I'd like," his mother interrupted brightly. "I'd like for us all to go out to a good dinner tonight. Oh, you, too . . . Mr. Kandinsky. You've been such a help to Kevin, I understand."

"I'll pass on dinner." Kandy shook his fuzzy wuzzy head. "I bet you folks want to talk things over."

"No, Kandy—" Kevin began to protest.

His parents remained mum.

"Look, I'm double-parked, not too cool at police headquarters. I'll be in touch." Kandy loped into the hall with a farewell wave.

"I'd like to go . . . home first," Kevin said. His mother looked blank. Only one place would ever be home to him in her mind—her own house. "Wash up. Change. Then . . ." His parents' faces looked old and drawn in the orange-reflecting fluorescent light.

Kevin grinned his surrender. "Then dinner . . . a good dinner. Yeah, Mom, that'd be great."

"Murray's Steak House," his mother said, beaming. The Blakes always dined there when they visited the Twin Cities—Murray's downtown steak house, noted for butter knife–soft steak and unpretentious service.

"Murray's," Kevin seconded, still not feeling hungry. But maybe he ought to go. None of his ex-cellmates, he knew, would ever take butter knife to beef at Murray's.

*   *   *

It is late Wednesday night, and Kevin is alone again, at last.

His parents have returned to their motel room reassured. He's wearing fresh jeans, shirt, everything. The old clothes lie in the icy dumpster at the back of his condo, exchanging essential scents with his neighbors' garbage. A remnant of scent shadowboxes with his senses. He's doffed his alien odor, but not the memory of it.

Kevin leans against his living room wall, looking through the open blinds at the parking lot below. It's an Art Deco abstract. He sees only black asphalt, grapefruit-pink sodium iodide lights and the streamlined humps of car roofs, hoods and trunks.

He knows if any agents are still watching him—or ever were—they can spot his silhouette against the over-lit room. He doesn't care. He doesn't know what to think, but he knows what he doesn't think.

He doesn't think he'll sleep without a night-light for a while. He doesn't think he'll stop smelling himself for a while longer. He doesn't want to think at all.

But he does.

He turns his head. His rooms comfort him. They haven't changed. Except . . . his eyes rivet to the spot in his bookshelves where the photograph of Julie Symons sat half-hidden by his old *Physician's Desk Reference*. Julie is gone now. Her gold metal frame sits in the same position. He wonders why his belongings look so undisturbed. He can't imagine Nordstrom bothering to reinstate the pillaged frame. Perhaps Turner's men were careful. Perhaps someone put things back.

On the coffee table an empty lunch meat package, brown beer bottle, yogurt carton and stainless steel spoon form a homely still life.

Nothing has been moved, touched, since Kevin came home, although his mother wanted to do it. No, he'd said, sounding sharp. No. Then he'd apologized and she'd said she understood. But she hadn't. It offended her nature to leave something undisposed of.

From purely housekeeping concerns, Kevin knows his mother is right. Mold is growing green along some yogurt slicks on the carton sides. Kevin knows he should throw the item away, along with the beer bottle and the curled plastic, but he can't. He is a highly retentive personality, which is a psychiatrist's way of saying stubborn.

His memory won't give up the ghost. Only Thursday night. Thursday night Jane was here, feeding herself, his memory tells him again. He calculates cumbersomely. Only . . . one hundred and forty-four hours ago.

Tonight only Kevin is here, feeding his illusions. He wonders if Turner lied about having caught Jane. He hopes Turner didn't, for what has she eaten since this pathetic picnic on his coffee table? At least in custody they feed you well.

He wonders if he should have agreed to work with Jane, if being violated by loving hands and minds isn't better than the alternative, although it doesn't seem to be for most people. He wonders what he could have done better.

Below his window sits a van. The parking lot lights pour onto its pale roof, buffing it to the color of wet cement. Kevin wonders if this is the van Kandy suspected of being a government watching post. Maybe the room is bugged. He looks around. It's been silent here ever since his folks brought him back from the restaurant and—somehow satisfied by eating out as a return to normal family rituals—said good-night and went away.

The snowbanks fringing the parking lot lie stark against the dark beyond it. Trees hunker along the street. Next to one stands a figure, a watcher.

Kevin straightens and focuses harder.

Not a furred figment of the imagination, not a particularly tall or heavy person, just an ordinary, vague figure stripped to the essential human silhouette. Something about the posture is female, something about the look of it is, is . . . Jane.

Kevin's hands crush metal vanes, push the blinds together to force them apart. He presses his face to the icy windowpane. Spiderwebs of frost sparkle in the corners of the glass, looking like fissures.

Jane, it *is* Jane! He knows it.

The night shifts. He is watching a scene viewed through a glass more darkly than the viewer had wished. Only trees line the street. Only phantoms footprint the snowbanks. Only empty cars squat on the snow-quenched asphalt.

She is gone. But he saw her. . . .

She is gone. Long gone. He's dreaming.

He saw her.

If it was Jane, she saw him, too.

She wouldn't have come, seen him, and left again. Not Jane.

She is not there, never was. Turner said so.

Kevin has to know.

But first, he has to know how to find Turner.

*   *   *

The mirror is still.

Jane's mind breaks its surface, diving into the chill silver—her face first feeling the icy brush of dissipating tensions, then shoulders, arms, hips. Legs and feet feel nothing, it is that cold in the mirror.

But quiet.

When she had tasted the full use of her powers before, amnesia had cleansed her palate afterward. This time an unpleasant aftertaste she calls "memory" lingers, but she is clean now, her mind rinsed of the recent episode.

So she forgets herself in her own image. Beyond the shape in the mirror she sees another. Her own other self, stripped cold and clean. Naked. She watches it jerk into life, move down the spirit streets of her memory, past campus buildings and department store windows.

It pauses, too. There are women in the windows— motionless, mute submerged women in holding tanks. Mannequins. Models. Dummies. Jane's naked self lifts fists against the plate glass. It rends soundlessly.

She is walking among the women on broken glass, stripping their frozen figures of everything weighted upon them. Sweaters, slacks, blouses, skirts. Like dolls they wear no underwear. Shoes and boots, though, they have, over-sized and forced onto iron-stiff feet. Even those she takes.

Their heads turn. She wrenches them off to take the clothing. Their hands fall and yearn up from the floor like drowning fingers. Their arms twist off and hang askew. Still they stand, rods of steel for a spine. Naked they wait under the undimmed fluorescents.

She dresses there; crouching amid their shambled selves,

she puts on pieces of them. The lights never dim, but no one comes to watch. Nothing is supposed to be happening here at night.

She crosses a moat of shattered glass to leap to the sidewalk again. Their painted eyes scream farewell.

At another window she stops again. The glass gives before her without waiting for her motion. She takes the long step up to the display window on chicly booted feet.

Here is winter wonderland, a forest of tall, elongated figures swathed in furs. Their haughty heads are crowned with erections of satin and rhinestones. Spiders sit their eyelids. Among them she walks, her naked hands moving down their furred arms to touch the plaster flesh.

Finally, she stops behind a mannequin clothed in amber fur and pulls the coat off the shoulders. The dummy's arms come with it. She pushes and pulls the severed limbs out through the satin-lined sleeves, then dons the thing herself.

For a moment she waits, one with them. Then she steps away, over broken glass—it is mirror glass, she sees now—into the dark, empty street. No one notices. There is no sound. There has never been any sound. It is a dream without a voice.

Jane watches the woman in the mirror walk toward her. No longer naked, there is dignity in her movements. She has gleaned well. She knows what she needs and where she is going. She calls to Jane, as Jane calls to her. She is getting closer.

Jane's hand rests on her chest, over her heart. She feels the beat. Its rhythm matches the steps of the woman in the mirror. Her hospital gown feels coarse and flimsy at one and the same time, like a dishcloth. Her fingers clench in the fabric. It is not enough. It is not yet enough. Something more must be done. She must . . . assemble more of herself for—for something.

Jane lies back slowly to go to sleep. The woman in the mirror marches on, her figure sinking below the frame's horizon as Jane's head sets on her pillow. Whiteness billows up, scattering sleep on its foam. Jane sleeps. Jane dreams. The silence finally stops.

Chapter Thirty-two

"I'm not going crazy—so help me, Freud."

"Of course you're not going crazy," Kandy soothed. "You *are* crazy, Kevin, just like the rest of us. Stop fighting it and enjoy."

Kandy, draped in the smoke of a slow-burning marijuana joint, was sitting cross-legged in his cluttered apartment, playing shrink.

Kevin, the play patient, was nursing a Scotch as stiff as Johnny Walker's cane and served in a chipped pottery mug that deadened all its bite.

"I saw her!" Kevin insisted. "I wasn't hallucinating. It wasn't just wishful thinking. She was there!"

"Look, you've just come off a pretty bad trip—five days in the county jail. And your preppie ex-classmate, Nordheim, injected you with God-knows-what before you went in, you admit that. You don't even know what you *said* under the influence of his needles, much less what you saw . . . maybe she—Jane—was a flashback."

"It's Nord*strom,* and if he'd gotten anything out of me he'd have crowed to Kingdom Come about it. Besides, that was six days ago. You've ingested worse in the name of recreational drug use, for Chrissake, and lived to tell about it. I saw Jane last night, that's all there is to it. In my condo parking lot."

"All right." Kandy nodded, running long, double-jointed fingers through his Rasputin beard. "Then we'll have to decide what to do about it, okay?"

"Okay." Kevin heard the tension drain from his voice. Here, in this crazyquilt Never-Never Land of Kandy's apartment where the window shades were always drawn, sanity seemed oddly attainable.

Something sprang from the eternal twilight. Kevin's shoulder tightened to ward it off, then relaxed.

"Hey, Kitty. . . . this isn't Blue?" Kevin uncurled the lithe furred body that had leeched onto his arm and was chewing ferociously. "He's . . . grown."

"Kittens do that. Besides, it's been a while since you dropped him off. Be glad he recognized you."

"Yeah." The feline face was worrying at his jeans now, sharp white fangs advancing and retreating staple gun-style. Kevin swooped up the kitten and brought its tiny face to his. Its unfocused bluish eyes had resolved into sharp-sighted hazel-green. A lank, preadolescent body dangled from his loose grip. "I've only been gone—"

"—almost three weeks. That's a long time in cat development."

"Three weeks." Blue, having fought and lost, curled into his lap and began indiscriminately licking its flanks and Kevin's hand. "Three weeks and my whole life's in the toilet. Probe's gone—And now Jane."

"Let's do personal inventory," Kandy suggested, inhaling until his eyes closed. "All right. Your condo okay?"

"I guess. A couple things are missing. Besides Jane."

"Your car?"

"How do you think I got here? Bailed it out of impoundment this morning. What about your van?" Kevin remembered suddenly.

"Got that back three days ago, as soon as they were done searching it. No sweat. And what about your folks?"

"Oh, we had a nice family dinner in a restaurant. Mom said we should do it more often. They kind of mellowed out when no charges were filed." Kevin looked at his wrist. "And when I got my goddamn watch back. They said they were sure it was a mistake and went home to Elk River."

"Cool. Then the only thing you're out of is a job, and you would have quit anyway, over Jane Doe."

"So I'm okay, you're okay. It still doesn't solve anything."

"Like whether you saw Jane?"

"Forget that. The real question is whether Turner—and Nordstrom—have her or not."

258

Kandy sighed. "What do you think?"

"I don't know." Blue draped himself over Kevin's thigh, purring. "I'm so bummed out I can't think anymore." Kevin leaned his head against Kandy's Victorian sofa's back, a throne-high swell of claret-colored velvet.

"Let me think." Long-legged Kandy, sitting lotus-style on the oversized ottoman, reminded Kevin of Alice in Wonderland's caterpillar. His life lately reminded Kevin of Wonderland, period. "How would they have caught her?" Kandy asked.

"Turner said . . . she was found like she was the first time."

"In Crow Wing?" Kandy sounded incredulous.

"Not there. But . . . naked. Underweight again, which sounds really unlikely. In the open—near the downtown railroad tracks this time. Turner figures she'd been mugged, stripped and left for dead. Nordstrom revived her."

"He has his uses, apparently. So Jane reprised her debut. *Verrry* interesting. At least the last time she played Lady Godiva it was August and hot as hell—how do you suppose she survives all this?"

A swallow of Scotch burned Kevin's esophagus. He stroked Blue's extended throat. "Maybe she's got nine lives."

"Come on, Kev, I told you my theories—Russian spy, resurrected icewoman. Tell me yours. After all, you're her shrink."

"Not anymore; maybe Nordstrom is now. Damn!" Kevin stirred on the couch, dislodging the kitten. It slid off him to the cushion, sprawling in sleep. "Okay, I might as well try my story on somebody."

Kandy jiggled his excitement like a kid. "This oughta be good."

"It is. Jane is . . . I think . . . a cloned human being."

"Then the Volkers *are* her parents! But whodunit? Who cloned her? The government?"

"The government hasn't even tumbled to Jane's being cloned yet, as far as I can tell. They think she's just your average all-American poltergeist—Jane the psychic discus-thrower."

259

"Wow, I get it. They figure she's a walking telekinetic tantrum in need of government guidance, like a missile. Is she?"

Kevin's face tightened. "Maybe."

"But if *they* didn't clone her, who did?"

Kevin took another slug of Scotch. It was loosening him up and bringing him down and he didn't care. "Them."

"Them, oh, sure. Uh . . . who?"

"The aliens."

"I knew it! I knew it was aliens! How alien?"

"I'm not sure. Never saw them. Saw their ship, though. They lifted Jane into it with a laser beam."

"And you never saw . . . them?"

Kevin shook his head and swirled the last of the Scotch in the bottom of his mug. Kandy's roach had burned to ashes in his cast-iron armadillo ashtray. His thin fingers twitched as if needing something to latch onto. They found his elbows.

"Heavy, man. You sure about this?"

"Think it over. The Volkers claim twenty-five years ago that they were taken into a space ship. Adelle Volker—barren for years—bears a child eight or nine months later. Lynn."

"You talking immaculate conception here?"

"No, Papa Volker was the father, but Mrs. Volker didn't even know she was pregnant until *after* the UFO incident, and then she never connected it with the alien visitation. But they—them, the aliens—could have taken a cell from her, just one cell."

"Well, *we've* done it with frogs."

"We've done it with lots of things, only we destroy the genetic material before we have to worry about the ethics of dealing with the results. The aliens didn't."

"So Jane grows up in the sky with diamonds—"

"Jane doesn't grow up. That's just it. She grows. From her recollection under hypnosis, she's . . . stored . . . in some semisuspended state. Fed information. Fed our language—whatever."

"That's why she was found so emaciated! She'd been in an induced coma!"

260

"And why she rebounded so fast under care. She's perfectly healthy, Kandy. Perfectly. Always has been. The aliens saw to that with every scientific means at their command."

Kandy lifted an excited fist and pulled on the ponytail frizzing down his back. "Then Jane's a . . . instant human! Just add IV and feed daily. God, what a concept. Maybe you *are* nuts, Kevin."

Kevin went on, almost to himself. "They dropped her on at least one other earthlike planet to 'glean' data. That's how she fixated on the fur coat she called Zyunsinth, probably haired hominoids—"

"The aliens used her like a portable tape recorder?"

"A biological probe, a living data recorder. It's not so nuts. Isn't that what we all are? Kandy? Input/output—food, information, emotions even? Our scientists tamper with genetic messages already. 'Engineering,' we call it. If *we* can depersonalize it, why can't the aliens? All that DNA is just so much circuitry to them. They send Jane out with her sensory skeins, then reel up her memory like a trawling line until all the little silver fishies fall to deck."

"That's . . . inhuman, Kevin."

"Yeah. It doesn't allow for complications, anyway. Like Jane's unforeseen emotional response to creatures even vaguely of her kind. Zyunsinth imprinted on her visceral level, even after she'd been wiped and the aliens had released her here."

"And you—you made an even better teddy bear."

Kevin nodded. "Me. I really gummed up the works. Jane began maturing—adolescently, emotionally . . . sexually. None of that alien software was designed to overcome a glandular storm like that. She was becoming human, not just acting like some preprogrammed automaton."

"But what about the special effects?" Kandy probed. "Jane's telekinetic abilities, Swanson's flying household object brigade? Frankly, Kev, I doubt the feds would give a ratshit about how Jane got here as long as they could aim her where wanted and fire when ready."

"But they can't, Kandy! Don't you see? The more human Jane becomes, the less predictable she'll be. Her . . .

powers are built-in defense mechanisms. The aliens want their expensive toys to get maximum mileage on their perilous journeys, just as we don't want *Voyager* to poop out for want of gas or a head-on with an asteroid."

"Fascinating!" Kandy had assumed a Mr. Spock tone. "And you actually *screwed* this phenomenon? Sorry, that just slipped out. 'Nother Scotch?"

Kandy collected the empty mug and strolled to the paper-littered dining room sideboard for the Johnny Walker bottle.

"That's the most understandable part of the whole mess," Kevin said bitterly. "Damn it, Kandy! Don't do a Dr. Cross on me."

Kandy shrugged as he dropped off the fresh drink. "I'm not surprised. Face it, Kevin, you wear guilt like a red flag. 'Sides, she didn't look too bad after she filled out some."

"I didn't 'screw' a phenomenon or a clone or a secret weapon. Jane was . . . is a woman. And she's different from any woman I've ever known—"

"I'll say."

"—she's new. She grew up without all the garbage childhood pours into our heads, that cultural imperative of 'shoulds' and 'musts.' It's *all* programming. Only Jane's alien programming, ironically, left her moral and emotional responses free to form a mature intelligence. She *was* fascinating. I was helping her—"

"I can imagine what Cross would say to that."

"He did. And I said back. God, I wish the old fart were still involved, I might be able to make some headway with him."

"You don't know where the Probe crew's gone?"

Kevin shook his head. "Scary how the government can make people vanish. . . . That's why I've got to find Jane! They wanted me to work with her, but I refused."

"Holy Christ! Why?"

"Jane doesn't need what they want from her."

"So you'd let a creep like Nordstrom pry it out of her! Kev, your judgment goes AWOL when you switch into noble mode. You could have jived the feds, worked with Jane your way."

"I never believed that they really had her."

"And now that you think you've seen her free, you're afraid they do? Makes a lot of sense, Blake."

"I know. But it was weird, seeing her like that. She didn't look quite real, almost seemed . . . naked . . . again, as if a past, helpless Jane were haunting me. Maybe she's—"

"Naw. She's engineered to survive, remember? Alien-guaranteed. Look, maybe you should find that government guy—"

Kevin looked up from his mug.

"I tried. This morning. I asked at the federal building— the one the cops took me from. Nobody there admits to having heard of Turner. I finally could use the bastard, and I've lost him."

Chapter Thirty-three

Absolute dark had fallen by the time Kevin returned to his condo. Minnesota winter evenings, like mercy killers, pulled the plug on light as well as warmth.

Kevin labored up the three flights of stairs from the parking lot. Only the snow-trampled middle section was passable, and even there footing was treacherous. Jane, he supposed, had tripped up these steps in broad daylight, sure as a mountain goat.

His key scraped at the lock. Despite spending all afternoon at Kandy's, he hadn't even gotten drunk, just numbed around the edges. It wasn't enough. The door swung inward without him. He followed it.

On his oversized forties Goodwill couch sat Turner.

Kevin's keys clattered to the glass-topped coffee table like a gauntlet. "I'd have more privacy sleeping in the park."

"What are you complaining about? I heard you were looking for me, so I found you."

Kevin came closer to study the government man. Turner looked almost as bad as Kevin felt. "What's up?"

"That should be my line, Doc."

"Never mind. What do you want?"

"Why did you want me?"

"I asked first, Turner."

"I want you to come with me to Jane Doe."

Kevin's shoulders slumped. He could no longer deny Turner's seriousness. Incredible as it seemed, in the few days they'd been separated, Jane must have been found as Turner had said—naked, again; lost, again; semistarved, again. Perhaps even memoryless—again. Kevin would be beginning, all over again.

Turner shoved himself out of the sofa's mushy mohair depths. "I think you're ready to come now."

"What about Nordstrom?"

"Nordstrom's . . . disabled."

Kevin, shocked, tried to read Turner's face. It remained blanker than a page in a Nothing Book.

"Come on, Doctor. You know you want to be there."

Turner walked to the door.

Kevin waited just long enough to wad together some self-respect before picking up his keys and following.

*   *   *

The room looked like they'd filmed a scene from *Porky's* there. It was an unholy mess.

Buckled vinyl floor tiles splayed every which way. The bed lay upside down, every strut of its functional metal undercarriage obscenely visible. A dried trail of sewage snaked through a partly open door. In the bathroom beyond, mirror shards tinseled the ceramic-tiled floor.

"It smells like jail," Kevin said.

"We found him at five A.M., pinned under the bed. He was caked with filth and not making much sense. You ever seen anything like this, Doctor?"

Kevin scanned the disheveled room, then looked down

at the vinyl tiles spun out of place. Enlarge them to the size of LP record albums and . . .

"Yeah. I've seen something like it. This all the damage?"

Turner stalked the bed, then wheeled to the nightstand to flourish a sheaf of manila folders.

"These documents—your medical records, background stuff—and some other . . . unrelated . . . papers were strewn around the room. The bulk of it landed in the sewage. We threw it out. It was mostly photographs."

When Kevin looked confused, Turner spelled it out as much as he cared to. "Black-and-whites of the camps. In Germany. After the war—and during. Pictures of . . . inmates . . . as they looked when they were liberated. And the bodies."

Kevin nodded finally, surveying the room piece by misplaced piece. When he glanced up again, Turner was looking away. He stared at the man until he had his eyes.

"And you let Nordstrom have her."

"We'd used him before."

"He used *you*! And now, Jane."

"Let's get out of here," Turner said gruffly. Kevin's eyes questioned his. "It's . . . making me sick."

In the hall, Turner thrust the manila folders at Kevin.

"What's this?"

"I told you. The documents in the case."

Kevin flipped open the top folder. Julie Symons's face stared at him, stared past him actually. She had always posed without looking into the camera.

"That's the only photo Nordstrom had that we can't identify," Turner said. "You know her?"

"I did."

"Who is she?"

"None of your goddamn business." Turner's and Kevin's eyes caught, held, held on. Turner didn't ask again.

Kevin turned Julie facedown. Behind her lay the newspaper likeness of Jane, and another sketch. He picked it up.

"New drawing," Turner explained. "Some woman made it at Brother Paul's House of Charity downtown. That's how we found her."

265

"Jane was at a soup kitchen?"

Turner shrugged. "She ate there at least, we presume, though it can't have been much."

Kevin's fingers traced the charcoal spirals depicting the hat atop Jane's head.

"A bag lady gave her that. Crazy character, walking hat rack. The hat wasn't on Jane when the police got there."

"What was?" Kevin turned and began walking along the phony corridor leading into phony hospital rooms, all empty. His tone was brisk. He was the doctor on the case finally called in and demanding a report on a patient.

"Nothing. She was naked."

Kevin stopped. "Completely? You weren't just jiving me before? Naked?"

Turner nodded. "Again. Even in the snow and cold. It was a miracle she was alive."

"Maybe not."

"What do you mean?"

"I think she can regulate her metabolism, even subconsciously."

"Another thing puzzles me. Was she . . . losing a lot of weight when you two were on the run up north?"

Kevin stopped again. "What the hell do you mean? Don't lay this weight thing on me. She was fine. I wouldn't let her starve; she wouldn't let herself starve. Jane's not anorexic. Never was. She's a survivor, first and foremost. More than you can imagine, Turner, Jane Doe is a survivor."

Turner's hands spread to deny whatever had offended Kevin.

"Where is she?" Kevin asked next. Demanded.

"You think you can . . . help her? Figure this out?"

"Haven't you read your Mother Goose, Turner? 'All the king's horses and all the king's men—'"

"You think . . . she did it." Turner's head jerked back to the room they had left.

"Don't you?"

"Yes, but what's wrong with that? Neither one of us gives a . . . plugged nickel about Nordstrom. At least it proves her telekinetic powers."

"Turner." Kevin looked away, then tried again. "Turner, Jane Doe's powers are purely defensive. Defensive. She's never . . . attacked anyone psychically. From a distance. She's incapable of it. That's not the Jane Doe I know."

"Then who—and how?"

"Maybe it's the Jane Doe Nordstrom made. I don't know yet. Let me see her."

Turner led him to a door that duplicated Nordstrom's.

"Convincing setup," Kevin conceded. "If I didn't know better I'd think I was in a hospital."

"You are, in a sense. We can get you anything you need."

"I need time, Turner. I need luck. I need what you can't give me—Jane before you and Nordstrom had a chance to damage her."

Turner hovered behind him anyway.

"I want to see her alone." Turner's face hardened. "Alone."

Kevin opened the door, went in, shut it.

It stayed shut.

The room was exactly like Nordstrom's, except for the large mirror opposite the bed. Kevin remembered the watching post Turner had mentioned in jail. He supposed Turner could be standing behind the two-way glass even now. He didn't care.

Kevin approached the bed. Jane lay on it, pale as the hospital sheets, her hair a charcoal smudge against the white. He didn't want to believe his eyes. She seemed to be a sketch of a woman—flat, empty, a mere likeness. The extent of physical regression in so short a time was unbelievable, the fact of it inescapable.

Kevin swallowed a spitball of sudden rage choking his throat. The brusque doctor-act was no defense against seeing this renewed nightmare in black and white. A recurring dream, a biological rerun. Total déjà vu. He was approaching a conundrum again, once again reduced to a clumsy, probing instrument that could destroy as well as salvage the delicate psyche.

"Jane?" He had whispered without meaning to.

Her eyes opened. They held the flat opacity of smoked Plexiglas. "Kevin." She smiled thinly.

He fought to keep his shock from infecting her. "You've . . . lost a lot of weight."

"I have, haven't I?" She lifted a bony hand to study it with a professional calm he envied.

Kevin reached out, his hand poised to grab hers, crush it with his caring, his pain, his guilt. The rash gesture froze, then his hand lightly clasped her wrist to take a pulse. Braced as he was for something—a tingle of telekinetic energy between them, her violent withdrawal—the fact that nothing did happen unnerved him more. She behaved so normally and looked so abnormal.

His mind routinely tallied the beats of her pulse while his emotions mimed silent screams for release. He could only regard this Jane through a bottomless well of despair. How far he had to take her again—could he? But he knew no course but caution, and couldn't face anything except one step at a time. One . . . heartbeat . . . at a time.

"How have you been?" His distress retreated behind med school inanities; bedside manner by Dr. Bob.

Jane's pulse throbbed steadily between his icy fingers. Sixty-eight beats a minute; low, but consistent with his hypometabolism theory. He calibrated her pumping heart on his handsome Swiss watch, wanting to hurl the gleaming watchface through the spying mirror, wanting to pull Jane into his arms and sob into her shoulder—My God, Jane, you're back where you began! What happened to you, what have they done to you? How could they hurt you so much so fast?

Instead he gently laid her arm on the sheet and pulled a chair to the bedside.

"You haven't said how you're feeling, Jane."

"Slow," she answered. "I've been waiting for you."

His heart stopped as he recognized something familiar in Jane—her serene faith in him. "Were you so sure I'd come?"

"Of course." Her eyelashes dropped as she looked away. "I didn't like Dr. Nordstrom. He was . . . inconsistent."

Kevin ached to blurt out what Nordstrom really was. Maybe if he named a villain he wouldn't have to confront the victim. He forced his voice to remain bland. "People

268

are sometimes like that. But I'm here now. I'll be working with you."

"Oh." She met his eyes with the first strong emotion she had shown—dismay. "Do we have to work? I remember everything we did in session before, and . . . I'm sleepy."

"Don't think of it as work. Think of it as us talking. You do still want to talk to me, don't you, Jane?"

A smile played tag with the taut corners of her mouth. "Oh, yes, Kevin. I've had . . . trouble . . . remembering recent things. I think it's because I used my . . . mind, because I had to use it. But I remember how we talked." Her hand finger-walked across the sheet to grasp his. "I'm glad you're back. I've missed you."

The words were sweet, but to Kevin's hypersensitive ears, they rang as counterfeit as his cautious small talk. He looked into her dark eyes and saw an abused stranger—looked deeper, and saw another stranger—the miniature reflection of himself and his uncertainty in her dilated, coffee-black pupils.

*   *   *

"Where's Nordstrom?" Kevin demanded afterward.

"You don't want to see him?" Turner asked incredulously.

"No, not now. I'd throttle him. Where are you keeping the bastard? Is it secure?"

"In a new room like hers," Turner said, "two-way mirror and restraints. We're watching him around the clock, believe me."

"But you weren't when you sicced him on Jane, were you?"

"No. We had no reason to. What do you think?"

"Think? I think you've done inestimable damage in an incredibly brief time. She's completely regressed."

Kevin began pacing the fake corridor in the fake hospital. He'd been driven here in a car with blacked-out windows, so he didn't even know where they were. "Jane herself admits to amnesia of recent events. I'll have to find out how far back it goes. I told you her powers were defensive, not destructive."

269

"What about my men?" Turner interrupted bitterly.

"They'd knocked me out, and I was Jane's only link to any safety. Besides, I'm still not sure exactly what she did. It was an accident at best; self-defense at worst."

"Don't you know, Doctor?"

"No. No one will ever know but Jane, and she developed amnesia about the specifics even then. That's why it's tough to figure what happened here. Even Nordstrom's nutritionless saline solutions can't account for a twenty-pound loss in a few days! God knows *she* can't say."

Kevin paused before leveling Turner with the guilt he himself felt.

"And her weight and memory aren't the only losses she's suffered—maybe they're the lightest. Emotionally, she's light-years behind where she was. My God, all the humanity, the growing strength of her assembling personality, her special vulnerability—" Kevin spun on his heel, his hands hitting his sides. "It's as if I were talking to a cipher again. It's Day One all over again, Turner."

"But she remembers you?"

"Yeah." Kevin spun away again.

"Does she still love you?"

Kevin stopped. "I don't know. Can't tell yet. Look, Turner, whatever the government wants from Jane, I don't need that, what you think I do. If the price of getting back the person she was becoming is Jane not loving me anymore, fine—I'll pay it. But I will not be made to use her, even by myself."

Turner's smile was bleak. "You always had the profile of a crusader. I believe you, Doctor."

"Believe something else. If I can get her back—and away from you and this godforsaken warehouse in human byproducts you've brought us to, I will."

"We'd have to stop you."

"Maybe," Kevin said, smiling grimly himself. "Maybe you can't."

Chapter Thirty-four

"What's the last thing you remember before you forgot things again, Jane?"

She and Kevin sat in chairs in a room other than her so-called hospital room. Jane was dressed. Clothes had been the second thing Kevin had ordered for her, after food.

Like the food, the clothing had appeared as if wafted forth by invisible hands in a fairy tale—slacks, sweater, and wear-scuffed Western boots, trendy outcasts of some urban cowgirl's wardrobe.

Jane's fairy godmother probably had been one of the women agents cleaning out the dregs of her closet. Kevin didn't care how Jane's wardrobe had arrived. The building, whose vastness he had glimpsed in passing, seemed equipped to support comfortably a large number of people for an unspecified amount of time. He had gotten used to seeing only its insides, and thought of it as a huge bomb shelter.

Jane looked better already, lipstick and eye shadow brightening her gaunt face courtesy of the "nurse," her hair combed. Right now she was twirling a loose strand around her forefinger, like the girl in the poem who could be very, very good, and was considering Kevin's question with flattering intensity.

"What do I last remember before I forgot?" Jane sipped one of the health-food milk shakes Kevin had ordered. "Dr. Nordstrom!" Jane declared, letting the impromptu curl slide through her fingertips. She waited for Kevin's approval.

"Dr. Nordstrom." Just saying the name slimed his lips.

He forced his voice to remain neutral—or what could pass for it. "What about . . . him?"

"He had strapped me down again—" She looked up quickly as Kevin's chair squeaked. "Why did he do that, Kevin? I wasn't going to go anywhere, except to the bathroom."

"He . . . he's a weak person, Jane. He thinks people only do what they have to do. He doesn't understand."

"I didn't like it."

"I know."

"But he was so fast. I didn't expect him to do it, not even the second time. That was wrong of me. I should have been . . . ready."

"What would you have done, if you had been?"

Jane regarded him with a crystalline gaze. "Stopped him."

Her reply stopped Kevin cold. She meant it. Jane knew how to aim her powers now, the ones he kept swearing were purely defensive, and—what was worse—possessed the inner rage to do it. A mental chill amplified Kevin's despair of ever resurrecting the Jane he had known—and loved—from this skeletal mockup of her.

"But you didn't stop him," he reminded her, and reassured himself. She still had free will and a moral hierarchy. "So that's the last thing you remember, Dr. Nordstrom . . . restraining you."

"No."

"No?"

"No. I lay there and thought for a while. A long while. I thought I saw myself . . . waking up. As if I finally knew what to do. I thought of you, Kevin, of finding you. And then it was night and Dr. Nordstrom came back."

Kevin studied his white knuckles. "Did he touch you, Jane?"

"A little. Mostly he talked."

"Talked?"

"About someone named Julie."

Kevin's breath hissed out. "What about someone named Julie?"

"I don't know. That's not anyone I knew at the dorm. There was Melanie, and Glenda. And Kim and Connie. Armajane and—"

"Arma-*what*?"

"Armajane. She was from New Prague. It's a town. I looked it up on a map. Kevin, what are you thinking?"

"That I didn't know much about your dormmates. If there was a Julie among them, I don't think Dr. Nordstrom meant that Julie anyway."

"What Julie did he mean?"

Kevin hesitated, then reached for one of the manila folders stacked on a table behind him. He extended the photograph of Julie to Jane, watching, watching hard . . . like a shrink. He wished he could watch himself.

"Oh." Jane tilted her head to study the picture. "I've never seen her before. Or this photo. She looks all stiff and funny."

"It's the pose. She was a dancer."

"Was?"

He smiled. Post-Nordstrom or not, Jane still had a lightning-swift uptake. "She's dead now."

"Oh. Like Lynn Volker. Then I don't understand why Dr. Nordstrom was talking about her the way he was, as if she were still alive. He said that she—I?—a woman could never be too thin or too cold. What do you suppose he meant?"

"He's sick." Kevin took back the photo, gazed into Julie's distant black-and-white eyes. He thought of bone and dirt. The wrinkles Nordstrom had crushed into the shiny paper still defaced the image, aging Julie's eternally young face. Kevin brooded on what hidden wrinkles Nordstrom had managed to pleat into Jane's psyche over the last several days.

"Maybe Dr. Nordstrom doesn't get enough to eat," Jane speculated, drawing noisily on her milk shake straw. "He didn't believe much in food."

Her analytical dispassion chilled Kevin. She seemed like the machine the aliens had intended her to be, that he had never been willing to see before.

273

He tried again. "And that's the last thing you remember —Dr. Nordstrom coming into your room at night and talking about Julie?"

"Yes," said Jane.

"Jane, I'd like to hypnotize you." He couldn't miss the way her body tensed. For an instant, she looked like a dancer about to dance.

"Why?" she wanted to know.

"Why not?" He had to find out how deep the new aggression she had unleashed at Nordstrom ran.

"Dr. Nordstrom tried to do it."

"Did he?" Very casual.

"Yes."

"Did you let him?"

"Of course. But—"

"Yes?"

"But he needed to know the word, you know. And—"

"So you gave it to him."

"Yes, but—"

"But?"

"It didn't work. Dr. Nordstrom didn't seem very happy."

Kevin sat forward. "It didn't work? But it had to, even for someone else. Why not?"

"I don't know. He asked for the word I thought of when I thought of you, and I said 'Zyunsinth'—"

Kevin laughed then and grabbed her hands. "You always did confuse me with the Missing Link! Listen, Jane, you gave Nordstrom the wrong word, that's why it didn't work. Don't you remember the word we used? What you called the ambulance by mistake?"

"Oh." Jane frowned, then smiled back at Kevin, as if his loosening up had released her somewhat. "Now I do. The . . . ec-na-lub-ma."

"Right. I could use that word and I could hypnotize you. Would that be all right?"

She thought about it, sliding her dark eyes sideways, looking to her hidden, eternally internal left. Such gestures activated the right, intuitive side of her brain. "All right."

Her retreat to intuition rather than logic relieved him.

Jane herself was still in there, somewhere. Time, she needed time. He began the hypnotic ritual, being as reassuring as a sensitive shrink could be. He even allowed some love to leak into his voice, damn unprofessional thing to do. She went under like a charm.

"Jane, after Dr. Nordstrom left, what did you do?"

"I waited. And thought."

"What did you think about?"

"About how he'd said I was to provide a demonstration of my power. I didn't want to, but then . . ."

"Then—?"

"Then I thought about Dr. Nordstrom. About how he came and went and how there was something in his eyes that sharpened itself on me. And he tried to contain me. This probe must not be contained." Her voice had hardened.

"This probe—?" Good lord, she was reverting to her original programming! Even at the University Hospitals, she'd never referred to herself in that cold inanimate way. . . .

"This probe must remain at liberty to fulfill its function," she recited at his prompting. "It must be free to Call and Recall. So it . . . so *Jane*—Jane thought. Jane thought through walls, through time. Then Jane made the room dance for Dr. Nordstrom. She did as he said. She provided a demonstration. And Dr. Nordstrom went away. Now Kevin is here. Kevin will not stop Jane. Kevin is . . . useful. Kevin is remembered. It is all . . . all right now."

Kevin let her warm fingers slip through his cold ones. He leaned back in his chair to rub a hand over his chin. His spine ached and he could use a shave. Funny. He had completely adapted to being beardless now. Odd how new habits so quickly assert themselves, and old ones desert one. No wonder Jane had changed, with all she'd been through.

He studied her as she sat before him in the serene expectancy of hypnotic trance. This . . . appalling disassociation between her current self and her old self, this reversion to probe status—it indicated regression so deep it pained him to contemplate it.

And now she had done the unthinkable—attacked without provocation. True, she'd been goaded by the sick baiting of Eric Nordstrom. Anyone would have responded to such a stimulus, himself included, but then "anyone" didn't have access to Jane's brand of electromagnetic mayhem.

Perhaps he was the fool for believing that Jane's lethal side was pure programming, Kevin told himself. Perhaps it *was* inherent, engineered into her genes. Perhaps Turner and the government knew what they were doing, and Jane was just the one to do it for them. Perhaps she had always been only a tool, and he was the evergreen optimist for believing she could be answerable only to herself, that he could love a being as bizarrely constituted as she, a biological probe first and a person second.

A thousand questions writhed to birth in his brain before he finally leaned forward and whispered the word that released Jane to waking consciousness.

*   *   *

"The man's a basket case."

"Dammit, I won't see him!" Kevin leaned back on the bed that was his. Turner had assigned him a pretty innocuous room—no Wonderland mirror, no hospital furniture. Kevin never believed he was alone in it for a moment, not even in his dreams.

"You're a shrink," Turner argued. "Maybe Nordstrom knows something that will help us. Or help you. Her."

"Yeah. I might look at the guy, but I can't! I'm much too . . . tied up in Jane's case. And Nordstrom's a counterforce in her treatment. Don't you see what he's done to her?"

"You can't be with Jane Doe every hour of the day!"

"Oh, but I am," Kevin said. "When I'm not with her, I'm thinking about the next stage of treatment. I'm wondering how to bring her along—or whether my own involvement is objective enough for her own good. Maybe even for yours, Turner."

"And—?"

"Some progress. She talks more like the old Jane—or

276

rather, the new Jane treatment pried from her shell once before. I can't risk my relationship—my professional relationship—with Jane by mucking around in Nordstrom's twisted psyche. You don't know how personally involved I am in this. Not just with Jane. With Nordstrom, too."

"I know Nordstrom knew you at Harvard, and apparently hated your guts."

"Do you know why?"

Turner shrugged. "You're likeable; he isn't. It figures."

"Thanks, but you're a lousy judge of human nature. I was the outsider, the 'unwashed phenomenon' from northern Minnesota. The scholarship student. Oh, I survived, but Nordstrom had all the aces hand-dealt to him.

"I suppose he gave you that 'poor me' routine. Don't believe it. He had it all. So did all the guys like him. That's really why Julie Symons picked me. I was the perfect antithesis to her successful father, guaranteed to drive old man Symons crazy. They call it adolescent rebellion.

"Julie was a little old for that, but her development had frozen somewhere in a preteen limbo, emotionally. I didn't 'take' Julie from Nordstrom like he imagines—she did! She picked me as bedside companion for her slow death from anorexia nervosa."

"Some honor." Turner shuddered a little, maybe not just for effect. Nordstrom had attuned him to degrees of sickness.

"Maybe it *was* a compliment," Kevin mused. "I wasn't threatening like her father, or predictable like the guys she grew up with—the rich, neurotic Nordstroms of the East Coast. I was good enough for her to kiss good-bye. Which she did.

"It took me a long time to figure out that Julie was giving her world the finger the only way she knew how. I was incidental. Nordstrom could never accept that, because that would have made him even more incidental. So he fixated on Julie, fixated on her death, on her way of death."

"And he's a shrink?" Turner sounded shocked.

"Ever hear the expression 'Physician, heal thyself'? It was custom-made for Nordstrom. Finding someone like

277

Jane simply intensified his delusions. You don't know half of what he put her through—starving her, restraining her so she'd have to soil herself. Trying to infantalize her, really."

"Blake—say, that's why . . . the feces, the vomit in his room. He ate it, did you know that? He licked it up like a dog."

Kevin digested the revulsion on Turner's face. "Don't feel too sorry for Nordstrom. He probably enjoyed it. The technical word is *coprophilia*."

"I'll never understand you shrinks."

"You'll never have to understand what we have to. Count your blessings and, in the meantime, do us both a favor and ship Nordstrom off to another head-shrinker. You and I've got our hands, hearts and minds full with Jane."

"It sounds like you're committed to . . . helping her, helping us."

Kevin grinned wearily. Turner wasn't so bad, if he hadn't had his job to do. "Watch your choice of verbs," was all he would answer.

Chapter Thirty-five

"Would it be all right if I taped our sessions?"

Kevin waved the tiny Japanese recorder under Jane's nose, then drew back internally to watch her. She eyed the mechanism, wrinkled her forehead, started to speak, then hesitated.

"I . . . suppose so."

"You still don't like recorders, do you?"

"No."

"Why not?"

"I'm—" He saw her mind searching for the right words. "They give me . . . bad vibes."

"Hmm. Sounds like another dorm phrase."

"But it fits. That . . . machine makes me feel like Dr. Nordstrom did."

"Which is—"

"Twitchy." Jane demonstrated by trying to outshrug her baby blue wool sweater.

"Okay. I just wanted to see where we stood. We're back to Square One, like I figured."

"I've disappointed you?"

"No, I've disappointed myself. I keep expecting life to pick up right from where it left off, like a comic strip. Nothing's like that. Everything is going back and back until we get it right enough to go forward."

"Is that what you mean by 'regression'?"

"Sometimes. The Hindus call it reincarnation." Kevin put the tape recorder away and kept his voice brightly professional. "So. What do you want to talk about? You don't recall anything that happened after I took you to the Crow Wing bluff top and the . . . others came and assumed you into their vessel. I'd give a lot to know what happened before they returned you."

"It's all so clear until then—Kevin, I'd tell you if I could!"

"I know." His hand tightened reassuringly on her arm, but his heart sank. He couldn't seem to get a firm psychological grip on this new Jane. Their sessions were cold, sterile. Maybe he expected too much too soon. Maybe he needed too much too soon. "You don't remember anything afterwards—oh, burying Zyunsinth, or the night in the motel?"

Jane shook her dark head, looking sad. Her fingers curled around his forearm, loosely. "Did I miss anything important?"

"No." He leaned away, letting her hand slide from his arm. Her question had provoked a sequence of pungent memories—the cheap outstate motels, the companionship of the van as it swallowed miles like krill, the cold, and Jane warm in his arms—those were suddenly, irrevocably the good old days. "We had our first fight, that's all."

"I can't imagine fighting with you."

279

"You did. You talked back. Argued."

"About what?"

"About clothes shopping. About . . . Zyunsinth."

"Oh. It's funny, I had a dream—" She stopped herself.

"About Zyunsinth?"

She studied him for a long moment, memory and calculation blending in her expression. "About . . . you."

"Listen, they don't pay me to hear about myself."

"They pay you?"

"No. No one pays me anymore. What did you dream about me?" His heart was thumping hopefully. Maybe *he* was Zyunsinth now, the key to her memory.

"We were . . . together. You know. Like before. Maybe it would help if we could do it again."

Jane broached his own unmentionable hope and he fled. "That's . . . past for now, Jane. I shouldn't have let it happen then. I have more reason to not let it happen now. We have to settle the present first."

"I thought *I* was there, too."

"You were. Only . . . I'm the responsible one."

"But you said, you *said* that I was to become responsible, that what I did . . . wanted . . . was because I was I."

"That's true."

Jane's eyes grew stormy. " 'I' wishes to be that I again. I miss Zyunsinth and I don't remember losing it. I miss you and you won't help me."

"Oh, God. Jane. . . ." Now. Close up on Jane's face. She remembers. Ecstatic embrace. Happy ending. Fade out. "Look," said the psychiatrist in him, cold as mirror glass, "you've been through everything I once hoped you'd be spared. It's hurt you terribly, though you don't know it yet. It's hurt me. We're—we can't just pick up from there. We have to give it time."

"How much?"

"Enough."

"You don't like me anymore!"

"No—" But *did* he like her now that he doubted her? Could he possibly love her again, or not love her, without hating himself either way?

"You're afraid of me!"

"No—Yes, afraid of damaging you! It's my goddamn job not to!"

Jane settled into her vinyl-seated maple chair that looked like it had escaped from a cafeteria. She absently scratched her back by swaying against the top strut, a motion all the more sensual for its innocence.

"I thought you liked to sleep with me," she said.

"I do! I did." That wasn't the answer. Life was never that simple, not even for clones. The image of Nordstrom's room—of what Jane had done to Nordstrom's room—surfaced in his mind, repelled him. He felt ashamed. "Things have changed."

"Me. You think I've changed."

"And me," he admitted. *Mea culpa, mea maxima culpa.* That's what you get for playing God.

"You always asked me to try to remember things, to think about them."

"Yes." He saw it coming.

"Think about that," Jane told him. "Kevin, I miss you. You're the one thing that made being here not seem right."

"Oh, Jane, I'm here now."

"Not the same."

"You don't miss Zyunsinth?"

"I've . . . forgotten Zyunsinth."

"That's wrong, somehow—"

"I haven't forgotten you."

"You're weak," he said, his fingers forgetting themselves long enough to brush her face.

She moved his hand to the side of her breast. His fingers felt only the ripple of ribs. "I'm getting stronger. A lot stronger."

*   *   *

Kevin saw Nordstrom that afternoon.

"Well, the young lion," the man greeted him.

Nordstrom had shriveled, everything but his head had shrunk. He looked like the fraudulent Wizard of Oz—a great, inflated bladder with no body.

"Apparently the tables have turned," he admitted. "I'm in the cage and you're the conquering hero."

"Hardly a cage." Kevin looked around the room.

"They took . . . my things."

"They should have."

"You've come to gloat? Or cure me, is that it? Dr. Schweitzer, I presume, come to minister to the poor ignorant savage—"

"Poor, no. Ignorant, hardly. Savage, yes. Nordstrom—"

"*Doctor* Nordstrom to you, Blake."

"Nordstrom, what did you want from Jane?"

"Past tense. My, we are overconfident. When the government doesn't need you anymore, they'll put you out to pasture, too."

"I'd have thought they'd have shipped you to a head joint in Virginia by now," Kevin conceded.

"Can't. Know too much. You do, too, Blake. Wait'll you see how they discredit you."

"You discredited yourself. What did you want from Jane?"

"Her . . . compliance."

"Jane isn't a terribly compliant person," Kevin said.

"No, but you did all right." Nordstrom's eyes glittered as he shrank back against his bed's metal headboard.

"I'm not going to hit you, Nordstrom. I'd like to, but I'm not going to. If you made me do it, you'd have won. I won't hit you and Jane won't—wouldn't—comply, isn't that right?"

"Yes, you're a fucking coward and she's a, a—free spirit." Nordstrom started laughing, a smug giggle that grated like chalk on a blackboard.

Kevin waited for him to stop before speaking again. "She made you eat shit. She made you hit rock bottom in yourself and then glory in it."

Nordstrom was silent, but near the nosepiece, his glasses fogged over with the fury of his seething breaths. Kevin automatically went to take his pulse, wary of hyperventilation.

The vast complex, whatever it had been originally, was habitually kept meat-locker cold, and the earth was still wrapped in the dead of winter outside this artificial miniworld.

282

Nordstrom jerked his wrist away. "Fast. I was hyperactive as a child. And I may be a . . . teensy . . . agitated now. So keep your filthy hands off me!"

Kevin watched the psychiatrist nurse his wrist, as if Kevin's impersonal touch had bruised it.

"Did you keep *your* hands off *her,* Nordstrom? Or couldn't you resist, another almost-dead body for you to fondle, as you did Julie's?" Kevin prowled around the bed, aiming insight like weapons, being a bad psychiatrist.

"How long have you been screwing your patients, Nordstrom? Your female patients? Or is that all? You like women bone-thin, boyish almost. Is that what it is—not a fixation with death but an obsession with sex turned inside out? Maybe you don't like women at all, in any shape or form. Maybe you like men and can't face it—"

"What about your stability?" Nordstrom struck back. "You picked Julie and enjoyed it enough to see her through the long, slow fade—"

"Dr. Cross's theories won't wash. Julie seemed normal when I met her. Besides, anorexia stems from an individual's desire for ultimate control, particularly for women—who are so often overcontrolled by environment and their culture. And Jane never was anorexic; she gains weight like a wrestler, given half a chance. You had to starve her to keep her at your needed perception of her. You're a mean bastard, Nordstrom; I bet your female patients would have a few tales to tell—"

Nordstrom brooded icily, pushing his chin down on his chest.

Kevin walked to the wall, where a print of Van Gogh's sunflowers hung too high and crooked. Someone had recently paid almost forty million dollars for the original that Van Gogh had never been able to sell. Kevin straightened the clone.

"There's a theory—about women and weight and the way our culture sees them, forces them to see themselves. Maybe you've heard of it." Silence. Kevin continued anyway.

"That theory is that the sight of those emaciated survivors of the Nazi death camps inspired the Western world's postwar mania for cadaverous women models. It's a fetish for death, sexualized into a cultural cliché. Extreme emaciation produces an asexual image, blurs gender, flattens womanliness. It's the ultimate victimization, the ultimate depersonalization. You don't have to answer to a corpse."

"Shut up, shut up, shut up!" Nordstrom's hands cradled his ears. "I won't listen to your obscene fantasies! And no, I didn't touch your precious Jane Doe; filthy, she was filthy.

"I've never really touched any of them, the stupid bitches. They all did what I said. They're all filthy, carriers of hidden foulnesses. You can wallow in their steaming, diseased bodies, if you like. I . . . covet their minds. I take them without touching them. I am morally superior, Blake, morally superior!"

Kevin was at the door, fading fast, but he'd learned what he needed to know. He also understood why Turner had left Nordstrom's room on the verge of retching after finding him. And he knew why Jane had done what she had done.

*   *   *

Kevin dreamed again that night. He was wearing rimless eyeglasses and screwing corpses. He flung the bodies from himself before each act could be completed. But corpse followed corpse, brides of Dracula and Poe, every embodiment of woman as death that the mind of man could conceive, monuments to the male sex's perverse love affair with death and war and violence—monuments . . . and victims.

He woke up, grappling with enlightenment and one last entwining cadaver. Call it a dry dream.

"Jane!"

The room was dark, but he knew her touch.

"I was tired of being 'I' by myself," she complained, wrapping her arms around him.

Kevin's hands skimmed the warm skin of her spine between rungs of strings up her back; she wore a hospital gown still—apparently no one had dug up any conventional nightclothes for her.

She was ladder-thin, thinner than any Jane he had made

love to before. He held her away from him like china and tried to think.

"Kevin. It's not new. It helped me before; maybe it will help me now."

"Is that why you want it, to help yourself?"

"No . . . I want it because I want it. I want . . . you."

"Jane . . . I don't want to be like him, like Nordstrom. Yet by caring for you, I somehow always risk exploiting you."

"Maybe that's always the way it is. I don't feel exploited."

She was snuggling expertly against him, her palms running down his sides, his thighs. He found his hands undoing the stingy bows along her back, then molding her fragile body to their warmth and hunger.

Her mouth fastened on his by some mutual impulse in the dark. It was warm and sweet and deep, nothing like the carnal pit Nordstrom feared. Kevin began to appreciate the wonder of what he was free to feel, of what he and Jane could weave between them. It was sex, but it was life, not death. It was desire, but it was love, not envy. It was right.

"Jane . . . I've missed you. God, I love you." He rode the bare bucking back of his need now, forgetful of his profession, her supposed vulnerability. Jane responded in kind, her body twining with his, her words and gasps echoing his own.

The sheets twisted with them; even the spiraling dark seemed to merge in the dance. Jane's hand found the spire of his erection. His penis prodded the archway to her vagina, retreated to advance—and encountered a thin, ungiving inner door of membrane.

Kevin felt caviar beads of sweat all over his body turn rock-crystal cold.

He balanced over the dark beneath him, poised to surrender to its unseen shape, to be shaped by it. His penis nosed forward. The barrier gave, then tautened. He rolled away, his fingers exploring with a physician's expert dispassion even in the dark. They probed a satin-slick cavity—and met ungiving membrane.

A hymen. Again.

"Jane." He whispered. "Jane, you remember the first time we—?"

"Of course. I'd never forget that, Kevin."

"You had a—barrier in your body."

"My hymen." She sounded possessive. "You broke it and it hurt. But it hurt more not to have you inside me."

"Once it's gone, it stays gone. But you . . . have it again, and you're not supposed to. A hymen isn't a renewable resource."

"Really? I wasn't supposed to have it in the first place, was I? The girls in the dorm didn't seem to know about ever having one."

"But . . . you had one, and then you didn't—not even when we last were together, in the motel, remember? Since then, it's . . . grown back. Did you know that?"

"Motel? Remember? No . . . I don't remember the motel. And how could I know it grew back? I wouldn't feel it, would I? It's not the kind of thing a woman feels. You are. Kevin, come in."

"I know your memory's grown new blanks since we've been separated, like a hymen, I guess. I can accept that: You don't remember the motel, okay. I can't accept a . . . brand-new hymen springing into place. I've got to know—when, how . . . why?"

"Oh, Kevin. Not now. You've always got to know. I just want to—"

"I know what you want. But—" His fingers slid from inside her. "I don't know . . . you anymore. Maybe I never did."

"Kevin," she complained. "It's not fair."

"It's not fair, but it's life. I can't now, anyway."

"Can't?"

"I'm . . . not operative. Listen, Jane, if you've regrown your hymen, it means you've felt damaged—far more deeply damaged than you think or I can begin to imagine. I can't ignore that kind of trauma."

"I told you! I didn't even know!" Her hand flailed in the dark and finally captured his penis. "Oh."

"I told you. I can't."

"But I'm all right. I feel fine. I want you to."

286

"I'm not all right. I can't do it again, can't take responsibility for your virginity over and over, every damn time. Your body is unconsciously defending itself. There must be a reason, even if you don't know it. That's more important than this. Jane, let go. Give it up."

He patted around in the dark until he found the discarded hospital gown. He stuffed her clinging arms into it and tied the strings shut up the back. At the end he embraced her shoulders, but she stiffened.

"All right," Jane said, her voice husky with hurt. She didn't know enough to feel humiliated, although she had a right to be. "All right. I'll go."

"Jane, please . . . the time's not right, that's all."

He never heard her leave, just knew from the quality of silence that she had gone as quietly as she had come, that he was alone.

Kevin threw himself back down on the bed, angry with his recalcitrant body, surprised by his resurrected nicety. Why did Jane's regrown hymen chill him more than anything else about this new, more potent, demanding Jane he simply didn't want or love as he used to, as he ought to, dammit?

He'd breached the barrier of Jane's virginity once—not relishing the act but doing it. Why did a second time make it all seem so much more premeditated?

Why the hell did he have to care, when she obviously didn't?

Chapter Thirty-six

"Look," Turner said the next morning, "I don't want to interfere with Love's Young Dream, but don't you think it's time to get down to the nitty gritty?"

"How'd you know?" Kevin asked. "Room bugged?"

"None of your business." Turner grinned. "Imagine me telling you that, Doctor. I believe you shrinks call that role reversal. If she's well enough to get it on, she's well enough to start coughing up her bag of tricks."

Kevin went to the window—a frosted glass expanse the size of a two-story wall—and sipped his herbal tea. The big echoing room was a kind of employee lounge for the place's government staffers. Kevin guessed he was a kind of government staffer by now.

"Blake, don't go all broody on me. I'm counting on you to produce results. Why do you think I gave you so much rope? Now that you and Jane have kissed and made up, maybe we can all get our minds on business."

"We haven't," Kevin said over his cinnamon-scented steam, trying to disguise his surprise at Turner's ignorance of the particulars. Then his room must be bug-free. . . . "It was no go. Nothing happened. Honest, daddy."

"I don't need to know the gory details, but why not? *She* visited you. That looks like clear consent, if you ask me."

"Nobody's asking you!" Kevin turned so fast that hot tea sprayed his hand. He wasn't about to let Turner in on another of Jane's anomalies. "I'm not supposed to screw my patients, do you get it?! I wasn't supposed to before and I'm not supposed to now. Maybe I can't live with that, all right?"

"That's all that went wrong—your conscience acted up?"

"Yeah." Kevin tried to sound convincingly defensive. "'Course you wouldn't know about that—"

"No need to get personal, Doctor." Turner was brusque now, all business. "If you don't feel yourself capable of eliciting your patient's potential—"

"Oh, I'll 'elicit her potential,' all right. Just don't ask for any seamy details, because there won't be any. That's all over."

"I can't believe you mean that."

Kevin looked Turner dead in the eye. "I do."

Turner believed him because Kevin believed himself. Kevin sighed and sipped the boiling hot tea. Convincing this determined new Jane would be a lot harder.

Later, after Turner left, he lingered to analyze himself.

It didn't help that he felt Jane's betrayer in more ways than one. He had so easily converted to Turner's side. At times, living in this remote rural bunker, moving from one indoor area to another, he took this mock world so for granted that the outside world seemed unreal. He didn't even know what day it was now, or what date. The world turned without him.

They provided him with food and fresh clothing whose origins he never questioned. He came and went without visible surveillance, though he was sure Turner never for a moment underestimated his capacity to rebel. He could even resume a physical relationship with Jane with no static—the government didn't care about that, as long as he continued to probe her psychic abilities.

Sometimes Kevin fantasized that he would "confess" the whole thing. Commit truth. He would tell them that Jane's so-called psychic abilities were even more unearthly than they thought. She was a space-born clone, he would admit, a test-tube baby an alien species had Tinkertoyed together. A genetic erector set.

He would swear he had seen the alien vessel, swear that a UFO sat at the center of everything weird about this case. They could polygraph him, and the needles would write a thin, level line of truth under every one of his assertions.

But it wouldn't matter what the polygraph said. If Kevin claimed what he believed—knew—to be the truth, he would be as discredited as Nordstrom. They'd consign him to storage so cold and so dead even Zyunsinth wouldn't survive it. And Jane would be in other hands, subject to other obsessions than his own. He still seemed the least of several evils, even to himself.

*   *   *

Jane studied herself in the mirror that Kevin didn't like.

Kevin didn't like very much here, she knew, including herself. She blew out the hollows of her cheeks, her fingers pushing her flesh into a fuller configuration. It didn't help. Nor did her slowing herself, hoarding her body heat and limiting her motions. She was gaining weight, but it would still take many days for her to resume the appearance she last remembered of herself and that seemed to be so vital to Kevin.

As for the other thing . . . Jane frowned. She knew what a hymen was, but had never seen one, had never experienced it as other than something she felt the absence of more than its presence. It was hard to restructure a null.

In the end, she went into the tiny bathroom and probed until she found it, a tough wall of thin tissue. She finally forced her hand through, felt the unpleasant burning tear. Her fingers came away bloodied, but she washed them under the tap water. She didn't have the proper equipment the girls at the dorm had given her on the other occasions she had bled like this, but the red rinsed away as fast as it had come and she knew she had no hymen any longer.

She had hoped some magic would make this renewed absence result in Kevin's presence. But he didn't seem inclined to touch her in that way again, and something in herself—something alien—balked at telling him what she had done. She would have rather done it as she was used to doing things—from within, subtly. She would have wished that he had done it, as before. Now, Kevin would be angry at her alteration of herself for himself, Jane sensed. Something in her wished not to anger Kevin, and something in her was—slowly—becoming angry with him.

"Jane," he said later in the day that she'd freed—or bound?—herself for him. "I guess I've got to ask you to try to . . . move something. Turner will boot me out if I don't put on a show for him. I know you can do it now, much more consciously. Will you try?"

"What shall I move?"

"What do you feel like moving?"

"Sometimes . . . everything."

"I've never seen that in you before."

"What?"

"That . . . adolescent . . . rage."

Jane was silent.

"Well," he asked. "Will you?"

"You always ask the wrong questions."

"That's a heck of a thing to tell a psychiatrist."

"The table."

"What?"

"I'll move the table."

Kevin glanced to the hospital tray-table pushed against the wall. Jane ate with him now, in a different room, like a grown-up girl, like a well person.

"Okay." He sat back to watch, half disbelieving, half reluctant to see her reduced to doing parlor tricks. "How do you do it?"

"I begin by seeing it. Then I let it see me."

"I . . . see." He nodded gravely.

Jane didn't so much look at the table as look within herself. The table didn't so much move as . . . sparkle. Kevin stared. He saw it shimmer in its position, glimpsed the ceaseless atoms randomly colliding yet holding a shape. He saw matter literally unravel itself. The impression lasted a mere nanosecond. It registered on his brain only because that organ dealt in hypertime, too.

Then the illusion was gone. And the table, the table had jumped two feet away from the wall. Kevin heard the noise of its motion from a distance, as if the hand of time had muffled reality for an instant.

"That's wonderful. Carolyn Swanson would have given her best starched lab coat to see that. Can you . . . show someone else?"

"Yes—"

Kevin rose, went to the table, touched it. The Formica surface felt slightly warm, as if sun-baked. Otherwise, it looked perfectly normal. As did Jane. He turned to look at her.

She was sitting on the edge of her bed, her feet crossed at the ankles, her hands in her lap. An expression he didn't want to read sat uneasily on her face. She looked slight and young and too powerful to psychoanalyze.

"Jane . . . I'm sorry. I had to ask you to do it."

"Kevin—"

"No."

"I did what you wanted."

"Sometimes, that's not enough."

Her expression intensified. "I could . . . move you."

291

"Jane, no! That would change me. And us. That's not the way."

For a moment he read unbridled power in her expression. His body tingled all over, as if every cell were snapping its electrical fingers.

"Jane . . . you don't want to—alter me."

"I altered *me*! But I still don't know how—how to be me anymore," she complained.

He went to her and pulled her close as he stood there, pulled her face into the dubious comfort of the sweater Turner had provided him. Nothing was his anymore. He had fought them until he had become them.

"Jane—" But he had nothing to say to her anymore. He was not enough, and she was too much.

She wordlessly wrapped her arms around his hips, pressed her cheek into his stomach. He stroked her hair. It had never been soft, glossy. Always thick and strong. It was the kind of hair that grayed early. He was thinking of time passing, of survival—hers and his. He was thinking forward and there wasn't any future in it.

"Later," he said. "We'll do it again. For Turner and his cameras, is that all right? We have to show them something."

She tilted her head to look up at him. Nothing but emptiness filled her face. Kevin bent down to kiss her and left the room.

*   *   *

Jane studies herself in the mirror again.

So much is missing that she sometimes expects to see holes in her image. There is not only her amnesia, the missing memories of all the time with Kevin after the aliens returned her. There are missing feelings as well, instincts. She *knows* what she should know, but doesn't know how to use it.

Frustrated, she stares at herself until she sees the infinitesimal bits of that self disassembling, dissolving in the glass. Reality mimics the illusion. She sees another self reassemble—an old self.

A fur-coated Jane strides through the snow, booted feet

kicking small sprays of white before her so she seems at times to be walking on water.

This Jane is whole, healthy—her face soft, not harshly drawn. This Jane walks with her head up and her hands in her pockets. She comes on, her eyes oddly dreamy for a figure so intent, so energetic. She comes so close to the silver surface of the mirror that Jane thinks she can reach out to pet the fur—the Zyunsinth that was long buried, Kevin said.

This remembered Jane comes so close her frosty breath seems to fog the mirror, obscuring her own image, everything. Jane's feet stutter forward, bring her eye to eye with the misty surface. She pushes a forefinger through the condensation, wiping the mirror clear again.

In the cloud of fog that remains, Jane's forefinger traces a design she'd seen on the steam-fogged dorm bathroom mirror one day. "K.B. + J.D." Jane draws a big heart shape around it and watches.

In time, the steam evaporates and Jane goes to bed.

The Severing

January 22

*   *   *

". . . the fever of the bone . . ."
—T. S. Eliot
"Whispers of Immortality"

Chapter Thirty-seven

"Tomorrow," Kevin told Turner that night.

"Drink?" the government man asked in answer.

"Yeah. Drink."

Turner—perceptive—poured a full three fingers of Scotch into a tumbler. Kevin hoisted it.

"That all the government can afford?" He nodded at the bottle still in Turner's hand.

"All that's allowed for medicinal purposes. I guess you're a doctor, so you can prescribe for yourself. I congratulate you, against your better judgment. If you can produce any concrete evidence of Jane Doe's abilities, we'll really get some dough behind us. You can keep her as a patient."

"I've lost her," Kevin said, drinking. "I've sold her out."

"Somebody had to do it." Turner sat at the lunch table in the ground-floor lounge. He'd angled out one of the lower window squares so a blast of fresh winter air prowled the smoke-stale atmosphere.

"What did this place used to be anyway?" Kevin stared up at the high, relentlessly functional ceiling.

"Meat-packing plant. We're sitting in the employee lounge. The outfit went bust in the sixties. This was a one-industry town and it dried up."

Kevin laughed until Turner looked at him oddly. "What are you going to do with Nordstrom?" Kevin asked.

"Ship him out when we close down operations."

"Leave here?"

"Sure. Now that we've got something concrete, there's no reason she—you and she—can't go to Virginia and work with the pros—the PID parapsychology team.

297

They're top people, Blake. Academics. They're not Mind Wars engineers, just curious scientists."

"So were the Nazi doctors. Who knows, maybe 'curious scientists' are eavesdropping on us up there even now—" Kevin nodded beyond the concrete ceiling. "Maybe they'll experiment us into oblivion, like the ever-useful *drosophila*. Fruit flies," he added when Turner looked blank.

"You're tired." Turner stood, then drained the undiluted gold in his glass. "Better get some rest. You've got a big day ahead of you tomorrow."

"Right. In a minute."

Turner left him the bottle, a tall green bottle wearing a label full of blarney about its impeccable Scottish ancestry.

Kevin poured another three fingers into his glass. The Scotch was warm but its too-sharp bite matched his inner bile. He got up and went to the window, stuck his head under the slanted glass and inhaled the brutal wind chill.

A meat-packing plant. Turner hadn't even noticed the irony. An abandoned meat-packing plant.

The night was dark. Woods surrounded the plant; inside the trees lay a ring of unmarked snow. Kevin knew there was perimeter security—there had to be. He just didn't see it. So was it so much worse—how his kind would use Jane, compared to how the aliens already had?

He strained his neck out the opening, looking for sky, for stars. Only darkness yawned over him—either the sky was overcast or he couldn't see well enough. In his hand, the glass was turning to smooth ice. His knuckles felt burned. He tilted the glass and let cheap Scotch pierce the snow below, driving into it like hot piss.

He leaned back into the room, dully thinking that he should really shut the window for the night, Simple Citizen saving the government heating money.

And then he saw her.

Standing among the trees—a vague figure. He knew it was Jane.

He rubbed his eyes, as they do in turn-of-the-century dime novels. She was still there—worse, she was walking out from under the shadowy trees toward the building.

Jane, no. . . . Jane, yes. He didn't want her to be real.

298

She was coming closer, step by step, more recognizably herself with every advance. Behind her stretched a trail of footprints. Even as he watched, the snow blurred unnaturally in her wake, erasing the signs of her passage. Ghosts don't leave tracks, he told himself, and normal people don't erase their own imprints. It *must* be Jane.

Zyunsinth's long hair riffled as she moved. Kevin had seen no stars, but there must have been a full moon. Jane seemed as well lit as a church on a Christmas card.

A few feet from his watching post she paused, seeming to stare right through him. The wind tickled a few black threads of hair along her cheek, blending with the upraised hairs of the coat collar. Her hair looked . . . teased. No! She wore a hat. A mink pillbox.

Kevin waited for his dream to end or take a bizarre new direction. Instead, Jane turned. She vanished along the wall to his right, the holes of her footsteps closing up behind her in neat sequence.

Kevin went back to the table to contemplate the low-grade Scotch. He was shivering. Projection? he wondered. Jane wishing her old self back so much she had produced it? Or had he just glimpsed a figment of his own wish fulfillment? And what explained the bizarre clothing this phantom wore?

With his eyes shut, he envisioned Jane wearing her Crow Wing jacket and politely lost expression, Jane as one solitary figure in a bank lobby bristling with anonymous passersby.

Cold entered the room—not from the window. Kevin's opening eyes had already focused on the door. He had to get upstairs and check Jane's room. He arrived at the door just as it swung open. Jane herself stood on the threshold, her nose burnished red, her eyelashes whitened with ice.

"Kevin?" she asked, looking dazed, surprised and happy all at once.

He was too stunned to answer and, anyway, she fainted at his feet.

*　　　　　*　　　　　*

Jane sat at the Formica-topped lunch table, the satin

299

lining of her fur coat unfurled behind her, eating a baloney sandwich.

She wolfed it down—two slabs of whole-wheat bread, pickles, lettuce, tomato, mayonnaise and six slices of Peters' baloney.

The sight would have turned Nordstrom's stomach.

Kevin sat watching her, his face propped in his fists, his expression sandwiched between two seldom-paired emotions—parental pride and adolescent infatuation. It *was* Jane, he knew. *His* Jane. Back again as she was, only God knew how. Back from someplace she couldn't have been.

"You *walked* from the Twin Cities?" he asked.

Jane nodded broadly, chewing. "Mwfffaplssss," she corrected.

Of course. She came from Minneapolis, not St. Paul. Precise Jane. Surprising Jane. Jane. Really, truly Jane Jane. Again.

Then who the hell was that upstairs? His mind reeled, torn between two mutually exclusive truths. If he didn't force his eyes to focus, they kept seeing Jane . . . and Jane. Double vision. Somehow, she was two. That would explain the bewildering weight discrepancy, and why Turner's Jane had selective amnesia. . . .

Jane took a professional swig of the beer Kevin had fetched from the Company refrigerator.

Her eyelashes were dewy, as if she'd been crying. Kevin knew better. She'd been walking in subzero temperatures for hours—other than a slow heartbeat, icy extremities that were rapidly warming, and a Godzilla-sized appetite, she seemed fine. Her face and body seemed fully fleshed, healthy despite the ordeal.

"You want some more?" he asked.

Jane frowned at the few bread crumbs spangling her empty plate. "In a minute."

"I can't believe that you found me," Kevin marveled. "Where is this place, anyway?"

"I don't know."

"You must know if you found it!"

Jane shook her head. Her only makeup was the blood

rushing back into her lips and cheeks, but she looked terrific. She glowed. "I just . . . went where I had to go."

"Speaking of going—" Kevin swooped the empty plate into the stainless steel sink, where other used utensils still lay. "We better scram before anybody sees you." He'd suddenly realized that no one must see her and lifted the foreign fur coat off the back of her chair. "My place or yours?"

Jane stared at him, surprised, then winked.

The hall wore its usual air of desertion that Kevin never quite believed. Someone was clocking his comings and goings. He prayed whoever it was took naps. Their footsteps seemed thunderous in the stairwell, but no governmental lightning struck. They saw no one and no one spotted them.

"It looks like a hospital," Jane said when he got her—unseen—to his room. She was not being complimentary.

Kevin sat on the bed's fake blanket—some sort of foam matted into blanket shape. "It's better than county jail. Jane . . . my God, how . . . where have you been? If you only knew what's been going on here—!"

She sat beside him. "I don't know, Kevin. It's so confusing. I was with Panama Hattie and Boomer in the dumpster, and then the fire started burning the blankets and I—I lifted it.

"When we got out, everybody stood around and I remembered you were at the county jail and went to find you. It was dark and cold. It reminded me of that . . . other place that I can't remember. Then someone or something rushed at me, hit me again and again—and I can't really remember *that*! I woke up in the snow and the cold. I only knew that you were gone, Hattie was gone, all my clothes were gone—I felt this . . . pull. From myself, almost—"

"Shhhh. Don't hit me with it all at once. It's too mind-blowing. The police said you were mugged for your clothes. From what you say, it probably happened that way. Only the police never found *you*, but . . . someone else."

Kevin pulled her close. Jane was wearing an expensive sweater woven from long, soft angora fibers. She felt solid and damn good and like she needed warming up.

301

"Kevin, I'm so glad to see you, but—"

"But?"

"I don't *know* what happened to me. I remember walking, looking. Looking for something . . . my clothes, you, Zyunsinth—I was so cold at first until I made my body fight it. And I couldn't let anyone see me that way. I mean, I didn't even have a hospital gown. . . ."

"You did all right." He found himself laughing a bit too hard as he fingered the new fur coat. "You must have dug up this rig somewhere. Pretty toney. I'd been worried sick about you, but your survival instincts seem to have gotten more sophisticated." He threw the coat down on the bed, fur side up.

"They had to. I was . . . called." Jane's face sobered. "Oh, it's confusing!" Her fingers, smelling faintly of mayonnaise, brushed his lips. "I know what's not confusing. Being with you again."

Maybe it was the touch of her warming fingertips. Maybe the bittersweet certainty in her eyes. It was one of those moments nothing can stop, not even terminal confusion, and least of all six years of higher education.

They tumbled back on the bed together in breathless, mindless, heedless reunion. What did mere reality matter when they were caught in the inescapable skeins of their emotions, their marvelous, mutual love and lovemaking?

Moments passed like the continuum of a stop-action film. Moments new and moments remembered. Kevin felt his mind releasing the unanswered questions that tormented him, felt his body bucking off doubt and reticence.

He shed his borrowed clothing, and Jane her alien garb, in unconscious inches. Zyunsinth's furred breadth upheld their frenzied union. When Kevin found his body once again poised to merge with hers, he barely knew he paused.

A question began to form in her eyes, and was answered by completion. They were together again, in the way they required, oblivious to everything but each other for a few time-exempt moments. Feeling into feeling, flesh into flesh, and no barriers of any kind to their union and reunion. The euphoria of physical climax, when it came, seemed redundant.

"I hope Turner's getting his jollies." Kevin lay staring at the ceiling, reality convening over him like a thunderhead, feeling paranoid about surveillance equipment even though he knew the room was only watched, not bugged.

"Turner?"

"Don't sound so polite." He tweaked the tip of Jane's nose. It was red and a trifle runny. "Turner's a government man. He wants to—" Kevin sat up abruptly, pulling his clothes on. Reality was storming the door like gangbusters.

"What?"

Jane still lay naked on the rich brown pelt, no shadows of doubt pillorying her flesh. For the first time Kevin felt free to regard her nudity without flinching, without remembering. Yet sitting there, his head and hormones cooling again, he realized that he'd managed to forget a hell of a lot.

"He wants things from you neither of us can let him have. And—holy Christ . . . you can't realize what this— you being here, wonderful as it is—means! I'm confused."

"You're not confused. *I'm* confused. You're Kevin." Jane sat up and began pulling on her disheveled clothes. She wore no underthings, as she had started out in Crow Wing. Somehow Kevin found that comforting. "You always know the answers."

"Not this time. Besides, all I ever knew was the questions." He waited until she had dressed, debating confronting her with the incredible truth, debating facing it himself. As always, he decided to protect her from what he himself couldn't face yet. "Jane."

She paused in zipping up her wool slacks and tilted her head at him. The Jane tilt, deceptively docile.

"Jane . . . how exactly did you get here? Why?"

"I don't know. I feel as if I've . . . been where I began. I feel as if I'm going there again. All I know is that I woke up, and it was cold and dark again, and I had no clothes. So I went to find you and—"

"Me? At my condo? Did you go to my condo? Once before then? After I . . . lost you at the bank?"

"Yes."

"And did you eat something there? Meet my parents?" She looked at him as if he were crazy.

"Yes . . . of course. Then I ate the funny stew at the place with all the people in line. And I had some of Boomer's medicine. Then there was the fire and the pain and the emptiness. When I woke up, I was sleepy still. And cold—I had to get some clothes. First I tried to find you. I remember seeing your place again through a fog. There was a light in your window, but—"

"Oh, my God! That *was* you out there! If only I had—"

"But then . . ." Jane stared at the closed door to his room. Kevin pulled her into his arms, so her cheek rested on his sweatered shoulder. Her voice grew drowsy. "Then the Call came. It was as if I'd always heard it. What is the word you like to use? Subconscious. I was called and I came. Something had called me to your place, too, but I was too late."

"I was there, Jane! An infant could have seen my silhouette in the window! I remember thinking that Turner's people could see me if they wanted to, and I didn't care. Why didn't *you* see me?"

"You were there?" Her fingers tightened on his forearms. "No. There was only the small light, far away. And the dark and cold. And the Call. The Call came, and I went. I came—here. And now—now I hear the Call again."

She pushed free of him and got off the bed, turning slowly in the room. Her arms elevated slightly from her sides, as if she were thinking about trying to flap them and fly.

Kevin's fingers reached out to uphold her palms. The contact seemed to galvanize her. Jane's eyes jolted into his again, leaving their dreamy expression behind.

She said his name, her eyes and mouth burning, and leaned toward him. Even at the moment of meeting, he felt her body slacken, then twist in his arms.

"I've got to go," she said. "Somewhere. Somewhere else yet. It's not enough. The Call still screams. Like an ecnalubma . . . an ambulance. Up and down, over and over. I'm so tired—" She moved toward the door.

"No." At the threshold, he interposed his body between Jane and her Call. It worked. Her expression cleared, her eyes sharpened. As much as his ego wanted to believe that

304

his mere presence had drawn Jane here, he began to suspect that she'd been lured by another presence, almost as negative attracts positive, or matter anti-matter. To catch a thief, you use a thief. To disarm a probe, you send another probe. To destroy a clone, you use . . . a clone.

"Jane." He could hardly stop himself from shaking her. "Whatever this Call is, it's lethal to you, it's got to be. Listen. We're leaving. Now! Here's your coat; put it on. We're going to sneak out of this oversized pillbox. You and me. Together. Again. All right?"

Dazed by his swift decision, she nodded.

"That's my Jane. Come on."

Kevin had no outerwear; he'd worry about that later. No wheels, either. He had Jane and she was a damn good compass, he told himself; she'd found him, hadn't she?

His watch squinted the hour back at him: eleven forty-five P.M. The staff had taken him for granted lately, accepting his comings and goings as if he were one of them at last. Maybe he wasn't as worth watching as Nordstrom now. Maybe they'd all gotten careless.

He took Jane's hand in his. It felt cold despite the warmth of her fur coat. They walked down the faintly lit hall, their footsteps falling to the floor as softly as shingles from a roof. Kevin looked back as much as he did forward. Every second seemed to tremble with the potential of a door along the corridor opening, of Turner rounding a corner.

No one came.

In front of one particular closed door, Kevin hesitated. He felt his own "call"—part conscience, part terror. A thin snake of night light slithered under the door. Jane turned and lunged mindlessly for it, but her long midwinter odyssey had weakened her; she succumbed to his restraining embrace.

"No," he said—sharply, as he would command a dog. "Not there. Anywhere but there."

Jane's attraction for that particular door only strengthened Kevin's resolve. His mind was shuffling the chess pieces around, coming close but still jumping the truth like a berserk knight. Like calls to like. Like is *used,* designed to call to like. Like lays in wait to destroy like. Some instinct told him that Jane must never encounter what waited behind that door, what had been *sent* to encounter her.

He hustled Jane down the hall, rushing her through a door he'd never seen anyone use, looking for escape in any direction but the ones he already knew.

Jane went with him.

Chapter Thirty-eight

Nordstrom's thumb and forefinger sawed the sliver of metal against the frayed canvas webbing.

The steel pressed red welts into his skin. He had so little grip on it, and his fingers felt so numb from pinching it, that sometimes he doubted it was there.

He kept on sawing, back and forth, tiny worrying motions.

Nordstrom had to twist his wrist back on itself to reach the restraint, but he had a genetic advantage. He was double-jointed. He had used the anomaly to disgust certain middle-school girls in his youth and had never found it useful since.

Now it was coming in . . . handy.

Nordstrom giggled.

Sweat squeezed from behind his glasses' plastic nose-pieces. He remembered when his imprisoned hand had first discovered the razor blade. At first his forefinger had swung over a raised surface in his mattress, back and forth. It had felt like a staple. And then . . . and then Nordstrom had set his idle mind to working the staple out. And out. And out.

When he had freed it and contorted his upper body enough to glimpse his prize, he found himself holding a fresh single-edged razor blade. He had never needed a razor blade until now.

Nordstrom's fingers pressed tighter and he sawed faster. He owed it all to Jane Doe. Jane Doe and her telekinetic talents. *She* had sent the blades flying from their safe harbor in the bathroom medicine cabinet. *She* had imbedded one in the mattress—exactly positioned to meet his questing fingers when he lay bound in the bed.

Then Turner had ordered Nordstrom's original, specially requested bed brought to his new room, probably because it was the only restraint-equipped hospital bed—besides hers—they had. Trust the government to run a cheesy operation.

Now Nordstrom sawed away, a victim of the bonds he loved to inflict; by the play in the material, the webbing hung by only strands. He didn't know what he'd do when he got free; it was interesting enough to get free, given the obstacles. Perhaps he'd visit *her*. With his razor blade. It would be a bit dulled but still should . . . suffice.

His hand pulled away from the side of the bed, trailing a ribbon of frayed canvas. Unbuckling himself in seconds, he slipped to the floor. Cold tiles chilled the soles of his feet. They'd given him a stupid hospital gown, and when he checked the closet, he found it empty.

That gave him his goal: to slip down the hall and get some clothes. Then . . . He glanced at the blank stare of mirror across the room. Supposedly, they were watching him through it. But Nordstrom was a watcher, too. He knew how numbing surveillance can get, especially when the object of one's vigilance is bound hand and foot. Very, very boring.

He gambled that they'd locked him away and forgotten about him. People were always forgetting about him, to their regret. Look at Kevin Blake. Only Julie hadn't forgotten him. Julie. He studied the slim blade in his hand. Jane Doe had awesome powers, but if she could be taken by surprise, with her powers sleeping . . .

Nordstrom smiled. It was a fine night for a stroll. He

plumped his pillows into a semblance of himself, then cracked his door open, listening for any alarm. None came. The hall was empty, puddles of thin light spaced at regular intervals.

He slipped through the door, shutting it behind him. He began padding down the hallway on icy feet, a draft drilling up the back of his hospital gown. He wondered which door he'd hit on first—his old room. Or hers.

At a turn in the hall, he paused, sensing something. Some noise. Some . . . motion.

His heart speeded up, but he poked his head around the corner. The door ending the corridor was just closing on the back of a woman wearing a fur coat. Curiouser and curiouser, Nordstrom thought. He skittered down the hall after her, his feet barely whispering over the tiles.

Chapter Thirty-nine

Beyond the rats' maze of cubbyholes erected to imitate hospital rooms and the spartan staff living quarters, the complex swelled to inhuman scale.

Kevin and Jane passed through sound-stage-sized arenas. Kevin kept expecting a megaphone-amplified voice to shout "Lights, camera, action!"

But he and Jane seemed the only moving targets traversing the vast interlocking chambers, and any cameras were concealed. Worklights shone just bright enough to throw spooky shadows into far corners, onto bare pipes and huge iron tracks suspended from concrete struts. Echo and distance and emptiness occupied everything.

Their boots clicked over the cement floor, every footstep amplified. The place smelled of forbidden zones from Kevin's youth: afterdark gymnasiums, janitors' domains in school basements, abandoned buildings.

Lines of rail-sided chutes and idled conveyer belts ended in empty troughs. Abandoned tools—saws, electric probes, curved knives with seven-inch blades, and massive cleavers —littered the slaughtering stations. The crude sinks and instruments inevitably reminded Kevin of a back-alley abortionist's setup in the bad old days. Obviously, the packing plant had been unused for years.

Yet it reeked with the imagined scent of fresh blood and still-warm guts. Kevin half expected the iron rails high above to begin vibrating, announcing the imminent arrival of what the building had trafficked in—carcasses on meat hooks. At any moment he dreaded confronting a row of headless, limbless beef torsos swaying on some ghostly production line, or shaking to the mock-serious cinematic jabs of a Sylvester Stallone.

But the laundry line of hooks above them remained vacant, the metal curves reflecting intermittent scythes of light until they seemed to swing like wind chimes.

Jane shared none of Kevin's memories or fears, whether primitive or sophisticated. She stumbled behind him, her boot toes scuffing into periodic troughs in the concrete floor—runoff trenches, Kevin supposed, and then considered what sort of runoff a slaughterhouse would produce.

"Kevin. I'm tired."

"I know. But we can't stop. They may be after us already."

"I can't go any farther. Please. I'm . . . so . . . tired."

"Jane—" He stopped, reaching for her in the dark.

He grasped slick, uncontainable fur. She stumbled against him as if semiconscious. He had seen these symptoms before—at Professor Neumeier's cabin. Jane's master cellular programming was again superseding her native human instincts.

"I'm . . . sleepy," Jane repeated drowsily. "And I belong back there. I'm getting . . . too distant."

"No! You don't belong back there. Come on—" But she resisted his tugs, and Kevin finally felt too beat to propel them both. "Okay. Sit for a minute. Here. Here's a . . ." —he found a metal-topped table in the gloom behind them—"a resting place."

309

Jane slumped against the table. By the meager light, Kevin could just trace the familiar jigsaw of her profile.

"There's . . . something behind me." She twisted to study the dimness.

He leaned on the table, too, talking rapidly, softly. "There *is* something behind you. More than you want to know about right now. More than I want to think about, even. You've got to resist that pull. It's not you; it's *them*. It's . . . her. My God, Jane, I used to think I was crazy for feeling the way I did about you, knowing what you were. A clone—"

"A coed clone," Jane corrected, her voice energetic enough to convey irony.

"A coed clone. A creature of the Eternal Now, with only a coil of mutated DNA for a past. A personality filtered through an infinity of genetic mirrors, through information perceived but not experienced. I thought there must be something missing in you—or in me for loving you. But I was wrong. What we consider human 'personality' may be only neurosis. What's missing in both of us is what's right."

"I'm confused again."

"Welcome to the human race. And you are human—I know that now. The best of what's human. I don't want to change you."

"Then . . . let me go back."

"Why?"

"The Call. I can hear it now." A new, adult tone leaked into Jane's voice; Kevin recognized its ruling emotion from every childhood occasion he'd been told he couldn't have what he wanted—weary compassion. "The Call didn't bring me to you, Kevin. You just happened to be here. It brought me to something else, something I can't quite see, but I can feel. I've got to go back and face it."

She pushed off the butchering table. In Kevin's mind that's what it was; the nicked steel surface screamed to him of old blood even as his palms braced on the chill metal, hemming Jane in.

"Not back, Jane. You don't know what's there."

"What Calls is there. Kevin, please."

She struggled against him until his palms lifted off the table's cold surface. Kevin recognized unarguable compulsion when he felt it. He knew her strength.

"Jane, I'm going to have to—don't fight me!" He heard his own voice soften to sweet reason, bitter untruth. Somehow lies always sound more deceptive in the dark. "Jane, you said you were tired. Sleepy. So sleepy. I believe you. You must rest, you know what's best for yourself. You must rest right now."

He said it, hoping he held a psychological talisman stronger than the Call scribed into her genes. "Jane, you must sleep . . . ecnalubma."

In the dimness, he couldn't tell if she had fallen into hypnotic trance. Her body still tensed against his. They stood frozen in conflicted isometric embrace waiting for what their next breaths would bring—

A sound of soft palms, clapping. It could have come from anywhere; it echoed from everywhere.

Kevin whirled to confront the darkness.

"Nicely done, Doctor," came an eerily unseen voice. Nordstrom's voice. "Oh, so nicely done. Quintessential Svengali, yes. Or simply the ultimate Trilby? Who knows —who cares? Not the Three Little Pigs. Not Mary's little lambsy . . . they're all *chops* by now."

"I thought they gave you a taste of your own medicine," Kevin answered, hoping for hidden loudspeakers but knowing the darkness probably concealed only the man himself, just as the man's mind hid only darkness. It was all out in the open now—madness and method. Kevin tried to anticipate what form they'd take. "I thought you were all tied up."

"So did they. Interesting place, this . . . cavern. A veritable university of higher knowledge. *My* university. *You'd* never matriculate there—no, no. Only the dead can be said to truly matriculate. . . . If only I'd brought my Brownie and a time machine. I've found some fascinating new toys here, though—see!"

Before Nordstrom had finished, Kevin heard a rising metallic hiss. Some instinct made him snatch Jane away from the table rim just as a spinning meat cleaver skidded down the stainless steel, its cutting edge revolving in the faint overhead light.

Kevin grabbed Jane's hand and she came without resistance. Together they leaped a chasm of darkness, their feet clattering in the silence. They ran until they ran into a wall.

Kevin stopped and looked back. Nothing was brighter but he could see more than he wanted to. A troll in a pale nightshirt had leaped atop the table, eyeglass lenses glittering in a slice of distant lamplight.

"I can see you," it singsonged into the dimness. "I can find you! You're It." Nordstrom's right hand lifted, the cleaver shining silver. "This little piggy went to Harvard and *this* little piggie stayed home. And this little piggie made a fine sacrificial lamb. And then there were none."

While Kevin watched, Nordstrom hurled the cleaver toward the ceiling. It somersaulted, glittering with every rotation, then lunged into the downward pull of gravity. Kevin hoped that Nordstrom's balding skull would be graced with a new Mohawk. Instead, the cleaver plummeted harmlessly to concrete.

Nordstrom leaped down into the darkness after it. Kevin tensed to move, and heard his sole scrape cement. Nordstrom was barefoot. Silent. Kevin felt behind himself. He and Jane were backed against a row of shed-high wooden crates.

"Walk softly," he instructed her.

"And carry a big stick," she finished by placid rote, an association she might have dredged up in hypnosis.

"Don't I wish," he muttered, still unsure if Jane was under. But when he tugged her hand, she followed.

They edged along the wooden row, their boot soles sanding the floor. Echoes and imagination magnified the sound into the slither of a gigantic snake. Perhaps, Kevin thought, echoes disguised where the rasp originated. He heard no other sound but theirs.

The wooden wall they crept along ended with unseen space yawning behind them. In Kevin's mind, an invisible and utterly psychotic Nordstrom loomed there, meat cleaver on high. They backed together into the unknown any-

312

way. Danker air breathed heavy across Kevin's neck. His exploring hand brushed a cold metallic expanse and followed it to a horizontal lever.

The configuration nudged an association in his brain, but the connections refused to dovetail. Kevin pulled the lever anyway. With a sound like a giant's breaking femur, the door cracked open. Beyond it lay only ultimate darkness and no exit.

Kevin's impressions finally had assembled into ice-cold certainty. No escape there. He jerked Jane back from the doorway. Maybe, he thought, if they kept quiet enough, Nordstrom would stroll into the trap Kevin had almost tripped himself.

"A mistake, Blake." Nordstrom's voice echoed from everywhere, "Blake-ake-ake-ake" rat-a-tatting off the hard walls like machine-gun fire. "Tom, Tom, the piper's son. Stole a pig and away he run—" Footsteps. "Fee, fie, fo, fum, I hear the blood of a dead man mum. Shhhhhh, walk softly, yes . . . death is so quiet. Death comes on little cat feet and leaves bloody paw prints. Someone has to straighten up after, no?

"Jane Doe will go gently into that dark night. She will be still, you know. I'll see to that. You should have let her languish at the beginning. She had such a head start on perfection when you found her!

"But a fool like you must meddle. You must waste your opportunities, fatten her like a sow, turn a delicate disembodied balance on the very edge of existence into mere gross humanity. Smell the old blood here, Blake, the matted hairs and slack bowels! The essence! A magnificent arena! Lions and Christians—and you're It!

"Get this right. There is such fever in the bone, the blood, the bright, severed hair. I am fever-breaker. I make all things well—as they should be. Julie saw that, yes, she did.

"Julie smiled at me, you know. In the parlor where she received guests. Even the lipstick they waxed on her lips couldn't keep her from smiling when she knew that she had achieved perfect . . . quiet. But don't *you* keep too quiet, Blake. No, let me hear you scramble. Too bad Mr. Turner couldn't be here. We're all alone. We can play without him."

Nordstrom's voice rebounded from concrete and metal, from everywhere and nowhere. Kevin and Jane cowered in a corner formed of wall and crating and so dark Kevin couldn't see Jane. Her hand—limp—warmed his.

He hoped she was under; then she'd only heed his voice and escape the sick aria of sound reverberating around them. Nordstrom could burst into "La Marseillaise" if he wanted to, and she wouldn't respond.

Silence held the darkened stage, then Nordstrom's bare soles were softly brushing step by step over the concrete. Kevin glimpsed a ghostly white blob weaving toward the open metal door.

"Even if you tippy-toed out of this place, there's only the next one," Nordstrom was singsonging. "We all live in ticky-tacky boxes inside ourselves. Cells. Brain cells. Brain fever and here comes Dr. Death with a cold compress." Nordstrom's laugh was a malicious gnomelike giggle. "You can't escape forever, Blake. You'll make another mistake-ake-ake-ake," he shouted, infuriated again.

Nordstrom's figure was clarifying as it neared. Kevin held his breath. Beside him, Jane's breathing suspended, too, perhaps in unconscious imitation. If only Nordstrom didn't hear them. If only Nordstrom didn't see them. If only Nordstrom walked right into the meat locker. . . . Then Kevin could jump out and close it. Lock it. Bottle Nordstrom like a beetle.

Silver flashed as it sliced the light. The cleaver blade. Nordstrom faced the doorway, his free hand clawing the deeper darkness, his pale body fuzzing in and out of focus in Kevin's strained eyesight.

Now, a few more steps, a second or two more for safety's sake, then . . . Kevin poised to rappel off the wall and slam the heavy door shut on Nordstrom's half-bare backside.

A light high above went supernova—exploded like a Kleig-light flashbulb—then shone hyperbright. Kevin looked up to find his eyes dazzled by the sight of a new sun in his dingy firmament, disbelieving his bad luck.

A light on the area's opposite side repeated the performance. One by one, each by inevitable each, the distant utility lamps flared into high power. Every exploded light bulb added its amplified candlepower to the overall illumination.

Tones of gray washed the floor now. Light glared on Nordstrom's eyewhites and the cleaver blade, on his puckered nightshirt and pale-fleshed limbs. Light even seeped into the corner where Kevin and Jane sheltered.

Kevin pushed Jane farther behind him, wondering how to tackle Nordstrom without encountering his cleaver. Invention came up empty.

But Nordstrom wasn't watching Kevin. His light-dazed eyes had lingered on the corner only long enough to note Kevin's presence. Now Nordstrom stared in another direction, admiration and pleasure tightening his expression.

Jane was walking along a center trough in the concrete, hands in her jeans pockets, following the depression foot in front of foot as if balancing on a railroad track.

Jane—dressed, awake, in perfect control.

It was the Jane Turner had found . . . the Jane Nordstrom had tried to break . . . the Jane Kevin had been brought here to help. To love, honor and treat.

The Jane he had hoped he would never see again.

Chapter Forty

Behind him, Kevin felt Jane—the real Jane, as he now thought of her—stir.

Ahead of him, the other Jane stopped to glance around. She hardly noticed Nordstrom, but her eyes fixed when they met Kevin's. She blinked her surprise.

"Kevin?"

"Yes," he answered carefully, watching Nordstrom.

"You should . . . be in bed," she said.

"So should you."

"No." Her hand lifted as if to dislodge a veil before her face. "I must come. I heard the Call. I heard the voices. There is an anomaly present—"

"Nordstrom is the anomaly," Kevin said.

Jane glanced to the psychiatrist, her features finally registering recognition, or at least distaste. "You were to be bound," she told him. "They promised me."

"They lied," Nordstrom jeered back. "I unbound myself. Better than you did. You were helpless. But I might have unbound you later. If you were good. I might have come in with my unbinder"—Nordstrom twisted the cleaver blade until it chimed against the meat locker door—"and let you loose."

"I don't care what you might have done, Dr. Nordstrom." The anger in Jane's voice ebbed. "I . . . don't care about any of that anymore. I am Called and must Recall. I must—"

"Don't you care about me, Jane?"

She looked at Kevin, confused. "Of course I do. But I heard the voices and there is something I must do."

"Voices! You hear that, Blake?" Nordstrom grinned and cradled his cleaver. "You think *I'm* kinko shrinko. But *she* hears voices. She's a bloody Joan of Arc, and you know what happened to *her*! If Turner only knew his precious mind-mover was a schizo!"

Kevin held his peace. Nordstrom was too unhinged, and Jane's double too disoriented, to spot Jane herself in the dim corner behind Kevin. And Jane herself had certainly kept mum, possibly thanks to "ecnalubma."

Kevin was still trying to juggle all the pieces of the situation when Nordstrom acted. He sprang into the space between Kevin and the second Jane. There he crouched, cleaver cocked, the back of his hospital gown gaping incongruously.

"Come on, Wonder Woman," Nordstrom cajoled. "Let's see your tricks. The lights—oh, impressive, but you'll have to do better. Better even than razor blades and broken glass. I'm ready for Kevin's little lamb this time. Oh, yes, Julie, I'm always ready to tend to my best patients."

316

"Nordstrom—" Kevin warned. If just seeing her duplicate could harm Jane, as he believed, seeing her duplicate hacked to death would be worse. Somehow, he had to stop Nordstrom.

"Stay out of it, Blake! You fake. This is between me and her. It always was. I have plans for her. Before I'm through with her—and after. Always better after. For them. For me."

Nordstrom hoisted the cleaver and made a pass toward Jane.

She didn't move, didn't even take her hands from her pockets.

The wooden handle spun from Nordstrom's grip so fast he shrieked as it burned his palms. After violent withdrawal, the cleaver paused in mid-swoop, turned its edge toward Nordstrom and poised there.

"How does she do it?" Nordstrom spoke with a momentarily saner awe, rubbing reddened palms on his nightshirted flanks.

"I don't know." Kevin was as surprised as Nordstrom.

"Swanson knew. Poor Dr. Swanson, cheated of her best subject. You were always a spoiler, Blake. But Swanson knew. 'You will believe a woman can make things fly.' Yes, I believe. Why didn't you? It's your job to know why."

"Swanson didn't provoke such . . . spectacular results." Pleasant as it was to see Nordstrom cowed by his own weapon, the sight of a lethal Jane was far less palatable. "Jane, let the cleaver down," Kevin instructed.

She did not. But behind Kevin, the hidden Jane murmured her hypnotic confusion at the illogical instruction—a small sound, barely discernable. Somehow, Nordstrom heard.

He twisted to face Kevin, staring right through him. The man's face shifted through a wardrobe of expressions, all of them more or less mad. The last was an unholy blend of greed and mad cunning.

"*Two!* 'E two, Brute.' Mengele would have killed for this. Twins!"—he glanced back at Jane and the suspended cleaver—". . . a Doppelganger. And there, behind you, is

317

the one, the one who . . . I saw it, going through the door, long muskrat hair—"

Jane had tired of upholding the cleaver. It smashed to the concrete. Now Nordstrom elevated in the weapon's place. He resembled a bizarrely attired magician's assistant, lacking only the telltale flatness to his body that revealed a board, or the tents in his nightshirt formed by invisible hooks.

Nordstrom simply hung in the air, three feet off the ground. He curled into a fetal ball, his oversized head seeming even more gnomelike, and glowered Rumpelstiltskin-style.

"Let me down, you stupid bitch! You can't do this! It's a trick, a trick—"

Kevin involuntarily stepped forward. "Jane . . . listen to me—"

She didn't. She listened to Nordstrom, who pointed.

"Look. Look-see. Look what he's hiding, your precious Kevin. Hide-and-seek and you've been It. Another you! Look, look, Jane, look."

Kevin froze, torn between turning back to safeguard Jane herself and shutting up Nordstrom.

Nordstrom giggled, his lenses flaring like high-beams. "How does your garden grow them, Blake? Is there a magic formula, a secret word? Of course. . . . " A cleaver-bright gleam stewed in Nordstrom's eyes.

"Nordstrom, my God, no!"

"Ah, wrong word, that's right. But *now* I have the right word—I overheard it. You told me yourself!"

"Dammit, Nordstrom, shut up!"

"Ec-na-la . . . la . . . la . . . lub-ma! That's what I heard. Ec-na-lub-ma-a-a, Jane—" he crooned.

Nordstrom plummeted to the cement, hard, and was still.

Kevin didn't care. He turned.

Jane was moving from the twilight corner. She almost seemed to be moving out of the wall, or out of herself. As she left the trance state, her eyes clarified with an emotion Kevin had never observed in them before—disbelief. Raw, wholesale disbelief.

Jane had accepted so much—a version of the planet Earth aliens had spoon-fed into her nuclei; Kevin's newer view of a more fully human world. She had accepted it all—growing, expanding, learning. She had never yet encountered anything that had forced her to shrink. Her identical self would—did.

That mirror image stiffened as Jane neared.

"You . . . me . . . *you* are the Call," Jane said in wonderment, drawn closer to her selfsame opposite.

"No!" the ersatz Jane commanded as if fearing contact. The wood crating behind Jane herself quivered, then flattened toward the floor.

Kevin lunged for her. A force field stopped him. Jane heard the shattering wood and lifted fur-muffled arms over her head. By a split second she sidestepped an avalanche of boards and rusted nails torn from their moorings.

Splinters frosted Jane's dark hair, but the fur had cushioned her from injury. She stared at Kevin, frozen in his helplessness. He felt like God called to account for the ills of the world. The real injury was in Jane's eyes.

"This is myself—?" she began, staring at the other Jane.

"No." The harder Kevin lunged against the force that held him immobile, the stronger it got. "Another self."

"That's not possible, Kevin. You said the self is the supreme individual. That I-ness stands alone. That we are all one. How can I be two?"

"You're not. It's only . . . science splitting atoms again, splitting hairs and letting all hell break loose. You're you. Always. She—" Kevin made himself regard his captor. The other Jane seemed imperiously calm, in control, her expression inflexible. "Jane," he begged her. "Free me."

"You are safer held," she answered like a parent confining a child.

"I don't want to be safe!"

A vigil light of doubt flickered in her eyes. "*I* want you to be safe."

"Yet you want to harm *her*."

"Want to? No. I must only . . . Recall. It is my reason, my purpose. My . . . I-ness."

319

"No. It's them. Those who made you. They made her, too. They want to unmake her."

"*I* want to unmake *him*." The other Jane glanced to Nordstrom moaning down private corridors of semiconsciousness on the floor.

"Yes, but you won't do it."

She thought about it. "No. It is not my purpose."

"And I don't want you to do it."

She nodded. "It's easy to do what you want me to, Kevin." Her expression struggled into a frown. "It's not easy to . . . not do . . . what I must." Her face turned toward its mirror image, sunflower to sun. The two Janes' utter likeness was striking, awesome even.

"Jane . . . ," Kevin implored, keeping his attention focused on Jane's clone. Something in his voice arrested her. She faced him again, confusion fracturing her features.

"You call her 'Jane,'" his Jane noted analytically, no accusation in the tone.

"Yes. I thought she *was* you, for a while."

"And she is not?" Jane was deadly serious.

"No. . . ." He found himself smiling as only Jane could make him do. "You're unique, Jane. Not to be duplicated, not even by scrambling a few genes to formula. Her memory duplicates yours only to the point when . . . they . . . came and took you away for a while.

"She doesn't . . . share any of the rest with you. Or me. And she doesn't *feel,* Jane, the way you do. I sensed it the minute I began working with her, but didn't know what I was picking up—or why. She's only a baby, an infant, with a ready-made brain and no . . . soul yet. What progress she's made *he* twisted to conform to his own kinks." Kevin glanced hopefully over his shoulder.

Jane was tilting her cheek into her fur collar to regard Nordstrom's sluglike writhing on the concrete. His lenses had smashed into spiderweb fractures. His knees and elbows were scraped raw. They both contemplated Nordstrom, Kevin torn between revulsion and unwanted pity and wondering what Jane thought of such a poor specimen of humanity. They had forgotten the second Jane, but she hadn't forgotten them.

Something picked Jane up and rammed her against the meat locker door, so hard the force of her body slammed it shut.

"Jane!" Kevin's arms and legs fought his immobility. It was like swimming in epoxy Jell-O. He moved but accomplished nothing; only his voice and face could express his distress.

The other Jane's eyes were darting from Kevin to Jane to Nordstrom, her confusion multiplied by the necessity of controlling three people instead of one.

"Did you do that? You'll hurt her," Kevin rebuked.

"I don't want to hurt. But . . . I hear the voices. I must do what I must do. I must Recall the failed unit. And I must . . . erase the flawed recording. I must undo."

"You can't undo humanity. She's as real as you, with as much right to exist—as she is—as you have now. More . . . she was here first."

"No! I remember. You remember. I woke up in the hospital, and you said, 'Hello, I'm Dr. Blake. I'm here to take care of you.' That was the first. I was always there."

"Not *you*. Her *memories* poured *into* you. Your own true memories started where you thought your amnesia began: when you were found in the snow in Minneapolis and taken into custody. The aliens dropped you there to . . . hurt Jane, empty Jane, return her, maybe—only Jane was hurt herself at the time . . . unconscious. You missed one another.

"That's when you were born, when you lay naked in the snow. That's why you couldn't remember anything beyond the moment the aliens lifted you into their ship on Crow Wing bluff—*you* weren't there. *She* was! They could give you her memories only up to the moment they released her."

"We share the same memories?"

"To a point, yes. But you don't *feel* them in the same way she does. She lived them. You . . . swallowed them. Whole. If you hurt her, erase her, whatever, you consume your source. Jane . . . they're wrong, those genetic missionaries from outer space. They can't undo what happened to her. She outgrew her use to them, that's all. You can, too."

"You . . . love . . . her."

"Yes."

"And me?"

"I . . . care about what happens to you."

"But we are the same, she and I. Why don't you love me, too?"

"Because . . . it confuses me. Because I loved her first. Because she *is* different from you, no matter how much the same. Because she is Jane."

"*I* am Jane."

He nodded. "Another Jane, who's already stockpiled her own individual memories. The voices can't override that."

"They can." Jane herself pushed away from the wall. "I've heard them, too . . . all along, ever since we left the bluff. I can't escape them. I haven't ever, not for a moment. That's why I came here, Kevin. *She* drew me, not you."

"But that's all they can do—draw you to her," Kevin argued. "We'll leave, go so far away the Call can't reach you—"

"She won't let us."

He confronted the second Jane for a grim moment, reading the raw necessity in her eyes before turning back to the first.

"Jane, you must . . . fight. I can't fight for you anymore. You have to defend yourself."

"Against myself? I can't harm *myself*—"

"She is *not* yourself! She's an illusion of self. She's much more in their control, for instance. She won't be able to stop herself. *You'll* have to stop her."

"Stop her? Destroy her?"

"To save yourself."

"Save . . . myself." Jane's eyes rested sadly on the other Jane.

"No," Kevin groaned. "Don't confuse yourself with her! Do what I say, Jane. Stop her."

"I have always done what you say, Kevin. Unless it has been what they said. Yet I have respected the I-ness in myself, and must respect the I-ness in another—"

A sound like stage thunder reverberated across the

light-spangled ceiling. Kevin looked up. An iron track was tearing loose above them, driving toward the floor—not above *them*. Above *Jane*.

"Jane—no!" He wasn't sure whether he appealed to one, or both.

The fur coat bristled around Jane's form. Silver light tipped the amber hairs. Her arms lifted slightly from her sides, as they had in Lynn Volker's bedroom.

The plunging track paused, its long metal arms twining like licorice in midair, and floated to a sand-soft landing on the concrete floor.

"How did you do that?" Kevin was impressed.

"I practiced," Jane said simply. "On a dumpster."

Her other self had not been idle. Metal scraped concrete. The massive girder of dead metal moved. Twisted rails shifted, inched forward. Above them a freight train of empty meat hooks began rattling down their aged tracks. The fallen beam scraped several feet forward, lumbering toward Jane herself like a metal dinosaur.

"Save yourself!" Kevin shouted.

Jane, confused, turned from the oncoming metal to her own image. Her counterpart stood rapt, her arms also slightly extended, her eyes cast up until the pupils were nearly obscured, her bobbed hair lifting all around her face.

A humming droned along the animated metal and the rattling hooks, a buzzing even Kevin could perceive. The other Jane's lips moved, vibrated really. Kevin could almost hear words in another tongue, a distant, alien litany being chanted.

Both Janes tilted their heads in concert, as if tuning in to a radio wave only they could receive.

"Observe the data slate—they coincide again."

"And both are fully conscious this time. One must neutralize the other."

"Perhaps. The outcome is always debatable when action is left to a single entity."

"Our duplicate probe lacks the attachment to the Zyunsinthians that hampered the first."

323

"But not an attachment to the male humanoid."

"Moot. Their programming meshes into synchronicity. They will merge into genetic eclipse and one will eat the other."

"But can we be sure which?"

"The slate will say."

"And then?"

"Then we are done meddling."

"What of the surviving probe?"

"Let it glean until it collapses."

"Stop it!" Kevin urged the silence he suspected was not one. He focused his will on the original Jane, pleading. "Stop *her*."

Jane debated. "Hurt . . . her?"

"So she won't hurt you! I didn't teach you that, but sometimes one's I-ness strikes at another's. They knew that, your makers. They programmed you to survive. They gave you the power. Use it, Jane!"

Kevin saw the slow-motion working of Jane's mind and heart on her face, saw that lightning intelligence slowed to molasses by a moral dilemma he could barely comprehend. It was suicide of a sort he urged on her, and he had taught her too well to avoid self-destruction.

Two tons of twisted metal ground toward Jane like a giant steel slug while she weighed her right to stop it at its human source. Its motions rasped like grinding gears, like giant jaws masticating. With all the racket, Kevin only saw Nordstrom move; he never heard it. Neither did either Jane.

Nordstrom skittered across the floor on all fours, something hacking into the concrete with each crawl forward. He rose to his knees, then elevated a grinning metal blade and let it fly. The meat cleaver spun with the same rhythmic grace as before, heavy head pulling it over and over itself to its target.

The blade sank deep into a field of fur, lost itself in golden ripples, in a gasp of surprise and the infinitely endless sinking of a body to the concrete.

Chapter Forty-one

Kevin was dreaming. Every constraint had fallen from him. *He* had fallen—endlessly, to a cold gray floor. He had fallen upon something white and mushy on that floor, something he loathed so much that he was mashing it to pulp to escape it and only miring himself further in its sticky web.

Someone was shouting every obscenity in the language. Someone was echoing it back. Echolalia, the psychiatrists called it. Pain teased the edges of his awareness. He felt only a terrible numbness expanding from his center and freezing everything around him, freezing even other people.

His dream reversed the commonplace paralysis nightmare. In it, only Kevin moved; everyone else was paralyzed. Only one someone else was here, though; he looked at her and saw double.

What was under his hands was not a someone, but a something. He crushed it. In his power and his insane sovereignty over time, he dragged the red-splotched white spider through a trench thick with an imagined river of guts and blood to a door that opened on utter darkness.

He pushed it through, for its own sake as well as his, and slammed the silver metal shut. Kevin stared at the door, at its old-fashioned refrigerator-style handle. You might call it a meat locker. A blood-stained white cloth drooped from his hands, something he had acquired for no good reason he knew.

He turned back to the frozen scene to feel his muscles freezing now, just as time and those trapped within it resumed their feeble flows.

Jane stood in the middle of the empty trough, looking at

him. Jane lay heaped in fur on the concrete. Kevin's arms began to sting with what some distant sense told him were bite marks—a lot of them. Other things hurt. Nothing hurt as much as seeing Zyunsinth lying still on a cold hard floor.

Kevin's legs didn't want to work. He lurched over to Jane anyway, threw himself down beside her, pushed his hands up one sleeve feeling for a pulse.

He parted the coat, the matted bloody fur. The cleaver still bit into her midriff. He hesitated, then pulled it away. Blood spurted, his hands pressing the red tide back, trying to stem the massive, mindless pumping of the abdominal aorta.

The flag of surrender in his hands became a winding sheet, a tourniquet. You couldn't tourniquet the whole bloody thoracic cavity, a voice told Kevin, jeering. He nodded. There were many voices here. He heard them now.

"Kevin?" said one.

"What?" croaked something near him on the floor. He remembered claws at his throat, choking, choking. He remembered not breathing, not *needing* to breathe, only needing to throttle back. . . .

"Kevin."

She, the fake, stood near him, shock painting her features slightly green.

He looked up. She seemed ten feet tall. He thought he was trapped in a hole, a depression rapidly filling with blood. His greasy fingers slid off one another as he tied the . . . the cloth (*Nordstrom's nightshirt*, the Voice whispered beside him) tight around Jane's gut.

Her closed eyelids flickered in a dead white face.

"Jane . . . my God, didn't you see it coming? Why didn't you stop it?"

Her head shook slightly.

"I didn't do it," False Jane said.

Kevin shut her out of his sight for a moment. "You were supposed to. Well, aren't you going to finish your work?"

"I—" The duplicate Jane knelt beside him, tilted her head to study her duplicate. "I . . . feel no compulsion anymore. The anomaly is removed. The voices are silent."

326

"She's still alive, dammit, somehow—!" Desperation made him face the unfaceable. He stared at the second Jane. "You! Can you . . . stop the bleeding? Make it clot. Folk-medicine hacks can do it, surely you can. Here, your hand—"

She would have held back, but Kevin forced her palm to the blood-soaked bandage circling Jane's body. The tremor he felt in her arm only disgusted him.

"Power; that's what they all want, but you've got it. Use it! Save her. The bleeding, slow it, stop it." He kept repeating the words, the commands, shouting at the simulacrum of Jane as Jane lay dying beneath them both.

Jane herself took a raspy breath. Her eyes, dulled with systemic shock, focused briefly on his. "Ec . . . ec-na—"

His emotions fisted into a baseball in his throat. They always cling to some non sequitur, the dying. "I know the word, Jane," he soothed. "I know . . . I know you always did your best—"

Her head shook, impatience brightening her eyes. "Ecna . . ." Her breath sighed to silence.

Beside him, her living duplicate squatted miserably, her hand pressed to the bloody cloth and accomplishing nothing.

"Oh, my God." Kevin shook his head to clear away the crosstalk of voices—Nordstrom's screeched obscenities; his own inner voice of self-accusing, unbridled fury; other voices less easy to isolate. "Of course—!"

"Jane." Kevin hung close enough over her face to kiss it. "Jane, I'm putting you under. You're going to rest now." He collected his dispersed self, wadded his will into something that would function. "You're going to rest when I say the word you know so well. Ecnalubma."

Nothing altered in her face. She was far too weak to show the slightest relaxation into trance. Her body had cast its own spell on her ebbing senses, and would not be denied.

"Jane," he said, he coaxed, his voice so calm, so professional. "Jane, I'm going to ask you to slow down your body. Your metabolism. I know you can do it. Just . . . slow it down. I know you're stressed, but slow, the blood is pumping more slowly now. It's thickening. You can feel it.

327

Like molasses, so lazy, so . . . slow. It doesn't want to leave you. It wants to rest, as you do. It wants to pool, to clot, to lie quiet as still waters. Peaceful. It is untroubled now. Calm, as you are. So still."

He glanced to the bandage. Old flow still darkened it. Whether his hypnotic charm had worked, he couldn't say. Certainly conventional medicine could do nothing for her—nothing Turner had available in this almost-hospital would help her. Yet to rely on Jane, feeble as she was, to perform psychic surgery on herself before the internally seeping blood could drown her was wishful thinking.

Kevin leaned back on his heels and sighed. His own blood pumped wildly, throbbing at a dozen sore points on his body. He began to remember parts of the violent tussle with Nordstrom, his . . . mauling . . . of Nordstrom—and vice versa. His shoulders slumped as adrenaline dissipated. He was tired, like Jane. He needed a rest, like Jane.

A hand plucked at his jacket sleeve. Jane's. And not Jane's.

"Kevin. I didn't mean to hurt you, only to hold you. But I couldn't hold you any longer. And you got hurt."

Her hand reached for his face, but he twisted away.

"I'm fine. As fine as can be expected. And you're fine. Just dandy. Apparently you no longer feel a need to wipe your other self off the face of the earth."

She simply shook her head, more confused by the bitterness in his tone than his meaning. "Kevin, what's wrong? I feel like I'm . . . lost. Or loosened. I feel—light. Maybe I was glad to see you hurt Dr. Nordstrom like that."

"Were you? Bully for you." Kevin absently rubbed his forearm. Bite welts swelled under his fingertips. His eyes remained on Jane, his Jane.

"I've got to think. She seems . . . to be holding. But a wound like that—nothing in Turner's pseudohospital set-up can save her. We forget how lethal knives can be, how some wounds drive too deep, are too internal to staunch."

Kevin bent over Jane, then worked his hands under the coat's lush folds. He staggered upright, Jane swagged in his arms.

"Where are you going?"

The woman kneeling at his feet seemed about three inches tall now. Maybe *she* was the Alice in Wonderland, shrinking and expanding on command. Jane was heavy, but the empty space around him felt heavier. He knew where he had to go, but he didn't have to tell anybody. Anybody.

"I'm coming with you!" The woman was standing and shouting far away behind him. He was walking toward a door. He couldn't see it yet, but he knew there was a door. And behind it lay another door. There was always another door. He would find all the doors and go through them one by one.

"Kevin, wait!"

He passed the metal door. Behind it, nails scratched and Nordstrom was muling and puking. Nordstrom was locked in. He could pass no doors until he was found. That was . . . good. That might buy . . . time.

A door, lit by the intensified overhead lights, jumped into Kevin's path. It was a broad, metal-sheathed door, rust-eaten, with a push-on metal bar that was a hopeless barrier to an armless man.

Kevin paused. If he could not loose Jane, he could not unloose the door. He could not unloose Jane.

He stood there, balked, until she came up behind him.

"I want to go with you." Her soft, husky voice would have been poignantly familiar had it not been so alien. "I have nothing left to do."

"Open the door," he said finally.

"How?"

"Any damn way you please. And then think about what you can do with an internal combustion engine."

"What internal combustion engine?"

"Any one you choose."

She threw her frail weight onto the door's bar and slowly shoved it open on darkness. A ray of light from the room they were leaving burnished her platinum-pale face.

"Where are we going?" she asked as he walked past her and into the next cavernous, ill-lit space, draped in Jane, blood and Zyunsinth.

He didn't answer.

329

Chapter Forty-two

Déjà vu.

The words echoed in Kevin's head as he drove the dark winter road. He was in a van again, with Jane again. With two Janes.

They were on the run again.

Just like old times.

Jane lay on a pallet of fur behind the front seats. She seemed tranquil. Not dead. Only sleeping. His hand kept reaching down to her face, the backs of his cold fingers warmed by the flush of life still pulsing in her capillaries.

The van was new, equipped with state-of-the-art surveillance gear Kevin knew nothing about. He remembered its exhaust huffing into the midnight darkness as the engine had rolled over in the presence of the other Jane's concentrated regard. Now, it drove like a dream through the dream landscape.

"Highway one-sixty-nine," Jane on the front seat sang out. Her voice grated on his nerves, but he'd asked her to report any road signs she saw.

"You ever see a state map?" he asked now, his voice still hoarse. Nordstrom had half strangled him.

"Map—?"

"Of Minnesota. When you . . . she . . . did all that speed reading at the university library, did she ever see a map of Minnesota?"

"Yes."

"All right. Remember it. Take me to Crow Wing."

"Back again?"

"Back again," he said. "Don't tell me you don't feel a pull—a 'Call'? Isn't your automatic alarm clock buzzing?

Aren't 'those gentle voices singing,' calling you home again now that your mission's accomplished?"

"Why are you so angry?"

"I love her, and she's dying! She's my patient, and I can't save her."

"But *I'm* here. I . . . love you, Kevin."

"You're a record album. A compact disc. Perfect reproduction, but not the real thing. You can't help it."

"Maybe . . . they don't want me anymore."

"Why not?"

"I . . . feel unanchored. I always felt anchored before. Now I feel cast loose. In some ways, I like it."

" 'You like, you love'—what a . . . travesty of life. Just be quiet and tell me when there's another road sign. Any sign."

Her silence might have signaled hurt, but Kevin doubted it. The mere existence of a duplicate of Jane reminded him of how easy it was to mimic humanity. An awful lot of humans were good at it, too. The time he and Jane had spent together had evoked too much humanity in her. In his own way, Kevin had made her as much as the aliens had.

He had made her vulnerable, he saw that now. They had equipped her to survive. He had taught her to think and feel. She was no match for the Jane a harsher reality had shaped. Neither was he.

"Deer crossing," that Jane announced obediently.

"You remember that map yet?"

She nodded in the fleeting brightness of a highway light. "I've been there before. Just follow this road. I'll tell you where to turn. I can find where you want to go, Kevin."

"Two stars to the left and straight on till morning," he mumbled.

"What?" she asked.

"Nothing."

Roadside trees rushed by, fading hitchhiker-fast behind the van. Occasional oncoming headlights probed the darkness, enlarging and then popping past without challenge.

Only red taillights gleamed in the rearview mirror, shrinking to dying embers of light.

A roadside sign flashed by cue-card quick: "Crow Wing, 17 Miles."

He wondered why such signs always marked awkward distances—"64 Miles," "128 Miles." Why couldn't miles count off in neat decimal-system blocks, like decades of the rosary? Fifty. Ten. Five. Bingo!

The van fishtailed as he rounded the first corner in Crow Wing. Brakes squealed. Beside him, Jane clenched her hands on her seat cushion. Behind him, Jane rolled limply with the motion.

He charged the sleek, ice-blanketed road leading to the top of the bluff, gunning the gas at any hesitation, forcing the heavy vehicle up the empty, unwelcoming incline.

It was quiet up top. Bushes wore unshaken bonnets of snow. Only the henscratchings of birds scarred the smooth, winter-whitened surface.

Kevin stopped the van and jumped out, sinking into drifts to his knees. There had been much less snow when he'd last brought Jane here. He wrenched open the van's side door and bent to examine her in the dim overhead light.

She was still alive—a little. Conscious—just barely. Kevin picked her up and waded into the whiteness that capped the bluff in winter.

He was too weary to lift his legs, but pushed them through the drifts, making a jerky set of deep tracks. Jane's fur coat, gaping open, trailed like wings on either side of his footprints, brushing delicate almost-Oriental characters over the surface snow.

A waning moon hung askew in the west, its Bing Crosby profile beaming vacuously. Its light threw a Rinso-white blue cast on the snow. A ring of ice crystals throttled the moon. Drifting clouds formed another, less geometric ring around the moon.

Kevin drove his way to the bluff's center and stared up at the sky.

"Kevin? Kevin, it's cold."

She stood on the edge of the empty circle of snow, near the van, her hands in her jean pockets, her shoulders hunched. Like himself, she had no outerwear. She must have been cold, but Kevin had forgotten how to be cold. He felt only fire inside; flames of inner denial snapped sky-high at the moon.

"Kevin—?"

She was treading in his drunken tracks now, coming behind him. He wished she'd stay away.

"What are you doing?" she wanted to know.

He stared up at the heavens.

They *would* come, whatever they were. They had meddled from the beginning and they would be unable to resist doing it again now. Especially now, when they had not only her, but him.

"Kevin, please. . . ."

She was circling him, a shivering snowbound gnat. She paused to stare into Jane's milk-white face as it lolled against his shoulder.

"I could try—," she offered.

"No." He spun so she could no longer see Jane's face, or see his own. Still he looked up. "It's too late for what you or I could try. There's only one thing that can save her—what they can *do*."

"Do you think they know?" She looked up.

"Know? Of course they do! They set it all in motion. They keep records. They . . . grow . . . people. They splice genes and play tiddlywinks with DNA—they know."

He ranged in a circle, half to keep watch, half in hopes that motion would keep him from falling.

"This time," he murmured, "they can have her. Maybe I was wrong to keep her from them. Now, I don't have any choice. They've won. You hear that?" He shouted to the starry night sky, to the sunken-cheeked moon. "You can have her. Come on! Come on! Even an immortal can run out of time. This unit needs fixing—this unit is too valuable to lose. Come on; you've won. I admit it. Take her!"

His words, the effort of speaking, had driven him to his knees in the drifted snow, Jane sinking with him. He seemed to hold her up in water, atop the thin crust of the snow. She seemed to float on it, almost weightless. He couldn't feel his arms and legs.

Something churned through the drifts to his side.

"Kevin. I don't . . . sense . . . anything. There's nothing there this time. My voices are silent."

He stared at the embodiment of Jane beside him. "They're there! They have to come. I've . . . given in. I'm doing what they wanted in the first place. They can have it all—you, her—me. I'll go with them. New blood for old bodies. A live, unaltered specimen must be worth something—"

"Kevin. They've withdrawn. Left. Left us alone."

"What do you know? You're programmed to think what they want, say what they want."

"I don't think they want anything of us anymore."

"Don't think!" he said savagely, twisting so she couldn't see Jane past the shield of his shoulder.

If Jane couldn't see Jane, he reasoned with ritual superstition, perhaps both did not exist. Perhaps only one did. The right one.

"Kevin—"

"What?" he shouted.

This time Jane herself spoke, her lips barely moving. Her eyes glimmered through the spikes of her lashes.

"What?" he whispered, bending close. She sank as his strength failed. Jane sank into snow, her weight bearing his arms down to the hard earth below. "What?"

"I don't want to go with them," she said.

"Then let them . . . fix you. We'll make them free you again—"

"They never freed me in the first place." She spoke calmly, and her sentences were whole again.

She stretched out an arm, brushed her naked hand softly through the snow, her fingers driving faint furrows in the sparkling surface.

"They can save you," he argued. "Call them. Ask them. Beg them."

"I am tired," Jane said, looking up at the empty sky. "Too tired to open doors in hopes that there is something better behind them."

"You could," he accused. "You could help yourself; call them."

She didn't answer at first. "It's warm in here," Jane said, "warmer than it's ever been before. I can hear my blood sing. I can see the moon at the back of my eyes."

"Jane . . . for God's sake! Don't talk like that."

He shook her, the crazy, insane fool he was shook her.

"I told you that someday I could go so far away I could never come back. The doors are closing, Kevin."

"You're letting it happen!"

"I'm not stopping it. I'm tired of stopping it. I'm tired of acting always on my I-ness. What of their they-ness? Don't you ever wonder about that? I'm tired of I's and they's. And of cold. It's a cold place you live in, Kevin."

"Death is the coldest season of all. Jane, fight it!"

She sighed.

"You can't choose not to be!"

"Kevin, you said I can choose anything."

"Except that."

Her lips curved, then relaxed. Her eyes flared wider. Jane smiled at him, past him. "I was right. I *do* have a sister."

Kevin stared at the other Jane. She looked as flat and surreal as the altered photograph of Lynn Volker.

"She's not real; she's not you."

"I have an infinity of sisters," Jane said, and shut her eyes.

She was warm in his arms. The cold came and wooed away her body heat. It went willingly. Her slack limbs grew chill, then frigid. Finally stiff.

The sickle moon grinned, sinking farther down in the sky but never when anyone was watching it. No one watched it. Kevin didn't look up anymore. No one— nothing—came.

Jane's body grew heavy. He pulled his arms out from under her. They were numb, as were his legs; he could finally feel at least that much, that not-feeling. Much later, he stood and lifted her again. This time he walked to the edge of the bluff.

Just beyond the lip of wind-curled snow at its rim, a small ledge protruded into the dark below. Kevin jumped down to it, reaching up to pull Jane's dead weight down beside him. He shook a small avalanche of snow from the bushes clinging to the bluff's side, shook them snow-free down to their dark narrow bones, then climbed up again and pushed more snow over the edge.

The dark figure in the snow—Jane in a shroud of fur—gradually disappeared.

Kevin straightened, feeling like hell. He drove his legs through the drifts again, back to the empty center of the bluff. An impression remained there at the hub of his track marks—an impression something like a swollen snow angel.

He looked up to a limpidly black night sky, knowing he'd never look up and wonder—or hope—again. Now, he knew.

He moved in the direction of his previous tracks. Behind him came the silent figure that had followed him through every ritual. It followed him, like a moon its planet, and he could do nothing about it.

Some sound began churning in the distance, echoing from the base of the bluff. Gradually, his ears ascertained their associations, his brain deigned to name what his senses perceived.

Car wheels grinding up the slick slope. A lot of car wheels—four-by-fours, and plain front-wheel drives. To his own kind, at least, he was still eminently predictable.

He froze in the freezing cold, and waited. Headlights popped over the horizon line like hot, greedy moons—two, four, six, eight, ten. . . .

The vehicles revved over the brow of the bluff, drove through the drifts, formed a grinning circle blocking the one road down.

Kevin stood pinned by the lights, blinking at the diamonds glinting off the snow. A shadow stood beside him. He didn't—couldn't—look at it, but he knew it was there. He knew it would always be there.

This time, he was not going anywhere quietly.

"All right," he said, addressing the shadow he could not face. "You put the lights on once; let's see what you can do to put some lights out."

One by one, traversing the automobile grilles from right to left, the headlights began winking out in chorus-line sequence.

Epilogue: April 11
Before

In the center of the clearing, twin patches of barren brown ground poked through the dissipating snow like eye sockets in a skull.

The snow itself was mushy; their boots pressed it into mud.

"This is crazy." Kevin stopped walking to look back where a parked van tilted on the highway's edge. No cars came by.

He stuck gloveless hands in his jacket pockets. He wasn't wearing a cap, and the raw wind tousled his hair. He did wear a beard—an untrimmed lumberjack frizz that brushed the zipper pull at his throat.

Jane stomped around the clearing, leaving mud-brown prints behind her. "I think this is it."

"How could it be?" he said. "You never saw it. You never were here even if this *is* it. You don't even have an innate attachment to . . . the damn thing! Our so-called sessions have proven that."

"I tried." She had stopped to study him instead of the landscape. "And I have this . . . feeling . . . that I can find it again."

"Not again." The edge had returned to his voice. "You're not her."

"I'm like her."

When he was silent she came back to him, treading carefully in her own footsteps.

"Kevin."

He shut his eyes. She was sorry. In the cloud-hazed daylight, his eyes had looked very blue. A brushstroke of new gray cut an off-center swath through his dark brown beard.

She waited until his eyes met hers again.

"Kevin. I *know* I can do it."

"It's impossible. Worse than that, it's unimportant!" He eyed the van, jittering on his feet. "And I don't like us playing sitting duck for nothing."

"Kevin, please." Her hand left her pocket to reach for his face. He shifted away.

"All right," he said, not looking at her. "Poke around. Satisfy yourself. You won't find anything."

She immediately turned back to the clearing, starting at dead center and scribing wider and wider circles in the melting snow that thinned like spent soapsuds on dirty dishwater.

Kevin crossed his arms to watch her, ashamed of his own remoteness and angry at her insistence. His anger was irrational, for there was so little she insisted upon.

He glanced back at the truck, always anticipating the suspicious vehicle stopping behind it, the highway patrolman pulling over. In its back window, he could glimpse a placard bearing the temporary license number issued to new vehicles.

He'd been lucky to lift a truck license from the Chevy in Swan River. Even luckier, the Chevy already wore new plates, so the owner wouldn't report the loss of the temps. And the van was fresh enough to cruise for months under a brand-new guise.

"Kevin. Look."

She was standing on the clearing's southwest side, holding up a small purple flower.

"It's a crocus. Sun must've hit there."

"Pretty," she tried.

He grunted, and she went back to circling the clearing.

Kevin surveyed the sharp pine tops. This could be the

place. So could any of hundreds of clearings along Highway 61. Even he didn't remember where they had stopped. Zyunsinth had truly found an unmarked grave.

He watched her pursue her quest, feeling like a bored parent humoring an even more bored child.

They had lived in the wilds all these weeks—months, it was, he guessed, since the Crow Wing bluff top. In his dreams, he could still see the darkened government cars spinning helplessly apart like record albums as he gunned the van down the open road, a Jane of sorts beside him.

If Turner still followed, he had never found them. Kevin had learned how to steal more than temporary license placards, and to stay away from people. He'd even learned to camp out. Wilderness living proved no problem for . . . her. She could tune her metabolism for any climate. Sometimes, he got damn sick of the cold.

Still, the Boundary Waters Canoe Area at the top hook of Minnesota was ideal terrain for hide-and-seek—isolated and underpopulated. Kevin had found and broken into Neumeier's abandoned cabin. He'd ruthlessly raided it for supplies, even ripping the quilt off the bed in which Jane and he had slept the first time Jane had heard . . . the Call. Kevin didn't want to think about the Call.

He'd also scavenged decent sums of money—rolls of bills tucked in the bottom of coffee cans and under floorboards. Professor Neumeier had seemed too sophisticated an old lady to have squirreled money away like a kid, but Kevin assumed that precaution was a legacy of surviving the Holocaust.

Another legacy of the Holocaust was living off the dead, which Kevin supposed he was doing, in his own way, just as Nordstrom had in his.

He pictured Neumeier squinting until the lines in her face became grooves as she drew on one of her Lucky Strikes and said indulgently, "Spoiled Child of Untold Postwar Affluence, don't be an ass. Take it all."

Kevin looked around for his charge. She was kicking at the snow now, her dark head down. The snow had melted

339

enough to reveal instantly what she sought if it was there. She was walking in circles in more ways than one.

Kevin turned from the sight, from the strong scent of ghost tobacco in his nostrils. The van was okay, and what harm did it do to let her try? Kevin was past trying, even when, on occasion, she turned to him. Even when something in him trembled response. He wasn't into surrogate sex.

"Kevin!"

"What?" He slogged over, ready to call off the expedition and resume the endless journey to nowhere.

She pointed at a particularly handsome pine tree. "There. I think it's there."

"The snow's almost all gone."

"But it was left under a tree, wasn't it?"

He paused, then nodded. He hadn't told her that. Lucky guess. She needed no more encouragement, but waded into the Dairy-Queen-soft snow mounded at the fir's base, digging with bare hands.

Kevin superimposed another image, another woman, over hers. Jane laughing and trotting like a pony about the snow-filled clearing. Jane crying and clinging to Zyunsinth and then himself. Jane leaving. Jane never coming back.

She was on her hands and knees now, spraying snow to either side. The fir's broad shadow had kept spring sunlight at bay; the snow was still surprisingly deep here. She dug like a dog looking for a forgotten bone repository.

"Kevin—Kevin!"

He leaned down to look. Long amber hairs protruded through the snow, either a dead fox or . . . Zyunsinth! Kevin fell to his knees, not feeling the cold snow through his worn denims.

"My God—how did you . . . ?"

She was shoving more snow away now, baring the stiff length of a fur coat.

Kevin saw another fur coat in the snow, saw spring's relentless softening fingers driving deep into the fur's center, driving decay and disintegration back into the earth it sprang from—the red, Indian earth of Crow Wing.

340

Jane would be found soon, if she hadn't been already, true skin and bones this time, presenting yet another unsolved mystery for the state's newspapers to exploit.

As the woman before him sculpted the dormant shape out of the snow, so Kevin saw Jane being stripped, revealed, destroyed. Again.

"This is it, isn't it? Isn't it, Kevin?"

He forced himself to look at the familiar fur coat she pulled from the snow. He forced himself to look at her. Her eyes radiated brunette warmth. Slightly chapped lips smiled over Pepsodent-perfect white teeth.

"That's it, all right." Excitement tingled in Kevin's stomach despite himself. "That's . . . amazing. That you found it. You never were here. You never had those memories of Jane's to draw on. How—?"

"Kevin. I *am* her."

"Not—really."

"As much as anyone can be. And I'm free of *them* now. They don't want me any more than the Volkers did her."

Kevin took the coat from her hands, brushed snow off the chilled hairs. Suddenly, he swirled the coat over her shoulders.

"I guess it's yours now. Finders keepers. Jane has her own fur coat."

She hugged it close, staring over each shoulder in turn to study the coat. "It still doesn't mean anything to me. Why, if I have all of her memories up to the point we—she—went back into the space vessel? I should care about Zyunsinth as much as she did. And I don't. I care about you, but not about this—"

"The aliens probably realized that early contact with the race of Zyunsinth had helped Jane disregard her programming. They stripped you of that dangerous emotional response as a safeguard. That's all."

Her hand stroked the wide, free-hanging sleeve. "It's soft and pretty, but something is . . . missing. Will there always be something missing?"

Kevin stared into her eyes. "Maybe. There will be for me." Her eyes lowered. "But, hey—you found it! That's

341

really something. That's a phenomenon that Turner and the PID would spit into the wind to document. I didn't think you could do it, and you did."

"Maybe there are other things you don't think I can do that I can."

"Impudent patients don't get gold stars." He pinched the coat together across her chest and pulled her up. "But you deserve a reward. Behavior modification therapy, reward positives. Finding this is progress. How about—?"

His arm around her shoulders was guiding her back to the parked van. The fur felt housepet-familiar to his hand; it even smelled familiar, like a wet dog, as his body heat—and hers—warmed it. Sun was leaking through the clouds, pouring down on them like tepid skim milk.

"How about we go somewhere definite for a change? Easter's coming up and—"

"Easter?"

"Holiday. Religious. Remember all the chocolate rabbits we saw sitting in the shredded cellophane at the convenience store? That's for Easter."

"Rabbits are religious? I didn't know that," she began seriously.

"Only at reproduction." Kevin laughed. She stopped walking to watch him. He hadn't thought it had been that long since he'd laughed. "No, rabbits are the secular part of the holiday. The religious part is about miracles."

"I know what a miracle is. A miracle is—," she began to recite.

"A miracle is finding a fur coat you never lost." Kevin smiled and squeezed her shoulders. "Maybe we should go someplace special for Easter dinner." She nodded hopefully. "Maybe . . . Elk River." She waited. "To my folks' place."

"Folks are . . ."

"A nicer way of saying parents."

"What are your parents like, Kevin? What are any parents really like?"

He stopped and stared at the anonymous van with the stolen license placard. "People. Just people. They worry a lot."

"Like you worry about me?"

"Sort of. Sometimes."

They turned back to view the clearing.

"Will it be . . . dangerous . . . to go there?" she asked.

"Maybe. Maybe they're still watching the place. Maybe I don't care anymore. I'm tired. I'd like to sit down after Sunday dinner with a newspaper—I'm tired of hearing about the world over a car radio . . . voices in the dark. I don't even know what happened in the Twin Cities after we got away, if they found anything in Crow Wing yet—"

"I can do dishes," she said.

"What?"

"After Sunday dinner. I can do dishes."

He stared into her serious face. "No." He grabbed her arms and shook her a little. "*I'll* do dishes. You can read the newspaper."

"I like to read, too."

He just shook his head.

"Will your parents like me?" she wondered. "The Volkers didn't. I mean, they didn't like . . . her."

"They were afraid of her. That's nothing new. She . . . you turned out different than they expected. That's nothing new, either. Yeah, my folks'll like you; they'll have to. What they'll *really* hate is my beard!" He tugged on the offending hair.

"I like it," she consoled him automatically.

"You like everything," he teased back.

"No. There are some things I don't like at all." Her eyes darkened.

Kevin guessed that she was remembering Nordstrom and the force she had loosed on him. She was more lethal than her predecessor—and knew it. She smiled into his dawning guilt. "But I like you."

He turned away, bent down and pressed damp snow into a soggy ball. He hurled it at a distant pine trunk. *Thwunck!* It hit dead center, splattering like a Big Bang universe.

"Why do you want to go to Elk River, Kevin?" she asked.

"Sometimes, Jane, it's just time to come in from the cold and go home." He nudged her arm. "Come on, sourpuss. I'll race you to the truck!"

He was sprinting away from her, but she stood there frozen amid the shrinking snow.

Jane.

He'd called her Jane. For the first time since . . . She didn't want to think about "since." She wanted to think about now, about going home, whatever that was. It sounded nice.

Laughing at last, she clasped the bulky fur coat around her and began running through the soggy snow toward the road.

THE BEST IN SCIENCE FICTION

THE TOR DOUBLES

Two complete short science fiction novels in one volume!